The Horse Keeper

by

Robyn Braemer

Halstad House

Chapter One

Southern England

Present Day Somewhere

Kara held her head high, struggling to maintain her most serene expression as she faced her uncle's rage at the news she had just told him. It was not easy to appear calm. Her jaw ached from the effort of keeping her face set in a composed expression. Kara tried to form an image in her mind of a peaceful scene with a gentle waterfall and bright yellow butterflies fluttering about her in a sun-dappled green meadow. That did not work so well. Memories of sweet scented fresh air and sun warmed grasses were overpowered by the reality of the scents filling the great room, of charred meat, rancid fat, and the ever present odor of man sweat. Centuries of wood smoke permeated the stone walls and damp days released the aged odor.

Her uncle's men followed the traditional custom of bathing as seldom as possible. Perhaps they had become immune to the smell but Kara had not. Imaginary butterflies fluttered away, to be replaced by the reality of a dozen dogs wandering between tables, a few intensely scratching at fleas and of several chickens picking their way through the rushes with bobbing heads and irritated cackles. The odor of cooked cabbage lingered from the last meal and the smell of dog permeated the very stone under her feet.

The Great Hall could hold hundreds of people with ample elbow room during a feast. Now about thirty men sat on benches at the closest tables scattered around the lord's table on its raised platform, Lord Roffe's table. Men laughed and argued as they cleaned weapons, wrapped bow strings, and ate a late lunch from the stew pot hanging in the gigantic fireplace on the far wall. A game of Knuckle Knife being played at a table in the back of the hall had attracted an audience. Laughter and swearing erupted in waves from the men watching the daring game. Except during meal times the women of the manor seldom lingered in the great room, preferring the women's solar for a bit more sedate, less aromatic afternoon activities.

Smoke occasionally drifted back into the room when an especially strong gust of wind raced down the chimney. Two servants carried pitchers of ale and mead to fill drinking cups as needed. This was the quiet time of the day in the hall. By evening almost every table would be in use and over a dozen servants would be scurrying about to serve the diners. The manor was prosperous and of a generous size and population.

The Great Hall was never truly empty at any time of the day. Often bodies slumbered along the walls or on benches late in the night, traveling men wrapped in wool blankets accepting what shelter they could get. Occasionally the snoring piles stretched out on the cold stone floor were occupants of the manor who drank too much ale and slept where they fell. Lord Roffe had little patience for drunkards though and if a man did wake before daybreak and did not have the sense to finish sleeping off the ale somewhere else or did not have a buddy who was kind enough to rouse him before the sun rose, the punishment was memorable.

Kara felt drained to her bones and travel dirty after five days of hard riding on dusty roads but she had not gone to her rooms first to clean and refresh herself, choosing instead to immediately seek out her uncle upon her arrival at the manor. Kara longed to take off her boots and sit on something that was not moving beneath her. The last thing Kara wanted was to be standing in front of her uncle fresh from the road with layers of sweat and dirt coating her but she had chosen to face her uncle before seeking the comfort of the women's solar.

Her uncle barely tolerated Kara on good days. His rage would be even greater if Kara had made him wait to hear the news she carried. If she gone to the solar first to refresh her uncle would have two reasons to be angry with her, delivering bad news and making him wait to hear it. Or worse, if he heard rumors from the men who had escorted her during her trip to France of the news she carried before he heard the actual story from Kara.

The barbarians were flooding into Europe. That should have been the news that held Lord Roffe's attention. The continent was struggling to raise a line of defense to keep them from invading further. First, the invasion could impact the horse trade even if the barbarians weren't at their door. Kara had heard chatter about increasing the need for horseflesh for war use being a boon to the horse breeders but she was concerned of the possibility that such a demand would come from the monarchy without receiving payment. Second, eventually they could themselves be facing an invasion. Too many men thought England safe from the barbarians because it was an island. Kara did not understand why so many men she heard discussing the barbarian topic thought that the channel would stop the invasion. The channel would only delay the barbarians if they made it to France's shoreline.

The stories Kara heard of these mystery invaders raised the hair on the back of her neck. There had been royal couriers crossing the channel when she came over. Though they had not talked to her they had talked within her hearing. King Guy of France hoped to form an alliance with King George of England, one that involved King George sending men to make a stand at the eastern French border. If the murdering hordes made their way through France then England would be next so it was in England's best interest to aid France instead of waiting for France to be annihilated before England rose to arms.

This news of a threat to his country, livelihood, and home did not seem to concern Lord Roffe however and he brushed it away with a wave of his hand. The French could deal with the barbarians. Kara feared this attitude would be the common attitude of the English barons. It was Kara's other news that impacted Lord Roffe directly and held his attention. As she expected, he blamed Kara.

History showed that too often it was the messenger of unpleasant news who lost their head. Since *she* was the one delivering this very unpleasant news to her uncle, the chances of Kara bearing the consequences of Angel's actions just because she was the one who played messenger to such bad tidings increased dramatically. In fact, they increased to the point where Kara had no doubt in her mind that she would pay the price somehow. When Kara told Lord Roffe what his daughter he had done he had been so stunned he had been speechless. Then a silent rage took him.

Trust Angel to go against her father's wishes and leave Kara as the messenger of such ill news. It was bad enough that Angel had done what she had done but in doing so Angel had also gone directly against her father's decision. Lord Roffe looked like his head would burst. His face was red, the flush spreading down his neck. Veins bulged in his neck. Lord Roffe's hand clenched so hard around his eating knife that his knuckles were white. Sweat glistened on his forehead and along his upper lip.

Normally Lord Roffe was a fairly attractive man, closer to his middle years now, tall and broad shouldered with no excess weight and a wrinkle free face though more white hairs covered his head than black hairs remained. The family resemblance between Lord Roffe and his niece Kara was noticeable when they stood near each other, the slightly square jaw, straight nose, and brilliant blue eyes were Roffe family traits. Though Kara could not remember much of her mother, she had been told often that she was a taller, auburn haired version of her mother. Kara had the same oversized eyes with a lilt at the corner, high cheekbones, and pointed chin. What made the resemblance to her mother stronger were the gestures and facial expressions that Kara was unaware of doing.

Lord Roffe's face grew redder and redder as the impact of what Kara reported sank in fully. Kara imagined Lord Roffe, her esteemed uncle, father to her cousin Angel, getting so angry that his head really did explode. The thought almost allowed a smile to slip out. Kara would not smile. Smiling would be a catalyst to an already volatile situation. It was not humorous, not in the least. Knowing how her uncle would react to any hint of humor from her at that time sobered her mood instantly.

"She what?!" Lord Roffe bellowed, spittle flying.

"My lady cousin has requested that I tell you that she will remain at Crow Bend and cannot marry Lord Hawkstead," Kara said slowly and gently, for the second time.

"I'll drag that damned vixen to Hawkstead by her damned hair!" Roffe yelled. He rose to his feet as if he meant to do it that very moment.

Here it was, the hammer blow. Perhaps she should have told this part at once but it made her stomach twist having to say the words. "Uncle, she has wed Edward Williams," Kara said softly. That Angel had wed Kara had already told him. The second part of the story Kara had held back for a few minutes to allow her uncle to absorb the impact. The second part was the hammer blow. Kara took a deep breath. "She is already with child."

Roffe stared at Kara in disbelief. His mouth moved but nothing came out. The red began to fade. The shock faded quickly though and anger returned. "But I promised her to Hawkstead." He slammed his fist on the plank table. "Stupid twit! I promised her to Hawkstead."

Kara chose to remain silent. There was nothing she could say to diffuse the situation. Any attempt to do so would only fuel his anger. If Kara could have slipped away unnoticed she would have done it. The next best thing was to try to become invisible. Hopefully he would forget that she was there. Kara remained standing in front of Lord Roffe's table, hands crossed in front of her stomach, as still as a statue. Kara was still dressed for travel so she wore a simple blue wool dress. Despite the current fashion requiring a wimple for a head covering, Kara's head was bare and her auburn hair was in a long, thick braid down her back. Kara could almost pass for a cast statue at that moment, a demure angel frozen in lapis blue wool.

Lord Roffe could refuse to acknowledge the marriage between Lady Angel Roffe and Sir Edward Williams. Since Angel was a minor the marriage was not valid without her father's permission. Angel had been smart enough to keep the marriage a secret until she knew that she carried a child. Even if Lord Roffe had the marriage between his daughter and her chosen husband annulled it would mean dealing with the resulting child. Lord Roffe could not wed Angel to Hawkstead while she carried another man's child, if Hawkstead would even still have Angel. Kara would have thought Angel marrying someone else while betrothed to Hawkstead would have been enough to destroy any agreement Lord Roffe had made with Lord Hawkstead but Angel was convinced that getting pregnant was also necessary to free her from the betrothal.

Angel had explained all this to Kara when charging her cousin with the task of delivering the news, so Kara knew that Angel had carefully planned the whole situation. Kara grudgingly agreed that it was a sound plan, for someone who wanted more than anything under the sun to avoid marrying the man. Angel was certainly securely out of Hawkstead's reach with her new husband and expected child. Angel had even managed to avoid confronting her father with the news.

Kara chewed on the inside of her cheek, a nervous habit. Kara had never met Lord Hawkstead, newly named Earl of Greenestone. What little information Kara had learned of Hawkstead was enough that she felt that he was not the type of man who would take mildly to his betrothed secretly marrying another man under his nose. It was difficult to imagine any man accepting as wife someone who dealt his pride such a severe blow. The only reason Kara could think of that would cause Hawkstead to agree to marrying Angel after she married another but had the marriage annulled by her father was if whatever Lord Roffe promised him with the betrothal was worth more than the bruise to his pride. Kara was not sure how strongly Hawkstead wanted this alliance. Kara had no idea what business Lord Roffe and Hawkstead had together.

Whatever promises had been made between the two men in exchange for Angel's hand certainly would not be enough for the man to swallow his pride and accept Angel as wife if she became again available. Kara concluded that Lord Roffe having the marriage annulled would not be enough to salvage the Hawkstead marriage plans even without a child involved but Lord Roffe would have likely still had had the marriage annulled as an annulment would keep Angel as a future asset in another marriage agreement. Lord Roffe would also be keeping a sharp eye on his daughter to avoid another surprise. The pregnancy was the unavoidable wedge Angel needed. Married into a strong family and carrying her husband's heir eliminated Angel from her father's plans for her.

Lord Roffe would likely have to pay a penalty of some sort for breaking the betrothal. Kara wished deeply that she had been included in discussions over the agreement between the two men. Normally Lord Roffe hid nothing from her in the business side of things but in this he had been uncharacteristically close-mouthed. Kara felt certain that it was because he knew that she would not like what he had offered Hawkstead as part of the marriage arrangement with Angel. Foolish, since it was imperative that Kara be involved in any such decisions. Lord Roffe blindly offering a contract was potentially ruinous. Kara wished she had paid more attention months ago when Lord Roffe first showed such interest in Hawkstead. Kara vaguely remembered Lord Roffe talking of little else for weeks but it had coincided with foaling time and she had been too busy to pay close attention to why Lord Roffe was so fascinated with Hawkstead. Now that the information was relevant the content of the conversations fluttered just out of reach of her memory.

Then there was Edward's family, a house as powerful as Roffe. They had accepted the marriage between Angel and Edward as a done deal and celebrated the impending arrival of the new baby. They would not meekly stand by and let Lord Roffe bastardize Edward's heir. Really, the match Angel had made was quite acceptable despite the lack of a contract to benefit the two houses. It was not like she had run off with the cook's assistant. However, her cousin Angel was a valuable commodity in the marriage market and Lord Roffe having his daughter securely married to a good family was secondary to what he could have gained with the marriage.

Angel had always had a knack for leaving chaos in her wake. Kara inadvertently let a subtle, cynical smile tug up the corner of her mouth at the thought of Angel's ability to stir up trouble even when she was not there, unaware of how Lord Roffe's eyes narrowed ever so slightly when he noticed the small change in Kara's demeanor.

It was all politics, this marriage Lord Roffe had arranged between Angel and Hawkstead. Kara was grateful that she did not have to worry about being traded in a political marriage. Kara did not need her uncle's constant reminders that she would never marry because she knew that he would never risk Kara getting married. Lord Roffe would not allow her to marry as long as he was her legal guardian. Kara getting married would ruin Lord Roffe. Kara had accepted the situation for what it was

Hawkstead had gained enough of a reputation that even Kara had heard rumors of the man. Visitors to Roffe Manor spoke of the man who had been given a new title and large estate at the whim of the king. Kara had made horse trading trips to London four times as well as two trips to the continent in the past year and Hawkstead's name had come up at each trip though she had not met the man. During her last trip Kara had learned that Hawkstead had been making the rounds in search of the right horses for some program he was starting.

Hawkstead meant to gain something from the marriage also, whether that be a beautiful wife from one of the most established families in the country or because of the horses. Horses might be a higher possibility than Angel's angelic charms. Hawkstead had gained his reputation as a man of battle and no one raised better horseflesh than the Roffe Stables. Of course, Kara just realized, it was all about the horses. Another secret smile tugged at the corner of her mouth. How ironic if Hawkstead was willing to wed Angel for access to the Roffe Stables. Kara would not expect Roffe to inform Hawkstead of the truth behind Roffe Stables.

By trying to wed Angel to a man who she feared and detested Lord Roffe had gained nothing but potential fighting on two sides. Lord Roffe should have known that Angel would continue to refuse to marry the man. Angel had returned from that visit to meet her future husband full of loud objections, yelling throughout the hall that she would never marry the brute. Angel had thrown out quite a few descriptions of the knuckle-dragging, walking mountain, none good.

When angry fits did not move her father, Angel used the pleading and begging angle. Though Lord Roffe treated his daughter with consideration and never raised his hand to her as he did to Kara, in this matter he remained firm and would not consider any option but that Angel would marry Hawkstead. Kara was under the impression that her uncle thought he was doing Angel a favor by pushing marriage to Hawkstead. Angel did not see it that way.

Lord Roffe patiently ignored the rages. Lord Roffe patiently ignored the pathetic pleadings. When Angel realized that none of her tactics worked to convince her father to back out of the marriage she became quiet and thoughtful. Angel was the definition of the obedient daughter for several days. Lord Roffe took a deep breath and relaxed, thinking that his daughter had finally seen the logic in cooperating with his plans. Kara, as well as anyone else who knew

Angel, watched with interest, wondering what she was up to with this little charade.

When Angel asked her father one evening during dinner if she could be allowed to go visit her mother's family before having to subject herself to a life locked away in a prison guarded by a hairy troll, Lord Roffe had actually agreed to that suggestion with a sigh of relief. Lord Roffe thought Angel had accepted the marriage and that he was gaining a few months of peace and quiet before the event. Lord Roffe expected further drama nearer the actual wedding but a break from his daughter's tirades was enough to eagerly send her on her way. Kara did not realize that she again let a small smile pass her guard at the idea that her uncle thought some time away would improve Angel's opinion of the marriage.

Lord Roffe caught Kara's small smile and a change settled over his demeanor. The red faded from his face. The outraged shock slipped away, to be replaced by a cunning, thoughtful expression. Seeing her uncle's change of attitude, Kara quickly composed her mask of serene nothingness but it was too late, the damage was done. Lord Roffe smiled. Kara shivered. That little slip of movement of the corner of her mouth had succeeded in shifting Lord Roffe's rage at his daughter to the cold hatred he seemed to most often feel for his niece. Kara's uncle stared at her intently for several long minutes, a thoughtful gleam growing in his eyes. Around them the normal hustle and bustle of the hall faded into a distant hum. Kara jumped when Lord Roffe chuckled.

"Ah, Kara, my beloved niece," he said softly.

Kara instinctively took a step back. Lord Roffe laughed outright. Kara froze. Several men in the room looked up in surprise when Lord Roffe shifted from angry yelling to laughter but everyone maintained their distance. The experienced ones knew that Lord Roffe laughing at Kara boded nothing well and shook their heads in warning to anyone without experience who showed interest in the discussion between their lord and his niece. Kara stiffened. It was a mistake to show him fear. She knew that. He fed on her fear. Yet it was not easy to hold her ground. Lord Roffe settled back into his chair, looking very relaxed. He stroked his jaw with a long forefinger and let his gaze drift away for a moment, staring at some point above Kara's shoulder.

"My brother gave you his look so there is no denying your parentage," Lord Roffe said thoughtfully. Kara frowned at him but he was still staring off in the distance as he spoke, as if to himself more than to her. "Your mother gave you your outlandish spirit, so wrong in a woman," Lord Roffe said. He leaned over the table, turning his gaze, cold as steel, directly on her. "So Angel sent you to me. She probably knew I'd beat the child out of her body and if she lived still send her on to Hawkstead. Were you prepared to take her beating?"

There it was, the anger shifting to her, the blame shifting to her. Though Kara had no part in any of this except to deliver the news, it was she who her uncle blamed. Kara had known that she would be the one punished. Kara dug her fingernails into the palm of her hand, clenched in fists at her sides. She would not show fear to this man. Yet Kara was afraid. No matter how hard Kara tried to tell herself that she could be brave, he made her feel fear. Kara felt a familiar tingle above her lip and a slight roaring in her ears.

It was the fear of experience. It was the fear of never quite knowing what would trigger his rage. It was the fear of knowing what would trigger his rage and not being able to avoid it. It was the fear of being humiliated in front of others. It was the fear of the physical pain when he put action to his rage with her. Kara knew what her uncle was capable of doing. She had scars to show how he physically took out his frustration with her. Though the physical beatings hurt, the pain faded, whereas the mental beatings hurt and continued to inflict pain long after the words were said. Kara wanted to be brave but no matter how hard she tried, when it came to her uncle she felt fear.

Kara could barely remember her parents, vague shadows, images, her memories entwined with stories of memories shared by those who had known her parents as she grew up in what was now her uncle's household. Her father had grown up in this very manor. Her mother had arrived as a blushing, young bride, vivacious and in love with her bridegroom. Kara even had fond memories of her uncle from those days. The death of her parents had changed her uncle as well. The almost kind and soft spoken man Kara remembered from childhood memories had not been exactly a loving man but that gentleness had been replaced with a growing resentment and cold rage.

Kara could still remember when her uncle first spoke harsh words to her, just a few weeks after her parents had died. The incident had been so shocking to her that it left a lasting imprint. The first time he struck her was a few months after that. It started as a slap to the face, the occasional cuff to the head, and then severe beatings until his rage was spent. Each passing year brought stronger hatred from him.

While her parents lived Roffe Manor had been a friendly, warm environment and many a servant smiled fondly at memories of those times. Not that they would complain about her uncle. He was a fair lord, most would say, even amongst themselves, fair but firm, not one to coddle his servants but not unreasonable either. A firm task master was a blessing when it kept them fed and warm and safe in the walls of the keep when it was a cold, harsh world outside the walls. Everyone knew this to be true. So if Lord Roffe was a bit firm that was all right because in the end they were safe behind the walls and armed men Lord Roffe provided. They were fed because they had armed men watching over them as they worked in the fields. They were alive.

Armed men were needed to watch over people working in the fields because danger lurked at all times. Nightfall sent everyone behind walls, whether it was within a keep, walls around a manor or walled villages. Travelers required armed escorts to travel anywhere.

This was known by all, even those who never ventured more than ten miles from their birthplace their whole lives. There were lords of other houses who did not treat their people so well. Stories of life in other estates and villages tended to travel even if those residents did not.

Lord Roffe might resent his niece's spirit but he respected her bravery. That was what Kara told herself every day. As long as Kara showed a brave face she would be safe. The brave front seemed to hold his rage at bay at least. Lord Roffe would go weeks without doing more than taunting her, reminding her that she was still unmarried and falsely telling her that she was living under his roof at his generosity. There was no benefit in pointing out to him the lies of his statements. Her uncle liked to point out that no man would suffer a wife with her spirit, hence her lack of suitors. Try as Kara did, the spirit part was not as easy to control as the brave face and the serene mask when facing him. At least Kara thought she managed a brave face and serene mask. Her face was much more expressive than she realized.

"You look like her," Roff muttered after several minutes of contemplative silence. He leaned back in the chair. "I never did like that look. Well, if Hawkstead breaks your nose it won't hurt your looks any."

Kara struggled to remain expressionless. His criticism of her looks was nothing new and Kara was used to the jibes he liked to throw her way. Being told that she was unattractive because she looked like her mother was almost mundane. Kara knew that her uncle thought a woman's looks were all she had so he sought to hurt her by saying that she was unattractive to men but it was the one thing that he did that Kara could shrug off as meaning nothing. If Kara was curious to know how or why her uncle thought Hawkstead would break her nose she was not going to ask. Kara would find out sooner if she kept silent. Knowing her uncle, it was a threat meant to scare her. He enjoyed tormenting her with possibilities.

Angel might be afraid of Hawkstead but Kara could not imagine the unknown man breaking Kara's nose just because Angel did not want to marry him. If anything, it was Lord Roffe's nose in jeopardy of being broken, along with a possible split lip. One could only hope. Kara wondered how Lord Roffe would tell this infamous Lord Hawkstead that his betrothed had run away rather than marry him.

Roffe chuckled again. Whatever he was planning gave him great joy. Kara felt the hair at the back of her neck stand up. She shivered. "You get to play messenger again," he said. "I will deliver the news to Hawkstead in a letter and you will deliver the letter to him in person."

That surprised Kara but she simply nodded once in understanding, too upset to utter even a single word in acknowledgement. Lord Roffe was too pleased with his private agenda to pursue that she was taking his news in stoic silence. Kara had been away on her travels for the past month and that her uncle would so callously send her back out on the road so soon to do his dirty work upset her more than anything. The detour to collect Angel had added to her travel time. Knowing him he would expect Kara to leave within a few days, not really enough time to fully rest. More importantly, Kara would not be here when the new horses arrived.

"I see you're wearing wool again. When you approach Hawkstead you will dress as befits your station, not like a merchant," Lord Roffe said.

Lord Roffe waved his hand in dismissal, drifting into thinking how he would word his letter to Hawkstead. Kara wasted no time in escaping his presence. Very regally Kara stepped away, head high, shoulders straight, hoping she did not trip on the rushes covering the floor. The moment Kara was out of his sight she hiked up her skirts and ran through the hall and up the stone staircase to the solar. Once within the safe confines of the solar Kara dropped to her knees, her back against the oak door, her legs trembling so badly that she could not stand another minute longer.

Katherine Smythe and Jenny Collins were sitting at embroidery hoops in the solar, a large glass window at their backs. The window allowed sunshine to fill the room at their backs. Bits of dust floated above their heads in the bright light. Glass that large was a rare and expensive luxury. The two young girls were both so startled at Kara's abrupt entrance and collapse against the door that they both stared at her speechless for several moments. Then in unison they rose and hurried to her.

Kara assured them she was unharmed and waved them back to their embroidery. The girls were both being fostered at Roffe Manor along with another dozen gentle born girls. The girls had witnessed Lord Roffe's treatment of Kara before and immediately assumed that Kara had suffered at her uncle's hands. After giving Kara another long, scrutinizing look Katherine settled back onto her stool and picked up her needle but her gaze remained on Kara and not on the framed cloth they had been working on prior to Kara's abrupt entrance. Jennie remained standing over Kara.

"Even if you be all right, you won't be for long, sitting on that cold floor," Jennie said in a chiding voice.

Kara nodded, but did not move. The floor was not really that cold. Thick wool rugs covered almost every inch of the solar. She looked around the nearly empty room. There should have been a dozen girls of various ages as well as the two adult gentlewomen residing in the hall in the solar. Kara had not seen any of them in the Great Hall or hallways. "Where are the other girls?"

"Jonny found a late patch of blackberries. They are all out picking what they can scavenge," Katherine said. "We hope to have blackberry cobbler tonight. If any berries make it into the baskets."

"Why did you not join?" Kara asked.

Katherine sighed. "Lady Lullan said we could better use the time working on our embroidery."

"How were your travels?" Jennie asked, settling onto the floor at Kara's feet, forgetting her own advice about the cold floor.

Her uncle was sending her to Hawkstead, to deliver a message
which he hoped would earn her a beating not to be avoided a second
time. Kara was to deliver bad news to Hawkstead, a man who so
terrified Angel that the girl burst into tears at the mention of his
name. Kara had heard Lord Roffe discussing Hawkstead long before
Roffe had decided to visit the man with Angel in tow. Some
information had stayed with Kara. Hawkstead had earned additional
lands and titles from the king. Hawkstead had supposedly contacted
Lord Roffe about horses. Kara still was not sure what had happened
regarding that.

Though normally Lord Roffe passed any business information
related to the horses to Kara he had not shared any information
regarding Hawkstead in combination with Roffe horses with her.
Kara had heard whispers and hints and though she waited for her
uncle to bring up the topic he never had. Kara was not about to ask
Lord Roffe. Her uncle did not mention Hawkstead in connection
with the horses but he had mentioned that Lord Addington's second
son was doing well, being granted Greenestone Keep from the king
as well as the title Earl of Greenestone.

When Addington's firstborn son and heir, Peter, was killed boar
hunting Lord Roffe suddenly became *very* interested in the new heir,
Addington's second son, Hawkstead. The Earl of Addington's
estates were in the same county as Roffe Manor. Lord Addington
was Lord Roffe's overlord. Lord Addington was not a fan of Lord
Roffe and Kara had though the sudden interest in Hawkstead

stemmed from a desire of Lord Roffe to have the Addingtons as in-laws. That was why Kara thought her uncle was being so secretive about the betrothal terms. Kara realized that she should have known it would have something to do with the horses.

It was clear that Lord Roffe had gone visiting Hawkstead's granted estate for the sole purpose of offering Angel in marriage or he would not have brought her with to visit Hawkstead at Greenestone Keep. When Angel found out that Kara was not to accompany them she had begged her father to allow Kara to join them. Though Lord Roffe often gave in to his daughter, he had adamantly refused that request, even when Angel threw a fit. Instead he had included ten year old Matilda as Angel's travel companion.

Kara did not know why Lord Roffe was so adamant about not having her in the party but she did not begrudge it in the least. Kara had waved them off with a big smile. The trip to Hawkstead gave Kara weeks free of the company of her cousin and her uncle and she had enjoyed the quiet time. Angel had taken her cue from her father years earlier and treated Kara less as a beloved cousin and more as a figure of disregard. Kara did not blame Angel for her behavior but it was a nice respite to have her out of the manor.

So one lovely spring day Angel had ridden out with Lord Roffe, sulky and pouting about having to go and about not having Kara along. When they had returned a few weeks later it was with a sulky and pouting Angel unofficially betrothed to Hawkstead and a pleasantly happy Lord Roffe. Though Kara did not know what it was about Hawkstead that had inspired Roffe to go seeking him as a future son-in-law she knew that nothing cemented a martial bond as strongly as a marriage. The growing wealth of Roffe Manor actually attracted attention that Lord Roffe did not want. The strong walls and a large contingent of fighting men, including three knights, kept things secure but it was costly.

The last wave of the Black Death that had ravaged the country yet again was now but a memory to that generation of her grandparents, the longest period without sickness since it had first appeared. Its impact was still felt with empty villages, empty manors and criminals roving the countryside without enough population to keep them in check. Abandoned estates provided shelter for many gangs and it was up to local barons to flush out these havens for criminals. Worse, some of these gangs were growing so strong that they were acting as feuding barons and violently seizing occupied halls.

Such news started as a distant problem for others until word reached Roffe Manor of a gang within the county. Having Hawkstead for a son-in-law could be enough to keep lustful eyes from looking at Roffe Manor covetously. Or perhaps Lord Roffe felt that Hawkstead would be recruited to purge the area of any existing gangs. Kara could only guess at what Lord Roffe's interest was in an alliance with Hawkstead. The news about the barbarians was just another issue in a long list of issues making life precarious.

Kara hadn't met Hawkstead and Angel had been surprisingly tight-lipped about meeting him, other than the bombardment of unpleasant descriptions. It hadn't taken Angel long to hatch up the plan to go visit her deceased mother's family and within a week of arriving had singled out Edward and managed to coerce him into this secret marriage. Poor Edward could not have known what he was getting into. Kara was sure that Angel had chosen to wed Edward simply because the girl could convince him to actually do it. Having met Edward twice, Kara was not impressed with the young man, at eighteen only two years older than Angel. Edward might be a knight and from a powerful family but he was weak, pliable clay in Angel's determined hands, a safety net to save her from Hawkstead. Angel needed a strong husband who would stand up to her when she got wild ideas into her head.

Kara looked over at Jennie, slowly realizing she was waiting for an answer to her question. "I'm sorry, girlie." Kara took the girl's hands in her own. "I have a lot on my mind. I missed you. It was a good journey. Twenty new mares." Kara smiled. "From LeRouget." The news of the barbarians wreaking havoc on the continent was not a topic for the girls.

"You look exhausted," Jennie said, pulling on Kara's hand to suggest she get to her feet. "There's warm water in the basin. Kat, would you arrange a bath for Kara?"

"I'm more hungry than dirty," Kara said, stumbling to her feet. She walked across the room to the stand holding a porcelain water pitcher and basin. The pitcher was half full with tepid water. Kara poured some water in the basin, cupped her hands, and splashed water on her face. By the time Kara finished washing her face and neck the water in the basin was quite black. A full bath with warm water would be so wonderful. "Yes, a bath sounds lovely," she said.

"You must be starving then," Jennie said.

A brisk knock at the door startled all three of them. Kara quickly wiped her face dry with a clean towel while Jennie opened the door. One of Lord Roffe's pages peeked into the room, a boy of about twelve. "He says be ready to leave within the hour. He'll have the letter ready in an hour and you're not to waste any time letting the ink dry."

Kara raised her eyebrows in surprise and then nodded. "Thank-you, Bridges."

"My Lady," he said with a brisk nod.

"Bridges, have the servants prepare a bath for our lady," Jennie said, nose in the air with her most imperious voice.

Bridges' eyes widened. "But she's to go within the hour."

"Then you'd better tell them to hurry," Jennie said, shutting the door in the boy's face. Kara smiled fondly. Jennie would have no difficulty taking the reins in any household she wed into.

"Nonsense," Katherine said once the door was shut. "You can't leave within the hour. You just arrived. You need food and a bath." Kara looked at the girl fondly, finding it endearing that the twelve-year old had so much spirit.

Kara was tired to the bone and the idea of riding back out almost immediately was almost overwhelming. She hadn't even had a chance to visit the stables. Kara had been so looking forward to arriving home, eager to see Banner and the horses. It had been a month since she left to visit France with the slight easterly detour to Dover to collect Angel. A month on the road with not even a day to recover before returning to the road to carry news her uncle should by rights be delivering was almost too much for Kara to bear to think about. This was insane, even for her uncle.

As long as Hawkstead did not slit her throat or beat her to death she would live to return to her uncle's keep again. Kara had only half a year until she reached her majority on her next birthday. Until then Kara was under her uncle's command. The thought of reaching that majority was all that kept Kara going some days. This was one of those days. Not much longer, she thought. When she reached her majority there would be many changes.

"What does he mean *go again*?" Katherine asked. "And where is Angel? Is she following you? Why is she not with you?"

"Angel is wed and not returning home. I am straight out on my way to tell Hawkstead the jolly brilliant news."

Jennie and Kat exchanged significant glances. Kara was too tired to delve into what had the two giving each other knowing looks and there was not time. Angel had probably confided her scheme to someone in their hearing before leaving. If they had been aware that Angel was up to something did not matter now. What was done was done. Even if the girls had believed that Angel was about to do something stupid they would not have been able to stop her anyway. Kara was just too tired to care. There would be plenty of time to find out details when she returned.

Another knock on the door announced servants bearing Kara's trunks. Four men set the two trunks just inside the door with a loud thud and left without a word. "We can repack while you bathe." Jennie said, gesturing to the trunks sitting near the door.

Kara shook her head. "No. Just leave them. There is not time. I'll just bring them all with again. I did not sort out the gifts for you girls along the way or the fabrics so will have to wait to give them to you on my return. Oh, there is one thing I can give you though." Kara opened one of the trunks and moved a few bundles to expose a red tin box nestled amidst clothes and fabric bundles. She smiled and pulled out the tin. "Be sure to share the sweets," she said, handing the tin to Jennie.

Jennie smiled and opened the tin, squealing slightly at the delicious assortment of sweets packed into the tin. Kat joined Jennie in studying the box of tins. Eventually they each picked out a piece of candy and popped them into their mouths. The kitchen boys arrived with the copper tub and a quick succession of boys carrying wooden pails of hot water followed. Kara watched them for a moment then made the decision to make the time to visit the stables while the bath was prepared.

"I have to go see Banner before I go," Kara said.

"What about the bath?" one of the boys who had just lugged in two buckets of steaming water asked. He stood frozen in the act of emptying a bucket.

"Just wait on adding the cold water until I get back."

"What about Elyse?" Jennie called after her.

Kara stopped in her tracks. She had forgotten about Elyse. The poor woman had headed straight for her room and did not know that Kara had to go straight back out on the road. Elyse would have to go with or she would have to drag one of the girls with her. No, if she brought one of the girls it would have to be Jennie or Kat since it could be hours before the rest returned from gathering blackberries. Kara looked back at the two girls. At fourteen years old Jennie was the elder and Kara had heard that her father was in the last stages of arranging her marriage. Though Kara was only six years older than Jennie, she felt ages older and only saw two young girls standing there watching her. Kara could not drag either of the girls along on such a task. There was no knowing what awaited them outside the manor walls. It would have to be Elyse. Kara sighed. Even if she thought to spare her companion from more traveling it was not likely Elyse would listen to her anyway.

"Yes, have someone tell Elyse what is happening," Kara said on her way out the door.

He resented her. Kara nearly ran all the way to the stables, ducking down back staircases and halls reserved for the servants to avoid any congestion. Lord only knew why but Lord Roffe resented her. Sending her to bear bad news gave Lord Roffe pleasure. Her uncle would be smiling for days thinking about her reception at Hawkstead's hands.

Kara slowed to a steady walk through the back courtyard, her healed riding boots beating out a steady staccato on the cobblestoned yard. Kara chewed on her lower lip as she considered the fact that Lord Roffe knew Hawkstead and seemed convinced that she would receive a beating. No wonder Angel refused to wed the man. Still, it was difficult to believe that a stranger would feel he had the liberty to physically abuse her. A stranger did not have the right.

Kara ducked into the stable, taking a deep breath of leather tack, sun-warmed straw, hay, and the warm bodies of prime horseflesh. Large, roomy stalls lined the building, each one holding a horse. Kara stopped at several stalls to say a quick hello to the equine occupant, a quick pat for one, a kiss on a velvety nose for another. Kara wished she had more time to give her beloved animals but it was Banner she was here to see and she had to hurry. Kara found the aged groom about halfway down the center aisle, checking the legs of a pregnant mare.

"Missy!" Banner said in delight, looking up, instinctively knowing Kara was there before she had a chance to make a sound. There were no formalities for his high born mistress from the man who technically was a servant. Banner leaned heavily against the mare's side to help him slowly straighten up from leaning over, his aged muscles protesting. He sighed from the effort necessary just to stand straight.

Banner was a slight man, sinewy muscles over a bony frame. As long as Kara could remember Banner had always been there and had always been old. His thin gray hair stood out in tufts over his head. Wrinkles made his face sag around an overly large nose. Deep brown eyes sparkled when he looked upon Kara. Until his accident he had been as spry as any stable boy though. Banner was not dealing well with being infirm and continued to go about his duties as if nothing had happened. At his age to properly heal the doctor wanted Banner lounging in bed for a few more weeks, or at least resting to give his body a chance to heal.

"Twenty mares from LeRouget, Banner," Kara said. "They're beauties. All bred with his Long Dancer."

"And to Mael?"

Kara glanced around. Though Banner would know who was in his stable she could not help it. No one was in sight. "Ten mares bred with Long Dancer and ten mares bred with Scescero. I just hope this threat of the barbarians does not interfere with my plans."

"What's this? Barbarians?" Banner asked.

"A massive horde. They are coming from the east and the south. I heard so many rumors that it's hard to know what's true, except that most of Italy is fallen but Rome is holding out. And they have conquered several provinces in the United Provinces of Poland. The Pope has sent out requests for aid and delegates from Germany were in Paris to discuss an alliance if they reach the German border, which prompted King Guy to turn to England."

Banner looked worried but he shrugged. "When the rumors get sifted out of the truth we shall decide our needed course of action."

"You and my uncle," Kara said in exasperation. "I could have strangled Angel when she told me her news on top of learning about this barbarian threat. I could barely sleep nights for worry. I heard horrible stories. They are not a conquering force. They are a destructive force. Could there be another plague? One that rots men's brains and all they think of is killing and destruction?"

"It is not always a plague," Banner said. He sighed. "I hope they are stopped before long. Even maniacs can only go so far. For our part we should look at supplying more stock to be trained as destriers and renniers so that the men facing these barbarians have the advantage of good horseflesh."

"Yes," Kara said, nodding. "It is my thought also. But it takes time, Banner. Hopefully they will be stopped long before that. Two years to even have stock old enough to start training. I can't imagine the state of the continent if they are still dealing with the barbarians in two years."

"And Benjamin worked out well, did he?" Banner asked changing the subject. Benjamin was his grandnephew and though Banner had confidence in the young man he still wanted the confirmation. This was the first horse buying trip that Kara had gone on without Banner at her side.

"Brilliantly. We constantly brought up that he was your nephew and that satisfied everyone that he had learned well from you. No one gave me a second thought," Kara said lightly.

Banner smiled in pride and nodded his head. "Good. Good. And you practiced the finger signals?" Kara nodded. She took his arm and led him slowly out of the stall to a stool near the door, bearing his weight as he settled onto the stool.

"No one suspected anything," Kara said. "Many asked after you." Banner smiled at hearing that he had friends asking about him. "I assured them that you were just too busy to make the journey this time," Kara said. Banner did not want anyone to know that a horse had gotten the best of him.

"The doctor says I'm not a young man anymore," Banner said with a chuckle and shake of his head. "Taking longer to heal. But I'll get there, dearie. I'll get there."

"I have no doubt," Kara said softly, looking at the old man fondly. He looked like he had aged twenty years while she was gone but at least he was moving around now. "I think you'll be dancing by the time I return."

Banner frowned. "Return? What's this?"

"My uncle is sending me out on an errand. I don't have much time so we'll have to go over the lists when I get back. Benjamin can give you adequate descriptions for now. He will do well. He is very sharp. I hope I'm not longer than a week. In exchange I promised the same number of mares carrying foals so we must make the list."

Chapter Two

It actually became two hours before Kara was on the road again, her uncle's letter stuffed into her skirt pocket. Elyse grumbled and muttered under her breath from the moment she stormed into the solar to the moment she settled into her sling in the wagon. That Kara was being sent to do what Elyse considered a lord's business was bad enough but that they weren't to be given even a day to rest had her back up like a cat facing a badger.

Elyse was Kara's second cousin on her mother's side. When Kara's mother had died Elyse had been living in the manor as a foster child for many years and had stepped up to take on the role of mothering Kara. Despite her grumbling, Elyse went everywhere with Kara and normally enjoyed traveling.

The twenty man guard who had escorted Kara on her travels had been replaced with twenty fresh men. Lord Roffe hadn't wanted to send his men back out without a rest. Kara would ride horseback most of the trip. Unless it rained or turned bitterly cold, riding on horseback was much more comfortable than riding in the old, stiff wagon beside Elyse. Kara could never convince Elyse of that fact unfortunately, so the wagon made the trip every time though it slowed them down dramatically.

The most common vehicle for travel was a wagon with a canvas covering the top and sides. Their wagon had higher than normal wooden sides and a covered roof, much like a moving sitting room, though most often there was not much room for sitting. The space between the sides and roof had canvas hung to cover the gap, which could be pushed aside to allow air to circulate when it was hot and tied down when it was raining. The chests and crates they had brought back from France had been removed. The assorted chests and crates were packed with seasonings, food stuffs and other supplies for the manor such as the French lace destined to edge bedding and gowns. Only Kara's personal chests had been returned to the wagon, plus the supplies needed for the week's journey there and back, so this time there was plenty of space in the wagon. At the front of the wagon a sling was strung from side to side and this was where Elyse spent her time on the road except for the few times she would walk beside the wagon and even fewer times she could be coaxed onto horseback.

A stable boy stepped forward and offered a leg up. Kara stepped into his cupped hands and vaulted into the saddle of her mount. The mare tugged at the bit half-heartedly but otherwise waited patiently. The mare would have preferred a longer stay in the stable as well. Kara snuggled her face into her fur collar. The fall wind carried a nip to it that afternoon. Around her the yard was chaotic with twenty men readying to ride out. Kara knew the names of most of them and the faces of the rest. The men chided each other as they checked pack animals and double checked their equipment. Kara smiled at some of the ribald comments floating around her head that she was not meant to hear.

The days were already becoming noticeably shorter as well. They had several hours of light left in the day and the first leg of the road was well known and suitable for traveling at dusk. Hopefully they could push through to Derby Town that day yet. Kara studied the gray sky with misgivings. She hoped it did not snow before they returned. Kara had no desire to be stuck at Hawkstead's longer than it took to deliver the message. Kara took a deep breath through her nose, relishing the brisk scent of winter in the air. Quite often the wind blew down the scent of winter from ice covered hills to the north weeks before snow would make its appearance in the area but she had not been home to know how the weather had been behaving over the past weeks.

The men acting as her escort must have felt something in the air as well for they set a steady pace to Derby Town and kept an eye on the sky as well as the surrounding countryside. They reached Derby Town in record time, with a few more hours of travelable time left in the day. Kara grimaced. At this rate the nearest town when dusk settled over the land would be a small village without an inn. To her surprise the men rode into the yard of Derby Town's largest inn. The escort's knight in charge saw her surprised face as she sat on her mare staring at the inn like she expected a trick. His name was Sir Jack Bullton and had been born and raised at Roffe Manor.

"We set the pace," Sir Bullton said. "Simon's mount lost a shoe." When Kara tilted her head and gave him a look of skeptical disbelief he sighed. "Rest, girlie."

"As much as I appreciate it, I'd rather get there before bad weather hits. I have no intention of being delayed at Greenestone due to bad weather," Kara said.

"Ah, sky is a bit gray is all. We'll ride out of it in a day or two," Sir Bullton said with a shrug. The knight attempted a stern expression and added gruffly, "Don't think every day will be like this or it'll be Christmas before we arrive."

True to his word, the pace was much harder the following days and though they rode northwesterly, the sky cleared and the weather remained mild with no hint of snow. On the third day they turned south. Kara spent most of the morning of the third day in the wagon with Elyse just because she was so exhausted. The sling was big but not so big that she could stretch out with Elyse sharing the sling so her legs were draped over Elyse's crossed legs. The road they currently followed was in fair shape and the sling's rocking motion almost lulled Kara into sleeping. Almost but not quite. Kara stared out through a gap in the canvas, pondering her steps when she returned from playing messenger to Hawkstead.

Elyse busied herself with needle and thread despite the bouncing and jarring of the wagon on the rough road. The sling absorbed most of the bouncing and Elyse was well accustomed to the rocking motion of the sling. "You should at least try to apply yourself to sewing," Elyse chided. "It is a wifely skill."

Kara wrinkled her nose. "You know that whatever I sew will fall apart after one day of wearing the garment. I would not do that even to Angel. Though it is most tempting. Trust her to put us through this and still convince you to make her maternity clothes."

"It is better than sitting here staring out at the trees morosely," Elyse said, looking at Kara pointedly, who was sitting staring out at the passing trees morosely.

"I have a lot on my mind," Kara said in her defense. "I have been puzzling over Hawkstead's name."

"His name?" Elyse asked. She set her sewing down and stared at Kara, quite perplexed. "What about his name?"

"Well, he's Lord Addington's second son, right? So his name should be Addington. Even before becoming heir. And he was made Earl of Greenestone. So where did Hawkstead come from?" Kara asked. "Did he just make it up out of thin air?"

"I could care less," Elyse said, picking up her needle again. "You should be thinking of more productive things."

"Less than a year, Elyse. I must be ready before Uncle realizes that I have looked into this," Kara said. "It's all I can think about. That and the barbarians at our door."

"They aren't at our door," Elyse said, wiping sweat from her neck.

"It's only a matter of time," Kara said. "You heard the king's men on the ferry. They came out of nowhere and are already nearing France's border. If they push through France as quickly as the other countries they will be here by the end of next year."

"Let us hope they don't get through France then," Elyse said. "Only a few days ago it felt like winter was around the corner and today it's boiling hot," Elyse muttered, wiping the sweat from her forehead.

"Take off that wimple," Kara muttered. "I am totally comfortable."

"I would not," Elyse said in shock.

"No one is here to see you," Kara pointed out.

Elyse glanced around, noting that the riders were only visible from the waist down. She shook her head. "No. A lady does not go about with her head bared to the world."

Kara shook her head from side to side and made mocking sounds. "A lady this and a lady that," Kara said scornfully. "I would think a lady would prefer to have her head bared to the empty road than sweat like a prune."

"A prune? Really? That's the best you can come up with?" Elyse chided. She laughed. "Child, I can't seem to get angry with you, though you do push me at times."

"When I reach my majority I will ban all wimples from all my estates. It's a stupid custom," Kara said. She stared out the window as she talked and suddenly saw something in a break between trees that caught her attention. "Look! Are we on the road to Crowborough?"

Elyse rolled her eyes and shook her head. "What makes you think I know?"

"Because you grew up here," Kara said. She stuck her head out the window. "I wish to ride, stop the wagon."

"I thought you were going to rest?" Elyse chided.

"I can't find rest in this wagon," Kara muttered, swinging her legs off Elyse's lap and almost falling off the sling in the process.

The wagon rattled to a halt. Kara grabbed Elyse's skirts to keep from sliding under the sling. Her escort immediately took up defensive positions and scanned the woods surrounding them. They were more vulnerable when at a stop. Kara crouched on the wagon floor, adjusting her skirts as she waited for someone to bring her mare up then jumped out of the wagon. The mare threw her head back in surprise when Kara jumped out right in front her. Kara patted the mare's neck and apologized for startling her.

"A lady does not jump out of a wagon," Elyse said in horror.

Kara looked up at Elyse and grinned. She vaulted into the saddle with the assistance of a leg up from one of the grooms. As soon as she was astride the wagon driver cracked the reins and the wagon started forward again. Kara guided her mare up to walk next to Sir Bullton, who was leading the way.

"Tell me, Sir Bullton, how far now to Hawkstead's hold?" Kara asked, studying the countryside. Something about the terrain gave her the sense that she should know the area. There, through the trees, a glimpse of a rusted skeletal structure high above the tree tops.

"God willing, we'll reach it late afternoon, my Lady," he said.

"Do we continue south?"

"Aye. For a few hours yet, then we'll change back to a westerly course, my Lady."

"That's the Glass Building, isn't it?" Kara asked, pointing at the top of the gutted building in the distance. "I have never seen it from this side so it looks different. But it is, isn't it?"

"Aye," Sir Bullton said, nodding as he gazed out across the trees. "That be the Glass House. About thirty kilometers, I think. Though there hasn't been glass for ages now. I've heard squatters have been using the area though. No lords left in the area to keep an eye on things."

"We are near Mael, then?" Kara could not control the tinge of excitement in her voice. "It felt like we were going in the right direction but I was not sure. I didn't have time to look at the map before we left."

"Aye, another long half day's journey north, past Hawkstead's hold. Half a day with that blessed cart rattling its way, that is. A few hours without anything with wheels. If that's what you mean by near."

Kara nodded her head and let her mare fall back a few steps behind Sir Bullton as she settled into deep thought. The plan was to deliver the news to Hawkstead and immediately turn around and leave for Roffe Manor. It meant a rough journey but then she would be done. Now Kara toyed with a better idea. Kara closed her eyes, trying to recall the map and estimate their position against the geography she knew. After delivering the news to Hawkstead she could ride on to Mael early on the morrow and still have most of the day to review the conditions at her estate.

Some of Kara's exhaustion faded with the excitement at knowing that it was almost over and she had been given the unexpected opportunity to visit Mael before spring. Banner should be able to get things started at Roffe Manor. A few extra days at Mael would actually save her time. Kara wished she had known that Greenestone Keep was south of Mael.

They should arrive at Hawkstead's hold by that evening and then in the morning she could ride on to Mael. Kara did some mental juggling with time and decided she would not lose more than a day or two even if she stayed for several more days since the road from Mael to Roffe Manor was better, more direct, and traveling would be faster. The road was better so traffic was higher which meant more chance of running into bandits but their group should be intimidating enough to prevent possible attacks. Kara hadn't been to Mael in almost a year and this was an opportune time to make a visit. It was a good omen.

Elyse stuck her head out the wagon's canvas window and called Kara to her. "I'm thinking that if it's a beating waiting for you some cushioning is in order," the woman said.

Kara stared at her in confusion. "Cushioning?"

"Aye. A few layers of stout wool should dampen the blows."
Elyse smiled at Kara's reaction to her enigmatic statement.

Kara returned to the wagon more out of curiosity than anything.
Once again the wagon halted, the escort took up their positions, and
Kara handed her horse's reins to a groom before crawling up the
short ladder into the wagon. At first Kara thought it was a stupid idea
but as Elyse explained her plan and they looked through the clothes
made for a pregnant Angel Kara threw her hands in the air in
surrender and let Elyse have her way. Elyse's project took several
hours, hindered by the jarring, bouncing wagon ride but Elyse
strained herself in her effort to protect Kara from Hawkstead's
anticipated abuse.

The road wound past a walled village ahead and Sir Bullton told
Kara that the keep was not far from the village. The road was better
maintained here, almost bump free. Kara glanced around, suddenly
feeling uncomfortable. A strange knot twisted in her stomach and
she stared at the village visible a few miles up the road. The village
looked normal. Kara studied the forest to the left. Tall, straight white
birch trees lined the edge of the forest. There was a quarter mile
cleared between the road and trees, providing no hiding spots for
anyone. Kara looked to her right. There were trees to the right but
not a forest, apple trees and filbert trees growing in straight rows.
There was no threat there either. Yet she felt anxious. Maybe not

quite anxious but a strange feeling of exhilaration mixed with fear warred within her. She would rather be anywhere but here.

They reached the village and several people stepped up to the road and waved and watched in curiosity. Double walls surrounded the village. The outer wall was neatly stacked stones about six feet high. The inner wall was almost ten feet high and made of whole timber. Most of the trees cleared from the sides of the road had gone into making that wall. The gates were still open for night had not yet fallen. Two men preparing a fire pit with cords of wood just outside the gate looked up and waved. Several children laughed and shouted and ran beside the wagon for a few minutes. The strange knot in her stomach untwisted as they passed the village.

"One last touch," Elyse said, digging out a wimple.

"I am not wearing a wimple," Kara said.

"It will protect your head," Elyse said.

"My head?"

"What if he punches you in the head?" Elyse asked.

"I suppose that's possible," Kara said slowly. "Do you think he will really hit me in the head?"

"I don't know," Elyse said. "It's better to be safe than sorry. In fact, knights wear metal helmets."

"Oh, no," Kara said, eyes widening when Elyse held up a pot. "I am not wearing that on my head! Give me the stupid wimple."

Thus Kara rode up to Hawkstead's keep well-padded with layers of dresses and fabric tied and pinned into place, covered by an over-sized silk dress meant for Angel's later stage of pregnancy. Lord Roffe had been specific that she must not greet Hawkstead wearing wool. Elyse had padded the headdress beneath the wimple now covering Kara's head but the pot was still in the wagon. Kara might be talked into padding against a possible beating but she drew the line at wearing a pot on her head no matter how much Elyse tried to convince her that she could camouflage the pot.

Hawkstead could still break her nose. Kara was convinced however that even if he took a quarterstaff to her anywhere else she would not feel it through all the wool padding. Unfortunately, she was already starting to sweat profusely. She could feel it running down her back.

Kara looked up at the massive walls surrounding the keep as they approached the gates. The place was teaming with activity even though the day's light was ending. It was an impressive sight, this keep. Scaffolding covered a large stretch of the wall facing the road. Workers were in the process of fixing an expanse of wall that had either been damaged or was crumbling from neglect and it looked like they were expanding the wall by almost half its length again. Flying buttresses and guard holes lined the wall that one had to strain their neck to look up at such close proximity. Guard towers soared another hundred yards above the wall at each corner and at the gate. Greenestone definitely earned the title of keep. Roffe Manor had high, thick walls of stone and brick surrounding the manor and several acres surrounding the manor house but those walls suddenly seemed so fragile compared to the walls guarding this keep.

Suddenly Kara felt absurd, stuffed like a hen for the oven, prepared for a rage that might not happen. Maybe Hawkstead was a different man than her uncle. Kara knew that not every man beat defenseless women. What if everyone was completely wrong about the reception Hawkstead would give her? It was too late to change her attire now. Kara felt the thick paper in her pocket. Her uncle had some trick up his sleeve and when it came to her uncle Kara always seemed to come out on the wrong side of the stick. The wagon rolled up to the gates of the keep. Sir Bullton galloped up ahead of the wagon and its escort of armed men. He raised Roffe's banner. "Ho the Hold!" Sir Bullton called. Kara sighed. This was it.

A handful of Hawkstead's men rode out of the hold's gate to greet them, then escorted Kara and her group inside once they had been identified. Dusk was quickly taking hold now and torch bearers were making their rounds to light braziers filled with stacked wood stretching out in both directions from the entrance. The bonfires served as warmth for the men guarding the gates as well as light. The light was not for the guards but to illuminate anyone approaching the walls. It was too late to leave the keep yet that night but she still hoped to deliver her news immediately and leave at first light in the morning.

Kara dismounted from the wagon with assistance. Lord, but her added bulk made her feel awkward. She prayed the padding did not slip. The last thing Kara needed was to leave a trail of dropped articles of clothing. Roffe's men noticed her sudden bulk with mixed reactions. Some looked quite confused and some shrugged it off as a female thing. Sir Bullton looked like he was going to ask her something, his mouth moving without sound, then he grinned and shook his head and let it go.

A tall, slender man approached. He bowed formerly. "Lady Roffe, welcome to Hawkstead Keep. I am Lord Hawkstead's steward of the hall, Nelson."

Kara nodded her head in greeting. There was something different about him that caught her off guard. The man was very polite, very proper, yet something was lacking. It took her a few minutes to figure out that it was a lack of the spark of interest that normally lit men's eyes when they met her. Odd how she had never given it thought until it was missing.

"Thank you, Nelson," she said with a smile. "Is your lord in residence?"

"Lady Roffe, indeed he is," Nelson said. "Your men will be taken to the barracks. How many knights in your party?"

"Just Sir Bullton," Kara said.

"Lady Roffe, Sir Bullton, this way, if you please," the man said, gesturing to the massive double doors serving as the entrance into the keep proper. A tall, slender young man strongly resembling Nelson stood in the doorway. "My Lord will wait until you've had a chance to freshen from your arduous journey. A room is being prepared for you and your companion. Sir Bullton, I hope you don't mind sharing a room with Sir Andrews, another guest. A meal will be sent up in a few minutes. Our chamberlain, Kevin, will take you well into hand. Ah, here comes Kevin now."

Elyse trailed behind them, ogling the giant doors as they walked across the cobbled courtyard and up three stone slabs serving as steps. Kara barely noticed her surroundings, though the massive doors did warrant a second look. A giant could use them without ducking his head. Kara was busy trying to decide how to handle her encounter with Hawkstead. It was very tempting to put off confronting the lord of the keep until the next day. Very tempting. Kara paused at the doorway. A man who looked remarkably like Nelson stood just inside the doorway to greet them. Nelson introduced him as Kevin, the chamberlain. The two men were clearly related, probably brothers, and gentle born.

Kevin stared at Kara in fascination. Nelson coughed twice and Kevin immediately averted his eyes. Kara had never had anyone stare at her like that before and was confused until she remembered that she wore several layers of clothes and padding that did not conform to the normal shape of a woman's body.

Kara had every intention of delivering her message without delay, yet now it seemed she was being given an opportunity to delay the meeting. If she followed Nelson's instructions and walked to the right and up the staircase she could put off the encounter with Hawkstead for at least a few more hours. To the left was the corridor leading to the keep's Great Hall. Kara could not see who occupied the Great Hall but she could hear the murmur of voices, the general turmoil of an operating keep, with occasional bursts of laughter and shouting. Sir Bullton and Elyse had already ascended the staircase, chatting idly, led by a young page. Kara could no longer see them but she could still hear their voices. If Kara followed the chamberlain to the right, she would lose the courage to face Hawkstead. Already her legs trembled in nervousness. Kara took a deep breath and squared her shoulders.

"I'm afraid I'm not a bearer of good news," Kara said. "I must request an immediate audience with your master."

Nelson and Kevin exchanged glances. Nelson definitely looked unhappy. Kevin looked interested, like a boy just told there was a cat fighting a mountain lion in the courtyard or maybe a bear wearing a hat in the hall. "Can it not wait 'til the morrow, my Lady?" Nelson asked.

"Nay."

Nelson grimaced. "I was afraid you would say that. Very well."

Nelson led the way down the dark corridor towards the Great Hall. Kevin sighed and trotted up the stairs after Sir Bullton and Elyse. Duty called. The light from the Great Hall was the only source of light in the corridor so as they approached it became easier to see, though it was still quite dim. The main sources of light were a few torches burning in metal holders along the back wall and a fire roared in a massive fireplace. A few tables had pots of burning oil as well. Kara slowed, giving her eyes time to adjust to the meager lighting.

Tapestries, weapons, and dead animal heads hung on the stone walls. More weapons hung on the thick timbers supporting the ceiling. Half a dozen men sat at a table on a dais centered to the fireplace. Rough plank tables scattered around the room also had men seated at them, some playing dice or chess, some eating, and some cleaning weapons. A few dogs wandered about the room, rooting for dropped food or smelling something of interest.

All heads at the raised table looked her way when she entered behind Nelson. The boisterous laughter faded but a steady hum of speculation continued to fill the hall with noise. Nelson approached the table and spoke in a low voice to a man who sat with his head down, chin on his chest. The man stood abruptly and Kara involuntarily gasped in surprise before composing herself. This must be Hawkstead. He was a giant of a man. No wonder Angel was afraid of him. If Hawkstead shared Roffe's temper Kara would not survive a beating from him even bound in layers of wool.

Hawkstead's strong, square jaw was covered with a neatly trimmed goatee, framing a well-formed mouth. He was not just tall, he was massively built with muscles that bulged beneath his tight fitting clothes, the clothe straining with every movement he made. Hawkstead was too far across the semi-darkened room for Kara to see many details, yet he exuded strength, power, and magnificence. For a moment she felt he could see through her to her very soul as he stood there staring boldly at her. Kara blinked and the moment passed.

Hawkstead wavered on his feet. He held up his goblet and had some difficulty coordinating his hand and mouth as he tried to drink. A goodly amount of ale slopped down the front of his shirt. Kara's eyes widened in shock when she realized that the man was drunk. He hadn't been looking into her soul. He had been trying to focus to even see her form.

Nelson spoke again, more urgently. Hawkstead frowned and squinted his eyes as he stared blankly at Kara. "So, whad's dis?"

The man was drunker than a wasp fallen into a wine barrel. Kara stared at him in silence as she debated on her course of action. Hawkstead wobbled some more then flopped back into his chair. This was obviously why the steward had tried to divert her from seeing Hawkstead right away. By all rights she should wait to deliver her message until he was sober. It was the better choice. Yet, who was to say that the man was ever sober?

Kara stood where she was, thinking of her options as she rubbed her thumb across the impressed wax seal on the letter from Roffe. She could hand him the letter, tell him that it was with regret that Angel was no longer free to wed him, and leave in the morning while he was sleeping off his drunkenness. If her visit was a bit hazy for him on the morrow he had the letter as physical evidence. There was his steward to witness any message as well. It was so easy. It

was not her problem that she had arrived to find the lord of the keep
in a drunken state.

Kara knew that the right thing to do was retire to the room set
aside for her and wait patiently until the man was sober enough on
the morrow to give her his attention. If he spent the night drinking
who knew when he would rise on the morrow? He could possibly
sleep the whole morning away and that would mean waiting and
possibly losing another full day. Plus, she would have gone to all the
work of turning into a stuffed sausage for nothing. Kara chose the
direct way.

Nelson was busy trying to talk some sense into Hawkstead, who
was frowning and shaking his head a lot while trying to get more ale
into his mouth than down the front of his shirt. Kara took a deep
breath. Time to face the storm. Kara crossed the room and presented
the sealed letter from Roffe. Even if Hawkstead could not read,
someone in the keep should be able to read it to him. Her uncle had
not said she had to witness the man reading the letter, only that she
was to deliver it to Hawkstead. "If you are Lord Hawkstead then this
is for you. It is a note from Lord Roffe."

Now that she was closer to him she was struck by how
handsome he was. Even drunk with bloodshot eyes he was striking.
His nose was straight and not too long nor too short. Overly long
eyelashes framed eyes so blue that they almost glowed with an inner
light. Soft, light brown hair curled ever so slightly around his ears
and down the nape of his neck. Angel had never mentioned that his

features were fair enough to suck the air out of her whole body. The bloodshot eyes and jerky, wavering movements were the only sign that he was drunk. He was not the first drunk man Kara had seen, though her uncle was very strict on drunkenness in his hall. Men made stupid decisions when filled with spirits.

Hawkstead frowned. He stared up at her in apparent confusion before taking the letter in his thick fingers. He looked between her and the letter several times, blinking. "Whad's dat?"

Kara sighed. All that beauty yet the man must have had a head injury, or he was slow. She leaned closer, trying to not announce the news to the whole hall. "I regret to tell you that there will not be a marriage between you and my cousin, Lady Angeline Roffe," she said in a low voice.

Hawkstead stared blankly at her. Kara wondered if he'd heard her. She straightened, chewing the inside of her cheek out of habit. Kara did not want to shout. Men and their pride was a touchy thing sometimes. If Kara had been doing things right she would have requested a private audience when he was sober. She did not think anyone else had heard her though, except maybe Nelson and the man sitting right next to Hawkstead, who she just noticed. He looked familiar. For a moment Kara was distracted as she tried to place the face of the man sitting next to Hawkstead. Maybe she had seen him at a horse fair for she could not produce a name to go with the face.

Hawkstead continued to stare at her, his frown drawing furrows across his brow. His gaze went from her head to her toes and back up again. Whatever he saw made his frown deepen. Hawkstead slid his large finger under the seal and used his thumb to flip open the letter, never taking his gaze from Kara. A dog bumped against Kara's legs and licked her fingers. Kara automatically stroked the dog's head. It was comforting to have someone at her side, even if it was just a dog.

The man next to Hawkstead reached for the letter when it appeared that Hawkstead was having difficulty getting it open. Hawkstead brushed the man's hand away without even looking. "Who's are you?" He glanced at the dog licking her hand and grunted. "Damned dog."

"Lady Kara Roffe," Kara said, startled to realize he had just referred to her as a dog. She did not notice that he had actually been looking at the dog when he spoke. It felt like a tight band of iron wrapped around her chest.

Hawkstead blinked. He took a long swallow of ale, sighed, and settled back in his chair to read the letter. Hawkstead read a few lines, then frowned and started reading at the beginning again. Halfway through the letter he choked as he took another swallow of ale. He slammed his goblet on the table, spraying ale everywhere. Whatever he was reading was seeping through his drunken cloud and he sat up a little straighter. Hawkstead glanced between Kara and the letter ominously. Kara felt sweat running down the small of her back as well as her temples. She was ready to vacate the Great Hall and this hulking man's moody drunkenness and leave him to Roffe's letter in privacy.

Kara tried to speak but her throat was suddenly dry. She had to clear her throat with a small cough to be able to speak. "I know you were counting on an alignment between Roffe and Hawkstead houses but Lord Roffe regrets to tell you that Angel cannot--"

Hawkstead interrupted her with a bellow. "Bloody arse gives me you 'stead."

Kara blinked. She was not certain what he meant. She could not have heard him right. Was he upset that Roffe had sent her instead of coming himself? Several of Hawkstead's men were looking at her and chuckling at some joke Kara did not understand. Hawkstead stared at her in drunken amazement. He shook the letter at her then tossed it onto the table in disgust.

"Thought I was getting an angel and got you tossed at me 'stead." He jumped to his feet, startling Kara into stepping backwards. "We gonna take it, men?"

Several voices yelled "No!" collectively. A few stragglers added their voices in a delayed response. Hawkstead hadn't been the only one dipping too deeply into the ale that night. Kara looked around the room more closely. Quite a few heads drooped onto chests and quite a few bodies had toppled to the floor. Other than serving girls she was the only woman in the room. It was time to retreat. Kara glanced around for Nelson. She hadn't noticed him leaving yet Nelson had vanished.

A sober voice sounded from behind her. "Hawkstead, let me see the letter." Kara glanced over her shoulder. Nelson had fetched the newcomer and now waited patiently beside Kara while the man approached Hawkstead.

Hawkstead waved his hand at the letter. "Help yerself, Richard."

The newcomer, Richard, picked up the letter and began reading, eyebrows rising a few times. He was older than Hawkstead, perhaps an uncle as there was a strong physical resemblance between them. Kara felt relieved that there was someone in authority, someone in charge at last. It helped that he was sober. It would have been much simpler if this sober man was Hawkstead instead of the man who was actually Hawkstead. Richard looked up at Kara thoughtfully then went back to reading. When he finished reading he carefully folded the letter and held it instead of putting it back on the ale-puddled table.

"Your name, child," Richard said gently.

"Lady Kara Roffe," Kara said slowly. She should have said her full title but this did not seem the time or place.

"Do you know the contents of this letter?"

Kara shook her head, not trusting herself to speak. She wondered what Roffe had written. Her fingers itched to snatch the letter out of the man's hands to read for herself what was causing such a commotion. Though her uncle had anticipated a reaction, she hadn't expected this type of reaction. She should have read it before they arrived, Kara realized. It had never occurred to her to do that.

Hawkstead drained his cup. He stared at her through narrowed eyes, grunted, and refilled his cup. Richard frowned at Hawkstead for the briefest moment before turning back to Kara. Richard smiled gently at Kara.

"It is a shame this discussion could not have waited for the morrow," Richard chided, though his gaze drifted past Kara to Nelson. Nelson shrugged and grimaced. "Do you know why you were sent here, child?" Richard asked.

A goblet flew past Kara's shoulder, spraying ale everywhere. A scuffle broke out between two men and Kara stepped to the side to avoid being knocked over. What a barbaric place this keep was! The sooner she could be on her way the better. Kara hoped there was a way to bar the door in the room she would rest in that night. They would leave at first light. When Nelson escorted her to her room she would tell him to let her men know to be ready early in the morning.

"Lady Angel Roffe has married another. Since there was a growing understanding between my uncle and that, that man, my uncle requested I deliver the news. I did not expect to find this, this man, drunk but I must be urgently on my way at first light so did not care to wait to find him sober," Kara said, meeting Hawkstead's glowering gaze with her own angry gaze.

Richard nodded thoughtfully. He turned to Hawkstead. "I suggest you seriously consider the offer."

"Excuse me," Kara said. "What offer?"

"Pardon my manners," the man said. "I am Richard Westgate, cousin to Lord Hawkstead. And oftentimes sober advisor. Your uncle--"

"Bring a priest!" Hawkstead yelled, interrupting Richard. He staggered to his feet, swaying where he stood. "I'm gonna marry me a lumpy dog 'stead of an angel!"

Kara's stomach dropped to her feet. Hawkstead thought Roffe had sent her in Angel's place. It was the last thing Kara expected. They must have misread the letter. Roffe would never do that. It did not make any sense. Roffe would not allow her to marry. He had too much to lose if she married. He had gone out of his way to prevent Kara from marrying all these years. He would not now suddenly throw her at Hawkstead. It did not make sense that Roffe would have offered her in place of Angel. Neither did it make sense for Hawkstead to agree to such a sudden marriage proposal.

Kara would not do it. She would not marry a drunken lout who despised the sight of her. Kara turned and ran. Richard gestured. Kara did not get very far. Two very strong, sober men blocked her way. Each took one of her arms and dragged her back to stand next to Richard. The priest arrived within minutes. Kara looked more closely. Most likely the priest had been one of the bodies snoozing with his chin on his chest until someone had roused him only moments ago. Wine stained his sleeve and shirt front. The hair on one side of his head stood out sideways.

"No," Kara whispered. She closed her eyes, took a deep breath, then faced Richard with pleading eyes. "I can't."

"You have no choice, child," Richard said. He patted her hand. "It will be all right." He stepped aside to speak privately with the priest for several minutes, showing the priest Roffe's letter. The priest nodded and left the room. He returned shortly, wearing formal robes in preparation for performing a marriage ceremony.

Held in place by two men and ringed by several other of Hawkstead's men who were sober enough to stand, Kara listened to the priest recite the marriage litany. Twice the priest paused in his recital to take a deep gulp from a wine chalice to clear his dry throat. The room seemed to spin. The air was thick and yet sparse. Hawkstead again sat slumped in his chair. He blinked when the priest addressed him, struggling to focus. He glanced at Kara, then looked at Richard. Hawkstead shrugged.

"Sure. Why not?" he muttered. Richard kicked him in the shin. "Yes, yes," Hawkstead said in exasperation.

The priest turned to Kara. "Do you take Lionel Henry Gabriel Michael Hawkstead as--"

"No. Never," Kara said firmly.

Startled, the priest hesitated, mouth opening and closing like a fish gasping for air. Richard held up Roffe's letter. "Her guardian gives permission. We can do it by proxy if necessary."

The priest nodded, took a deep breath, pronounced them married, and reached for his wine chalice. The chalice was empty.

He tilted it over in dismay. A kind hearted drinking companion shoved a cup of ale into the priest's hands. The priest downed the contents and wiped his chin. Kara's knees buckled. She sagged between her two guards. Someone brought her a chair and her guards eased her onto the seat but maintained their hold on her arms. Kara wondered where Roffe's men were during the entire episode and if they were aware of what was happening, then decided that even if they had stepped in to protect her, the wily Richard would likely convince them that it was Roffe's orders. Maybe it was Roffe's orders. Kara still felt she should have had some say in the matter.

The whole event was surreal. Kara had arrived intending to deliver the news about Angel no longer being free to marry Hawkstead and now she was suddenly married to the man. Not only had she never anticipated such a thing, she still could not believe it had actually happened. Kara regretted not reading the letter. If she had known the contents she would have handled delivering the news differently. What could she have done? Burned the letter? Sent the letter and continued on to Mael? Mael would not have kept her hidden long, unfortunately. It would be the first place Lord Roffe would look. It had to be a mistake. When everyone was sober in the morning they would have to listen to reason.

Hawkstead continued to drink ale while his men slapped his back in congratulations. Some made ribald comments about the upcoming wedding night. It did not take long before the crowd decided to drag the newly married couple upstairs and toss them in bed for the bedding ceremony. Hawkstead thought it a good joke and willingly let them pull him to his feet. Kara did not think it such a good idea but one of Hawkstead's burly companions did not bother to give her a chance to voice her opinion. He simply picked her up and slung her over his shoulder, leading the way up the stairs at a brisk trot.

The master bedroom was dominated by a massive oak bed with a red velvet canopy tied back to the bed posts. Kara did not have a chance to see anything but the bed before she was dropped to her feet and shoved in the general direction of the bed. Hawkstead came stumbling after her, being held upright by many supporting arms. When Hawkstead reached her he pulled her against his hard frame and planted a wet, drunken kiss on her cheek. He had aimed for her mouth but missed when Kara turned her face. He fumbled with the ties of his drawers, nearly causing Kara to faint when she realized what he was about to do. Panic gave her strength and she pushed against his chest. Hawkstead lost his balance and they both toppled backwards onto the bed, eliciting cheers from the crowd. Satisfied that the couple had things in hand, and with Richard's cool voice ordering everyone out, the room soon emptied of the onlookers.

Hawkstead had landed on top of Kara. She gasped for air under his crushing weight. Kara pounded on his arm but he did not move. Desperately she used all her strength to push and wiggle until she could at least breathe. After a moment to catch her breath, Kara again pounded on his arm to push him off her. Hawkstead grunted and rolled onto his side. Within seconds he began to snore. Kara lay where she was, on her back, staring up at the canopy over the bed frame. Hysteria brought tears to her eyes even as she laughed silently in disbelief. Kara had entered a nightmare.

Kara wiped the tears from her eyes then struggled to sit up, tugging her skirts in an effort to get them from under his body. Both her added padding and his weight made it difficult and she paused to sob in frustration. There was enough light from the candles burning on a side table against the wall for her to see the drunken man who was now her husband. Kara studied his features in the candlelight.

Never had Kara even been near a man as large as this one. Even in repose his arms bulged with muscle. His long, muscled legs dangled over the edge of the bed, long and hard. Everything about him was hard. Kara tugged her skirts out from under Hawkstead's legs at last and clambered off the bed.

Kara paced the length of the room angrily. How dare he! How dare Roffe trick her like this. It was humiliating. How dare that priest still perform the ceremony despite her protests? How dare Hawkstead call her a fat dog? How dare the man still marry her when he thought she was so horrible on his eyes? Kara was not foolish enough to think that she would marry for anything other than political or financial reasons yet it still hurt to hear him refer to her as a dog. It was not what she expected of a gentleman. Kara glanced at the man lying on the bed in drunken slumber. He did not fit any description of a gentleman.

Kara sat in the single chair in the room, a wood armed chair with a padded seat designed for enough room even for her padded girth. In the morning she would wake and find this was all a bad dream. It could not be true. Roffe had always been determined to not allow her to marry. It did not make sense that on some whim he would hand her over to Hawkstead. It had to be a misunderstanding. If this marriage was a misunderstanding it would be Kara who Lord Roffe blamed, no matter that she had no desire to be in this position and had tried to avoid it. If this marriage was a misunderstanding Roffe would be *madly* enraged at her. Roffe probably did not realize that she knew the extent of her inheritance but she did know. If he lost guardianship of her he would lose too much. It had to be a misunderstanding.

Kara covered her face with her hands. She had less than a year to reach her majority. Kara had visited with a solicitor in England the first time when she was eighteen, where she had learned her full inheritance and that when she reached her majority she could make certain decisions herself. Kara had quietly been investigating her own marriage arrangements, to a nice young man who would provide his name and support but otherwise let her live her life as she wished. He was also in need of a convenient marriage to live his life as he wished. They had only touched on the topic but Kara felt confident that they could come to a firm agreement within the year.

Now she wondered if Roffe had learned of her plans. Could her uncle plan her death to hold what he had? Kara did not know where that idea came from and was so startled at the thought that she jumped to her feet and paced once again. Roffe needed her. Losing her meant his losing too much. Kara often thought that Roffe's anger with her stemmed from the deep resentment he felt in knowing that he was so dependent on her. She had thought on occasion that he would try to marry her to someone he could control or he would hold her hostage in some room in the keep once she reached her majority, but either choice would eliminate his greatest source of income. It made no sense for him to give her to Hawkstead. One thing she knew, if this was some misunderstanding Roffe would punish her.

In the morning she would leave for Mael and stay there. Kara looked at the man the world would call her husband now. They weren't really married until it was consummated. She would go live on her estate and avoid her uncle and her new husband who was not her husband. At Mael she would be free of uncles who hated her and men who thought she was ugly and married her anyway. Tears ran down her cheeks. It had hurt to hear him say that she was a dog. It should not matter, yet it did.

If she could not annul the marriage she would be trapped for the rest of her life with a man who could not bear to look at her without grimacing. It was a horrible thought. It was bad enough growing up with her uncle's abuse, she was not ready to go from that to a miserable marriage with a man who hated her. At least the situation with her uncle had had an end in sight. This marriage to Hawkstead would be for the rest of her life.

"Enough," she whispered, wiping her tears with a determined hand.

Feeling sorry for herself would not change anything. Since Hawkstead was not happy with her she should be able to convince him that they were better off not being married. Kara sat up straighter. Of course, when he sobered he would possibly listen to reason and agree to annul the marriage. Concentrating on what she would do instead of concentrating on what was happening to her helped ease away the feelings of panic.

Kara fell asleep in the chair. She woke with a stiff neck to the sight of Hawkstead standing over her. He definitely was not happy. The anger in his eyes made her sink back against the chair. His height was impressive across the room, with him standing over her, looming in such a dark, sour mood, he felt even more impressively large. A spark of anger flared in her own eyes at his trying to intimidate her but the spark quickly faded. The man was an imposing sight. Knowing the damage her uncle did when he struck her, Kara could only imagine how much worse it would be from this man. Kara suddenly felt very small and insignificant against so much might.

"So, Roffe sent you to replace the daughter," Hawkstead said in a deep, low voice. "One ugly chit and not even a virgin."

Kara stared at him in surprised horror. "What?"

He waved at the bed though his gaze did not leave her. "No virgin sign from our wedding bed."

Kara bit her lip to keep from responding to his false assumption. The idiot had been so drunk that he did not even know that he had passed out without doing more than slobbering on her cheek. The promise of a new day was starting out to be as bad as the day before. She had barely gotten any sleep all night. Her eyes felt puffy from lack of sleep and crying. Kara was so hot from all the extra padding that she had sweated barrels of sweat and she could smell her own body odor. Sweat beaded on her upper lip. If he was going to beat her Kara wished he would get the beating out of the way. Anticipation was always the worse.

Chapter Three

Hawkstead visibly slumped. He ran his fingers through his hair. "I'm sorry," he said, sounding sincere. Kara's eyes widened in surprise. Most of her anger softened. "I'm sorry I chose yesterday to get drunk," he added, still sincere. Kara's eyes narrowed in renewed anger.

Hawkstead rubbed his temple. Kara felt no sympathy for him if he was suffering the pangs of the after effects of too much drink. His eyes were still bloodshot and now he had dark brown bags under his eyes. His hair stood in tufts across his head and his constantly running his fingers through his hair did not improve matters in the least. Kara stared up at him. Her wimple had slipped and twisted and pressed against her right eye, making it difficult to see out of the eye. Hawkstead was still the most handsome man she had ever seen.

"Well, the deed is done," Hawkstead said. He paced the room twice before facing her again. "I needed a wife and I guess you are it. You're not to my taste. I won't be touching you again." He grimaced and glanced at a spot on the wall. "At least I won't be touching you for a while."

Kara did not say a word. She did not move a muscle. Each word out of his mouth cut her deep inside. Kara had never given much thought to her looks despite her uncle's constant barbs. It should not matter what Hawkstead thought of her, yet it hurt. Hawkstead had said he needed a wife. What if he would not release her? He must release her. Then he would be free to wed someone he actually wanted. Kara tried to think of a way to convince him that he could be free of her, without offending him.

Hawkstead stared at her for several minutes. He frowned and stepped closer. Kara flinched when he reached for her but all he did was raise her chin with his finger. Her wimple squished her right eye almost completely shut. "Funny how your face does not match the rest of you," he said. Kara remained frozen in silence and he sighed as he stepped back. "The marriage is a fact. I have no desire to be husband to you but we are wed. I will expect nothing of you. Do you understand?"

Kara licked her dry lips. "You want no child then?"

"Since I need an heir I have no choice but to sire one upon you. Perhaps a child resulted from last night? If you turn out to be pregnant I shall be counting carefully. I have no intention of being forced to raise another man's bastard." Hawkstead paused but Kara remained silent, glaring up at him sullenly. "If you're not pregnant we can discuss children in the future. First I want to be certain any child is actually mine." His gaze drifted down the length of her lumpy, padded body. "And I feel no desire for you. But in the dark I suppose I could bring myself to perform the necessary deed."

"*Forced?*" Kara mouthed the word. Fire lit her eyes, startling Hawkstead with how much her face changed. Kara sat up straight, hands clenched on the arms of the chair. "Forced?" she said aloud. Hawkstead took a step back. "I had no desire to wed you. Or did you forget your men dragging me to stand before your whine-soaked priest? Did you forget my being *forced* to marry you?"

Hawkstead frowned, distracted by a sudden interest in the woman sitting in front of him with fire in her eyes. Vague memories returned of his new bride refusing to marry him and Richard telling Father Tom to do it anyway. It did not make sense that the lumpy woman sitting in front of him would not want to marry him. Most women would line up for the chance to be his wife. Hawkstead certainly would have chosen someone besides her to wed. She should have jumped at the chance to marry him, not fought so hard against it. Though Roffe was wealthy it would surely drain even his vast coffers to find a suitable match willing to take her as wife. Or a drunken idiot.

Hawkstead shook his head to clear the images of Hans and Jonathon dragging her back when she tried to run. That could not be right. Yet, married they were. He stared at her, wondering if there was more to her than he first thought. If it was not for her sweating bulk she might be worth investigating. Still, he would not claim a child that was not his.

Hawkstead had the worse hangover. He was not use to drinking such quantities of ale as he had drunk the previous night. His head pounded. A steady throbbing clamored between his ears and he could not shut it out. The pounding was distracting his thoughts. Hawkstead felt like someone had dragged him behind a wagon the length of the county. Hawkstead was also remembering what had prompted him to get drunk in the first place.

Usually Hawkstead was a reasonable man. He knew he was currently being unreasonable but he could not stop himself. He had no desire to be reasonable at the moment. Hawkstead felt irritable as well as angry with himself for being too drunk and marrying the chit while drunk and unreasonable. He looked down at the girl sitting in front of him. Perhaps he was being too harsh on his new wife. He would be reasonable another day.

Guilt added to the harsh tone he used. "Well, you're a fool to think you had a choice who you marry," Hawkstead muttered. Kara's eyes narrowed in anger. "Matters not," he insisted. "Wed we are. I have no intention of playing some doting husband role. I have matters to attend. Once my head gives me peace."

Kara pushed the wimple up away from her eyes. As he berated her an idea had been forming and taking shape. If the man wanted nothing to do with her it could actually work to her advantage. At first this marriage had seemed like an end to all her plans and dreams when in reality it could instead be an answer to her prayers. Everyone, including Hawkstead, thought her married to him in all sense of the word, while she knew that since it had not been consummated they really weren't married. Hawkstead did not know it but he had just given her the time she needed. Lord Roffe could not make any other arrangements and she could safely pass the time under the net of Hawkstead's protection.

Kara chewed the inside of her cheek. The honorable thing to do was tell him that he had passed out before he had performed his intended deed. The better thing to do was to keep that information to herself so that she could use this marriage fiasco to gain her the time needed to be free of her uncle's control. Kara felt a twinge of guilt at the idea of using him so. It was just a twinge, however.

"On top of my other tasks now I have to learn what I have gained with this marriage," Hawkstead said. He paused in his ramblings and glanced sharply at her. "You did bring something to this marriage?"

Kara shrugged. "Aye, I suppose. I have property, yes."

Hawkstead nodded thoughtfully. "I'll have my steward look into it. That would just add to the rub if I don't get anything out of this."

Kara stared at him in disbelief. The man was incredible. She had never been subjected to anyone so lacking in empathy for another human being in her life. All he seemed to care about was how this affected him yet he was the one who had put them in this position. Not once in his tirade had he taken into account that she might be feeling a bit used, abused, and overwhelmed. His attitude could work to her advantage, she reminded herself. Though a piece of paper now said they were husband and wife they were complete strangers. They could remain strangers. Any guilt at using him evaporated.

"If this is such an encumbrance for you, why did you marry me?" Kara asked.

"Everyone gets married," Hawkstead said with a shrug. "It was expected for me to get married."

Kara decided to not pursue the topic of illogical attitude she had the urge to discuss in depth with the man. "Where will I sleep?" she asked.

"You'll share my solar. It would seem I'd put you aside otherwise." He snorted when she bristled at the idea of sharing his bed. "Don't worry. I can resist your charms."

"I prefer not to share a bed with you," Kara said in a flat voice. "Since we won't live as husband and wife it does not matter what anyone thinks of our sleeping apart."

"I am trying to protect you," Hawkstead said, patience slipping.

"I think not," Kara said. "If anyone asks, tell them I snore. I am not worried about what anyone thinks."

"You may not be worried but I care," Hawkstead said. "I do not want you to be under questionable behavior at the outset."

"Under questionable behavior? I was just married by a priest who ignored that I did not agree to the marriage and you think my not wanting to share a bedroom with a man who I just met last night is what is questionable behavior? I may be the only sane person in this keep!"

"There are no rooms open," Hawkstead said, voice rising. "Why won't you just do what I say?

"I will not share a room with you. Where do I sleep?" Kara insisted.

"On the other side of the keep!" Hawkstead snapped, patience gone.

"Good," Kara said calmly. "Then we are agreed that until we learn if I'm pregnant and it is not yours we do not share a bed?"

Hawkstead's head pounded. His face turned red. "So you admit you might carry another man's child?"

"No, not at all," Kara said calmly. "But for your sake I want you to be sure."

Hawkstead stared at her with so much anger that she was surprised he did not either punch her in the jaw or burst a blood vessel somewhere critical. Hawkstead looked like he wanted to do just that. Instead he turned his back on her then stalked out of the room, slamming the door behind him. Kara felt immense relief when he left the room. She struggled to her feet and stretched. Her neck was stiff from sleeping in the chair, trapped immobile by all the padding. Kara needed to bathe and rid herself of her cumbersome outfit. She needed Elyse to help her get out of these padded clothes since Elyse had sewn her into them. There had not been time to fashion fasteners.

Hawkstead was wrong. Somewhere in this keep was a room where the steward had planned to put her before the impromptu marriage. That would be where she would find Elyse and her trunks and that's where she would stay until leaving this place.

What a mess. What had her uncle been thinking? It had to be a misunderstanding. Kara wanted to read that letter. First she had to bathe. Some food in her empty belly was a good idea as well. She had not had anything to eat since the previous midday. Normally Kara would have expected to be presented with a meal upon arrival even if a small, light snack but with the way events had unfolded last night there had been no opportunity for food. It would have at least been hospitable to be given a tray of food at first light for breaking her fast but she would not fault any servant for not daring to enter the room that morning.

Hawkstead must have had reasons for marrying her. Obviously rushing to produce an heir was not the reason. The reason he gave her minutes ago made her snort in disbelief at the idea. No one rushed blindly into a marriage simply because marriage was an expected life event. Kara firmly believed she had been forced into marriage with an idiot.

For a moment Kara wondered what it would have been like if he had not decided to marry her on a drunken whim. If Kara had come to Greenestone Keep anticipating meeting her future husband she would have been pleasantly surprised by the sight of Hawkstead. A sober Hawkstead would have been an impressive encounter. Kara sighed. That was the night before. In the light of a new morning Hawkstead was not her idea of the man she wanted at her side the rest of her life. Appearances only went so far.

Daydreaming about a more pleasant initial contact did not change the fact that the man may have made the alcohol induced decision to marry her even though he found the sight of her repulsive and had no qualms about letting her know. Kara frowned. Being dragged as an unwilling participant into a marriage was bad enough but what were the odds that she would be forced into a marriage where the man did not even find her attractive when there had been so many men who found her attractive. Kara could not imagine sharing a bed with a man who found her repulsive. At least when the time came to tell him that they weren't exactly wed he should be happy to see her go.

At Roffe Manor they had a bath house near the kitchen. It was a luxury that she took advantage of often, when there was time to fill and heat the pool. When Kara made trips to buy and sell horses she found that regular bathing was not common even in wealthy estates. At one place she had stayed there had not been a single bathtub in the manor since the lord and lady of the manor bathed twice a year in the river in their underclothing. The lord and lady bragged that they did not force their people into the habit of bathing either since the local belief was that dirt protected against illness.

Kara hoped that this keep did not share such primitive thinking and at least had bathtubs. She would haul the water herself if necessary. Kara smiled. If there was not a bath house now she would see that one was constructed soon even though she did not plan on staying permanently. The keep and its people would be better for it.

Kara faced the door and squared her shoulders. Though Kara dreaded facing what lay beyond that door she dreaded even more facing her new husband again should he return to the room. Kara opened the door. A man who she remembered from the night before as the steward stood facing her, hand poised to knock. Startled, he stepped back. "Lady Hawkstead."

Kara automatically glanced behind her before realizing that he addressed her. To the rest of the world she was no longer Lady Roffe. She was now Lady Hawkstead. What a formidable name to acquire without any warning.

"You are the steward? Kenneth was it?" Kara vaguely remembered him from the night before.

"The chamberlain. It's Kevin, m'lady," he said politely.

Kara's stomach growled. If it had been a real marriage there would have been a feast and merrymaking with guests and a special dress. Trays of food would have been set out so that the newly married couple could nourish themselves during the night and into morning without leaving the room. Though food was on her mind, more important than food was the urge to bathe and rid herself of the bulky, hot clothing. Kara needed to feel like herself again.

"I need to bathe," she said, watching his face closely for signs of shock at the idea of bathing before some local annual bathing custom.

Kevin nodded. "The river is just out the east door, m'lady. The man at the gate will see that you are left undisturbed in the bathing area."

Kara felt disappointed at his news. The river would be too cold now. "You have no tubs? I prefer warm water and some privacy."

"My mistake in not being clear. The bathing house is a private area next to the river. The river is diverted and warmed as it flows into a pool," Kevin said. "The keep has many unexpected comforts. I suspect you will be pleasantly surprised with the bath house. If you wish to go there now I will have your companion sent to you with fresh clothes as well as a breakfast tray."

"I suspect you are a very competent chamberlain," Kara said.

Kevin smiled very subtly and bowed before offering his elbow. "If you are ready now I shall escort you to the east gate and then return for your companion. I have also selected several likely candidates to act as your personal maid. After you have bathed and eaten will you be available to choose which girl you would like to use?"

"That sounds well," Kara said. She felt something hanging outside of her wimple and subtly reached up to feel what was hanging on her forehead. Without a word she tucked the sock back up under her wimple.

***

Hawkstead left the solar in a sour temper. He was not a man who usually drank too much ale and that morning he was paying the price. Besides being saddled with the unappealing woman who was now his wife he was suffering with a head that felt like a storm cloud, complete with thunder. If Hawkstead had not been drunk he would have never listened to Richard and married the twit. Though Hawkstead knew he needed to wed he would not have married her on the spot if he had not been so drunk.

Vaguely Hawkstead remembered feeling that it did not matter who he wed so he had dived into the idea of taking Roffe's challenge. Hawkstead frowned, trying to remember exactly what Roffe had stated in that letter. Hawkstead had felt like a challenge had been thrown at him but now he could not remember what. All Hawkstead remembered was the feeling that he had been completely insulted and it was that overly plump, lumpy, red-faced, defiant-eyed vixen's fault. Now he was not even certain that Roffe had given him leave to marry his new lady wife. Richard would have stopped him if he had not been given leave to marry the twit.

Hawkstead now wished that he had pressed the matter with Roffe's daughter, Angel, when they had visited. Hawkstead had dragged his feet at the time. The daughter was fair enough but something about her bothered him enough that he could not bring himself to commit to a betrothal. Hawkstead vaguely remember that when she could put two words together to speak to him they had been curt, cutting words. It was almost like she did not like him. Lord Roffe's avoiding making a commitment regarding the Roffe horses had made the biggest impact on Hawkstead's delaying the betrothal.

Hawkstead stopped in the hallway and pressed his face against the coolness of the stone for a few minutes. The cool stone almost helped clear his head. At least it kept the fog at bay for a few minutes. Faced with having to marry Roffe's heir who was quite striking he should not have balked when the result was being saddled with Roffe's neice, who was quite unappealing. Hawkstead did not remember Roffe mentioning horses in his letter. Being saddled with the lumpy twit and now possibly not even having a chance at the Roffe Stables was ill luck. Hawkstead straightened and continued down the hall in the direction of the Great Room.

Waking up to find the girl as unappealing as he remembered the night before did not help his mood that morning. Bad enough that he had married her. That had been no virginal marriage bed. If she birthed before a full nine months passed he would send the babe to Roffe. As soon as he had realized it had not been a virginal wedding bed his first thought had been to kick her large arse out of the keep that morning yet.

Then his new wife had looked up at him, her eyes red from hours of crying. Hawkstead was certain a sock was hanging out from her wimple but it was possible he still had ale flowing through his veins. The twit was lumpy and over-sized in all the wrong places. Yet something about her had turned his insides to mush. There she sat, all lumpy, with fear and bravery both shining from her eyes. Hawkstead could not just kick her out. At least the rational side of Hawkstead knew that he could not just kick her out. That was what he told himself now. It was not that she had some impact on him.

Hawkstead had himself a wife. That was what he needed. It was really too much to expect her to be attractive. Hawkstead did expect that the twit at least brought some value to the marriage. Hawkstead found Richard in the Great Room eating breakfast. Richard looked up, smiling at Hawkstead's miserable face. "Ah, the newlyweds. Or at least one of you. Where is your new bride?" Richard asked, looking past Hawkstead but not seeing the new Lady Hawkstead.

Hawkstead scowled at his cousin. "I am not her keeper."

Richard's smile faded. "Tell me you did not storm out of your solar, leaving your new bride on her own."

Hawkstead scowled and settled onto a chair across the table from Richard. A servant immediately slid a trencher in front of him with cheese and roasted meat. Hawkstead ignored the food. "What did you get me into, Richard?"

"A marriage," Richard said in a bland voice.

"What happened to that letter?"

"I had Kevin put it in the strongbox. You'll need that. I had him make two copies and one will be on its way to London soon."

"I need to read it. Just not right now," Hawkstead muttered. He rubbed his face, grimacing at the pain filling his head. Hawkstead had a sudden flash of memory from the night before, of his bride turning and running when he had drunkenly announced he would marry her. Hawkstead swore under his breath. It had been a bad time to be drunk. He did not even know her name. "I don't remember Roffe having a niece."

"Brother's daughter," Richard said. "Better for you. She inherited wealth from her mother as well as her father's properties."

"Properties? That's something anyway," Hawkstead said. More of the dark cloud lifted. He picked up a piece of cheese and carved a chunk. "Since the deed is done it's good to know something came of it."

"Plus she's beautiful," Richard said. Hawkstead made a face in disagreement, surprising Richard. "You don't agree?"

"She's not exactly to my taste," Hawkstead said, trying to be polite.

Richard's left eyebrow rose. "You jest?"

"You jest," Hawkstead snapped. "Good lord, man, did you look at her? She's, well, lumpy, for one thing. And prone to weeping. She spent the night crying, which did nothing to aid her appearance."

Richard leaned back in his chair and studied Hawkstead intently. "Are you still drunk, cousin?"

Hawkstead glared at Richard. "She better be very wealthy. She did not come to that bed untouched. I prefer to be sure any issue is mine."

Richard leaned forward. In a very hard voice he said, "You slander her. I warn you, I won't hear that from you again."

Hawkstead was stunned. "Cousin? You would turn against me to defend her? Do you play a game to defend your bad advice to marry the twit?"

Richard's cheeks flushed in anger. "I thought to do her a good deed. Don't prove me wrong." Richard stood. "I would have wed her with a joyful heart but I am not lord of an estate like Greenestone."

Richard walked away in anger. A black storm cloud descended over Hawkstead's head again. Hung-over and riddled with regret, his cousin's attitude seemed the irrational attitude in this situation. Hawkstead chose not to continue the argument until his head cleared so let Richard walk away without protest. Hawkstead did not seem prone to win any arguments that morning. Hawkstead was prepared to admit that he was not in the best frame of mind to deal with any discussions at that time. Food helped. By the time he finished his trencher he felt more stable. Men wandered into the room seeking food to break their fast before going about their business. Many clapped Hawkstead on the back, congratulating him on his marriage. Hawkstead grimaced with each slap but nodded and accepted the congratulations with a lordly face.

Eventually Hawkstead calmed and assessed the situation more rationally. Hawkstead would never have said what he said about his new wife to anyone but Richard, yet Richard was right, she was his wife and deserved respect outside his chambers. Hawkstead should not have introduced even a hint of disrespect against his new wife's character. A twinge of guilt wormed its way into his thoughts. Hawkstead had behaved very badly to her since laying eyes on the twit.

First, he had been drunk. Then Hawkstead had married her without her permission. Hawkstead did not remember how he had performed in the marriage bed but suspected that he had not been at his best. Then Hawkstead had started out the day telling her how much she pained his eyes. The woman had done nothing to him to deserve such treatment from him. It had been that damned letter that had set him off and she had been the focus of his rage.

Hawkstead decided that he would make amends for his churlish behavior. He could spend the day smoothing her ruffled feathers, pat her on the head, and then find some business to deal with at the farthest corner of his estate to give her some respite from his bad humor. First he would bathe. Bathing would help clear his head and make him more presentable. Hawkstead would even suggest to his new wife that she bathe, get her used to regular bathing. By the smell of her the twit followed traditional habits of annual bathing.

The guard at the gate did not tell Hawkstead that someone was bathing at the river. The man nodded his head several times, congratulated his lord on his sudden marriage, and stood grinning at some private joke. "You got an eel in your pants?" Hawkstead asked, looking at the grinning man suspiciously.

"Good one, my Lord," the man said, chuckling.

Hawkstead frowned but did not pursue it. The previous owner of the keep had built a tiled pond near the river and diverted part of the river through clay pipes that were heated so that warm water flowed into the tiled pond. Wooden walls around the tiled pond and the garden area surrounding the pond provided privacy from the river side. A tent could be erected over the area during inclement weather so even in the winter the bath house could be used. White smoke drifted into the air from the fire pit used to warm the pipes. The brick wall gave privacy from the river but only minimal privacy once entering the garden, hence the guard. The bath house was off limits for anyone but the lord, highborn servants, or guests to the keep who might want to use the tiled pond so Hawkstead was caught off guard to realize that someone was using the bath house. Hawkstead stopped in his tracks when he saw her.

The bather had her back to him so he did not know who she was. Hawkstead ducked behind a tree and watched for a moment. At least he intended to linger only a moment. In truth he could not stop watching her. This was a private bath so no one had the right to use it without permission. Perhaps the mystery bather traveled with his new wife. Hawkstead did not remember much of the party's arrival the night before so he had no idea who traveled with Lady Roffe.

Whoever the woman was, she was physical perfection, finely
toned, long, lean limbs and a cascade of auburn hair down her back
drew his attention fully. Hawkstead could not tear his gaze away
from her form. The mystery bather turned slightly, that wavy mass
of hair sliding across her face to prevent an opportunity for
Hawkstead to identify her but he caught a glimpse of round, high
breasts above a flat stomach. Hawkstead smiled. Curves were
definitely nice.

A female voice spoke and the bather replied in a soft chuckle.
Hawkstead decided he had better leave before this mystery woman
caught him spying on her. Hawkstead glanced over his shoulder as
he started to leave. The woman stretched languidly, arms above her
head, twisting her head to loosen the muscles of her neck.
Hawkstead nearly tripped over his feet in his rush to get away before
he did another stupid thing of the day. All he could think about was
her stretching beneath him in the same way.

"Why did you not warn me that someone was bathing?" he
asked the guard.

The guard looked confused. "But 'twas your lady wife and her
companion, my Lord. Did not think naught of that. Thought you
were joining her." The man's smile slipped right back into place at
the idea of the newlyweds using the bath house together.

"Aye," Hawkstead muttered.

Hawkstead had not known his wife had brought a companion.
He wished he had stayed at the bath house long enough to see her

face. Well, no matter. His new wife should only have one companion
and he would meet her soon enough. Perhaps Hawkstead would not
venture out across the estate just yet. Hawkstead had thought to get
away from the new bride but he could stick around. Hawkstead
longed to meet this mysterious companion.

It was the nature of things. One wed for necessity and then
tumbled the maid. Sometimes wives were not so quick to turn a
blind eye to their husbands bedding their own maids or companions
however. Hawkstead could be discreet. He hoped the companion
could be discreet as well. Hawkstead hoped the companion did not
have some odd idea of loyalty to his wife. If the companion had
some sense of loyalty it would take some work to convince her that
they both could enjoy an encounter. Hawkstead started planning the
seduction of his wife's companion. The thought of engaging with the
mystery companion perked up his mood and his head cleared
noticeably.

"Send a boy to me when the bath house is available,"
Hawkstead said. "I'll be at the stables."

Hawkstead walked with a lighter step as he made his way to the
stables. Hawkstead noticed that his new wife had brought a palfrey
mare who was a prime specimen of the renowned Roffe breeding
program. His mood improved even more. The mare was a reminder
of why Hawkstead had been agreeable to considering a marriage
with the Roffe house. Hawkstead had one year remaining to get the
keep in order and send the first round of trained destriers to the

king's stable. The Roffe horses would guarantee success in that king's edict.

His original discussions with Roffe had revolved around access to those horses, though Roffe had been strangely noncommittal about expanding the breeding program. Nothing Hawkstead had learned of Roffe since meeting the man indicated that the man had such talent for producing the best horseflesh in the country. Still, there was no denying the result. The mare was perfection. With a woman such as the mystery bather to please his eye it should not matter which Roffe woman graced his name, he decided.

One of Roffe's men approached Hawkstead. "Lord Hawkstead, good day to you. I am Sir Bullton." The man barely waited for Hawkstead to respond with a greeting. "We have heard that you wed Lady Kara upon her arrival last night. Is this true?"

"Aye," Hawkstead said. He noticed several other men of his wife's escort lounging about the stable, letting Bullton speak for them but clearly paying careful attention to what was being discussed.

Bullton nodded thoughtfully. "Indeed. We have a bit of a dilemma then. We had intended to continue on today to Mael, per Lady Kara's orders, despite her uncle's instructions to return immediately with Lady Kara to Roffe Manor. We be thinking we won't be required to escort her to Mael today. With you wedding her. But you can see our confusion?"

Hawkstead tried to sort out the odd request. "If my wife need go to Mael I'll see her escorted. You may linger another day to rest. There is no need to rush back immediately."

Bullton nodded. "Indeed. I thank you for your hospitality. Now since Lady Kara had no chance to breathe between her arrival from France before heading here we thought a delay would be in order to give her a chance to rest but since we won't be bringing her back with us there's no need to be dawdling. Yet we're thinking maybe we should at least wait a little while longer."

"You just came from France?" Hawkstead asked.

"Nay. Not us. Just Lady Kara." The man rubbed his chin. "Indeed. Mind you, I'm of a certain mindset you would not be marrying Lady Kara excepting Lord Roffe gave permission to be doing so, yet seems a might odd with his history regarding the idea of the girl marrying and on top of that I get the right, strong impression that he wanted us rushing back with her. You see my dilemma?"

"I see," Hawkstead said, though he did not see at all. Hawkstead had not completely managed to follow the man's conversation beyond that his new wife had recently been to France and Lord Roffe expected her to return with these men.

Bullton rubbed his chin with his thumb thoughtfully. "Indeed. Odd that. Pleased to see she's in good hands as I always had a soft spot for the girl, er, Lady Kara. She deserves a fine, young, strapping fellow like you. Been asking around and your people have nothing

but good to say about ya. Mighty fine. Mighty fine. All right then.
We'll take your hospitality another day. Gives me a chance to talk to
Lady Kara before we're on our way back to Roffe Manor."

"You'll be leaving without, uh, my wife's companion?"
Hawkstead asked, not sure why he suddenly felt so guilty asking
after the mystery bather.

"Companion? Oh, Elyse? Aye. She won't be wanting to leave
Lady Kara. Been with her since before her parents died. Raised the
girl. Elyse did."

Hawkstead frowned. The man said a lot of words but Hawkstead
was finding it difficult to sort out the relevant words. "The
companion *raised* my, uh, wife?"

"Aye. Stuck with her in Roffe's household though she be a free
woman," Bullton said, nodding his head for emphasis. Bullton
seemed to just notice that they were standing in front of Kara's
horse. "Fine mare, isn't she? Lady Kara is mighty proud of her. Calls
her Rhinney. Out of Nobe by Fastener's Clutch." Bullton turned
back to Hawkstead and something outside the stable door caught his
eye. "Ah, there goes Elyse now."

Hawkstead turned quickly to see the companion, eager to put a
face to that glorious body. Though Hawkstead turned his head as
soon as Bullton said the words he was too slow to catch sight of the
auburn haired woman. All Hawkstead saw through the stable door
was a tall, rigidly stiff-backed, older woman at least in her thirties
crossing the courtyard, her arms clutching a bundle of clothing.

Hawkstead could not tell if she had auburn hair because she wore a wimple and not a single strand of hair escaped the head covering.

Could she be the mystery bather? It seemed unlikely. Hawkstead watched the woman walk past the stable as long as she was visible through the door. Even with the enveloping dress and head covering this woman did not match what Hawkstead had seen in the bath house. This stiff-back woman appeared too small and bony to match the vision Hawkstead had witnessed. A strange, sinking feeling settled in the pit of his stomach. Perhaps it was a lingering effect of the overindulgence of ale he had consumed the night before. Maybe it was because everything about his new wife felt overly complicated.

"Well, since we won't be escorting Lady Kara to Mael we'll be out of your way come morning. Do want to chat with Lady Kara first, mind you," Bullton said. He winked at Hawkstead. "Mael might be a good location for a newly married couple, aye? Of course, I heard you have a lot of work here so maybe you won't have time to visit Mael. Maybe we'll ride up there first, deliver the news of Lady Kara's marriage. Then we can come back this way, make sure everything is going well."

Mael? Hawkstead stared at the man in confusion. Perhaps he had a thick head yet. It hadn't registered that Mael was Kara's intended destination, only that she planned on leaving. He knew of the estate. Who did not? It was the largest estate between there and London. What reason could his wife have for going to Mael? Before

Hawkstead got too worked up about his wife planning on leaving that morning to Mael he realized that Bullton hadn't seen her yet that morning so she had made her plans before the marriage.

Sir Bullton's long rambling message also slowly registered on Hawkstead when it sank in that Sir Bullton was trying to explain that Lord Roffe expected Lady Kara to return with this escort. Hawkstad grimaced. Lord Roffe certainly hadn't expected an immediate wedding. Well, the deed was done. It was time he learned more of his wife. Hawkstead had been so distracted with interest in the mystery bather that he had forgotten that he was going to make an effort to be congenial to his wife that day.

While Hawkstead was making an effort to be nice to her he would also learn what he had gained with her. Hawkstead was not happy with his drunken action to marry the lumpy twit but he decided that it was not really her fault and if she brought to the marriage what he needed then he would make the most it. Hawkstead had to marry and now he had his desired connection to Roffe Manor. It was horses he needed, not an attractive wife.

Chapter Four

Kara stepped into the room and shut the door. The room was suitable, just big enough for a bed for her and Elyse both to sleep on comfortably and her trunks pushed up against the wall. Private rooms were extravagant and tended to be small when available. Kevin had raised his eyebrows but said nothing when she had told him that she would stay in the room instead of moving into the master solar. Elyse had been surprised to hear of the impromptu marriage and confused that Kara would not be sharing the master solar with her new husband but kept her tongue at bay for now. Kara knew the scolding would come when Elyse realized that the sleeping arrangement was not a temporary situation.

"My prayers be answered," Elyse had said in greeting to Kara that morning in the bath house. "Long past time you escaped that man. And now you have a strong husband to stand up against your uncle."

"You heard then?" Kara said.

"The entire keep is talking of nothing else."

The bathing house had been a pleasant surprise. Not only was the pool tiled and screened from observers but the water was warmed. Elyse had arrived within minutes of Kara entering the bath house and had been smiling since. Clean and dressed in an elegant silk gown with trailing sleeves, Kara felt herself again.

While she bathed Kara considered her options. Now that she had had time to think about it she concluded that this marriage could indeed be beneficial. Kara felt her spirits lift as she washed away the dirt, sweat, and grime. Her plans took shape as she dressed. Elyse had been so happy and talked nonstop as she combed Kara's hair and dressed it into elaborate braids. Kara barely heard anything Elyse said, deep in her own thoughts.

Kara just needed to decide if she should approach Hawkstead with her proposition or if she should just not say anything to him at all. All she needed was the protection of this marriage until she reached her next birthday. Despite his behavior that morning Kara was not sure if he would agree to release her. He thought them married and if she told him that they hadn't completed the ceremony he might decide he wanted to remain married and take the step to finish it. Kara chewed on her lower lip. It was tempting to tell him right away in the hopes of improving his mood. No, better to wait. If she told him now that they weren't in fact truly wed he might go the other way and not wait to release her from the marriage and then she would be under Roffe's control again.

"You are quiet," Elyse said, stepping back to observe her efforts dressing Kara's hair and noticing that Kara was lost in thought. "I hope you are not planning something devious. Or is it the wedding night that has you so distracted?" Kara shook her head. Elyse frowned. "I heard he was drunk. Men do not perform well when drunk. It will get better." Elyse's frown deepened as she looked around the room. "I do not understand this room either. You should be housed in the master solar. But you are wed and in time I am sure you will appreciate what that means."

"It has been a lot to take in," Kara said slowly. She wanted to tell Elyse the truth but did not know how the woman would react.

"And no food to break your fast," Elyse chided when Kara's stomach growled.

"Kevin was having a tray sent. Perhaps they went to the solar instead."

"I will go find out," Elyse said.

Elyse had only been gone a few minutes when the door opened and Kara turned to see Hawkstead standing in the doorway. He looked baffled. He glanced around the room, as if looking for someone else then his gaze settled on her. The room felt very cramped with him looming in the doorway. Hawkstead stared at her in silence for an agonizingly long time. Kara braced herself for another round of cutting barbs from her new husband's lips. Her upper lip tingled and breathing became difficult.

"What game do you play?" Hawkstead asked in a low, angry voice.

Kara was taken aback. "Game, sir?"

"The witch speaks!" The anger in his voice made her wince. Hawkstead stepped further into the room, studying her, glaring at her hair. "You arrive of a girth and yet I see a water nymph bathing in the pond. Now I discover the nymph is my own wife."

Kara's face burned. "You watched me bathe?"

"You changed into a different woman."

Kara raised her chin. "I am the same woman who did arrive yesterday, sir."

"Nay," Hawkstead said. "I was not so drunk last night nor yet this morn to not know what I saw."

Kara frowned. "Do you mean because I had on so many clothes?"

"Clothes?" he sputtered. "What?"

"Ah," she said slowly. She stared at his feet, unable to meet his eyes. "Was cowardice, my Lord. I expected a beating for delivering bad news so I sought to cushion the blows."

Hawkstead did not say anything for so long that cautiously she glanced up to look at his face. His gaze was so intense that she blushed. Never had she met a man like him. He made her feel mixed up inside. He was the most handsome man she had ever seen yet he had also treated her with total lack of consideration. Kara wanted to relax her guard and tell him all her secrets but hard lessons had taught her to keep things to herself. Kara wanted to lean on him, let him share some of her burden but she did not know if she could trust him. Hawkstead was a stranger. Kara dropped her head to stare at his feet again. She could not share her secrets with him yet, if ever. He filled her head and heart with conflicting thoughts. Hawkstead reached out to cup her chin with his hand and she flinched.

"Damn," he muttered.

Kara bit her lower lip. She hadn't meant to flinch. Anticipating the blows was always the toughest. Kara did not know what to expect from him. Hawkstead always seemed to be angry with her but he had yet to strike her. Kara wished he would hit her and get it out of the way. Her legs trembled. Her knees threatened to buckle. Kara closed her eyes, willing him to hit her or leave her be. A low rumble filled her ears.

Hawkstead caught Kara when she fainted though he was so startled that she almost slipped past him to the floor. For several heartbeats he stood frozen, Kara dangling in his arms like a rag doll. Eventually he gathered his thoughts and swept her into his arms, cradling her against his chest. Hawkstead was not exactly certain what to do when a woman fainted. For that matter he was not sure why a woman would faint.

Hawkstead glanced at the bed. The room felt so cramped and the bed so small but the alternative was to carry her through the keep to his solar. Hawkstead laid her on the bed. He stared down at her. He just did not know what to do with a fainting woman. What caused a woman to faint? There was the possibility that she was ill. Or pregnant. Hawkstead raked his fingers through his hair. His new wife looked so different freshly bathed and not wearing those bulky clothes. She looked so vulnerable. Hawkstead did not know what to think of her. He definitely desired her now though.

Pregnant women fainted. If she was with child he would know if the child was his. He could not touch her until he knew for certain. It was too early for her to faint from pregnancy if it resulted from the previous night. Even Hawkstead knew that much after he gave it some thought. Realizing that she was likely indeed pregnant from another man was a very disappointing idea. Kara continued to lay unmoving on the bed.

Perhaps if he loosened her clothes it would help. Kara stirred when he touched her. Her eyes fluttered open before he'd done more than decide which ties would actually loosen her clothes. When Kara saw Hawkstead leaning over her she held back a startled gasp. The resulting sound came out sounding like a choked chicken. Hawkstead had been concentrating on how to undo the ties of her dress and her choked gasp made him jerk back in alarm.

"I, uh, um, was, well, you fainted," he said, backing away.

"I'm sorry," Kara said.

"What? No, no. I'm sure it was not your intent," Hawkstead said.

Tears ran down her cheeks. Hawkstead shifted his weight from foot to foot. The only thing more uncomfortable than a fainting woman was a crying woman. Kara did not make a sound. She just laid there, looking up at him with large eyes glistening with tears that pooled before sliding down her cheeks. Hawkstead resisted the urge to gather her in his arms and comfort her.

"You are exhausted. Rest," Hawkstead said slowly. Crying for no reason was another sign of pregnancy. For some reason he felt disappointed that this lovely creature had come to him besmirched with another man's child in her belly. "I am sure it isn't your fault you are in this condition."

Elyse entered the room, carrying a tray with bread, cheese and fruit. "What is this?" she asked, seeing Kara on the bed and Hawkstead standing over her. Elyse hurried to Kara's side and set the tray down on the bed next to Kara since there was nowhere else to put it.

"Your lady has fainted," Hawkstead said. "See to her."

"Fainted?" Elyse asked in surprise, choosing to ignore that he treated her like a servant though she was a lady of a house that far outranked his titles. "Fainted? Did you strike her?"

"No," Hawkstead and Kara said in unison. Hawkstead threw his hands in the air in frustration. "Why are you people convinced I beat women? I would never strike a woman."

Hawkstead left the room without waiting for any further drama. Frustrated, he strode through the keep without looking to left or right until he reached his office, where he found Richard working on the ledgers. The office was a small room at the back of the Great Hall with a door that could be locked. Hawkstead's cousin looked up when Hawkstead entered, studying him thoughtfully. Hawkstead scowled and settled into a chair at the table that served as a desk, opposite of Richard.

"It is a good harvest," Richard said, turning back to the ledgers. "Everyone shall have full bellies all winter as well as extra coin. Much better than they had last year. This will further cement your stature among your new tenants."

Hawkstead nodded, distracted. "I need to take some men out soon to hunt. Did you get a tally of the livestock yet?"

"Not completed. When we collect the last of the rents on the eastern border it'll be complete." Richard looked up from the ledger, studying Hawkstead. "Are you five or five and twenty? Why are you sulking now?"

"I am not sulking, cousin. I am wholly distracted. My impromptu marriage is off to an ominous start. Where is that letter from Roffe? I hate to think of the consequences if we misread his intentions," Hawkstead said. "His men thought to return today with the lady in hand, not leave her as new bride."

Richard opened the strongbox and pulled out the letter. Richard handed the letter to Hawkstead, who immediately read it again and then read it again, eyebrows raised. What he read was worse now that he was sober. "Hell, Richard, if I hadn't been drunk last night I'd have thrown this offensive work directly in the flames and thrown that lady out on her arse the same night. Why should he wish to goad me so?"

Richard shrugged, taking the letter and placing it back in the strongbox. "I have my thoughts," Richard said. "The important thing is that he said you could have her as wife."

"Could it be that the man can't read and whichever clerk did the writing thought to play a trick on his lord?" Hawkstead wondered aloud. "You know Roffe better than I do. My new wife perhaps suffered at his hands?"

"Roffe confided in me once that he never intended to let her marry."

"Yet he threw her in my face? That makes no sense."

"You'd have never married her sober," Richard said. He considered then nodded thoughtfully. "I think I have an understanding. Perhaps. After you chased her out she would have returned to Roffe, who would have told her that he had offered her to you and she had been rejected."

"Phff. That makes no sense," Hawkstead said.

"It would if you knew how much Roffe delights in torturing the lady and how determined he is to keep her at hand. There were men lined up wanting her hand in marriage. Roffe refused them all. Refused to let any approach her."

Hawkstead shook his head. "Why would he not want to marry her off? What good does it do to hold her at hand?" Hawkstead sat up straighter. "Does she bring Roffe Manor?"

"Aye, it is rumored that it is hers. But it does not matter because the wealth comes from the horses," Richard said.

"Aye, the horses," Hawkstead muttered. His mood lightened slightly. "At least there are the horses. First choice every season and unlimited use of my pick of stallions. The original agreement with the daughter was twenty mares carrying foals as a wedding gift so I will be expecting the same with the niece."

"There were rumors that he wanted his brother's wife," Richard said. "I was but a boy but I remember that there was some conflict over that. Mael came to your bride through her mother. As I said, you wed a wealthy bride."

"Ah, yes, Mael. That is why the knight was rambling on about Mael." Hawkstead nodded. He had inadvertently married an heiress of the highest order.

"You realize what it means that she owns Mael?" Richard asked, watching Hawkstead's face for when the information made its way into the hung over brain.

"It's a fine estate," Hawkstead said. He looked up at Richard in surprise. "And she's a duchess?"

"Aye," Richard said, nodding.

Hawkstead whistled under his breath. "She cleans up well also." It almost hurt him to say it but he owed Richard that much.

Richard grinned. "Seems you owe me."

Hawkstead grunted but a grin escaped. "She may be a shrew." His grin faded. "*And she may have arrived in his keep already pregnant*," he said to himself.

"It would only be fair if she turns into a shrew," Richard said lightly. "Already you're too lucky. Back to the business at hand, there's a pack of wild dogs terrorizing one of the villages. Toby can probably deal with that. It'll give him some experience and you should spend a few days concentrating on your new wife. Where is she?"

"I don't know," Hawkstead said, slightly embarrassed that he had not considered her whereabouts since leaving the bedroom. Hawkstead debated on whether to tell Richard more then decided to drop the subject of his wife for now. "I still haven't made it to the bath house and I need it. Anything else pressing?"

"No, not anything that can't wait or I can't deal with," Richard said. "The kitchen is preparing a marriage feast for the keep tonight and in a few days another feast for the serfs, give them a chance to see the new bride as well. When do you plan on introducing her to Mrs. Smith?"

"Tomorrow," Hawkstead said. He hadn't actually thought about handing over the household duties to his new wife but it was customary. Mrs. Smith ran the household in perfect order and he saw no reason to disrupt that but if it had to be done it had to be done. Hopefully his new bride was a competent housekeeper. Mrs. Smith would retain the title but the lady of the house had the final word on anything affecting the household just as the lord of the house had the final word on anything affecting the keep and estates.

"That reminds me, the butcher's wife is due to have her child any day," Richard said.

"I'll want to accompany Mrs. Smith when the babe is born," Hawkstead said. "*After* the babe is born. Not during the birth."

"Toby misunderstood. You won't have to deliver the butcher's child. Your lady wife will accompany you as well?"

"That would be appropriate," Hawkstead agreed after consideration. He hadn't thought of that. It was going to take some time to get used to having a wife.

"A messenger arrived this morning from the king. French, German, and Spanish ambassadors are visiting him with news about the barbarians moving across the continent," Richard said, handing a sealed letter to Hawkstead. "He is in the kitchen. Do you have time to talk to him now? He told me a majority of the news but I am sure he's held some things back to tell you personally."

Hawkstead nodded. The barbarians moving ever westward was a great concern. They slaughtered whole villages in their path, leaving no one alive. They lingered only long enough to strip the land bare of food and wealth before moving again, like a human band of locusts devouring everything they came across, leaving bare desolation in their wake. The past decades had been tough already with the great diseases wiping out a majority of the population. The country was only beginning to show signs of recovering. This new threat could set them back decades.

Hawkstead was at the east gate, at last on his way to bathe, when Elyse confronted him. "My Lord, a moment," the older woman said, hurrying towards him.

Hawkstead groaned. Was he ever going to get his bath? "Elyse is it?" he said in greeting.

"I am not a servant, my Lord," Elyse said, taken aback with his familiar greeting. "I am Lady Ashton." Elyse took a deep breath and smiled demurely. "I wish to thank you for your patience with my lady," Elyse said. "Right now she is exhausted and overwhelmed. In time her mood will settle. She had no chance to rest before her uncle sent her right out again and the marriage was a complete shock to her."

Hawkstead stared down his nose at the woman. "You have been with her a long time?"

"Aye, her mother was my cousin. When Diana passed I took the role of raising her, so you will understand that I have a very motherly feeling for the girl. She is quite headstrong, as youth often is but she has a good heart and I think you will be quite pleased, given time."

Hawkstead felt the arrogance stiffening his back drain away. "And you feel the need to stand up for her now, Lady Ashton?"

"Aye. This business of sleeping on the opposite side of the keep is not a good start to a marriage, even if it was an impromptu marriage. Kara is satisfied with the arrangement but I am not. Not at all. One night might pass but no longer mind you."

"What?" Hawkstead asked, slightly distracted as he studied the edge of her wimple for a possible stray hair. The woman's eyebrows were a light brown with no sign of red but Hawkstead knew from personal experience that facial hair did not always match the hair on a person's head. Though he knew it must be his wife he had seen bathing he could not help but wonder what Elyse hid under her wimple and dress.

"Are you not listening? I think your marriage to her is right for her. It won't work if you keep separate beds," Elyse said. "Since you are almost my son-in-law you have my leave to use my given name, Elyse, in private."

"Thank you for the kindness," Hawkstead said. He bowed formally in acknowledgement of the honor of being given permission to use her name. "And you may call me by my given name as well, Elyse." Elyse stared at him, waiting to hear just what that given name would be. Hawkstead did not appear to notice that he hadn't supplied a name. "It is my wife's decision to sleep apart. I am not sure what you expect of me."

"Hrumph," Elyse said. It was more the sound of the wind getting knocked out of her and escaping through her mouth than an actual word. With that she turned and strode purposely away, leaving Hawkstead staring after her rigid back thoughtfully. Hawkstead was convinced that Elyse was not the mystery bather. Up close the woman was older but not elderly. Hawkstead did not dare ask the woman her age but he would guess that she was not much more than thirty.

While he bathed Hawkstead mulled over the day and what led up to his gaining a wife while too drunk to think rationally. The king had given him two years to get his new estate into order and at least have an heir on the way before stepping into his appointment as marshal over the southern region. That appointment meant spending at least a few months out of the year in London. Now that rumors of a barbarian horde sweeping across parts of Europe had reached England there was the possibility that King George would send him out to deal with that.

The idea was to have a competent wife in place to take the reins while he was in London but since he had Richard to manage the estate he had not been in a big rush. Perhaps he had delayed too long. A year ago two years had seemed like a long time down the road so it was possible Hawkstead had not been in as much of a hurry as he should have been with what was in reality a tight timetable for his tasks. Instead of having a leisurely two years Hawkstead was beginning to feel that the remaining year might not be enough time to have everything needed in place.

Hawkstead had not actually committed to a betrothal with Roffe's daughter though he had seriously considered her so he was surprised that Roffe had felt obliged to send a message. Roffe must have felt they had agreed to something more than Hawkstead felt they had. Hawkstead frowned as he stood and reached for a towel, water running off his hard body. Hawkstead rubbed the towel

brusquely over his body, arms, and legs then threw the towel to the

stone flagging.

Roffe was not the only one who had shown up at the

Greenestone door with daughter in tow. Hawkstead had been

bombarded by visitors hoping to convince him to an alliance through

marriage. Hawkstead had been tempted by Roffe's offer because of

the Roffe Horses. The daughter was attractive enough but after a few

days Hawkstead could sense that he would not feel secure leaving

her to run an estate the size of Greenestone, even with Richard at

hand to help with managing things. That feeling had been what held

the logical part of him from agreeing to an official betrothal. There

was just something about the girl that he did not trust. The access to

the Roffe Stables had been what stopped him from saying no

outright. Obviously Roffe had taken the lack of a no as a yes.

Now Hawkstead had a wife and knew nothing about her at all.

All his caution and planning had been thrown out the window by one

drunken act. Hawkstead dressed quickly, his breath creating small

clouds of steam. The water flowing into the pool was warmed by the

fire pit over the clay pipes but the bath house itself was not heated.

Well, the deed was done and he had to live with it. If she carried

another man's child he would send her to the nearby monastery until

the babe was born and then she could start supplying his heirs. Heirs

and horses were what he expected of her. How she would perform managing the estate in his absence was something he would have to wait to find out.

The keep was a beehive of activity, even more than normal. A marriage feast on such short notice had the whole household in an uproar, especially the kitchen. For some reason everyone seemed to think Hawkstead cared about the details in preparing the celebration. They were wrong. After the fifth time he was stopped and asked an inane question Hawkstead decided to ride out with a few men and avoid the commotion. It was beyond him why servants thought he cared whether they served duck or goose. Whether there were cashews in the red cabbage. How many barrels of ale should be unsealed? Should there be both beer and ale?

When Hawkstead reached the stables he was surprised to see his wife talking to his head groom, Allan. The two stood at the stall of a mare that Hawkstead felt had great promise to breed with his war horse. Their voices were a distant murmur amidst the whinnies and occasional hoof hitting a stall wall. One of the horses nearest Hawkstead rattled its feed bucket with its lips, the wood hitting wood drowning out even the soft murmurs he had initially heard. The mare they were discussing lipped Kara's hand and his wife laughed softly at the tickle.

Hawkstead debated on avoiding her but realized that would appear rude so he went up to the two. They both fell silent when they noticed him and watched him warily as he approached. Hawkstead frowned, wondering what they were up to. Hawkstead could think of no reason for his newly wed lady wife chatting with his groom.

"My Lady," Hawkstead said gruffly. "Allan."

"My Lord," Allan said.

Kara just nodded her head then mumbled a good day in greeting almost as an afterthought. Hawkstead stared at her, finding it difficult to believe that she was the same woman who had arrived the night before. Hawkstead was not even aware that he was drinking in the sight of her with his eyes like a drowning man seeing land. Kara stood with her eyes slightly downcast, her long, thick eyelashes framing her blue eyes. Blue eyes were not that uncommon but her eyes were not the blue of a washed out summer sky, they were the blue of a deep and turbulent ocean Hawkstead was fascinated by them. Her freshly washed hair was in a long braid down her back but wisps of hair floated around her face. Hawkstead broke the spell he was under with a small shake.

"Am I interrupting something?" Hawkstead asked when both just stood still quietly. Hawkstead felt like they were waiting for him to be on his way so they could continue a private discussion. His new wife had no need for private discussions with his groom.

Allan glanced at Kara. Kara stood with her gaze locked on the straw littered cobbled floor. When Allan realized that the lady was not going to speak he rushed to fill in the awkward silence. "Just talking horses, my Lord," he said.

"Ah," Hawkstead said, glancing around the stable. He was quite proud of his horseflesh and it pleased him that his new bride showed an interest in his horses. "I hadn't realized you were interested in horses," he said, causing Kara's head to jerk up in surprise. She opened her mouth to say something, then snapped her mouth shut, teeth clicking. "I suppose horses are a popular subject at your former residence." Kara lowered her head again to stare at his feet. Hawkstead frowned. "Well, Allan does know horses. I'm sure he can teach you a few things."

Allan looked very uncomfortable. "Ah, the lass knows a few things, my Lord," the groom said. He looked at Kara again, as if expecting her to say something. "I have tasks. Excuse me, my Lord, my Lady."

"Thank you, Allan," Kara said with a smile.

Hawkstead stood staring at his wife. Hawkstead suddenly realized that he could not remember her given name. Angel was the daughter and this one was the niece. Hawkstead was sure the name started with a K but it could be T. Was it Kendra? Or maybe Karin? No, it might be Tara. "I'm not sure if Allan told you but I have also started a breeding program. The king has appointed me as royal marshal because of my skill and knowledge of horseflesh."

"How kind," Kara said softly.

"Kind? It is not kindness which prompts the king to set such an appointment," Hawkstead said, irritation evident in his voice. She frustrated him. How could the chit not find favor with such a great accomplishment? The chit should be happy that she was married to a man of great accomplishment. Hawkstead wracked his brain for something that would bring a spark of interest to those blue eyes, something that would bring her attention up to him and off the floor. "I will present you to the king when we go to London. Will that excite you?"

Kara looked up at him. "I have met the king, my Lord."

The chit spoke matter-of-factly yet the statement annoyed him. How was he to impress her when she would not be impressed? She already knew something about horses. She had already met the king. Why could not she just smile at him in adoration? Why was she being so difficult? Women liked compliments. Hawkstead wracked his brain for a compliment.

"Now that I see your great beauty I am more inclined to enjoy this marriage," Hawkstead said. Kara frowned at him. Hawkstead felt his irritation rising. "It would help if you would cooperate."

Kara stared at him in disbelief. She did not even know how to respond to the back-handed compliment and insult that came out of his mouth within seconds of each other. "Now you see my beauty? I am the same woman who you did call a dog the night I was forcibly wed to you."

"No, you aren't. You arrived, of a girth," Hawkstead said, holding his hands out to show how wide she had been. "Besides, I am sure I did not call you a dog. I couldn't have been that drunk."

"You thought you could treat me so vile because you thought I was fat?" Kara asked in confusion.

"I did not treat you so vile," Hawkstead protested. He hesitated when he realized there were gaps in his memory of that night. "At least I did not mean to. It was the drink. And you did look, well, lumpy."

"What difference does that make?" Kara asked. "I am still who I am. If I had come missing an arm would you have treated me with such disdain? After a few children I shall likely be quite matronly. Will that give you leave to treat me as less?"

"You looked lumpy," Hawkstead muttered. "But now that I see you are not lumpy, I am looking forward to sharing the marriage bed. How can you not be flattered that I desire you now?"

"Now. Even though you think I already carry another man's child?" Kara asked, an angry gleam in her eyes.

Hawkstead did not know if it was lingering effects of all the alcohol he had consumed the night before but later he would point the blame to an extreme hangover. Hawkstead did still have a thick head plus he found it difficult to think rationally when in her presence. Hawkstead could feel the wrongness of it yet he could not stop the words from coming through his lips and as soon as the words were out he wished he could take them back. "Tell me who your lover is. I would know who has gone before me."

Kara's cheeks flamed red. "You're an ass." Without waiting for a response she slipped past him and stalked out of the stable. If she had been a cat her tail would have been slashing the air.

Hawkstead took a step after her then stopped himself from following her. He actually was being an ass. Hawkstead could not help it. The thought of the chit he had married on a whim sharing her luscious body with another man stirred feelings deep in his gut that made him mad with jealousy. In one day he had gone from wanting her out of his sight to wanting to see all of her. It seemed that Hawkstead hadn't managed a rational thought in his head since meeting her. Allan returned cautiously, quietly waiting for potential orders.

"What were you and my wife discussing?" Hawkstead asked Allan, gaze on the door she had just stalked through.

"She was just returned from France, my Lord," Allan said. "Brought mares back from LeRouget."

"Indeed," Hawkstead said. He had been trying to work with LeRouget and the man was not cooperative.

"Thought we had a good start here. Seemed mighty pleased that you show promise," Allan said. The groom looked like he wished he could take the words back when Hawkstead turned his head to stare at Allan with a hard glare that could freeze the most seasoned warrior in his tracks and yet make his knees tremble at the same time. "Uh, maybe I did not say that right, my Lord. My Lady was pleased at the great work you are doing. Yes, that is better. Pleased with the great work." Allan swallowed, or at least tried to swallow as his throat seemed to have constricted. "Are you in need of a horse saddled, my Lord? Should I saddle Ajax?"

Hawkstead's gaze landed on his wife's palfrey mare two stalls from where they stood. "Saddle the mare. I'd like to see what she's got."

Allan frowned, following his master's gaze. "The Lady's mare, my Lord?"

"Yes, the Lady's mare. She is my wife so I think I have the right to ride her mare."

"It's just, well, are you sure, my Lord?" Allan asked, struggling with questioning his master's decision but definitely questioning the wisdom of his request.

"Just do it, Allan," Hawkstead insisted.

"She's a grand mare," Allan said. "But she's been ridden--"

"Just do it, Allan!"

"Aye, my Lord," Allan said, shaking his head. Hawkstead was his master and when Hawkstead issued a command there was no argument to be made. Not even when there was a need to argue. Allan knew that Hawkstead was not himself at the moment. First the boy then the rushed marriage had the lord on edge like Allan had never seen. Allan led the mare out of the stall and summoned a stable boy to bring a saddle. "It's a shame about the boy, my Lord," Allan said while the boy fetched the tack.

Hawkstead nodded but did not respond, the grief still raw. The boy Allan referred to was Robin, the eleven year old foster boy who Hawkstead had only recently chosen to start training as his squire. Death was a part of life, yet the unfairness of a strong, strapping young life being snuffed so early by something so simple as a cut on the leg from a rusted piece of metal hidden in the grass was as frustrating as it was painful. Maybe if the boy had said something before the infection grew so deep, maybe they could have saved him. The dying had not been a clean, painless death either. The boy had suffered a lingering death as the infection spread through him.

When the suffering had ended the day before Hawkstead's suffering had intensified and all the ale he had consumed did not chase the feelings of loss away. Not only did he feel the boy's loss but he also felt frustrated that a life could be taken by something so minor as a scratch. There were stories from the Golden Time that doctors could even reattach severed limbs. It was all lost. All that knowledge was lost. The boy was gone before his time should have been up.

Hawkstead settled back in the saddle and let the mare find her gait. The palfrey ambled so smoothly that it felt like they were not even moving yet the ground was eaten up quickly. Hawkstead had only brought two men with him, both riding jennets, sturdy little horses that had to break into a canter to keep up with the mare's amble. No wonder the palfrey stock Roffe produced were so in demand despite the high price. Palfreys were expensive as a rule and

Roffe palfreys were higher priced yet again above average. Hawkstead had only been aware of the quality of their destrier stock and had not realized that their palfrey stock was also beyond compare.

They had almost reached the village reporting the problem with feral dogs, the closest village to the keep. The thatched roofs were in sight below the hill they were about to crest when the mare skipped a beat and stumbled slightly. Hawkstead frowned and paid careful attention to the mare's gait but she ambled along smoothly. When they reached the village Hawkstead dismounted and looked the mare over. The horse's legs trembled slightly but she stood with head high, showing no sign of weariness.

"Wonderful horse," Toby said, walking out of the village. "I'm surprised you decided to ride her considering your wife asked the groom to make she was walked three times a day without a rider but otherwise kept in the stall. Seems the mare has been ridden nonstop for over a month and your lady wife wanted her to rest."

"I did not know that," Hawkstead said. He immediately ran his hands down the horse's legs, feeling for any swelling or problems. Allan had tried to tell him but he would not listen.

"Head still thick?" Toby asked. He laughed. "Or head on other things? I'd like to accidently marry a beautiful heiress."

"Head's not so thick that I don't know a solution," Hawkstead said. "Since I'm here to deal with the dogs you can walk the mare back to the stable. And I mean walk, not ride at a walk. I'll take your horse."

"Damn. Gotta learn to keep my mouth shut," Toby said. Toby took the mare's reins, patted her on the withers, and without another word headed back to the keep, mare trailing behind him. Toby could be heard talking to the horse as he walked. "I'll bet all the stallions give you a neigh, eh?"

Hawkstead felt bad immediately. "Jarad, go with him. He can ride pillion after a mile. He gets the mile of walking for opening his mouth."

Hawkstead spent the good part of the afternoon riding in the area looking for the feral dog pack without luck. The hard exercise and fresh air helped clear his blood of the alcohol and he felt himself after a few hours. When they found no sign of a dog pack gone feral having become established in the area it was a relief. Hawkstead wondered if someone was building a dog pack for hunting, which was strictly prohibited. Another possibility was that the dogs belonged to several people but had been running loose and formed a temporary pack. There were many possible reasons for reports of a dog pack but no sign of a dog pack.

They were several miles from the village when there was a loud crack, then two more cracks sounding in the direction beyond the village. Hawkstead pulled his horse up and tilted his head to listen but no further sounds broke the air. His men were all fairly close to him, within hearing distance anyway.

"What was that?" Hawkstead wondered aloud, looking in the direction of the village.

Everyone had stopped to stare off in the distance but it was Toby's younger brother, Terrence who answered. "Sounded a lot like a tree exploding in deepest winter."

"It's not winter, Terrence," Hawkstead said.

"I noticed that, too," Terrence said. He shrugged. "Quiet now."

"It's time to head back anyway. Maybe someone in the village knows what it was," Hawkstead said.

Hawkstead and his men rode back to the village. The villagers were as puzzled by the noise and a small group had already gone out to investigate out of curiosity. Terrence grinned when someone mentioned that it sounded an awful lot like an exploding tree in winter. Hawkstead put the noise out of mind and focused on the real issue at hand, the problem with the dogs. He questioned some people for more detail and after listening to several more villagers' version of the story concluded that it was most likely just two or three dogs passing through. One of the villagers rattled off breed, description, and owner of every dog in the area and only one of the reported feral dogs came close to a matching description.

"Yep, old Massey got that little border collie 'bout five years past, I suppose," the man said, bobbing his head. "She had two pups in the first litter. Gave Tucker a male and kept the female. Both had black muzzles. Old Massey is up to three dogs now. Got himself a shepherd when that potter traveled through last year. Fine dog. Fine dog. She is almost solid black except for her brown legs. Not a herder, mind you. But lets old Massey know when anyone is coming. Old Massey does not hear so well these days. Noisy dogs, shepherds. Now Davie has got two short haired collies. Long noses on those dogs. Heard they can stick that snout into a badger hole and the black tip can be seen at the exit door."

Hawkstead let the man ramble on but tuned out his voice. Instead of being irritated that it had been a wasted trip, the focus and exercise helped clear his head at last and he spent some time overseeing what was happening in the village. Besides, he wanted the villagers to be in the habit of keeping him informed about any problem so that something major did not pass by without his being aware of potential problems. The sun was heading for the horizon by the time Hawkstead was ready to leave the village and head back to the keep. Hawkstead was suddenly aware that he had a feast to attend with him as the guest of honor.

Hawkstead had just mounted the jennet when one of the villagers approached him. "My Lord, there are strange visitors. They were attacked by the wild dogs. Bakken is bringing them in now."

"Strange visitors? Serfs wandering?" Hawkstead asked, concerned.

"Nay, strange. Strange clothes. Definitely not serfs," the man said, shaking his head.

"Strange how?" Hawkstead asked.

The man threw his hands in the air. "I don't know. You'll see."

Hawkstead waited atop the horse. The small party of men and women carrying two litters between them was visible only a few minutes after the villager bade him stay. Despite walking uphill carrying a litter the two groups moved briskly. They stopped and gently set the litters down at Hawkstead's feet. Hawkstead did not know what to make of them. They were certainly not serfs who had wandered from their own lands.

The man was dressed in a light brown shirt and darker brown pants with pockets sewn in all sorts of odd places, such as sleeves and the legs of his pants as well as bundles attached to a leather belt around the waist. He was smaller than average and had a yellowish cast to his skin. His hair was so black it almost looked blue and he was clean shaven. The man's clothes had several bloody stained tears. Some of the fabric had been torn enough to see the severe bites from dogs as reported to Hawkstead, including one on his neck.

The woman was pale and blonde. She wore a pink blouse of a shimmering fabric that at first glance resembled silk because it draped around her smoothly but it was not silk. She also wore blue pants of a stiff fabric. Hawkstead frowned when he saw that she wore gold and silver around her neck as well as precious gems on rings of precious metal on her fingers. That much wealth worn openly was an invitation to bandits. Leather ankle boots covered her feet, the heel at least two inches high and the leather form fitting around the ankle somehow. Hawkstead could not help staring at the boots. No laces to pull in the leather yet it fitted snuggly at the ankle.

There was no way her foot could go through that hole, yet she was wearing them.

The woman also had a purple leather bag hanging at her side, a strap over her shoulder and across her chest holding it in place. More jewels and metal dangled from the bag. She lay with her eyes closed but no obvious signs of bite marks. Her hands were smooth and her nails long and oval. They were hands of a woman who did not perform manual labor. She was clean, polished, and smooth. One of the villagers who helped carry her was rubbing the fabric of her shirt sleeve between two fingers in, mesmerized by the feel of it.

Though the man's hands were not as smooth as the woman's hands they also did not look like the hands of a laborer. He had a nail bruise on his left hand but the nails had no dirt under them and were neatly pared short. He also had a callous on the outside of his left hand, just below his pinkie finger but no callouses on the palms of his hands common with laborers. His clothes were also clean and fitted. Hawkstead glanced out the way the villagers had come, looking for something, anything, that would explain why these two strangers would appear on foot so far from anywhere.

"The man clearly needs medical attention," Hawkstead said. "Why is she unconscious?"

"There's a goose egg on her head," Bakken said, gesturing to an area on her forehead under her hair.

"Those don't look like dog bites," Cory said, kneeling next to the man and examining the wounds. "There's only one hole at each wound. Dog bites? Definitely not knife wounds but they don't look like dog bites."

"There were no other footprints near them," Bakken said. "Just the paw prints and their footprints."

"There was no one, no one at all with them?" Hawkstead asked.

"No, m'lord," the villager said.

"Send some men out to look for runaway horses or sign of an escort farther out," Hawkstead said.

"Aye, m'lord," the man said. "But as I told ye, there are no tracks leading up to where they were found."

"What? I thought you said there were no other footprints around them. Follow their footprints back as far as you can."

"That's what I am saying, m'lord," the villager said. "There are no footprints from them either. It's like they just dropped out of the sky in the apple trees. But we'll take a scout around. See what we can see."

"We need to get them to the keep as quickly as possible," Hawkstead said. "Cory, ride ahead and make sure that Father Tom is warned. We'll lash his litter between two horses. A cart would likely kill him off at the speed we need to use and a sedate pace might not get him to the infirmary in time to save him."

The men hurried to follow his instructions and in a matter of minutes the wounded man was laying on a litter that had been strung between two horses and strapped in place. The horses were also tied together with a length of rope at the back of their saddles and bridles to keep them moving in pace. Jonathon scooted behind his saddle and the villagers handed up the woman to sit in front of him on his saddle. Jonathon wrapped his arm around her waist and her head fell back against his chest.

Hawkstead studied the strangers thoughtfully as they rode back to the keep as fast as the litter allowed, puzzled by their appearance. The jennet Hawkstead rode did not compare to the palfrey and he was reminded of the quality of his new wife's horse. Hawkstead was determined to get his hands on more Roffe horses.

Hawkstead was late for his own wedding feast. They rode into the keep in the last light of the day, having watched the sun set over the horizon a few miles out yet. The music could be heard even out in the courtyard and Hawkstead rode to the stable fearing that whatever feast had been prepared was either growing cold on the table or burnt left simmering on account of his being late. Hawkstead should have ridden ahead of the group. If Hawkstead had remembered that there was to be a feast to celebrate his impromptu wedding he would have ridden ahead of the group. They had not needed him to know what to do. He still had to change into more appropriate clothing also.

The two strangers had been taken to the infirmary with orders given to inform Hawkstead when and if there was any information on their condition. Though he was intrigued with their mysterious arrival on his estate, he had more pressing matters at the moment. At the last minute Hawkstead decided that what he wore was good enough to at least make an appearance. Instead of hurrying up to the solar to change into his best clothes he sauntered into the great hall in his every day clothes.

The Great Hall was packed with people. Upon entering Hawkstead looked immediately to the lord's table, to his wife playing hostess alone at the wedding feast. She smiled and nodded her head as people passed along the front of the table to congratulate the bride on her wedding. A small pile of gifts grew on the tabletop in front of her. Hawkstead stared at her for several minutes, unsure what he was feeling. At first Hawkstead thought that it was a feeling of pride warming his chest but it was more than that. His wife was a striking woman. Had he really told her the night before that she was a dog?

Hawkstead slid onto the bench beside his wife. She did not even look up at him. "You almost missed your own feast," she said, smiling at the steady stream of well-wishers filing past the front of the table.

"Something came up," Hawkstead said. "It looks like you have things well in hand. No one probably even noticed that I was not here."

That earned him a head tilted stare from those intensely blue eyes. "The groom missing from his marriage feast doesn't go unnoticed."

Hawkstead grinned until he looked down at his trencher. The fat in the gravy over his meat and smashed potatoes had congealed. He signaled to a servant. "I need warm food."

"Mrs. Smith saved this especially for you," the girl said. "Mrs. Smith said that after you finish your serving you will be allowed to have seconds from the pot."

Hawkstead ate the cold food without further complaint. The small penance from his housekeeper was a reminder that he had slid on his responsibility to his wife and he accepted that reminder. Hawkstead had barely finished the meager portion of cold meat and tubers when the same servant girl slid a steaming trencher piled high with food in front of him.

Musicians gathered at one end of the hall, creating a loud nerve wracking mixture of sound as they tuned and warmed up for a performance. Hawkstead was surprised that Mrs. Smith had managed to find musicians at such short notice until he looked closer and recognized several faces. Calling them musicians might be a stretch. They were recruits from the kitchen and stables who knew the right end of a musical instrument. Eventually a passable sound emanated from their side of the room.

Hawkstead noticed that his wife's head was bobbing, eyes grown heavy as her chin jerked ever closer to her chest. She jerked upright and gave herself a shake. Hawkstead really needed to find out his new wife's name. He considered calling her Lady Hawkstead but the formality was not appropriate at their wedding feast. "Wife, you look tired. Do you wish to retire for the night?"

She shook her head. "I cannot leave so soon. It would look odd."

"It is late enough," Hawkstead said. "If we go together it will not look odd."

Her eyes widened. "No."

"Then perhaps some more wine," Hawkstead said, lifting a flagon from the tabletop to fill her cup.

She put her hand over the cup. "If I drink another cup of wine I will be snoring with my head on the table."

"It is a feast," Hawkstead said. "Half a glass then."

"Very well," she said after a moment's consideration.

Elyse caught her attention while Hawkstead poured ale to the rim of her cup. "Kara, did you know that Richard is your husband's cousin? I was quite pleased to see him. He was fostered at Mael when your mother and I were children. I am sure you have met him at Roffe Manor."

"Richard?" Kara asked.

Elyse blushed. "Sir Richard Addington. He is the second son of Lord Addington's younger brother. I remember when he was knighted. It was just before I left for Roffe Manor, a year after your mother wed your father." Elyse reflected on her childhood memories for a moment, the thoughts softening her face. "I remember when he caught us in the dairy barn looking for kittens. We weren't allowed there, you understand. Feral cats carry disease and are not at all friendly to little girls trying to cuddle their babies. He crawled up into the loft and brought down two kittens for us to see. The mother cat was torn between rescuing her abducted kittens and guarding the ones remaining in her nest. Ah, that seems a lifetime ago now."

Hawkstead smiled. At last he had learned his wife's name without having to resort to actually asking her. Kara. His wife's name was Kara.

Chapter Five

Kara woke disoriented in darkness. Confused, she tried to sit up but could not. Something heavy held her skirts pinned to the bed. Gradually Kara became aware of the sound of someone else breathing. Alarmed, she tugged on her skirts to free them from the weight holding her in place. Hawkstead wrapped his arm around her waist and pulled her against him.

"Be still," he whispered in her ear.

Kara froze. Her heart thundered in her chest. For several long minutes she did not dare move a muscle. Kara lay on her back with her legs twisted sideways. The position was not very comfortable. Kara could hear Hawkstead's heart beating a few inches from her ear. Hawkstead grunted then turned her so that she lay on her side and nestled in the curve of his body. It was discomforting to feel his arm pressed under her breasts and to know where her rear end pressed. Kara was unable to fall back asleep long into the night.

Kara was so aware of his body. She could feel his heat beating against her back. Kara heard his slow, steady breathing. She could hear the steady boom of his heart beating within his chest that felt as hard as granite. He smelled of leather, wood smoke, and horse. Hawkstead moved in his sleep and she was aware of changes in his body where her rear end rested, aware of his arm brushing against her breasts. The sensations that flooded her were new and confusing. Eventually she slipped into a restless sleep.

Morning arrived with her alone in the bed. Cautiously Kara sat up and looked around her. She was alone in the room. It was not her room. It was Hawkstead's solar. Puzzled, Kara tried to remember the events of the night before that ended with her sleeping in Hawkstead's bed. There had been the wedding feast and then it became a little fuzzy. Kara thought she had retired to her own room but maybe she had fallen asleep before reaching her room since she was still wearing her clothes. Either way, Hawkstead must have brought her to the master solar.

Kara did not understand why Hawkstead would have brought her to his solar instead of just leaving her be. Kara hurried out of the solar and walked briskly down the halls to her own room. The room had been emptied of her belongings. Startled, she stared around the small cell in surprise. Kara heard a servant passing in the hall and stopped him.

"Where are my belongings?" she asked him sharply.

"I didna take them," the startled man said in surprised alarm.

Kara sighed. "Can you find out where my belongings have been taken?" She asked in a more gentle tone.

The servant hurried off down the hall, glancing back at her over his shoulder several times. Kara began to worry he had just run away from her but he did actually go in search of someone who knew what was going on because he returned. Another servant appeared, the first man hovering anxiously in the background. "My Lord Hawkstead said your belongings had been left here too long by mistake. They have been taken to your room and your companion moved closer to a new room."

"My room? Where is that?"

Kara followed the man, somehow not surprised when he led her right back to Hawkstead's solar. Kara forced a smile and thanked the servants. It was not their fault that their master was a black hearted oath breaker. Already Hawkstead had changed his mind. He had said he would not lay a hand on her, neither to strike her nor to love. Hawkstead had said that she would sleep on the other side of the keep yet here she was back in his room. Kara had no intention of allowing him to entice her into performing her wifely duties. Hawkstead might not find her attractive but she certainly found him attractive. Kara could not spend nights nestled against his manly form, aware of his strength and virility, without being affected.

Kara set about collecting her things, intending to have them returned to the room she claimed as hers. There was no sign of the trunks. Most of her clothes were in a wardrobe on the far side of the room. There was a matching wardrobe containing Hawkstead's clothes, as well as a hauberk and chain mail. Kara reached out and touched the chain mail, stroking the dents and dings with her fingertips. The chain mail had been used well. The scarred rings were near the heart. Kara slammed the wardrobe door shut and returned to the wardrobe holding her things. She pulled chemises and dresses from the wardrobe, tossing them on the bed. Many things were missing. Kara dropped to her knees beside the bed and lifted the coverlet to look under the bed.

"Did you lose something?" Hawkstead asked from the doorway.

"Don't you have anything to do besides stand over my shoulder?" Kara asked without thinking.

One eyebrow rose in surprise and Hawkstead chuckled. "I see some rest has restored your spirit, if not improved your mood."

Kara dropped the coverlet and stood, wiping imaginary dust from her skirts. A trundle bed took up the space under the bed. "I am looking for my clothes," she said. "Several pieces have vanished."

Hawkstead's eyebrow rose higher. "Under the bed?"

Kara waved her fingers in a nervous gesture, a soft sweep like a dove's wing. She almost told him how Angel used to hide her things under the bed they shared, under the other beds, in the stable, or just about anywhere. For some reason Angel thought that it was funny, especially if the item was personal and there were male witnesses. Kara kept her tongue still. She did not want to discuss Angel with him.

"I ran out of places to look," she said at last.

"Why did not you just ask?"

Kara's voice dropped to barely above a whisper. "I did not want to be a bother. By some mistake my things were brought to your solar. I meant to take them back to my room."

"Ah," Hawkstead said. He grinned. "You were sneaking out. It was not a mistake. This is *our* room."

"You said I would sleep on the other side of the keep."

"That was the effects of too much ale speaking. I spoke badly. As for your missing things, I told your new maid to go through your things that need to be laundered as today is laundry day."

"I was content to be on the other side of the keep," Kara said slowly.

Hawkstead crossed the room and took both her hands in his. Startled, Kara immediately dropped her gaze to stare at his his feet. "Look at me," he said. Hesitantly she looked up at him. "I was upset and angry when I sent you out of my solar yesterday morning. You would lose your standing in the keep if you don't share my bed. You would be the one to suffer if I banished you from my room the first day."

Kara laughed. A dimple appeared just below the right corner of her lips when she smiled. "Ah, sir, you will have me on the floor laughing. 'Tis not for me that you make this sacrifice."

"Is not a sacrifice."

"And how will I feel if you take back your word on the rest?" Kara asked, puzzled by his behavior but not about to give up the argument.

"Hopefully excited," Hawkstead said in a low voice. Startled, Kara took a step back. Hawkstead slid his arm around her waist and pulled her up against him. Kara blushed. She knew what it meant to be a dutiful wife. It would be so easy to submit to the urges surging through her body. He shut out the rest of the world when he held her against his long length. Kara felt only him, saw only him, smelled only him. The man was her husband. Hawkstead could satisfy the needs he stirred within her and it would be all right since they were married.

Then what? It was a strange game that he played with her, tossing her senses about like a ship on a stormy sea, first one way then the other and her stomach danced to match the upheaval. All Kara had to do was resist him and then in a few months the marriage could be annulled due to lack of consummation. Then she would be free. That idea gave her resolve.

Kara looked up, straining her neck so she could look him in the face. "So your word means nothing?"

Hawkstead's eyes narrowed. "I keep my word. Uttering a few harsh words when I was in a foul way was not swearing an oath. I will not strike you because I do not strike women. Eventually we will work on creating children, Kara. I never said we would never do that." He leaned down and brushed her lips with his, the briefest of kisses. "Unless you wish to discuss children now?"

Kara wavered off balance for a moment, her knees going weak. Hawkstead held her steady. "Not yet," she said.

"No. Not yet," he said with a sigh. He rubbed her back with his hand. "Perhaps our wedding night resulted in a child?" He did not seem pleased with the idea.

Kara did not know how to respond. She knew that no child would result from that night. It was strange to know that Hawkstead really did not remember that he had passed out. How could he not know that nothing had transpired between them? Kara could tell him that he had slobbered on her cheek then flopped onto the bed like a lined fish. The words choked in her throat and she was unable to bring herself to tell him what had not happened that night. It had been humiliating. First he had repeatedly told her how ugly she appeared to him, then he had passed out, and then he had started the new day with accusations and more barbs about her appearance. Kara shook her head. No, she would not tell him the words that would ease his mind.

"Why were you so afraid of me?" Hawkstead asked.

"I thought you would beat me," Kara whispered.

"Are you still afraid of me?"

"Aye." She nodded. "Please let me go."

"I don't know who fed you untruths about me. I am not a man who mistreats a woman," Hawkstead said firmly.

"Many men mistreat women," Kara said. "Angel must have had some reason to go to such lengths to, uh, avoid you," Kara said, trailing off when she realized what she had just blurted.

"Did your uncle mistreat you?" Hawkstead asked gently.

"I don't wish to be married to you, sir," she said in a rush. "I was not given any time to consider marrying you. Nor any man."

"Surely you knew you would marry eventually?" He continued to move his hand slowly up and down her spine.

"Nay. My uncle made it clear that I would never marry." His steady massage made her relax. "Do you not notice my aged position? I am past twenty years of age, sir. I am still stunned that he offered me in marriage. Certainly not to marry in the same hour I did arrive."

Hawkstead stopped rubbing her back but kept his palm in the small of her back as he considered what she said. "Why would not you ever marry?" he asked.

"As you said, I am an ugly dog compared to Angel," she said. "Nay, do not think I pity myself for I've long been accustomed to what I am."

Hawkstead winced. He looked down at her. Kara was one of the most beautiful women he had ever seen. Her thick, dark hair had coppery threads that glinted in sunlight. Her heart-shaped face accented her large eyes that turned up slightly at the corners, giving her an exotic appearance. Her full lips begged to be kissed. Her skin glowed. Yet he had indeed spoken those words Kara so calmly repeated back to him.

Hawkstead could prove to her right that moment that he desired her and leave her in no doubt that in truth she deserved to be worshipped. All he had to do was touch her amazing mouth with his lips and need would take over. Hawkstead held back. He could not do it. Hawkstead could not touch her until he knew if she carried another man's child.

"That's not logical," Hawkstead said. "Marriage has nothing to do with appearance." He felt Kara stiffen in his arms. He was starting to adjust to the idea that she was affronted by just about everything he said though he was not certain why. "Besides, I spoke in anger. I can't believe you've heard anything but compliments."

Kara gave a short bark of laughter. "Don't mock me." She twisted to get out of his embrace. "Release me. I do not understand the game you play but do not play at my expense."

Hawkstead released her. He did not understand her. So what if he had said some harsh words while drunk? Had he not already said that he had not meant it? Richard had said men lined up to marry her. She must have heard of her beauty daily. At least one man must have filled her ears with prose and compliments to allow him access to the treasure between her legs.

"Hawkstead is such a mouthful, what is your given name?" Kara said, crossing the room to put some distance between them. "I wish to call you something less formal."

Hawkstead grinned. "Hawk. You can call me Hawk."

Kara grimaced. He looked so like a twelve year old boy being clever, which annoyed her for some reason. "I shall not call you Hawk. What does your mother call you?"

"Lional when she's angry. Leo when she's feeling motherly," Hawkstead said.

"I remember one of your names was Henry," Kara said, the memory triggered when he said Lional. "I shall call you Henry."

Hawkstead rolled his eyes. "Must you be so contrary?"

"Yes," Kara said. She paced. "Why are you trying, Henry? I thought you were going to just leave me alone."

"We're married," Hawkstead said in surprise. "How can I leave you alone?"

Hawkstead raked his fingers through his hair and sighed. Roffe's letter had dared, taunted, and riled but Hawkstead had taken the wrong bait. Though he would not have beat her as she expected, he would have sent her back to Roffe with a clear message that he would not marry her if she was his only choice. Even drunk he was ready to turn her away until Richard stuck his nose into the affair. What a mess he had made. However it was not anything he could not fix.

"You are of good blood, have property, look to be healthy, and your current agitation is completely understandable so though your current mental state might be questionable, I'll give you some time to calm your stretched nerves," Hawkstead said. Kara stared at him with her mouth open in surprise. "Hopefully your household skills make up for the rest. I'll send Mrs. Smith to you. Mrs. Smith is the housekeeper."

Kara looked frantically around the room for something to throw at him. He surprised her with a quick kiss before abruptly leaving the solar. Kara collapsed back on the bed. The man was going to drive her insane. Kara stared up at the canopy draping the top of the bed. Had she really thought to manipulate him? She could not even understand him. Hawkstead did nothing she expected. There was only one thing that would work to take her mind of her problems, a visit to the stables and possibly a nice ride through the countryside. Mrs. Smith was forgotten.

Kara walked down the stalls until she reached a stall holding a large dun stallion, Hawkstead's destrier, Ajax. She was still irritated that he had so callously helped himself to riding Rhinney without even asking her. The mare was not to be ridden. Kara had given clear instructions that she wanted the mare walked without a rider for at least two days, to allow her to recover from the long journey, yet he had taken the mare out without a care to Kara's instructions. A groom came up to her while she studied the stallion.

"May I help you, m'lady?" the boy asked.

"Yes, saddle the dun," Kara said.

The boy's eyes widened. "I'll get Allan, m'lady." The boy immediately darted away to fetch Allan. Allan turned out to be the head groom.

Allan tried to talk her out of it but Kara was insistent. "If you can't saddle the horse I will do it myself. I will take an escort. Have two men ready to ride in ten minutes."

True to her word, Kara opened the stall door and slipped a lead rope onto the stallion and led him out of the stall. Allan dry washed his hands nervously but was also fascinated to see her so calmly handle the destrier, trained war horse, terror of the stables, and watched in amazement as the horse patiently stood while she collected tack and prepared him for a ride. Kara talked to the horse in French the whole time. Kara was ready to mount in less than ten minutes and the two riders designated to accompany her were ready and waiting.

"I pray to God that I survive the first year of their marriage," Allan muttered as he watched his lady give Ajax his head, racing out of the stable at a full gallop.

"Ho the gate," one of the grooms accompanying Kara shouted up at the gate tower as she raced through the open gate. "We return in an hour. Heading north." Before the man at the gate tower could respond the groom raced out of the keep before losing Kara.

Kara let the stallion have his head. The horse clearly needed to stretch his legs. After a few miles Kara slowed him and set him through his paces, wanting to see what he had. Though she did not train destriers she had bred and sold many horses to knights and lords who were able to afford the price and were willing or able to have them trained as war horses. During her initial visit with Allan she had learned that Hawkstead had trained Ajax himself and intended to train destriers at Greenestone. Kara agreed that Ajax was a good candidate for breeding future generations of destriers. Kara formulated a mental list of which mares she had that would make a good match with Ajax for breeding. No matter the breeding though, training was everything.

Riding chased away the turmoil of the events of the past few days. Kara eventually let the horse pick his own pace and studied the fields and people working the land near the keep. Her escort had not been able to keep up with Ajax and rode at a steady pace behind her but within sight. Several people waved and Kara waved back but did not stop. Kara did not know if they knew who she was but she was not riding to meet the tenants, she was riding to clear her head. Besides, she would prefer to wait to meet them with Hawkstead at her side. They circled the keep and then headed back. The keep was so large that she had been able to ride quite a distance and still keep it in sight.

A man stepped out from a copse of trees directly in front of her and Kara had no time to stop Ajax from running him over so she turned the horse and attempted to slow him, causing the horse to swing into a circle around the man as she pulled back on the reins in a downward motion. "Are you mad?" she yelled at the stranger. Ajax snorted and half-reared at her attempt to stop him.

The man smiled and stared at her in appreciation. "I was lost in your striking self," he said.

Kara frowned, taking in the man's strange appearance. He wore a black leather coat over a black shirt and black pants that had an unfamiliar cut and style. He was no serf, yet she would have sworn that he was no knight, though he had an air about him of a man extremely confident in himself as a man. His appearance was polished. Polished and clean. His words had been clear enough but sounded odd to her ear, slow and drawn out with an added lilt to the end of some words.

Kara's escort thundered up behind her, instantly wary at the sight of the man. When Hawkstead's men exchanged glances Kara missed it because she was still trying to urge Ajax under some control. What Kara did not know was that her escort had been at the village the day before and encountered two other strangers, also dressed oddly. The escort took up defensive positions, one on each side of her, wary but curious at yet another stranger appearing on the estate.

"You are alone?" Kara asked, glancing around for others.

"Yes, indeed," the man said. He bowed slightly, almost mockingly. "I am passing through. A wanderer, if you wish to know. You may call me Roger Murdock, if it pleases you."

"It pleases me to hear your real name," Kara said.

The man grinned. He was of average height and slender but muscular with wide shoulders. His hair was dark brown with a few gray hair highlights and trimmed very short. If he had one outstanding feature it was his eyes. His eyes were large and deep, deep brown with a thick frame of black lashes. He had a child's over-sized, large eyes that did not match the masculine harshness of the planes of his cheeks and jaw.

Kara felt that he was a dangerous man though she was not sure why. Perhaps it was the extreme confidence and even arrogance he displayed though he was alone and trespassing and facing armed men who belonged where he was trespassing. Yes, definitely arrogant, not at all the demeanor of a serf. He had enough arrogance to rub elbows with a king.

"My real name is Roger Murdock," the man said, bowing his head again briefly. "I became separated from my acquaintances. Once I find them I will be on my way. Have you seen other strangers in the past day or so?"

Kara shook her head. "No, you are the only stranger I am aware of."

"I believe you,' he said, nodding. Roger Murdock glanced at each of the two men escorting Kara. "And you men? Have you seen other strangers recently?" The hard face hardened even more when he addressed the two men, eyes narrowing slightly as he watched their faces. The two men stared at him expressionless, making no response. Roger Murdock nodded thoughtfully before turning his gaze back to Kara. Ajax had finally calmed and stood in place. Once again his face softened slightly and a smile tickled his lips when he looked upon her. "You are wise to ride with an escort. It is not safe for a beautiful girl to venture out in these lands alone."

The two men escorting Kara immediately took that as a direct threat and reached for weapons, though they did not pull swords from scabbards but just kept their hands on their weapons. Kara had no patience for flattery and took his words for false flattery rather than a threat and gestured for the men to stand down. The two man escort remained on alert, hands on weapons. Kara stared at the man standing in front of her thoughtfully.

"You should be careful of your words, sir," Kara said, deciding to address him as a peer. "That could be taken as a threat to my person."

"I would never harm you, child," Roger Murdock said. For some reason Kara believed him.

Kara did not know what to do with him. If the man was truly just passing through she saw no harm in letting him continue on his way but he had no business lingering about the estate and could be lying about passing through. Kara did not know how Hawkstead would manage the situation and since they were on Hawkstead's estate she did not want to overstep her authority as a visitor. She still had not wrapped her head around the fact that she was the mistress of this very estate.

"How did you lose your friends?" she asked.

"They were faster than me," the man said with another twisted smile.

Kara nodded politely, though she felt it an odd explanation. "Once you catch up with your friends you will either move on or present yourself to the keep."

"Exactly my plan," Roger Murdock said. He put his first two fingers of his right hand to his forehead and gave her a sharp salute then turned and trotted back into the trees.

"That is a dangerous man," one of her escort muttered, watching the man vanish into the trees.

Kara had to agree but she kept it to herself. "I will tell Lord Hawkstead as soon as we return so he can decide what to do about him," she said, staring at the place the man calling himself Roger Murdock had entered the copse of trees. "Hopefully he finds his friends and they move on with no further problems."

***

Hawkstead hoped to find Nelson in the main hall. Nelson was in the main hall. "Send some men to Roffe Manor to find out about my new wife. Make sure Roffe does not know about them," Hawkstead said to Kevin.

Nelson stared at Hawkstead in surprise. "What?"

"Have you started on the ale again?" Richard asked, coming up from behind just in time to hear Hawkstead's orders. When Hawkstead just scowled Richard added, "Anything in particular you want to know from your spying?"

"Hawkstead's scowl deepened. "It's not spying. I just want to know more about her."

"Does the past matter?" Richard asked.

"If she's carrying some other man's brat it does."

Nelson's eyes widened. Richard turned to Nelson. "Forget he said that nonsense. He'll come to regret that he uttered those words." Richard turned to Hawkstead. "You were too drunk to remember your wedding night. No amount of spying will give you the answers you want. I'm surprised you'd even think it. If you want answers, get your head out of the ale fog you've been wandering in."

"Do you intend to set her aside?" Nelson asked in a voice two octaves higher than his normal voice. Nelson cleared his throat and tried again. "Are you looking for evidence to set her aside?"

Hawkstead did not say anything.

"No?" Richard asked.

"No," Hawkstead replied.

"Then that's that," Richard said. He turned abruptly and walked away in anger. Hawkstead stared after Richard's retreating back in surprise. As always, Richard's was the voice of reason. He had not even considered setting her aside.

Nelson cleared his throat. "Um, Lord Roffe's men are still here. Should I question them?"

"If it can be done subtly," Hawkstead said after consideration. It now seemed a petty undertaking yet curiosity consumed him. "I don't even know what I've acquired with her."

"I'm working on that," Nelson said. "I've already sent runners."

"Anything else?"

"The two new boys arrive next week for squiring," Nelson said. He went on to tell Hawkstead of other normal, mundane news but Hawkstead drifted to his own thoughts.

Robin would have brought him a cup of ale. Always his shadow, Robin. The boy was sharp and quick, open without being too talkative when the need for quiet was more prudent. Hawkstead realized how much he missed the boy. The body had been sent back to his family for burial since they were within a day's travel. The son of a minor baron with moderate lands, the boy was being groomed to take over his own estate one day.

In a flash, Hawkstead could picture Robin's reaction to his mentor's current behavior. The boy would have had that surprised look on his face, the eyes widening and then the thoughtful look as he considered whether to say that he thought Hawkstead was behaving foolishly and then a more serious thoughtful expression as he considered *how* to tell Hawkstead nicely that he was being a fool. Robin would have said something clever, something that Hawkstead could not take offense at.

"Forget any spying," Hawkstead said. "It was a wild thought."

Nelson let out a loud whoosh of air in relief. "Thank you. I was not looking forward to spying."

"I still want to know what she brings to the marriage," Hawkstead said. "And I won't chastise you for gossiping with her men."

Suddenly Hawkstead grinned as it sank in what Richard had
said. Hawkstead did not remember his first night with his new bride
because he must have passed out within minutes of entering the
room. The little twit hadn't told him otherwise either. Since Nelson
had been telling Hawkstead that news had arrived that Baron Vespin
had recently passed away he was caught off guard by Hawkstead's
sudden grin and soft chuckle.

"Did you dislike Baron Vespin?" Nelson asked.

"What? Has something happened to Baron Vespin?" Hawkstead
asked.

Nelson sighed. Getting married had definitely turned his
cousin's head over his heels. "Your new wife is touring the keep
with Mrs. Smith," Nelson said. "I think they've reached the kitchens
by now."

Hawkstead jumped to his feet. "I think I will visit the kitchens."

***

Kara looked around the kitchens in approval. It was the last
building of Mrs. Smith's tour. Mrs. Smith had only taken Kara to
those places where she had domain, a complete tour through the
halls of the keep, the laundry, the linen rooms, the gardens, the
weavery, and now the kitchens. Everything throughout the keep was

neat and orderly. The servants respected Hawkstead and were
generally happy as they worked at their tasks. Women laughed and
chatted as they hung laundry to dry. The gardener hummed as he
checked on the last of the vegetables in the garden. Two boys
helping him cover strawberry plants with straw were getting as much
straw on them as on the ground. Even in the dairy barn the mood
was light and banter constant as servants milked the cows and fed
the goats.

"I'm sure you'll want our Lord Hawkstead to show you the
smithy and tannery and others," Mrs. Smith said.

Mrs. Smith was an elderly woman of aged plumpness and an
extensive bosom. She wore a plain wimple and steely gray hair
peeked around the edges. Kara liked the matronly woman
immediately upon meeting her. Elyse had joined the tour and also
seemed quite impressed with the keep's housekeeper. Elyse knew
the right questions to ask and with each answer Mrs. Smith returned
Elyse would nod approval.

The cook offered Kara bread fresh out of the massive brick
oven. The cook was a large, elderly man who wore short sleeves
under his apron but still sweated profusely down the back of his
neck. He waited, anxious that the bread pleased her, not out of fear
but due to professional pride. The kitchen seemed to have the largest
concentration of people in one area.

Boys turned the spit of a whole hog roasting with a slightly
older girl overseeing them. Both boys and girls were scrubbing pots.

A cluster of women were rolling out pastry dough but spending more time watching the cook with their new lady of the keep and whispering amongst themselves. There were boys chopping nuts and girls cleaning herbs and vegetables. Men carried in casks of ale and wine then teased two young women decorating cakes at another table by trying to snatch pieces of sweets. Two young men were using wood planks to pull golden, crusty loaves of bread out of the oven. The smell of roasting meat and baking bread and other fantastic smells of cooking food tickled Kara's nose with the promise of wonderful tasting food.

The servants were all relaxed in mood and appeared quite content with their situation wherever Kara had visited within the keep yet everything was neat and orderly. The servants greeted Mrs. Smith with a warm smile as they went about their tasks. They had been politely curious to Kara.

The whole atmosphere was so different than the atmosphere in Roffe Manor. Kara frowned as she thought about it. There everyone scurried about in fear if Roffe stepped into sight, trying to look busy. Even if Roffe was nowhere to be seen Kara was either invisible or treated with rigid politeness. If someone was foolish enough to be kind to Kara and Roffe learned about it they weren't foolish a second time. Everyone knew that Roffe had spies within the servants so everyone was always on edge. It was like a fairy tale here, everyone happy and even the sun seemed to shine brighter and the sunshine reached into all the corners of the keep.

The cook watched Kara's frown anxiously. "Is it bad, m'lady?" he asked.

"Oh! Oh, no," she said quickly. "It's wonderful. Uh, good job."

Kara tore another piece of bread from the chunk of bread the cook had given her and stuffed the piece of bread into her mouth to show that she was enjoying the bread. The cook visibly relaxed. He smiled and nodded in agreement then offered Elyse and Mrs. Smith each a piece of bread. The cook watched both women carefully as they tasted the bread. Satisfied that everyone approved of the bread he went back to working his dough for the next batch to go in the oven. Kara tore the last of her bread into two pieces and ate one of the pieces of bread as she watched the cook work, fascinated by the smooth, deft movements as the man sliced dough from a large mound of dough sitting on the table, patted it into shape and then repeated the two steps without missing a beat. He had several loaves ready to go into the oven before Kara stuffed the last of the bread into her mouth. Even more kitchen workers stepped up to take the loaves and slide them into the oven.

"You do not have a separate bakery?" Elyse asked. A general hush fell over the kitchen. Lord Hawkstead may be lord of the keep but Cook was lord of the kitchen.

"The baker comes in early for pastries and cakes and the like," Mrs. Smith said. "But Cook makes the bread when the baker is finished with his work."

"Very efficient," Elyse said, nodding her head. The kitchen visibly relaxed and chatter filled the air again.

Mrs. Smith led the way out of the kitchen and Kara followed with Elyse beside her. The kitchen floor was tiled, the walk to the main building cobblestoned, and then the floor in the keep was covered with fresh, clean rushes. Kara was struck anew by how well kept the keep was. Mrs. Smith was a special housekeeper. Even if she had planned on staying she would not want to interfere with the way things were being run now.

"Is the cook a sensitive man?" Elyse asked.

"Only about his kitchen," Mrs. Smith said.

"And it was his decision to not have a separate bakery?" Elyse asked.

"Aye," Mrs. Smith said.

"A separate bakery is something to consider," Elyse said. "I trust you will manage to find a way to convince the cook that it is in his best interest." Mrs. Smith nodded but did not say anything. "He will be in charge of both," Elyse said.

Kara had no idea why Elyse cared so much about a separate bakery. If it worked to have everything done in the same kitchen there seemed to her little point in changing things. In fact, Kara thought keeping all the work in one place even made more sense but she would not go into a discussion over it with Elyse in front of Mrs. Smith. Really, Kara did not care either way.

"A separate bakery means that the ovens can produce more bread and not be taken over by meat for most of the day," Elyse said, looking at Kara as she spoke. "I saw the old bakery and wondered why it was abandoned. There were enough people packed into that kitchen to enable the bakery to be managed."

"What was the reason for Cook to shut down the bakery?" Kara asked, trying to sound interested.

Mrs. Smith looked uncomfortable. "Surely he had his reasons. I shall indeed talk to him."

"Personal reasons then," Elyse said, nodding her head. "Emotional servants cannot dictate the running of an estate this large."

"Cook didn't strike me as an emotional servant," Kara said.

"He wants them under his wing so he can protect them," Mrs. Smith said quickly. She turned a bright shade of red. "He is very protective."

Elyse stopped walked. "Is there a danger to the kitchen staff? That should be dealt with immediately."

"I will talk to him about opening the bakery," Mrs. Smith said. "He will do as he is instructed. Now that Lord Hawkstead is lord of the keep it is a safe place for servants."

Elyse resumed walking and Kara trailed behind. Kara wondered what had happened that made Cook feel like he had to protect his staff. Slowly it dawned on her that most of the kitchen staff was young girls. It did not seem likely that Hawkstead would tolerate abusing girls in his keep so something must have happened before he acquired Greenestone Keep. If these servants would just talk to their lords it would make things so much better but Kara knew that it was not that simple. She pictured if a servant went to her uncle to complain of mistreatment from his men or guests and knew that no servant in Roffe Manor would be so daring. Lord Roffe would be livid that they brought a problem directly to his attention.

The normal course would be to have any issue escalated through the servant hierarchy and the steward would discuss the issue with the lord. Most issues were settled long before reaching the ears of the lord. Some issues might reach the lord's ears and still not be acted upon if the misdeed was done by a landed guest. The lord's rule in his estate was absolute. He only answered to the king. If Kara heard of any mistreatment of girls she would not stand by even if Hawkstead did but for some reason she felt that Hawkstead would never allow the mistreatment of his servants even if it was the king himself behaving badly.

Mrs. Smith stopped in front of a large tapestry hanging on the main hall wall. "Every lady of Greenestone has placed a bit of herself on this tapestry." Mrs. Smith smiled fondly as she looked up at the tapestry. "I hope you will continue the tradition though Hawksteads now reside where once Greenes resided. When you decide what will be your contribution I will have the tapestry carried to the solar."

"What? Me?" Kara asked, feeling uncomfortable with the idea.

"No hurry, dear," Mrs. Smith said, patting Kara's arm. "This star in the corner was the fourth Lady Greene's. It is said that she took forty years to decide. And died a month after it was finished. I was not here, of course."

"Of course," Kara murmured.

She was Lady Hawkstead, Lady of Greenestone. Strange. She still felt like Lady Kara Roffe. To the world she was Lady Hawkstead. Eventually she would no longer be Lady Hawkstead but would once again be Lady Roffe, so really she was just borrowing the name Lady Hawkstead for a time. Kara stared at the silver star in the corner. Had it taken that Lady Greene forty years to finally feel like she was Lady Greene and not Lady Whatever?

"What happened to the Greenes?" Elyse asked, studying the tapestry thoughtfully.

Mrs. Smith sighed and her smile faded. "Ah, a sad tale. The Black Death took most of the family. One boy survived. He was a third son and had been given to the monastery. Though he was too young to yet say his vows his heart belonged with his brethren and when he was returned to Greenestone to take his proper place as Lord of the keep he left his soul at the monastery and could not bring himself to marry even to do his duty and the line died with him several years ago." Mrs. Smith wiped a single tear from her cheek. "He was a lovely man who lived a very long life in the wrong position."

"Terrible times," Elyse said in somber agreement.

"Are you a Greene, Mrs. Smith?" Kara asked on a hunch.

"Aye," Mrs. Smith said slowly, cheeks turning red. "My mother was the last Lord's niece. But the sons held the line, of course. Lord Greene asked my mother to remain on the estate as housekeeper and I took over the role in time."

"But why did the estate not go to you after Lord Greene passed if he was the last son?" Kara asked.

"Oh, no," Mrs. Smith said, putting her hands up in front of her as if to ward off someone. "The king was wise to award the estate to a young man who has many years in front of him and can provide heirs. I had no children and even if I had the desire to take the management of this large estate there would again be no one to pass it to."

"It costs a lot of money to manage an estate of this size, Kara," Elyse pointed out.

Kara almost rolled her eyes but did not want to show her companion disrespect in front of the housekeeper. She knew very well the high costs of managing an estate, as Elyse knew she did. Without the horses Lord Roffe would not be living so well at Roffe Manor. He would be moderately successful since the estate was smaller but they would not be living in the luxury they currently enjoyed.

"Without the manpower to work the estate the costs would drag it under. Lord Greene managed to maintain the keep but perhaps not the full estate? I suspect Lord Hawkstead brought in more people?"

"Oh, yes," Mrs. Smith said. "Lord Greene did his best with what was available but so many people are needed to operate at full capacity. It was a very quiet keep before Lord Hawkstead came. He brought many of his unlanded relatives to help manage the different parts of the estate. And he also brought more serfs to work the fields. Free men to take over the tenant farms. He brought in young apprentices for the mason and blacksmith. I am not sure how he managed to find them all but he did. I could never have done that. I am quite content as my role as housekeeper."

"I have no intention of changing that," Kara said. "I can see you love this place and I think you do a wonderful job of managing."

Mrs. Smith looked uncomfortable instead of relieved. "It is your place, m'Lady. I would not dream of intruding."

Elyse gave Kara a sharp look then turned to Mrs. Smith with a warm smile. "What m'Lady is saying is that she hopes you will continue as you have until she has time to learn all there is to running such a large keep. Between the two of us we should be able to guide her in the right direction."

"Aye, that makes sense," Mrs. Smith said in relief. "I have some things to see to. Dinner will be served in an hour. Excuse me."

"Thank you so much for the tour today," Kara said.

"That's what I'm here for, dear," Mrs. Smith said.

"Isn't that what I said?" Kara asked Elyse once Mrs. Smith was out of hearing range. "I said the same thing you did. You just honeyed it up."

"You can't just throw something like that at her," Elyse said. "You are the lady of the house now and thus housekeeping is in your hands. Besides, you put her in an uncomfortable position suggesting she resented you owning her home."

"I never meant that," Kara said. It had never occurred to her that way.

"I know that but Mrs. Smith did not," Elyse said. "You can go twenty years without changing how it's being run but you can't just say it outright."

"Why not?" Kara asked. "We both know I will never take the reins of the household."

"Servants expect more than that of you. When will you learn that?" Elyse asked in exasperation. "I will take up the reins for now, of course, but it must be subtle."

"Yes, subtle," Kara said, studying the tapestry. "What a horrid mess this tapestry is, yet I suppose it has a charm in a way."

Elyse was not looking at the tapestry. "I wish to visit the garderobe before dinner. You'll be fine on your own?" Elyse asked even as she started to walk away, her gaze on something across the courtyard.

"Of course," Kara said at Elyse's back. "I am the Lady of the keep, am I not? If I am not safe alone here I am not safe anywhere." Kara turned back to the tapestry, grimacing as she studied it.

At one time the tapestry might have shown promise as a great piece of work but so many hands with different styles had disrupted the flow. Perhaps the original Lady Greene had died before finishing it to prompt others to join into its creation. Several hands had clearly contributed to the tapestry, different threads, different styles, and different skill levels. There was a dog. Or maybe it was meant to be a bear. A child's cradle hovered in the middle, crudely stitched and out of scale with everything else. Kara touched the cradle, wondering which Greene's birth had inspired this image. For all she knew it could have even been the birth of Mrs. Smith. Strange to think that the woman grew up as a lady in a great house and now was the housekeeper instead of lady of the keep. That the king could simply give the keep to someone else was not right, in Kara's mind.

Someone came up behind Kara and slipped their arms around her waist, one hand pressing her stomach. Kara hadn't realized anyone was behind her and jumped in alarm when she felt herself embraced from behind. Panic swept through her before she realized it was Hawkstead. Kara relaxed. Well, she tried to relax. He held her against his long, hard frame and it was difficult to relax when he was so close. A strange warmth spread through her, radiating from his hand.

"Maybe we've started a child already," Hawkstead said, staring over her head at the embroidered cradle she had been touching when he approached. Kara did not say anything. Hawkstead pulled her even more tightly against him and lowered his head so that his chin was resting against her temple. "Was I so rough our wedding night?"

Kara shook her head. "Nay. Not so rough."

"Did I please you?" he whispered.

"Please me? Very much! I hope every night is such as that," Kara said in as light a tone as possible though she could feel her face burning. The man was vain.

Hawkstead chuckled. "I don't know if I can promise that but I'll definitely try my best to always please you. I don't remember anything of that night so will have to trust your memory."

Kara felt increasingly uncomfortable. The topic was one which she wished to avoid and Hawkstead's hand burned against her stomach. This discussion of pleasing stirred thoughts and feelings inside her that she did not fully understand.

"You aren't angry that I was drunk on our wedding night?"

"What's done is done," Kara snapped. It was becoming difficult to breath. She tried to step out of his embrace but his arm was like an iron band. "I need to freshen up for dinner."

"How does one freshen up for dinner?" he asked.

"One gets away from one's husband in order to breathe normally so that one can digest one's dinner."

Hawkstead laughed. "Ah," he said with a grin. He loosened his grip. "By all means, go freshen."

Kara slipped out of his arms and he let her go. Kara hurried down the hall without looking back. His delighted chuckle rang in her ears. Hawkstead's behavior confused her, one moment cruel and petty and the next moment gentle and almost affectionate. Kara also hadn't expected the physical side of marriage, the way he made her body ache in a most peculiar way. While he held her she felt the need to escape yet once she escaped his embrace she missed the feeling of his strong arms around her.

Instead of returning to the solar Kara wandered aimlessly through the keep, lost in thought about the events of the past few days. Maybe it would not be so bad to be married to him. Kara had not considered marriage as an option while under her uncle's guardianship. Surviving the years to her majority had been her only focus. Even her consideration of marriage to Carlton was but a distant plan to maintain her freedom. Kara hadn't fully considered what she would do after that date arrived, regarding the potential to marry. In many ways she was relieved that her uncle refused to allow her to wed. Most of the men her uncle had initially considered for her could only be described as totally unsuitable.

Kara had been but fifteen when Lord Roffe had told her that he was considering Lord Bigglestone's offer for her hand. Lord Bigglestone was three score if he was a day, had already buried three wives and had twelve grown children and three nearer her age. In the days when Lord Bigglestone thought there was the possibility of a match with her he had followed her around, constantly trying to grope her and kiss her. Fortunately Lord Roffe had decided that he was not ready to allow her to marry yet and since Lord Bigglestone already had ample heirs he did not need a match with Kara.

Only a few months after Lord Bigglestone was Lord Freemont, fourth son of Earl of Casselton. Lord Freemont was a man who had no property, no interests, no manners, and no prospects. Kara found him the biggest bore she had ever met. Freemont had no interest in horses. His only interest seemed to be in fine food and wine offered at the tables of others. And himself. Kara still found it amazing that Lord Roffe could have seriously ever considered his suit. As the parade of unsuitable men went through Roffe Manor Kara began to wonder if Lord Roffe was only considering the most unsuitable prospects. Then the offers stopped. Or at least her uncle stopped presenting men to her as possible husbands.

At one time Kara had dreamed of the handsome knight, strong and clean in spirit as well as body, come to whisk her away from her tormented life. This mystery knight with no face or real image would bring her to a land of light and comfort, a life with joy. They would go for picnics in the garden, surrounded by their beautiful children, laughing and happy. Kara had approached marrying age at fourteen so the daydreams matched those of a normal fourteen year old girl. The most common age for a girl to marry was sixteen but by fourteen or fifteen any gentle born girl was at least betrothed. Eighteen was considered almost a late marriage and getting married beyond that age was very rare. Over the years Kara had pushed away any dreams of such a marriage, burying such hope deep, deep down inside her. She hadn't even thought about that dream for years.

It was a rough world Kara lived in. She ran her fingers along the rough stone wall in the garden. There was a reason why the manor was surrounded by a stone wall. Every village was surrounded by a wall. The keep was surrounded by double stone walls. If the threat was severe the keep was the last line of defense for the villages on the estate. The walls were for protection. What chance did she have alone in a world where armored warriors needed the protection of stone walls?

Two peasant girls walked past on the other side of the garden wall, unaware of Kara's presence, giggling and laughing. With her wealth and ranking Kara had less freedom than those girls. She sighed. Or so it seemed at times. Even peasant children had their marriages arranged by parents more often than not. Did they feel like pawns with no control over their own lives also? Kara was sure that those girls she envied would in turn think that she had a life far better than theirs.

Except for the first drunken night and the harsh morning after, Hawkstead had been quite kind. Oh, and except for the incident in the stable and when he took out Rhinney without permission. And when he accused her of being a witch because she was not as fat as he had thought. Other than that he was not too bad. If she must be married then Hawkstead would be an all right choice. He was kind on the eyes as well. Hawkstead could protect her from Roffe. Not just protect her until she reached her majority but also beyond that time.

Kara sat on a stone bench under a crab apple tree that still had leaves so late in the season. The keep was a comfortable place. People here were well treated, a reflection of their master.

Technically they were already married, well, mostly married. Hawkstead certainly had resented their marriage at first, which might have prompted some of his bad behavior. Hawkstead seemed to have accepted their marriage as a done deal and moved on. Kara rubbed her temples. There was so little in her life that she had any control over and it seemed that her marriage should be one thing she had some control.

Mrs. Smith found Kara. "Oh, m'lady, there you be. I'm to tell you that Lord Hawkstead is having dinner sent to your solar."

"Oh," Kara said, heart sinking in her chest. The news confused her after Hawkstead's friendly attitude only minutes earlier. Perhaps the talk of babies had reminded him that she possibly carried another man's child. After just considering accepting Hawkstead as her husband it seemed that he was the one now considering setting her aside. Why else would he banish her to dine alone in the solar instead of joining him in the hall?

Mrs. Smith was smiling. The older woman had been pleasant, polite all day but this was a big, pleased smile. Kara liked the woman. Kara was sure that Mrs. Smith's warm, motherly attitude influenced everyone in the keep. "It is so pleasing that m'lord has found himself such a lovely wife. Now dinner is waiting, so off we go."

Kara was not in such a hurry to rush up to the solar to eat dinner by herself. "So dinner in the solar?" When her uncle was in an especially angry mood with her he would often banish her to the women's solar to eat her meal in isolation. Kara could refuse the order. "He really said I am to go to the solar for my meal?"

"Yes, yes. Off we go," Mrs. Smith said. The matronly woman looked quite pleased with the order, which further confused Kara.

Kara let Mrs. Smith harry her to the solar. When they reached the solar door Mrs. Smith patted her arm then sauntered down the hall, humming a cheerful tune. Kara took a deep breath and stepped into the solar, stopping short when she saw Hawkstead waiting for her. Hawkstead stood facing the doorway, next to a serving table that had been brought up and loaded with food. Kara had not expected him to be there, in fact had expected to be dining alone. Though she had not been eager to dine alone the idea of dining one on one with him was even less appealing.

Hawkstead further flustered her by bowing formally and leading her to a chair. The meal prepared for them was wonderful but she had little appetite and could barely eat. Kara felt so torn about what to do, so uncertain of the consequences of what her choices would bring. Kara was not ready to face Hawkstead when she did not know herself what she wanted.

"What was it like growing up in your uncle's house?" Hawkstead asked as he poured wine for them.

"Complicated," Kara said. "This is very good bread."

"Why did you believe you would never marry?"

"Cheese."

Hawkstead was startled. "What? You would never marry because of cheese?"

"Could you pass the cheese?" Kara asked. She drank nearly half the wine in her cup with one swallow.

"Of course," Hawkstead said. He sliced off a chunk of one of the cheese wedges, using a wicked looking hooked knife. "Would you like a different type?"

"No. This is fine."

"It's just hard to believe that your uncle truly never intended you'd marry. Perhaps you misunderstood?" Hawkstead suggested.

"Mmm. There are onions in the pastry," Kara said.

Hawkstead growled. "Why won't you talk to me?" he asked. He poured more wine into her goblet. "I'm trying to get to know you, yet you seem to be preoccupied with food though you've only eaten two bites."

Kara looked up at him and met his gaze. He had amazing eyes, very open and sincere. "I don't know what to say, except the truth," she said at last. "I'm not so sure you want to hear the truth."

"Let me decide that," he said.

"Then it would be too late," Kara said.

Hawkstead grinned. "Logic. Very well. I take it upon my shoulders to suffer the burden since you have warned me."

Perhaps it was the wine. Perhaps it was his persistence. Perhaps it was his eagerness to get to know her. Kara told him what she had never uttered to another living person. "If I tell you that my uncle beat me whenever I did something wrong and when I did not do something right and when my cousin did something wrong, will that satisfy your curiosity? That he told me almost every day that he'd never give me to a man for wife because I would shame the Roffe name by having my infernal spirit interfere with my wifely duties, would that help you understand why I did not expect to wed?" Kara spoke coolly, calmly, simply stating facts.

"No matter how hard he tried to break me I could not help but resist. I am not suitable as a wife. Did you do something which caused him to dislike you? That he'd throw me at you?"

"I don't think he expected me to wed you," Hawkstead said slowly, carefully, absorbing what she had said.

Kara nodded then went back to pushing her food around on her trencher. Hawkstead needed time to absorb what she had told him. Already Kara regretted her outburst. Kara took another long swallow of wine. Kara was not sure what had released her normal reserve to so openly tell him. Kara felt like a large burden had lifted from her shoulders yet now that the words had passed her lips and she could not take them back but she wanted to take them back in the worse way. Now Kara felt exposed, vulnerable. Well, what was done was done.

Hawkstead spoke after several minutes had passed. "It is quite common for parents to thrash their children," he said. Kara raised startled eyes to stare at him in horror. He was staring at his trencher and did not notice her reaction to his words. As he continued to speak Kara composed her features to a bland mask. Kara had a lot of practice in that. "He most likely had his reasons. As for his telling you that you'd not marry for those reasons, why that would eliminate many a woman from marriage if that was true."

Kara felt like he had punched her in the stomach. Kara had opened herself to him and Hawkstead had swept it away as nothing. Hawkstead looked up at her and nodded in satisfaction at having explained away her confession. Kara knew the answer to her conflict. With or without his approval she would annul this marriage. How could he defend her uncle's actions?

"We don't have to stay married," Kara said in a low voice. "I'm sure you regret what you, well, what happened. We really aren't married."

"The marriage was real. The priest said the words," Hawkstead said.

"I mean, well, you fell asleep," she said in a rush. There, it was said. Kara turned pleading eyes up to him. "If you would just wait a few months, not tell, ah, anyone that we aren't, um, actually husband and wife, then when I reach my majority on my next birthday you, we, could annul the marriage. Then I won't have to go back to my uncle's guardianship pending reaching my majority."

Hawkstead studied her thoughtfully. Kara did not have her facts quite right. They were married and whether or not the marriage bed resulted in consummation did not matter. It was even possible to have the marriage annulled even after a marriage produced children.

Hawkstead knew this but chose not to clarify at the time. Getting an annulment was a long, difficult process but it did not matter because he had no intention of getting an annulment. Though the wedding had been a drunken whim Hawkstead considered them properly married.

"What would you do?" Hawkstead asked. "If we weren't married?"

"Then you will consider it?" Kara asked, perking up.

Hawkstead was clearly having a tough time understanding her desire to not be married to him. He could not get past the belief that she must marry someone. Kara would never be free to marry without approval, not with such vast, wealthy holdings. Though Hawkstead did not yet know the extent of her holdings he knew about Mael and that was enough by itself to warrant special attention to her. The king would have a say in the matter even if she outgrew Roffe's guardianship. Hawkstead was surprised that the king hadn't stepped in earlier to see her properly settled. Since Hawkstead was a favorite of the king he knew that she really had no choice and what her fate would be, no annulment and to stay married to Hawkstead.

"Is there a reason why you would not prefer to stay married to me?" Hawkstead asked. "Perhaps other plans?"

"I do have other plans," Kara said. "I would think you would be happy to annul this marriage. Not only did I have no say in the matter but you were clear that you only did it because you were drunk."

Hawkstead nodded thoughtfully. "I guess an annulment would suit your plans?"

"I did consider just going with that we are married but I am helping you as well. You don't know the consequences of being married to me."

"Consequences?" Hawkstead asked. He could not help but smile. "Let's just let things be as they are for a while and discuss this again when you are closer to reaching your majority," Hawkstead said. "Will that suffice?"

"It will," Kara said. Her mood improved dramatically and she even started eating her food.

Perhaps she had given her heart to another but if so she hid it well. Hawkstead did not understand why she wanted so much to not be married to him. He had always been confident in being an eligible, even desirable catch. Hawkstead could do as she wished but he rather liked the idea of keeping her around. Kara was his wife whether she accepted that or not. He had patience. Hawkstead would rather she liked the idea of being his wife.

"They say my mother went insane," Kara said. "I'll go insane one day. As well as any children I have."

That sounded so much like a threat that Hawkstead threw back his head and laughed. "Insanity? My family history makes anyone else look tame."

Kara chewed on her lower lip. "Truly?"

Hawkstead chuckled. "You're a jewel, Kara."

"I don't understand," Kara said.

"Indeed." Hawkstead leaned back in his chair and smiled as he watched her. "Nelson is listing your holdings. Once he's finished we'll tour your lands and see how they stand. I meant to anyway."

"Mael is mine," Kara said. "Funny, Nelson did not discuss it with me. I could have told him."

Hawkstead looked uncomfortable, almost guilty. "I had not thought about that route."

Kara knew her holdings. Kara could tell him but chose not to for now. It would make no difference since he had agreed to an annulment. Her eyes glowed in delight. Kara relaxed, actually wiping her trencher clean as she talked about the ride, the weather, her horse, her mother's home. Hawkstead watched her, amazed at the transformation when she became animated, more startling even than when she had shed several sizes the day after her arrival. The twit thinks he had accepted her offer, Hawkstead realized. He had no intention of seeking an annulment of the marriage.

"Mael was my mother's estate. It isn't far from here. I go there when, well, it's peaceful. It is a fine estate and the manor sits on a hill with a lake below." Kara paused, slipping into thoughts that made her smile. "Maybe the horses will arrive before we get there. We will go soon, right?"

"Horses?"

Kara blinked. "Horses? Um, I suppose I could tell you about the horses. You see, I had a message sent with Sir Bullton to inform me here when they arrived at Mael. If I am going to be here awhile I should consider bringing some here."

"Your uncle's horses?" Hawkstead frowned. "I don't want to go behind your uncle's back."

"No," Kara said slowly, trying to decide how and how much to tell him about the horses.

"Though delivery of horses was part of the marriage contract discussion with your cousin, I am not sure yet if the same agreement transfers to you."

"My uncle promised you horses with your marriage to Angel?" Kara asked, tone going hard.

"Yes, that was to be part of the contract, a specific number of horses each year," Hawkstead said. "I hope he honors that agreement with this marriage."

"He should not have done that," Kara said slowly, considering what that might mean. Since Lord Roffe did not own the horses he could not promise them to Hawkstead. Since Lord Roffe had not discussed it with her Kara wondered how he planned on fulfilling that promise. Lord Roffe could not hand over horses to Hawkstead without informing her. How had Lord Roffe planned on managing to try to slip that past her? He could not do that. A shiver ran down her back.

Before Kara could question Hawkstead further about the details of the arrangement he was making with Lord Roffe there was a knock on the solar door. Hawkstead got up and opened the door just enough to converse with the person on the other side. Kara could hear their low voices but could not understand the words being said. Hawkstead looked back at Kara. "I have some business to attend," he said. "I'll be back late. Don't wait up." The door shut behind him with a soft click.

Chapter Six

Kara stared at the closed door when Hawkstead had gone. The room felt empty without him in it. As lord of the keep Hawkstead was responsible for his people and any number of emergencies could occur to call him away. Kara was actually relieved at the interruption that called him away since it gave her the opportunity to decide what and how to tell him about the horses. The subject had sort of come up without planning on her part. There was something about the man that made her say whatever was on her mind.

Kara did not know how Hawkstead would react to learning that she was the horse keeper at Roffe Manor. She had almost blurted out a secret she had been holding for over half her life. Once she told him there was no taking it back. Kara had no idea how he would react to learning that *she* was responsible for Roffe horses. Being married to a woman who was behind a horse breeding program would be damaging to his reputation, especially if Hawkstead was intending to start a similar program at Greenestone.

Kara and Banner had gone to a lot of effort to keep it secret that she was the directing force behind the Roffe horse breeding program. Not only would the knowledge that a girl was directing the program have destroyed it before it could get going, even now that the Roffe horse lines were well established Kara knew that Roffe horses could still be shunned if it became common knowledge that a young woman was making all the decisions. Lord Roffe knew, of course, and was determined that no one learned that it was his niece responsible for the program.

Lord David Roffe, Kara's father, had started the breeding program. He was the first to notice that his daughter had a unique talent to assess horses. Lord David Roffe would discuss with Kara the direction he was going and often quiz her on her opinion, thinking it amusing that his eight year old daughter could assess horseflesh better than his younger brother. It soon became apparent that Kara could assess horseflesh even better than her father and his renowned groom.

When Kara's father was killed and Kara's uncle became the new Lord of Roffe Manor the horse program almost disappeared until Lord Roffe discovered that his young niece knew as much or more than her father about horses. Apparently Lord David Roffe had kept the information to himself. So Lord Roffe followed her advice on everything to do with the horses and the horse program had flourished. Eventually Lord Roffe had stepped back completely and let Kara run the business. Lord Roffe had no interest in the horses other than enjoying the benefits from the money that poured in.

There was more than wounded pride that drove Lord Roffe to keep it a secret that his niece was the one responsible for the horses. Women were not horse breeders, especially ladies. So much money poured into the Roffe coffers that he could not stop using her if he wanted to. The stigma attached to such behavior from a gently born lady would be devastating to the whole Roffe name. If Kara told Hawkstead her secret and he released her from the marriage then he would know the Roffe secret and could ruin her family as well as destroy the breeding program. If Kara did not tell Hawkstead her secret and he did not release her from the marriage then he would be outraged that she had kept the information from him.

Hawkstead returned to the solar several hours later when Kara was long asleep. He crawled into bed and pulled Kara's sleeping form against him. The movement woke Kara and she stirred. "I heard you took Ajax for a ride today," he said in a low voice.

"'Twas not a secret," Kara said, yawning.

"You are never to do that again," he said firmly. "When I find out who saddled him for you, that groom will be punished. So don't think anyone will be foolish enough to do so for you again."

"No one did the first time," Kara said. She tried to pull away from him but he kept his arm around her waist and it was like an iron vise. "I saddled him."

"You?!"

"I wished to ride him and your grooms seemed to all have feet of lead."

Hawkstead was silent for so long that Kara thought he had decided to drop the topic but he hadn't. "You saddled my destrier? Don't you realize how dangerous that was?"

Kara shrugged. "He's just a horse. I have saddled many horses."

"Why did you have the urge to ride my destrier?" Hawkstead asked.

"Why did you have the urge to ride my palfrey?" Kara responded.

"Is that what this was about? A petty need to show me something because I took out your palfrey?" Hawkstead asked, voice rising in anger.

"No, not at all. But I could not take out my palfrey since you so callously took her out the day before despite my request to give her the day without any exercise so I chose the destrier for my ride today," Kara said. "He's a decent horse."

Hawkstead snorted. "Decent? He is a war trained and war experienced destrier. He is the reason that the king has requested I personally train fifty more destriers before the end of next year and one hundred a year for five years after that. He is more than a decent horse."

"That's a lot of horses," Kara said in surprise. "How will you ever get that many trained every year?"

"I will be very busy." Hawkstead admitted. "Half will not pass training so I have to start with at least more than double."

"We did not train destriers but we have supplied yearlings to many for training," Kara said. "I don't think I could even supply that many and we're established. How do you plan on getting the stock in place?"

"Yes, that is why I want the Roffe horses," Hawkstead said.

"You would not lose half during training if you pick the right ones to begin with," Kara said. Hawkstead was quiet and Kara regretted giving the advice. Lying in bed in the dark had relaxed her guard over her tongue. "At least that's what I've heard."

"I'm sure everyone feels it's easier when they haven't done it," Hawkstead said.

They lay in silence for many minutes. Kara could feel that Hawkstead was still awake. Not only did she forget herself with him and say what was on her mind, half the time what she said seemed to offend him. Kara was getting tired of his constantly feeling that he could direct her life as it suited him without taking her view or opinions into consideration.

Kara felt at times that she was not a person to Hawkstead, just someone to follow his direction, someone Hawkstead felt he could control. It felt like Hawkstead had a preconceived idea of who she was and had not bothered to find out who she actually was. For some reason that reminded her of the man she had encountered on her ride. Though the man on the road was rude and gave her the creeps, she felt like the man saw her, really saw her.

"Oh, I forgot," Kara said. "I encountered a strangely dressed man today. He said he was passing through and would be gone once he found his friends."

"Yes, Cory told me already." Hawkstead's voice was still clipped.

"What are you going to do about him?" Kara asked.

Hawkstead was quiet for several minutes, considering his answer. "I will send men out tomorrow to see if he is still there."

"Ah, that is a good plan," Kara said. It seemed like a good thing to say to soothe his ruffled feathers.

Long after Hawkstead fell asleep Kara lay wide awake in his embrace, thinking about which horses would suit his needs. Kara had already made commitments for some of this year's yearlings and did not have one hundred horses to be available the following year old enough for training. There was such a high demand for her horses that often they were sold before they were even born. What Kara could do would be to help him choose good candidates from other breeders until she could ramp up proper stock for destriers. Kara did not know how Hawkstead would react to such a plan, however.

Roffe had probably known of Hawkstead's demands yet had said nothing to her. That surprised and irritated her because Roffe would know that he had to go through her to arrange the horses. Lord Roffe should not have promised what could possibly not be delivered. Kara decided that she could only make it work if she pulled back on other commitments, which she was not willing to do. Hawkstead would have to settle for what she had available.

Horses suitable to be trained as destriers brought good money so Kara had included them in the program, just not such high numbers, since the demand was not as high. In the morning Kara really would have to learn the arrangements Roffe had made with Hawkstead in this marriage contract. If there was no promise of horses with their marriage contract then Kara would do what she could to help him but was not obligated to endanger her existing commitments.

***

They spent the next few days in the same general routine. Hawkstead rose before her in the mornings and went about his business. With a large estate there was always something needing to be done and Nelson gone from the keep meant Hawkstead had to take up his tasks as well as his own. When Kara had learned that Nelson was away from the keep on some business of Hawkstead's she had decided to wait for his return to question the marriage contract rather than ask Hawkstead. On occasion Hawkstead sought out Kara to see how she was doing but mostly he left her to her own devices. They ate their meals together, along with everyone else in the Great Room. Hawkstead let her ready herself for bed in privacy, staying away from the solar until he was sure that she was asleep.

While Hawkstead was busy managing the estate Kara divided her time between the stables and horse pastures and dragging Elyse along while Kara pretended to try to learn the household demands. The truth was that Elyse was learning the household demands and Kara was trying to appear attentive even though what she felt was boredom and impatience so strongly that it was almost physically painful. Every minute spent following Mrs. Smith around was a minute she could be evaluating what needed to be done with the horses. Kara still had to make her list to fulfill her agreement with LeRouget.

Kara had promised mares carrying foals from two of her stallions, Red Dancer and Tornado's Circle, in exchange for the mares she had brought back with her. Though she had a general idea which mares to ship off she still wanted to evaluate each one. The reputation of the stable depended on it. It was difficult to be stuck at Greenestone when there was so much work to be done at home. Now she had the added burden of selecting potential destriers for Hawkstead. Kara would have to approach Hawkstead about her returning to Roffe Manor for a few months. Kara had a feeling that such news would not go over well with Hawkstead, yet there was no way to do her work from Greenestone when her horses were at Roffe Manor.

The housekeeper and Elyse discussed the points of linen napkins while Kara trailed behind them trying to remember how many horses in the south paddock would be suitable for her needs. The trio approached the kitchen and Kara smiled at the sounds greeting them. The cook was making meat and turnip pastries for the field workers and he sang in a boisterous voice that lacked anything pleasant to the ears. Kara thought that she recognized the song but he sang verses she had never heard before. He was so off-key that it was possible that it was not really the song she thought that it was. Mrs. Smith cleared her throat loudly and the cook looked up from his rolling pin. When he saw the three women he smiled.

"Ah, m'lady and m'lady," the cook said, a giant smile on his face. "And the charming Mrs. Smith. What brings you to my humble kitchen this fine fall day?"

Kara pointedly looked out the open doorway of the kitchen. Rain fell so heavily that the pathway to the main keep was a blur. It had been raining hard and steadily since the early hours of the morning. The ovens kept the kitchen warm and chased away the dampness that pervaded the rest of the keep.

"A messenger just arrived," Mrs. Smith said. "We are expecting a party of twelve in the next few days. I think only two servants. Four gentlefolk and eight men at arms."

The cook's eyebrows rose. "Names?" he asked.

"Is it important?" Mrs. Smith asked evasively, catching Kara's interest in an otherwise mundane task. Kara glanced at Elyse to see if she had noticed also. By Elyse's intense gaze on the cook, she had. Kara was happy to leave the running of the household to Mrs. Smith's capable hands but was performing her obligatory hour of pretending to show interest. Kara was impatient to head for the stables. Yet this was holding her interest.

"You know it is," the cook said. "No salmon for our lord's aunt. Capons for Lord White. I must plan. Who is it?"

Mrs. Smith still hesitated. "Can't you just make a variety?"

"Names!"

"Oh, very well. You'll find out anyway. Lord Burlington and his wife. Their daughter. And Sir Rotnase."

"Rotnase?" the cook asked. He stood frozen for several minutes. Slowly he straightened his shoulders as a man prepared to face his doom with a brave face. "Very well."

"No tricks, Hubert," Mrs. Smith admonished, shaking her finger at him.

The cook sniffed and went back to his pastries. Suddenly he remembered that Kara was there and his head jerked up in alarm, afraid he had insulted her. "My pardon, m'lady," he said.

"Granted," Kara said. She stepped closer. "Tell me, Cook, is there a problem with one of the expected guests that I should be aware?"

Hubert glanced at Mrs. Smith then glared down at his unfinished pastries. "No problem, m'lady. I know my place."

"You may speak freely, cook," Elyse said.

"Aye, m'lady. With your permission I'd like to get back to me pastries," the cook said.

"Of course," Kara said.

"I need to make sure those girls are airing out the loft," Mrs. Smith said as they left the kitchen. Two servants held oiled tarps over the women's heads as they walked back to the keep. "If you wish to have the tapestry down just let me know."

"Not now," Kara said. Mrs. Smith asked twice a day every day if Kara would like the tapestry taken down so that she could work on it. "What I'd like to know is why the cook is so unhappy about the expected visitors."

Mrs. Smith waved away the servants holding the tarp and gave her skirt a shake before facing Kara. She wrinkled her nose as she considered her words. "Well now, I suppose you have the right to know of it then. The cook's daughter was, well, pressed into service, you could say. Not by her choice. The lord frowns upon men forcing serving girls but some households don't allow the girls the choice, ya know. Well now, the girl got a black eye and a son. Cook suspects Rotnase but Betty never did say. Hubert'll behave himself. Rotnase might get a burnt scone or two is all."

"Poor girl," Kara said. "What happened to her?"

"She helps in the kitchen. I'm sure it's not for me to say but I have my suspicions about that Rotnase myself. Now I'm off. Unless you need me for anything?"

"You're free to go. I'll be in the stables," Kara said.

"You'll be wanting to bathe then. I'll have your maid bring clothes to the bath house an hour before dinner," Mrs. Smith said. The woman bobbed a curtsy and walked away.

"Hawkstead should have forced the issue," Elyse said, frowning after Mrs. Smith's retreating back.

"The girl probably felt too embarrassed to say anything until she could not hide the result," Kara said.

"That's no excuse," Elyse said, sniffing in anger.

"I'm not saying it's an excuse," Kara protested. "Poor girl. A servant and him a gentleborn. She probably felt she could do nothing about it."

"That's why it was up to the lord to do something," Elyse said. "You should say something to him. As a wife it is sometimes necessary to remind a lord of his responsibility to all his people."

"I have to go to the stables," Kara said, impatient to go. Her horses had arrived from Mael that morning and she was eager to see them.

"This is important, Kara. As the lady of the estate you should be taking care of your people," Elyse said.

"It is something that happened long before I arrived in this soddy keep," Kara said. "What am I supposed to do about it now?"

"You haven't consummated your marriage with him yet, have you?" Elyse asked sharply, gaze locked on Kara. When Kara blushed Elyse had her answer. "What are you thinking? I should have known. I should have seen it."

"Hush," Kara chided, glancing around to see if anyone was within earshot. "Whatever put that idea into your head?"

"Child, you probably have some elaborate plan to hold to your original goal but I'm telling you, do not destroy this chance at your happiness," Elyse said, taking Kara's hands in hers. "He is a good match for you. Do not sabotage this relationship."

"He is a self-absorbed ass," Kara snapped.

"Most men are, dear," Elyse said softly. "Just as you are being now."

"Me?" Kara stared at Elyse in shock.

"Yes, you. What reason could you possibly have for holding him at bay? No good reason," Elyse said. Elyse tilted her head in thought. "You think this is temporary? That is why you are holding back on building a relationship with this place and why you are holding back from your husband."

"This is not the place to discuss this," Kara hissed, seeing several men walking in their direction. "I must go to the stables. I have trudged through the household tasks long enough."

Elyse sighed. "Very well. But we will continue this discussion."

"No we won't. This is my business, not yours," Kara said.

"It is my business," Elyse said, face flushing in anger. "It is always about you. I grow weary of it always being about you." The woman immediately regretted her outburst and started to say she was sorry for uttering such harsh words but then straightened her shoulders and shook her head. "No, I will not take back those words. For they are true. Always I have been there for you and now that the end of my task is near I will not let you destroy both our futures."

"I don't understand," Kara said, feeling a knot tighten in her stomach. "You will always have a place with me. You have never said you wished for a future away from me."

Elyse slumped slightly. "I never thought of a future away from you, before." Elyse rubbed her forehead with the palm of her hand.

"I am finding myself overwhelmed." She glanced around them, noticing the foot traffic as people went about their business within the keep but no one encroached on their space. "Something has happened to me, Kara. Something I never expected. There is a man. He has my head and heart in turmoil."

"A man?" Kara mouthed the words in surprise. "You? But, but you are, well, old."

Elyse went rigid, staring at Kara with hurtful eyes. "Child, I am only 30 years old. I am still young enough to wed and bear at least one or two children."

"Who is this man? Has he proposed marriage to you?" Kara asked. Kara realized how harsh she sounded and forced a smile. "I am happy for you, Elyse." The words came out stilted. "But why have you said nothing? Who is this mystery man?"

"He, he…" Elyse's voice faded away and she stared off into the distance. A change came over her as she thought of the man who had opened her eyes to seeing herself differently, as a vibrant woman, not an old maid. For the first time Kara saw the beauty of Elyse, not the elderly mother figure. Elyse shook her head. "Not yet. Not yet. Go, child. Go visit your horses."

Instead of having a footman hold a tarp for her, Kara held one over her head herself and dashed to the stables as quickly as possible while hopping from place to place to avoid puddles. Kara dropped the tarp at the stable door and headed down the corridor to the rear stalls. Hawkstead's stable probably suited him but she missed her own stables. At least the head groom was capable and kept a clean, orderly building. The stable here was just too small to handle the volume of horses she managed.

The discussion with Elyse weighed heavily on her thoughts. Never had Kara considered the possibility of Elyse having any place in life other than being Kara's companion. Life was changing and Kara did not feel that the change was in a good way. Kara had not noticed any man showing a special interest in Elyse but then again she had been so wrapped up in her own problems that she might not have noticed.

Kara tried to think of possible suitors and lingered on Hawkstead's older cousin Richard. The man did follow Elyse with his eyes whenever the two were in the same room. If it was Richard then Elyse was very good at controlling her feelings because she had never given any hint to being interested in Richard. Except, Elyse had been excited to learn that Richard was at the keep, Kara now remembered.

Two of her mares had arrived that morning and were settling in well. Kara was expecting more any day. Kara had not made plans yet on what to do with her horses at Roffe Manor since she did not know where she would be in the months ahead but it had put before her the necessity of making those plans. The logical choice would be to gradually move them all to Mael. When Kara reached her majority she had intended to reside at Mael but it had seemed so distant that she hadn't planned out the details.

The longer Kara stayed at Greenestone the more she did not like the idea of leaving. Kara stroked the mare's velvet nose. It did not have to change. Hawkstead seemed content to leave her untouched. Thinking about Hawkstead made her feel all sorts of emotions boiled together with either anger or frustration or happiness or warmth ready to pop out without a moment's notice. When he talked his voice had such a warm, deep timbre that sent wonderful shivers down her back. When Kara looked at him she saw beauty in his nose, his rugged jaw, and that easy smile. Every night when he held her Kara ached for something more. Hawkstead made her feel something inside that she did not understand.

Elyse had been right. Hawkstead was a good choice for her. Kara suddenly felt how childish she had been acting, toward her impromptu marriage and to Elyse as well. Suddenly Kara wished that she could really be married to him. Kara paused in petting the mare. Fate or destiny had pulled her from her uncle's cruelty and tossed her into the lap of possible happiness and she had closed her eyes to the opportunities being married to Hawkstead would give her.

Kara had accepted that she would never marry because Roffe had said she never would, yet here she was married in name at least to a man who was strong, yet gentle, pleasing to the eye, entertaining to talk to, and who made her ache inside. Sometimes he made her blood boil and sometimes he frustrated her but they seemed such minor things compared to the warmth that filled her when she looked upon his face and form. Kara had grown so used to not wanting to feel the need to be loved that when the opportunity came she resisted rather than feel.

Kara heard his voice. Kara turned. Hawkstead was in the stable. Without thought she walked, then ran, in his direction. Kara stopped, composed herself before sedately walking the rest of the distance. Hawkstead saw her, watching her with a smile on his face. Thinking that Kara had come to the stable seeking him, he grinned from ear to ear.

"Miss me?" he asked.

Kara blushed. "Perhaps," she said in such a low voice that he was not sure if he had actually heard right.

"This is Ajax," he said, gesturing to the massive war horse next to him. "Don't get too close or he'll--"

"Hello again, pretty baby," Kara said, going right up to the horse. She held out her hands, palm up, and Ajax snuffed, blowing air through his nostrils. The stallion whinnied, a low rumbling greeting, then he nudged Kara with his head.

Kara looked up at Hawkstead with a smile that lit up her face. "He's magnificent."

"Magnificent," Hawkstead said in agreement though his gaze was locked on Kara. "Watch his teeth," he said automatically. The horse was a weapon in itself, a trained war horse that had seen battle and she had the horse purring like a kitten.

Hawkstead watched her in amazement as she talked to the horse, finding the right spot to itch. The horse stood with his eyes half-closed as she scratched right behind his withers. When she stopped scratching Ajax bumped her with his head. Kara laughed and kept scratching. Ajax literally shivered in delight.

The head groom joined them, nodding at Kara. "Me mother had ye gift," the man said. "This be the devil horse and ye got him purrin' like a puppy."

"He just acts tough because he's unhappy," Kara said. She tapped the horse's jaw when Ajax snapped at the groom. The horse closed his eyes and rumbled deep in his chest.

Kara twisted Ajax's forelock, gave the horse one final pat then turned to Hawkstead. A wise person did not turn their back to Ajax. Kara may have faith that the horse would not harm her but Hawkstead did not have the same trust in the horse and instinctively pulled her out of Ajax's biting range, right into his arms. Kara looked up at Hawkstead with a smile, a smile that warmed her face and lit a fire inside him. Neither noticed the groom chase the two stable boys out of the stable with a gesture and shut the door behind him. Without thought, Hawkstead pushed all thoughts of patience out the window and pulled her into an embrace and lowered his head at the same moment for a kiss. Their lips brushed lightly for a moment, then with a groan Hawkstead demanded more. Kara wrapped her arms around his neck and returned his kiss with all her heart.

Behind them someone coughed lightly. "Um, excuse me."

Hawkstead raised his head and glared at the man who interrupted them. Kara sagged in his arms, gasping for breath. Once she had gained her senses she glanced around Hawkstead at the man who stood there, smiling slightly, arrogant to his bones. It was the man Kara had encountered during her ride a few days before, Roger Murdock. Startled, she stepped back from Hawkstead.

"Newlyweds, eh?" he asked in his low drawl. He leaned an elbow against a stall gate and crossed his right ankle over his left, the image of a man relaxed. "I appreciate your hospitality while I search for my, uh, friends, but I am wondering if maybe you're holding back on me."

Hawkstead frowned. "What are you saying?"

"Well, I heard that there were two people, a man and a woman, brought in from a village a few days ago. I was hoping to visit them, see if maybe they saw any sign of my friends."

Hawkstead shook his head. "The two serfs are runaways from my father's estate. They were attacked by wild dogs and are in no condition to talk to anyone. Father Tom gave the last rites to one because it is not looking like he'll survive. The other is still unconscious. They are being kept isolated because I don't want runaway serfs giving my serfs any ideas."

Roger Murdock frowned, not certain whether to believe Hawkstead, yet detecting no obvious lie. "Strange coincidence, eh?"

he said, uncrossing his ankles and standing straight. "I'd still like to see them."

"I don't see how the business of my serfs is any business of yours," Hawkstead said coldly. "I've given you a roof and food for several days now. Either you move on soon or make yourself useful."

"You are offering me employment?" Roger asked in surprise.

"Stables always need mucking out," Hawkstead said with a shrug.

"Aye, indeed," Roger muttered with a smile. He shifted his gaze to Kara. "What do you think, beautiful girl? Should I stay longer and muck out stables for my supper or move on in hopes of running down my friends in another direction?"

"I think if you still haven't found your friends by now that maybe they don't want to be found," Kara said without thinking. The man made her uncomfortable.

He laughed. "That is also what I am thinking. But I am very determined to find them. Plus, I have found a lovely diversion within the walls of this castle. Very well, I shall work for my supper. I have better skills than mucking out stalls, however."

"For now all I have need of is a stall mucker," Hawkstead said. He felt no kindness towards the man who so casually addressed his wife as beautiful girl. "Let's see how you manage that and we'll go from there."

A loud commotion outside the stable doors drifted through their discussion and all three heard it at the same time, turning their heads in unison towards the doors. The head groom's voice could be heard arguing with someone just before the doors slammed open. The noise disturbed the horses and several grew agitated, whinnying and moving about their stalls. Lord Roffe strode purposely into the stable, eyes blazing. His anger flared even higher when he saw Hawkstead and Kara standing together with Hawkstead's arm around Kara's waist.

"What is the meaning of this?" Roffe yelled.

Kara opened her mouth but Hawkstead was faster. "That is my question?" he said. "You have no right to barge into my stable when you were clearly told that this was a private discussion."

"Bah, some chatter from a stable hand means nothing to me." Lord Roffe turned on Kara. "I expected you home, my lady niece," he said, gaze locked on her with so much rage that she cringed. Roger Murdock watched with interest. Lord Roffe never noticed him and Hawkstead and Kara forgot Murdock's presence.

Hawkstead protectively took a step forward, partially blocking Kara from Lord Roffe's view. "She is home. At your request I took the lady as wife."

Lord Roffe paled. "Nay," he gasped, gaze still fixed on Kara. He took a step back, looking at Hawkstead, battling to calm his rage. "Surely you mean you will consider her for wife. I have come to make apologies. I was upset when I, um, suggested the possibility of you considering my niece in place of my daughter. You are not bound."

"Aye. She is my wife," Hawkstead said firmly.

Lord Roffe's eyes blazed as he turned on Kara. "I expected you to resist!"

Once again Hawkstead stepped into the conversation Lord Roffe was trying to draw Kara into, saying, "Resist what? You gave her hand to me and she obeyed. She is a very obedient wife. I am pleased."

"Obedient? Bah!" Lord Roffe spit to the side.

Kara remained silent during the exchange. Though she wanted to hide behind Hawkstead she remained at his side, fingers clutching the sleeve of his tunic. Hawkstead was standing up for her and Lord Roffe was keeping his distance. Truly it was a miracle.

"We have not drawn up a contract," Lord Roffe said. His anger was cooling but he was not ready yet to back down.

"Nelson rode to finalize the agreement. I'm surprised that you missed him," Hawkstead said. Lord Roffe's eyes darted to the side at that, making it obvious that Lord Roffe was aware of Nelson's mission. "I know the lady's property."

Lord Roffe scowled, hand massaging his sword hilt. "Her property?"

"Aye. All of her property."

"I did not agree to this," Lord Roffe yelled.

"Aye, you did," Hawkstead said calmly. He pulled Kara back up beside him, tucking her arm around his elbow. "The letter from you has been sent to my father, your liege lord, and is already in his hands. As are the papers listing her property."

"I will not abide by this marriage," Roffe said. "You took it into your own hands to marry the gal and had no right to the deed."

"Aye, the deed is done," Hawkstead said.

Lord Roffe deflated slightly. Kara remained silent through the whole, amazed that Hawkstead had so firmly stood his ground against her uncle. Kara had never seen anyone do that before. Anyone. Roger Murdock slipped silently into the shadows.

"You and your men must be exhausted after such a long ride," Hawkstead said. He started walking out of the stable, Lord Roffe automatically falling into step. "Chippers, find a place for their livestock. Lord Roffe, you may walk with us to the Great Hall. Unless you wish to see to your own mount?"

The rain had stopped and only a light sprinkling continued. Lord Roffe walked up to his horse and removed a saddle bag then gestured to one of his men to take care of his horse. "Why do you think I'd care to play the groom?" he asked with a sneer.

Hawkstead frowned thoughtfully for a moment. "My mistake. As a breeder I thought, well, no matter," Hawkstead said. He gave no indication that he saw the sharp look that Lord Roffe gave Kara, which prompted her to duck strategically to the other side of

Hawkstead. "It is a fine beast you ride," Hawkstead said
conversationally as they walked to the keep.

Lord Roffe grunted. "Best in the stable. I always ride the best in
the stable."

Kara kept Hawkstead between her and her uncle as they walked
to the Great Hall. Hawkstead held back at the doorway but gestured
for Lord Roffe and his men to continue on inside. "I'll join you in a
few minutes," he said.

Hawkstead leaned down so he could speak in a low voice to
Kara for her ears only. "I shall entertain your uncle for the time if
you wish to freshen up before dinner."

Kara nodded. The longer she could wait to face her uncle the
better. Hawkstead promptly led her in the direction of the bath
house. Lord Roffe watched them leave, eyes narrowing. It was
almost a physical relief for Kara to be away from Lord Roffe. It had
never occurred to her that he would come after her like this. His
arrival was a complete shock to her.

"I'll send your maid with what you need," Hawkstead said when
they reached the bath house.

"You're going to leave me?" Kara asked in alarm.

"You're safe here," Hawkstead said. "Your maid will be here in
a few minutes and George will not let anyone pass."

Kara nodded grudgingly though she knew that neither the maid
nor George would be able to stand up to Lord Roffe. Maybe her
uncle would leave her alone now that she had Hawkstead at her side.

Yet Kara knew that her uncle was angry, angrier than she had ever
seen him before and Kara had seen him really angry. It was only
Hawkstead's presence that had held him back from striking her in
the stable. Lord Roffe did not care who was around when a rage took
him. Sometimes knowing that people were seeing her being treated
like a dog was worse than the actual blows. Kara looked up at
Hawkstead, her almost husband. Hawkstead would protect her.

Kara bathed quickly. Kara had just finished rinsing the soap
from her hair when she heard a step on the stones behind her. It was
a great relief to see Elyse and her maid when she turned and the
breath she had not realized she had been holding came out in a long
whoosh. The maid Kevin had found for her was a competent young
woman who had little to say. She immediately assessed Kara's stage
of bathing and grabbed a towel to cover Kara with as she stepped out
of the pool. Elyse was laying out articles of clothing in preparation
of Kara dressing.

"Do you not know?" Kara asked, watching Elyse going about
her task so calmly.

"That your uncle has arrived? Aye. What of it? You're married
now. He has no right to touch you. No right at all. Turn so I can dry
your hair."

"Someone needs to tell *him* that," Kara said, shaking her head.
"I don't think he realizes that."

Elyse allowed the maid to take the towel she held and watched
as the girl blotted the water from Kara's hair. "You are a competent

maid, child," Elyse said. "I should have gotten the girl a maid a long time ago."

Kara glanced at Elyse in surprise. There was something quite different about Elyse and the changes were becoming more and more noticeable. "You haven't been wearing a wimple, Elyse," Kara said in surprise.

"You just noticed?"

"Well, I have seen you without a wimple, just not out in public," Kara said.

"I have heard that it's a shame to cover this hair," Elyse said, stroking the auburn braid draped over her shoulder. She smiled at a private thought. "And so I chose to leave the wimple in my room."

"Whoever he is, I hope he is honorable," Kara said.

Elyse smiled. "Honorable? I am learning that there are many layers to honorable. Is it honorable to make a woman believe that she has no value in living once she reaches a certain age? You should be the first to understand what value you have other than breeding future lords and ladies." Elyse stood and handed Kara's underthings to the maid. "Let's get you dressed and ready to face the dragon."

Kara gripped Elyse's hands between her hands. "Elyse, I am only afraid that some man is toying with your affections and will hurt you in the end. If he was honorable in his attentions he would not be a secretive suitor hiding in the shadows."

"Yes, dear girl," Elyse said. "The benefit of being elderly is that I am aware of the traps of the heart and know that there is also risk. But without the risk one will never discover the good as well as the bad." Elyse took a deep breath and looked around her. "I wonder if there is something in the air here or maybe it is just the matter of stepping out from under a dome of darkness. I feel empowered. I feel that I should have done more to step between you and your uncle. Yet at the time I felt helpless. I feel like I should have done many things differently."

"He would not have let you stop me. I remember in the early years."

"Well, it's over now," Elyse said, shuddering as the memories left her. "Your life has changed. You used to dream of the day when you would reach your majority and be free of him. That day is here."

"Aye. But he's here. He's here and he's so very angry," Kara said.

"It is a terrible thing this man has put you through. It is over now," Elyse said even as the maid dropped Kara's dress over her head.

It made sense, yet Kara could not let go of the feeling of impending doom. Elyse walked arm in arm with her to the Great Hall. Soup had already been served and servants were entering with trays of the first course, baskets of steaming buns and freshly churned butter with little pots of a variety of jams. Kara avoided her uncle's burning gaze and settled into her seat next to Hawkstead.

Normally her uncle, as a family member would have been seated to her left but Hawkstead had seated him to his right. Elyse sat to her left instead.

Lord Roffe made polite conversation but often lapsed into periods of silence while he stared at Kara intently, the anger so strong that she could barely sit still. Hawkstead took her hand in his, entwining her fingers between his fingers in her lap. More than once he raised her hand to his lips and kissed the back of her hand. Every time he made the loving gesture Lord Roffe turned a darker shade of red.

"Relax," Hawkstead said in a low voice for her ears alone while Lord Roffe was distracted in conversation with Richard who sat to his right. "He dare not harm you under my roof."

Kara laughed without humor, a short bark of laughter. "You know not my uncle. He dare do as he please where he please."

"He has no reason to strike you," Hawkstead said.

Kara shook her head. There was no explaining to him. Lord Roffe did not ever need to have a reason for hitting her. At least Hawkstead was taking seriously the threat that she felt from Lord Roffe instead of just brushing it to the side as he had when she had first told him of her uncle's past treatment of her. Lord Roffe finished conversing with his table neighbor and turned back to Hawkstead, ending their brief private conversation.

"I'd like to stay around a few days, see the work you've been doing enlarging this keep," Lord Roffe said. "Your cousin said you have been working on it for almost a year now."

"I'm surprised you would prefer to stay," Hawkstead said. "I would think you would be eager to return home before winter settles in."

"You're sending me on my way?" Lord Roffe asked, eyes narrowing. "Your wife's uncle?"

"What I am suggesting is that you might want time to get your affairs in order," Hawkstead said. "My home is open to my wife's family. I am just surprised you want to linger when there are things needing your attention."

"So you plan on pushing me off Roffe Manor?" Lord Roffe asked. He glared at Kara. "No matter what this little bitch has been telling you, Roffe Manor is mine. It is mine by right."

"Do not call my wife names, Roffe. This is your only warning," Hawkstead said after taking a deep breath to gain control over the urge to put his fist in the man's face. "I understand that Roffe Manor is only under your guardianship for now. I am talking about what you need to do to maintain the breeding stables. We will need to come to some agreement about them."

"Um," Kara muttered, putting her hand on Hawkstead's arm. "Um, husband, ah, Hawkstead, you should know…"

"My breeding stable?" Roffe asked in surprise, looking around Hawkstead at Kara, glaring at her when he realized that she was trying to get Hawkstead's attention. "My breeding stable? Do I have your word that my breeding stable will not be touched by you?"

"They are mine," Kara said, sitting forward and glaring back at her uncle. She was not about to let him weasel his way into gaining the stables. "My uncle has nothing to do with the stables except to request a mount to ride. Even that he can't do adequately."

Hawkstead frowned. "You? But they are the finest animals in the country."

Kara gave him a tight smile, frustration boiling her blood at that moment. "Thank you." Kara sighed. "Maybe we should discuss this later, in private."

"No, we should discuss it now," Lord Roffe said. Servants appeared with more trays for the second course, spinach and mushroom pie. Lord Roffe paused to grab a pastry and take a long swig of his wine. "Do you really believe this chit has developed a horse breeding program to rival the country's most experienced breeders?"

"It is difficult," Hawkstead said slowly. Kara tried to pull her hand from his but he tightened his grip. "Difficult but not impossible."

"Why do you even want them?" Kara asked Lord Roffe. "Within a few years you would be wallowing. You don't even know which horse has value."

"Ah, but I do," Lord Roffe said with a smile. "Banner turns blue when I destroy the valuable ones. He only gets red with the less valuable ones."

Kara sucked in her breath. "That is a bad jest, sir."

Lord Roffe laughed. "You think it a jest?"

Kara was shaking. Her hands trembled. Her left leg shook so badly that her knee was knocking against the table bottom. "Even you would not destroy the horses."

Hawkstead studied Lord Roffe during the argument and made a decision. "Richard, sorry to interrupt your spinach pie but I'd like you to inform Toby to take ten knights and twenty men at arms to Roffe Manor. Their sole task is to guard the horses and someone named Banner until I come to collect them."

Richard stared at the steaming spinach and mushroom pie he had just taken a bite from. "Pie is dry anyway," he said. Richard stood. "Anyone in particular you want to send?"

"Tell Toby to pick men who have an idea about horseflesh. And take that visitor working in the stables as well. He was not too enthused about mucking out stables but he might appreciate this type of work." Richard immediately left the hall. Lord Roffe stared after the man's back, a frozen, sullen mask settling over his face. "A few days to linger here is actually a good idea," Hawkstead said, reaching for his wine. "Gives your men a chance to rest. I don't remember what you toured during your last visit but you'll have to let me know your opinion on the work that's been done since this spring."

Lord Roffe did not say anything. He was taken aback by how quickly and decisively Hawkstead responded and acted on the decision but feeling that his own response was quite limited. Lord Roffe could not stop Hawkstead from sending his men and to race out after them in the hopes of reaching Roffe Manor first would not accomplish anything but looking like a fool. The whole incident left him feeling like a fool. Lord Roffe's gaze settled on Kara. The sight of her gazing adoringly up at Hawkstead made Roffe see red.

Lord Roffe regretted not taking care of his niece long ago. He had kept her around because of the immense fortune generated by her almost inhuman knowledge of horseflesh. Lord Roffe was completely aware of her upcoming birthday which would release her from his absolute guardianship. He had been lulled over the years into a life of leisure and prestige and had only recently woken up to the fact that the status might not remain as it was forever. If only Kara would behave herself and do as he wanted then his life would be good but she never cooperated with him. Kara always had to be contrary.

Lord Roffe had managed to avoid her getting betrothed or married once she reached marriageable age but time had caught up with him and he had been working on securing a marriage for her that would keep control of Roffe Stables in his hands. His plan had been to have Hawkstead send her back crushed, where he would step in and force her to marry Lord Wasgrove, who had agreed to Lord Roffe's terms. He had not expected Hawkstead to marry the chit. Now Hawkstead's men were heading out to Roffe Manor to police the horses. Next, the horses would be removed from Roffe Manor and Lord Roffe would be left with nothing. If Kara would just have behaved as she should none of this would be happening.

The stilted silence in the Great Hall faded as men began to relax a bit and talk amongst themselves again. The tension had risen between Lord Roffe's men and Hawkstead's men, neither side knowing how Lord Roffe would react to Hawkstead's actions. Hawkstead's men were relieved that there would be no scuffle while Lord Roffe's men were confused that Lord Roffe would just sit there and take what felt like a brash insult. If nothing else, Lord Roffe's men were confused as to why Hawkstead would send men to guard the horses from Lord Roffe when they were Roffe horses. Hawkstead surely overstepped himself in ordering such an action. Lord Roffe stared at the table, deep in thought, rubbing his thumb on the stem of his wine goblet, occasionally shifting his glare to Kara.

Kara felt wonderful. The only thing intruding on her happiness was the worry that Roffe had somehow taken out his anger on Banner or the horses at learning of her marriage. Kara had reasoned out that her uncle would not have had time to do any harm since he clearly had ridden out immediately at finding out the news. On his return he would certainly have followed up on his threats and done some mischief to get back at her but Hawkstead had swiftly acted to prevent that. For the first time since her parents had died Kara felt safe from her uncle. Lord Roffe could no longer touch her, no longer torture her, no longer attempt to control her. Kara felt wonderful.

Father Tom entered the Great Hall, heading straight for Hawkstead. The priest nodded greetings at people as he passed them but did not slow his pace. When he reached Hawkstead he leaned close and said in a low voice, "She's awake."

Hawkstead looked up and immediately got to his feet. He paused and turned to Kara, "I have something to attend to. Please see to our guests."

Hawkstead was leaving her with her uncle. Some of Kara's elation faded. Kara forced a smile. "Certainly, husband."

Chapter Seven

Hawkstead walked from the Great Hall to the chapel with long, purposeful strides, covering the distance in only a few minutes. The infirmary was behind the chapel. The first few beds held people with various injuries or sickness. Beau Dippen lay in the first bed with a broken leg strapped between two boards being held immobile with a series of ropes and winches. Connie Middlesex lay in the bed next to Beau with a ruptured appendix, her complexion quite gray and the smell from the vomit bucket on the bed made Hawkstead hold his breath as he walked past her.

Two nurses were in the process of going from bed to bed with a pot of hearty broth. Father Tom only allowed his patients to eat broth while in the infirmary. The beds further back were empty. At the rear of the infirmary two beds had been sectioned off with wood screens. The man with the suspicious dog bites still lay motionless but the blonde woman was now sitting up eating broth.

Hawkstead's sudden appearance startled the woman and she dropped her spoon into the bowl of broth. "You are awake," he said in greeting. "Who are you and what were you doing in the village?"

The woman stared at him blankly for several moments. She calmly picked up her spoon and took a sip of broth before answering. "I am Julia."

Hawkstead frowned. She was very difficult to understand. Though her words were heavily accented he could not place the source of the accent. Even Murdock's voice was not so heavily accented. Despite what Hawkstead told Murdock, Hawkstead knew that there was a connection between the three strangers.

"Julia," Hawkstead said. He pulled up a chair and sat next to her bed. "We were visiting the village when the villagers found you and your friend. Were you attacked by wild dogs?"

Julia stared at him blankly again for a few minutes. "Dogs? We did not see any dogs?" She looked over at the man on the bed next to her. "Friend? He is John Cho, my escort."

"Are you runaways?" Hawkstead asked, gaze immediately going to the diamond ring on her left hand. That ring would not buy a keep but it would pay to maintain a full keep for a year or two. Serfs did not own such wealth let alone wear it for the world to see. Gold strands hung about her neck for the world to see. More rings decorated her right hand and a watch decorated with diamonds graced her wrist. It was almost like Julia was inviting robbers to pay attention to her. Though he did not believe they were runaway serfs he still had to ask.

"Runaways?" she repeated, confused. "I was visiting family in England. We, we, got lost." She stared at John Cho. "How is he doing? He does not really look good."

"Though he lost blood and the dog bites don't look infected, he isn't recovering," Father Tom said.

"Dog bites? He was shot," Julia said, setting her bowl aside. "Have you not removed the bullets?" She tried getting out of the bed but Father Tom stepped up to the bed to block her way. "Are you a doctor?" Julia asked before noticing his clothing. "Is there a doctor?"

"I am the doctor here," Father Tom said. He looked over his shoulder at John Cho. "Bullets? That is from the Golden Age, yes? These are dog bites. I have cleaned them and examined them for infections. Now we just wait."

"The bullets must be removed," Julia insisted.

"What are bullets?" Hawkstead asked Father Tom.

"In the Golden Age there were weapons that pushed projectiles with enough force to enter a man's body and do internal damage. I saw one such weapon in seminary in London but it was no longer capable of exerting such force. Bullets are the projectiles."

"No guns," Julia muttered. She looked around the infirmary, studying what she could see from her bed. "Very rudimentary hospital." She looked up at Father Tom. "The wounds were made with projectiles. Some may still be inside. I must see. I am getting up."

Father Tom frowned. Hawkstead shrugged. "Let her look to her friend, Father Tom."

"But I am the doctor," Father Tom protested.

"Yes, but it can't hurt for her to look at him, can it?" Hawkstead said. The words were barely out of his mouth when Julia pushed Father Tom aside and climbed out of her hospital bed. She stood over the patient, assessing the damage. He was still wearing his clothes. His wounds had been cleaned through the tears in the fabric. "His skin has a yellow cast," Hawkstead said. "Is he ill? Is this a new disease?"

Julia looked up sharply. "Yellow cast?" She looked down again at John Cho. "Oh. No. No. It is common where we are from."

"Sometimes babies have a yellow cast to their skin also," Father Tom said in an authoritive voice. "It often clears up however. An issue with the liver. If it does not clear up, well, then, well they grow ill. And persons fond of alcohol also get a yellow tinge to their skin but he looks too healthy to be succumbing to the drink."

Julie did not seem to be listening. She had looked at each of the wounds and now slid her arm under John Cho's back to examine the opposite side of the wounds. "The neck wound went through. Damn, he's lucky it did not sever anything. The wound in the leg did not go through. Bet it hit a bone or got lodged somehow. We need to open them up and clean them and get any bullet out."

"Open him up?" Father Tom asked, eyes widening. "You mean cut into him? We can't do that."

"Then I will," Julia said. She gently set John Cho back down and turned to Hawkstead, realizing he was the real authority in the room. "I am not a doctor but I can manage this. They aren't near anything major but will risk infection if left alone." She turned to Father Tom. "You did a fine job cleaning his wounds. I'm sure that's why he's still alive."

Hawkstead watched with interest. "You may attend to the needs of your friend, given the condition that you ask the questions I have for you."

"Fine, when I'm done with Cho I will answer your questions."

"No." Hawkstead shook his head. "I want answers now. Tell Father Tom what you need and while he's fetching the items you will answer my questions, honestly. If you lie to me then we will continue until I have my answers."

"You would let the man die?" Julia asked in surprise.

"No. You would let the man die if you don't cooperate."

Julia stared at Hawkstead. "Fine. I'll need a scalpel. Sharpest knife you've got if you don't have a scalpel, sharpest and thinnest. Disinfectant. Soap. Boiled water. Clean clothes. Needle. Tongs or big tweezers. Thread. Everything must be sterile."

Father Tom stared at her. "I will see what I can do. What is disinfectant?"

"What you used to clean the wounds," Julia said frowning. "They are amazingly clean and clear.

"That's the leeches," Father Tom said.

"Perhaps you could write a list so Father Tom does not miss anything?" Hawkstead asked, watching her response to the request to write. Few people could read or write.

"Of course," Julia said. "Do you have paper and a pen?"

"A pen?" Father Tom muttered. He walked around the screen and returned within a few minutes with a piece of light gray slate and charcoal.

Julie's eyebrows rose but she did not comment on the items, instead quickly scribbling out her list. Father Tom studied the list, trying to interpret her writing. He asked for clarification on a few items, nodding when Julia said the word out loud, muttering to himself as he left to fetch what he could. Julia watched Father Tom leave to fetch what she needed, not at all confident that he would manage to find more than the knife. Julia turned to Hawkstead.

"Those wounds are days old. If I only had a bump on my head why was I out for days?" she asked.

"I was not ready to meet with you yet," Hawkstead said. "Father Tom kept you sleeping. I have questions for you."

"Ask away," Julia said.

"Sit," Hawkstead said, gesturing to her bed. Reluctantly Julia sat on the edge of the bed. "Where are you from?" Hawkstead asked, studying her face.

"Chicago."

"Chicago," Hawkstead said the word. Though the word sounded strange the woman seemed to be speaking truly. "And what brought you to the village?"

"You said the villagers found us. So the villagers brought us to the village," Julia said. She was distracted with John Cho lying so still on the bed next to her bed and kept looking over at him.

Hawkstead frowned at what he saw as an evasive answer. "Very well. What brought you to my lands surrounding the village and this keep?"

"A keep?" she asked, growing thoughtful. She looked up at Hawkstead meeting his gaze directly. "I was on vacation. You know, holiday. I was going to Stonehenge but with a detour south, to visit family, as I mentioned. I saw someone I knew. We followed that person and I was attacked from behind and I woke up here."

"And this man was your only escort?" Hawkstead said, nodding his head at Cho.

"Oh, he's very good," Julia said. "I am capable as well. If we hadn't been ambushed we would not have been hit."

"The family you were visiting? Who are they?"

"Greenes," Julia said. Hawkstead's eyes widened slightly. Julia noticed the reaction and studied him thoughtfully. "Do you know them?"

Hawskstead chose to ignore the question. "Your friend, is he Roger Murdock?"

Julia laughed, an involuntary burst of laughter that she quickly stifled. "You would not know why that name is funny, of course," she muttered more to herself. "So you met him? I never said he was a friend. In fact, I suspect he is who ambushed us."

"A man called Roger Murdock was found near the keep, looking for his friends, a man and a woman," Hawkstead said. "Why would he attack you? Is he a thief?"

"He is no friend," Julia said, shaking her head. "Thief? No. He is just someone I know."

Hawkstead nodded thoughtfully. Murdock did not strike him as a thief and he had clearly not robbed them after attacking them. Julia could be wrong. Julia did not seem to know for sure that it was Murdock who attacked them since she hadn't named her attacker. "Murdock is from the same land as you? Chicago?"

"Chicago is a city," Julia said. She shook her head. "He is not from my land, no."

"And what land is that?"

Julia grimaced. "Illinois. Chicago is in the land of Illinois."

"Why do you think Murdock attacked you?" Hawkstead asked. Julia turned into a stone, clamping her lips together. "I would like to know if I have a criminal in the keep," he said, becoming irritated with the whole conversation.

"Did I say it was Murdock who attacked us?" Julia asked. "Perhaps I misspoke."

"Very well," Hawkstead said slowly. The woman was beginning to irritate him with her unnecessary secrecy. "You must know that this whole ordeal is odd. If it was not Murdock who attacked you I will do my best to find out who did. If it was not dogs then it was likely thieves. You are wearing a fortune in jewelry and would do better to cover it up or better yet put it away."

"It was not dogs," Julia said. Julia raised her hands, studying the rings as if seeing them for the first time. "A fortune? Huh."

Hawkstead leaned back in his chair. She hadn't lied to him yet her story made no sense. "Once your escort is well enough to travel you may continue on your way. Until he is well enough you have the hospitality of my home. You are free to move about as you wish as long as you dress appropriately. I will have my wife's maid provide you with clothing to use. For tonight you may remain in the infirmary and I'll send the maid in the morning."

"Thank you," Julia said, visibly relieved. "And Roger Murdock? Where is he?"

"I sent him on an errand," Hawkstead said.

Father Tom returned just then, arms laden with supplies. Hawkstead watched the two discuss the supplies and procedure with interest. Most of what the woman had said made no sense but he really was satisfied that they were not runaway serfs. She was a woman used to being in charge and did not have a single hint of any deference to anyone. Hawkstead also found it interesting that she claimed to be from another country visiting family in England. There were no Greenes left, of course. He would wait for another time to tell her that he was Earl of Greenestone. Julia Roberts did not seem to be looking for relatives at the keep, however.

The talk of the Golden Age made Hawkstead think of the relic room. It was more a closet than a room. He had been in residence at Greenestone Keep for more than a month before Mrs. Smith had shown him the collection. At Addington Keep his father maintained a similar collection of artifacts from the time before, though it was a smaller collection than at Greenestone. Most of the items were a mystery. Mrs. Smith said that many items required electrishity to function.

***

The keep was quiet. Lord Roffe had retired to his room to rest and his men were in the barracks. Hawkstead was still attending his task that had called him away during dinner. Kara was on her way to the kitchen to find Mrs. Smith but her thoughts were on what could have called Hawkstead away from her side at such an important time, leaving her to deal with her uncle alone. Lord Roffe had been angry the entire meal, a cold rage that normally would have made Kara wary of what was to come. Now that Kara was under

Hawkstead's protection she felt safe but still unnerved by that cold rage.

Lord Roffe stepped into the hall right in her path without warning. He grabbed Kara by the hair and dragged her into the storage room where he had been hiding without saying a word. It all happened so fast that Kara barely had time to realize that it was Lord Roffe and not a ghost who suddenly popped right in front of her.

Lord Roffe tightened his grip on her hair, forcing her to her knees. "So you married Hawkstead?"

Kara bit her lower lip to keep from crying out in pain. Roffe twisted his hand in her hair, forcing her head back. Kara had nowhere to look but up at his angry face. Kara instinctively raised her hands to try to reach the source of the pain. Lord Roffe jerked her head again and she dropped her hands to her side.

"Did you play the whore with him?" Lord Roffe asked. Kara did not answer. Lord Roffe jerked her head even farther backwards. "Did you?"

"We shared a marriage bed," Kara whispered, tears running down her cheeks.

Lord Roffe swore, pushing her away. Kara fell backwards but scrambled to her feet quickly. Lord Roffe stood between her and the doorway. "I had plans for you," he muttered, staring at the floor. "How was I to know he'd wed you? He should have been angry enough to slit your throat. Yet he married you on the spot. Obedient! Ha! What did you promise him to get him to marry you? Shameless whore! Did you bribe him with Roffe Stables? That's what he wanted."

Lord Roffe backhanded her. She reeled from the unexpected blow. Kara had not seen it coming. Kara wiped the blood from her lip. Kara should have seen it coming. For some reason Kara had let herself be lulled into thinking she had gained safety under Hawkstead's roof. Lord Roffe struck her again, knocking her to her knees. Before Kara could get to her feet he grabbed her hair, holding her in pace. Her uncle bent on one knee next to her so they were face to face.

"I told you that you'd never marry. Why did you think to go against me?" Lord Roffe asked in a dangerously low voice. The anger was a physical presence in the room.

"I, uh, I'm sorry," Kara whispered, keeping her gaze averted. As long as she did not meet his eyes it often helped diffuse his anger.

"Gwenlyth," he muttered.

Startled, Kara looked up at him for only a moment before looking away, gaze locked on a spot beyond his shoulder. Lord Roffe jerked her head back again. Kara began to fear he'd break her neck. "She's my mother," Kara said. "Gwenlyth."

"Aye, you're not Gwenlyth. You have her look. Especially when you're on your knees in front of me. You never beg though. I'd like to hear you beg."

Kara resisted the urge to struggle. Kara had learned long ago that she was no match for his strength and that struggling only fueled his anger more strongly. As Kara fought to ignore the pain of having her hair being pulled she wondered why her uncle hated her so much. He was a hard man but no one except her received his special attention on a constant basis. Even now that Kara belonged to Hawkstead he felt free to abuse her. Her uncle did not have the right.

Pain erupted through her chest, an emotional pain when she realized that she would never be free of her uncle. Lord Roffe would always be there to punish her for breathing, punish her for the sky being blue, punish her for the grass being green. Kara gasped when Lord Roffe suddenly stood, jerking her to her feet by her hair. Lord Roffe punched her in the stomach without warning.

"No!" Kara yelled in alarm, bending over.

Lord Roffe pulled her head up then punched her again, this time keeping a firm grip on her hair. Kara tried to protect her body by crossing her arms in front of her stomach, which angered Lord Roffe. He shook her head by her hair then punched her in the jaw. Kara saw stars. Lord Roffe released his grip on her hair and Kara sank dazed to the floor, barely aware of Roffe kicking her.

Mrs. Smith ran into the room just as Lord Roffe delivered another kick. The older woman screamed, startling Lord Roffe. He yelled at the housekeeper to mind her own business, confused that the woman had not meekly ignored that he was beating his niece. Lord Roffe's servants knew better than to question his authority in any action. Mrs. Smith did not see things that way. She rushed further into the room, wedging her way between Lord Roffe and Kara. Lord Roffe swore and backhanded the housekeeper.

"No," Kara muttered, struggling to get to her feet. Stars continued to dance in front of her eyes. It was a struggle to get to her hands and knees. Kara hurt. Kara hurt so bad. Kara could not let him hurt Mrs. Smith. Kara tottered on her hands and knees, shaking her head to clear it but the action made things worse. Kara groaned. She had to help Mrs. Smith but she could not. Mrs. Smith was not about to let Lord Roffe hit her without a fight. Mrs. Smith grabbed a broom and hit Lord Roffe across the shoulders with the handle. Lord Roffe roared in rage and turned back to the housekeeper.

Meanwhile, Mrs. Smith's scream had attracted attention and two of Hawkstead's men appeared at the door, followed by one of Lord Roffe's men and several servants. It took but a moment for Hawkstead's men to assess the situation and act. One man knelt beside Kara, placing himself between Lord Roffe and Kara, short sword drawn. The other man stepped between Lord Roffe and Mrs. Smith. Mrs. Smith stood behind the man at arms with chest heaving and broom still raised, ready to hit the man again if he came near her or Kara.

"Hawkstead isn't going to like this," the man defending Mrs. Smith said when Lord Roffe still tried to reach the housekeeper, matching Lord Roffe step for step. "You've made a serious mistake." Lord Roffe was not as eager to engage the armed man as he was the unarmed women.

"She is just a servant," Lord Roffe yelled. "She has no right to strike me."

"Ach, and you're daft. Don't think that will carry weight with my lord," the man said.

Mrs. Smith dropped the broom and rushed to Kara. "Take her to the solar, Max," she said to the knight. She turned to Lord Roffe, eyes blazing. "You may have bullied her under your roof. I've seen the scars. But here you do not touch her. If my lord does not whip you I shall." Mrs. Smith called to one of the kitchen boys peeking around the doorframe. "Aggie, fetch Lord Hawkstead and tell him what has happened here this day." The boy nodded and ran.

Kara tried not to cry out when Max picked her up but some small sound escaped for he apologized for causing her pain. Lord but she hurt. Each step through the keep shot pain through her bruised and battered body. Kara struggled to stay conscious though darkness hovered threateningly. Kara could hear Mrs. Smith's voice but she could not understand what the housekeeper said. It sounded like the woman was talking in a box far away. Kara sighed as darkness won and she slipped into it.

Mrs. Smith instructed Max to lay Kara on the bed when they reached the solar. "Are any bones broken?" she asked.

Max checked Kara's arms and legs then carefully felt her ribs. When he touched Kara's ribs Kara winced. Her eyes fluttered open for a moment before they rolled to the back of her head and she was unconscious again. "She might have cracked or bruised ribs," Max said.

"Aye," Mrs Smith said. "Nothing else seems broken? She'll be a mass of bruises though. Help me get her out of these clothes so I can dress her ribs."

"Me?" he asked in alarm. He backed away from the bed, gaze locked on the lord's lady.

Mrs. Smith sighed. "I can't do it myself, Max."

"Aye," he said. He did not move.

Hawkstead entered the solar, breathing heavily because he had run to the solar when Aggie told him that something had happened to Kara and Mrs. Smith was attacking Lord Roffe with a broom. When Hawkstead saw Kara on the bed unconscious, the side of her jaw already swollen, he hesitated in surprise for a split second before hurrying to the side of the bed.

"What?" was all he could say, gaze locked on Kara. She looked very beaten.

"Lord Roffe gave her a wedding gift," Mrs. Smith said. "Max is afraid to take her clothes off so you'd better do it."

Hawkstead looked back at Max, who shrugged in discomfort. "Why do you want her clothes off?" Hawkstead asked, the question directed at Max.

"Ribs," Max said. He cleared his suddenly dry throat. "Ribs are hurt bad."

"Where is Roffe?"

"Hold him?" Max asked.

"I'd like to talk to him. Make sure he does not do anything else foolish."

Max nodded. "Aye. I think Geoffrey had that in mind when he pulled the man off Mrs. Smith but I'll make sure."

Hawkstead looked at Mrs. Smith for the first time since entering the room, now seeing the split lip and reddened cheek. "You all right?" he asked Mrs. Smith.

"I'll heal," Mrs. Smith said. "She's my worry right now. He was kicking her when I came in."

Kara drifted in and out of consciousness as the two removed her dress. Hawkstead sat at the edge of the bed and propped Kara up by supporting her shoulders. When Mrs. Smith removed the chemise Hawkstead saw the white scars across Kara's back and shoulders. He looked up at Mrs. Smith in surprise. Their eyes met over Kara's head, Mrs. Smith surprised that he did not know about the scars, he surprised that she did.

Kara stirred when Mrs. Smith felt her ribs. "I'm sorry to be a bother," Kara said slowly, words slightly slurred. "Are you all right?"

"Don't you worry about me," Mrs. Smith said briskly. "It's your ribs, dear."

"Not so bad," Kara whispered. "I just need to rest. I won't be a bother. Just need to rest."

Kara slumped back against Hawkstead. Mrs. Smith frowned, touching Kara's forehead. Hawkstead realized Kara hadn't even been aware that he was behind her. "She's warm," Mrs. Smith said. "She should not be so tired."

"What's wrong?" Hawkstead asked.

Mrs. Smith shook her head. "I don't know. Maybe it's from being hit in the head. Maybe it's her way of dealing with the pain. Rest may be the only thing."

Elyse rushed into the room. "Oh, it's a bad one."

"I'll be back," Hawkstead said, gesturing for Elyse to take his place behind Kara. "There is a woman in the infirmary. I am going to send her here."

"What?" Elyse asked, looking up. "The runaway serf?"

"What do you know about a runaway serf?" Hawkstead asked, surprised. Elyse turned a bright shade of red but kept her lips pressed firmly together. "She knows as much or more as Father Tom about healing," Hawkstead said. "You two can wrap her ribs."

"Aye," Mrs. Smith said. "I'll do my best." She looked up at Hawkstead. "It would not do to kill him."

"Just do your task and leave Roffe to me," Hawkstead said in irritation. "This keep seems to be sprouting bossy women these days."

"Yes, my lord," Mrs. Smith said without hesitation in a tone devoid of any deference.

Hawkstead grimaced but let it go. There were more important matters to attend than a motherly housekeeper behaving in a motherly way. This marriage opened the door to change. First he married a woman who should have been raised and trained in the art of managing a household and tending her husband and instead only cared for the activity in the stables. Then a woman appeared out of thin air who had the personality of the king of England, no feminine meekness in her bones. Now Mrs. Smith lost her veneer of polite meekness. A shift was definitely in the air.

Julia arrived in the solar, now properly dressed in a simple wool gown. Her steady gaze took in the situation with a critical eye, dismissing the housekeeper and companion and focusing on the girl lying on the bed. The two women had wrapped her ribcage with strips of cloth then covered her nakedness by laying a robe over her rather than move her more to clothe her. Julia crossed the room and pulled Kara's eyelids back so she could see the pupil response. "What happened to her? Hawkstead merely said that his wife had been hurt."

Mrs. Smith stiffened. "Lord Hawkstead. She has been beaten. A fist to the face and repeated kicking."

Julia looked up in surprise. "Hawkstead did this?"

Mrs. Smith stiffened even more, so rigid she could barely speak. "*Lord* Hawkstead would never! We have no need of you here. Accusing the lord of such things."

"I am not accusing anyone of anything," Julia said firmly, attention back on Kara. "She has a concussion, I'm sure." Julia tapped Kara's cheek with her palm. "Wake up, girlie. I would like to talk to you."

"What are you doing?" Elyse asked, trying to put herself between Kara and Julia without actually touching Julia. It was not an effective method of intervening. Kara did not open her eyes but she frowned slightly.

"I want to see if she is responsive. I need her awake."

"Awake? She must rest," Elyse said.

"I don't mean for her to go out dancing. I just want to make sure she is responsive," Julia said. She tapped harder and Kara frowned, turning her face slightly to avoid the irritation. "C'mon, wake up. Let me see the color of your eyes."

Kara partially opened one eye, blinking as she stared up at Julia. "What? Blue. Leave me alone."

Julia smiled and patted Kara's cheek gently. "Go back to sleep then." Julia then pushed the robe away so that she could see Kara's stomach, shaking her head at the sight of a bruise in the shape of the bottom of a boot. Revealing Kara's nakedness agitated Elyse even further. Elyse tried covering Kara and Julia sighed. "Let me do what I need to do. If she has internal bleeding all that binding of the ribs will be for nothing."

Elyse frowned. "Internal bleeding? I don't understand."

"Exactly," Julia said. She felt Kara's stomach with her palm then pressed down firmly, watching Kara's face. "I can't be sure but I don't think anything has ruptured. I'll have to check again tomorrow." Julia gently covered Kara with the robe and straightened. "Do not leave her unattended for twenty-four hours. If she starts vomiting or is confused when she wakes, send for me. If she does not wake after a few hours, send for me. If she does anything not normal, send for me."

"Are you a doctor?" Mrs. Smith asked, some of her defenses dropping.

Julia shook her head. "No, just trained in field medics. Basic stuff."

"Field medics?" Mrs. Smith repeated slowly.

"Battlefield," Julia said. "I was in the military."

Both Mrs. Smith and Elyse stared at her as if she had said that she rode in the air on a rug. Mrs. Smith turned her gaze to Kara, considering. Having reached a decision, Mrs. Smith stood and offered her hand. "I am Mrs. Smith. I am the housekeeper. This is Lady Ashton, Lady Hawkstead's companion."

Julia took the hand without hesitation. "Julia Roberts. Pleased to meet you." She nodded at Elyse, who had not offered her hand. "Well, there's nothing more I can do here. I need to get back to Cho."

"Um, Miss Roberts?" Mrs. Smith said hesitantly.

"It's Mrs. Roberts," Julia said with a smile.

"Don't repeat that," Mrs. Smith said. "For some odd reason I have taken a liking to you so I am telling you for your own good, don't repeat that."

"Repeat what?" Julia asked.

"That you were in the military," Elyse said. "Women are not in the military. Men in the military are in the military for life unless they can buy their way out."

"That's right," Mrs. Smith said. "Don't ever tell anyone you were in the military."

"Women don't go into the military. Right," Julia said. The two women nodded vigorously.

"Where did you come from?" Mrs. Smith asked. "I am the housekeeper here and I was not aware that you were in the keep."

"I have been staying in the infirmary," Julia said. She studied the two women. "If it was not Hawkstead, er, Lord Hawkstead who beat her, who was it?"

"Was her uncle," Mrs. Smith said.

"Something he is in the habit of doing," Julia said. It was not a question. Julia had noticed the scars. Julia shook her head. "Women always seem to come out on the short stick when cultures are regressive." The two women stared at her blankly. Julia sighed. "Is it common for women here to be physically abused?"

"It happens," Mrs. Smith said. "I did not expect it to happen to his Lordship's new wife. He has no tolerance for his people to be brutal."

"You must be close to my age," Julia said to Elyse. "You could not step up?"

"Don't blame Lady Ashton," Mrs. Smith said. "Even though she is a mature woman she had no way of stopping Lord Roffe. Reaching a mature age does not grant special powers."

Lady Ashton blushed. "I am not so old as everyone would have me be. And I did what I could. You don't know. He is, well, he is an angry man."

"I am sorry," Julia said to Elyse. Julia meant the apology. She felt out of line having said what she said but cases of domestic abuse frustrated her and the chastisement slipped out. "It isn't easy when the law does not back you up."

"Now that Lady Roffe is married to Lord Hawkstead she is out of her uncle's house and the beatings will stop. It's just this first time, you see. Lord Hawkstead did not know." Elyse stopped short, staring at Julia in surprise. "I find it too easy to tell you my soul."

"I am sure it's been bottled up so long it was just aching to get out," Julia said. She patted Elyse's hand. "I too hope this young girl no longer suffers at the hands of her uncle."

Tears glistened in Elyse's eyes and she gripped Julia's hands tightly for a moment before pulling her hands away and resting them demurely in her lap. Julia was touched by how tragic the situation really was beyond the severely beaten young woman lying in the bed. These women were at the mercy of the men around them and if fortune put them in the hands of a brutal man there was not much they could do to prevent physical abuse. Julia felt tears welling up in her own eyes and quickly blinked them away. It was time to leave.

Julia did not mind when the same young man who had escorted her to the solar stepped into place beside her when she left the solar. Though Julia thought she could find her way back to the infirmary there were a few almost false turns caught when the young man hesitated when she would have turned or continued along the same path. Now that Julia was not in a hurry she looked around her surroundings more closely. The zippers were doorways through dimensions and were not doorways through time so something must have happened to stall time in this dimension. This dimension was the most stalled one Julia had ever visited.

They passed within view of the stable and Julia slowed when she saw a man standing with his back to her, leaning on a rake, talking to two other men. They all laughed in unison and Julia caught a clear look at his profile. Jensen. Julia cursed under her breath. Hawkstead had said that he was out of the keep on an errand yet there he was. As subtly as she could, Julia slipped to her escort's other side so that he was between her and the stable. Even if Jensen glanced that way he would not be able to see her face and she was wearing local clothes.

When they reached the infirmary Julia thanked her escort and went inside. The young man bobbed his head and wandered away, quite unaccustomed to being thanked for doing as he was told. Father Tom was standing over Cho. He straightened when he heard

Julia approach. Julia glanced at Cho. He was awake but still weak. It would be at least a few more days before he would be able to get out of that bed.

"How is our patient?" Julia asked. She knew that she made Farther Tom uncomfortable though she did not know why.

Father Tom took a step away from the bed. "Healing," he said. He studied her for a moment as she checked Cho's wounds before taking a deep breath as if he had to summon all his courage to ask her what he would ask her. "Where did you learn, well what you learned?"

"It was training," Julia said. She considered Mrs. Smith's warning. "I took the training to prepare for medical school but did not pursue a full degree, obviously."

Father Tom snorted. "Obviously. Women can't be doctors."

Julia decided to let the man's comment pass uncontested. "Obviously," Julia said drily. She patted Cho's shoulder and sat down on a stool next to his bed. "Maybe you can help me, Father Tom. You mentioned something about a Golden Age when we were talking about projectile weapons. What was the Golden Age?"

Father Tom smiled slightly and shrugged. "It's more a mythical time, of course. Wagons that moved without horses. People could talk to someone in France while standing in England. Lights that glowed steadily without flame. Buildings of glass that reached the clouds."

"Interesting," Julia said. "What happened? To end the Golden Age?"

"I don't really know," Father Tom said, ducking his head. "It was a long time ago. Many, many years ago. There was something called lectrishity that held diseases as bay. When the world lost this lectrishity the world was filled with diseases like nothing anyone had ever experienced before. The first plague wiped out most of the major cities." Julia and Cho exchanged glances. "It's been many years now since the last plague. Perhaps we are free of them at last," Father Tom said, crossing himself.

"Sent back to the Dark Ages," Cho whispered.

Julia felt a chill run down her spine. Images of medical labs across the world, protected with redundancies upon redundancies and security and a world dependent on electricity and computers to create those redundancies. A dimension that had advanced earlier but sent back to the dark ages, Julia realized. Stopping Jensen from returning before them was critical. Julia glanced at Cho, confirming that he heard and understood. Cho nodded before laying his head back and closing his eyes. They would have to be certain that they did not carry a plague back with them.

"This plague, what are the symptoms?" Julia asked.

"Well, the last plague was in my father's generation, so it's likely gone now," Father Tom said in a placating voice. "Don't worry about it."

"But I would like to know the symptoms," Julia persisted.

"Sometimes it's better to not know," Farther Tom said. "Sometimes worry can create false crisis."

Julia let the topic die. Father Tom excused himself and walked around the screens to the other side of the infirmary and Cho had fallen asleep, leaving Julia alone with her thoughts. She had told Hawkstead part of the truth. Julia was in England to visit Stonehenge but had gone south first to find distant family members. Julia had been on her way to visit Greenestone with John Cho when they had spotted Jensen at the train station and followed him. Jensen had not appeared to notice them following him but he must have known they were there because he had ambushed them as soon as they stepped through the zipper to this dimension. At least Julia assumed it was Jensen who had pushed her head first into a tree and shot Cho. She hadn't actually seen who had attacked them. Julia had stepped through the zipper and vaguely remembered a tree racing to meet her head but did not remember how that had happened.

Julia and John Cho belonged to a small, select group within the U.S. government that monitored doorways between dimensions called zippers. Their goal was to prevent people from using the zippers, not to use them themselves. The discovery by the government of the existence of zippers was made when a man named Daniel Thomas had used a zipper to remove an investigating FBI agent threatening his illicit use of the zippers. Thomas had used keys to open the zipper. The keys were various objects such as meteorites and everyday items, such as a porcelain poodle with a

jeweled collar. Tabitha Anderson was the first person in the team
discovered to be able to manipulate the zippers without needing a
key.

The team had been formed to prevent others from using the
zippers to enter the U.S. It had been decided that since the
dimensions reached through the zippers were not technically on U.S.
soil, there was not U.S. jurisdiction in the lands reached with zippers
so the mission was to monitor the zippers. It was a very small group
of people forming the team and an even smaller subset who could
manipulate the zippers. Only a few people had been found that had
the ability to detect and open the zippers. People with that ability
were described as having a purple halo. The existence of zippers was
kept in extreme confidentiality.

Jensen had attracted the team's attention when he used a known
zipper in Denver. All mapped zippers were being monitored. Zippers
that Thomas had used and had keys for were physically watched and
others that Tabitha found were under video surveillance. Jensen had
entered a zipper that Thomas had had a key for so the zipper was
being physically monitored. The action had set off all types of
alarms and garnered a lot of attention and the first step was to send
someone in after him. Julia had been that person.

Weeks after Julia had returned home without Jensen he returned
in the company of someone from the other dimension. It was not
clear how yet he had managed to elude the agents monitoring the
zipper. Those agents were never given details on why or what

exactly they were monitoring. Having someone step out of thin air was not something even a trained agent could prepare for without some warning. The incident with Jensen was the first case where a zipper was used since the monitoring began.

The incident had generated countless meetings and discussions on how best to monitor the known zipper locations. The resolution was to continue as they had been, rotating in agents for a tour of boredom because even if they weren't able to apprehend someone using the zipper at least they were in a position to note the use and leave it up to the team to chase down the intruder eventually. The theory was that Jensen had recruited a purple halo because a few months later the same person had opened the zipper and returned to their dimension.

As a result it was believed that Jensen traveled from dimension to dimension looking for people with the ability to use the zippers. At least that was what his file said. Why he recruited them was not known. What Jensen did with those people was not known. What the team members should do with this knowledge was not known. Their job was to monitor the zippers not hunt down perceived threats. Tabitha assured them that the team was so new that it could take time to iron out the administrative details. Tabitha was learning to talk like a politician. The truth was that keeping the zippers secret and also meeting their set goals regarding the zipper was experiencing growing pains. A lot of side stepping happened which anyone with a grain of common sense could see had no logic.

Julia had spotted Jensen at the train station. At first Julia was so shocked that she could not believe her eyes. Though Julia knew that Jensen was from England and that he had returned to the country she was taken aback to see him in the same town as she was vacationing. Without a second thought Julia had followed Jensen and Cho obediently followed her. Julia had not had a plan. Julia only knew that she needed to follow Jensen. Her goal was to catch up with him, not to spy on him. When Jensen opened a zipper in the park and stepped through, vanishing from sight, Julia ran to the spot where Jensen had vanished, located the zipper, opened it, and stepped through. John Cho had no choice but to follow at her heels. Julia vaguely remembered hearing Cho barking some order at her to wait, to proceed with caution, but she did not listen.

What happened after stepping through the zipper was still a blur. Julia had been struck on the head at the same time there was a sharp crack and Cho stumbled next to her. Or Cho stumbled next to her and then she had been struck in the head. It had all happened so fast that she was not sure. After that she had woken in this keep's infirmary staring up at Farther Tom's dour face. He spoke but she was not sure about what he said, only being aware of how much his breath stank. His hand was cold and clammy when he touched her forehead and then she lost consciousness again.

Since Jensen was still in the keep he must have found someone here already, if indeed he could detect a purple halo. Julia did not have the talent or tools to detect someone with the ability so she had no way of knowing who held Jensen at the keep, or if that's why he was there. Their team leader, Tabitha Anderson, had a tool to detect the ability but they had never been able to replicate the tool. Tabitha was not willing to allow it to be destroyed in an attempt to reverse engineer it so testing had to be done with the tool intact. And the testing had to be done by people who belonged to the team. If there were other people like Jensen who had the ability to be able to sense the talent within people, Julia had never met one.

Julia wondered if his ability was strong enough to distinguish the level within people, like how Tabitha could sense the zippers themselves. Julia could not sense the zippers unless she was within a few feet of them. Tabitha could somehow see the patterns that suggested a zipper was likely. Tabitha had tried to explain the process several times but Julia found that she could not wrap her head around it no matter how many times she studied maps. Tabitha insisted that it was just mathematics, yet Tabitha was the only one who could do the calculations and she did them in her head.

The problem with Jensen was that he was good at what he did. Jensen could turn into a ghost. Jensen was even better than Cho at predicting people's actions and eluding detection when he wanted to become invisible. In hindsight, Julia thought it might have been better to mark the zipper, guard it, and call in Tabitha instead of blindly dashing through the zipper behind Jensen. The man knew her and it was too strong a coincidence that he was in Greenestone when she was visiting the town. Julia realized too late that he probably meant for Julia to see him use the zipper, expected her to blindly follow him. Going back and calling in reinforcement to catch Jensen leaving was her secondary plan now, once Cho was well enough to travel back to the zipper. Once Jensen returned they would be waiting for him. At least they would be waiting for him as long as Jensen did not return through the zipper before Cho was well enough to get back on his feet.

Hawkstead seemed amiable enough. The girl that was his wife had been quite severely beaten. Julia had two daughters close to Kara's age and it was difficult to imagine either of her girls in that position. Julia wondered if Kara was who Jensen was hanging around for. There was no way of knowing who Jensen had spotted with a purple halo. That was what distinguished someone who could manipulate the zippers, a purple halo. Or it could be Hawkstead or the cook or a stable hand or anyone.

Julia paced restlessly. She had been honest with Hawkstead but only as forthright as absolutely necessary. Their team was going to investigate Stonehenge. Someone had come up with the question whether Stonehenge meant anything so anyone with talent had been shipped off to England. All members of talent on the team had assigned body guards so the body guards were shipped over as well. Julia had scheduled her trip a few days early in order to visit her family's origins and hope to find some distant cousins. John Cho was her current assigned body guard and though he was a quiet man Julia found his presence comforting. Julia glanced over at the bed.

The priest doctor must have been drugging him because she could not imagine why else Cho was so out of it. At first she had been concerned about infection in his wounds but they looked good when she dug out the bullet and they looked to be healing nicely.

**

Kara drifted in and out of consciousness for several days. When she woke she did not talk. She would stare up at the canopy over the bed, silently cry, and then drift back to sleep. Mrs. Smith and Elyse both tried to get her to eat something but only managed to get her to drink broth. Kara woke alone in the solar one day and tried to get out of bed and to get dressed. She managed to get her chemise on. Lord but it hurt. The chemise was snug over the strips of cloth wrapped around her ribs and chest and it took effort to ease the chemise down over the bandages. Her arms hurt. Her head hurt. Kara felt like the bandages were suffocating her. Kara could not stay in bed any longer. She had been in bed too long.

Hawkstead entered the solar to find her sitting on the edge of the bed, slumped over like a rag doll. Her rushed to her side. "What are you doing?"

Kara looked up at him. She winced. It hurt to look up that far. "I don't know," she said. "But I have to do it."

"What you have to do is get back in bed," Hawkstead said firmly.

Kara shook her head. "I need to go away. Somewhere Roffe can't hurt me."

Hawkstead clenched his jaw. He had failed her. She was his wife and he had failed to protect her under his roof. "It will never happen again. He will never harm you again."

"No. He'll always be there. I have to leave. Go somewhere safe," she whispered. Kara started to tremble.

Hawkstead lifted her legs and slid them onto the bed. He put his hands on her shoulders and firmly but gently pressed her back on the bed. He covered her with a blanket. "I'm sorry that he harmed you under my roof. It won't happen again."

Kara lay still, staring up at him. "I'm sorry. I have to leave. I just have to leave. Next time he will kill me."

"Where would you go?" Hawkstead asked, more harshly than he intended. Hawkstead took a deep breath and spoke in a more calm voice. "It won't happen again, Kara."

"Mael," Kara whispered. "I can go to Mael."

"Nothing would stop him from going to Mael," Hawkstead said. Hawkstead took her hand. "I'm sorry I did not take seriously enough your fear of him. I did not realize how severely he would hurt you. I thought a cuff to the head or a slap to the face... well, I guess I did not really think that much of it at all. As long as he is here you will always have one of my knights or myself at your side. You won't ever be alone."

Kara frowned. "Never alone? He's still here?" Some of her old spirit lit her eyes. She pulled her hand free from Hawkstead's grip. "What did you do? Tell him you would rather he not strike me again?"

Hawkstead's neck turned red. "He is your lord uncle. I could not have him whipped in the yard. Don't think I did not consider it."

Kara nodded slowly. "I see. Leave me, please."

"I hadn't realized you were such a blood thirsty little vixen," Hawkstead said. Kara glared at him. "Very well." Hawkstead stood, looking down at her. "Once you are healed from your injuries we should consummate this marriage. It is time to produce an heir."

Kara growled in exasperation. "Get out!" If she had anything within reach to throw at him she would have.

It was not that Kara wanted her uncle publicly whipped. Hawkstead could not do that even if he wanted to. She just wished Hawkstead had done, well, something. Kara did not know what. Kara did not know what Hawkstead could do. It just felt like by his doing nothing meant that it was all right for her uncle to continue beating her even now that she was married. Kara had started to feel safe. Now Kara felt that she would never be safe from her uncle's beatings. Even Hawkstead could not protect her from her uncle.

The next day Kara felt markedly better. Kara woke up with the sun shining on her face, feeling ready to get out of bed and start her day before she remembered what she had been through. For a few minutes Kara lay still, considering her sense of despair the day before. It did no good to feel sorry for herself, though she had been feeling overwhelmed. Most of the pain had faded though Kara still felt sore and with the lessening of the pain the depression had faded as well. Her uncle would not be at Greenestone forever, just a few days. Kara could avoid him for a few days. Kara was intensely disappointed that Hawkstead had not punished her uncle, not certain why she felt he would, just feeling disappointed that he had done nothing.

Kara climbed slowly out of bed, grimacing and muttering "ow" with each movement but eventually she was standing on her feet. Kara wobbled a bit but sucked in her breath and forced her trembling legs to cooperate. A head popped up on the other side of the bed and Kara shrieked in surprise. It was Elyse. Elyse had been sleeping on the trundle bed pulled out on the other side of the master bed.

Elyse rubbed the sleep from her eyes. "What are you doing?"

"Starting my day," Kara said. "I am starving. Once I break my fast I would like to visit the stable."

Elyse yawned and stretched. She got to her feet and went to the wardrobe to select clothes for Kara. Elyse had been sleeping dressed. She yawned again. "Something nice today," she said, studying the dresses. She pulled out a mustard yellow silk gown. "Yes, this will be perky."

"Perky?" Kara asked.

Elyse watched Kara slowly moving around the bed for a few minutes then brought the dress to her. "You are smart to get your muscles moving again but I think that breakfast in the Great Hall is the farthest you'll be walking today. The stable can wait until tomorrow."

"I will be fine," Kara said, grimacing when she raised her arms so Elyse could slip the dress over her head. Kara was panting by the time the dress covered her.

"Of course you will be fine to traipse on out to the stables," Elyse said, selecting slippers instead of boots. Elyse knelt beside Kara and raised each foot just enough to slip on the slipper. Kara had to brace herself against the canopy frame while Elyse put on her shoes. "Let's try the Great Hall first and see how it goes."

If Elyse had not been by her side Kara would never have made it as far as the Great Hall. Kara leaned against the wall on her right side and Elyse held her left arm as they went down one step at a time, the sleeve of her dress scraping against the course brick wall. When they reached the bottom of the stairs Kara had to pause to catch her breath. A headache was forming at the back of her head. Kara squared her shoulders and walked straight if not quickly down the hallway. It suddenly occurred to her that there was not an escort trailing her.

"Hawkstead said he was going to make sure I was to have an escort," Kara said softly. A strange twisting knot formed in her stomach.

"Oh, yes, the escort," Elyse said. "Instead of having you deprived of privacy, he thought it would make more sense for Lord Roffe to never be left alone. Two men trail him constantly."

"Oh," Kara said in surprise. The knot in her stomach untwisted a bit. "My uncle must resent that immensely."

"I believe he does," Elyse said with a smile.

Kara was starving and the smell of roasted sausages and fresh bread mixed with other food smells made her stomach growl loudly. They made their way into the Great Hall, Kara relying heavily on Elyse's supporting arm. The general hum of noise slowed only slightly as men nodded greetings to her. Looking around the large room filled with men Kara realized that this keep was lacking greatly in gentlewomen. It would be up to her to remedy that. It was good to foster girls of lesser houses in a larger house. There was currently no shortage of fostered boys underfoot. Perhaps without a mistress in place no family desired to send girls to Greenestone, Kara wondered. Getting girls to foster at the keep would be her task now.

Kara settled onto the bench at the lord's table and even before Elyse had a chance to be seated next to her, a servant placed a trencher loaded with food in front of her. Two more servants set down steaming bowls of bacon and sausages as well as a pot of honey and the last of the season's fruit. Elyse used a wooden spoon to drizzle honey on a crispy top crust of fresh rye bread and handed it to Kara before preparing a piece of honey bread for herself.

"My Lady," Richard said in greeting as he came up to the table. "I wish you good morn and I wish you well on your road to recovery."

Since Kara had just taken a bite of the bread and her mouth was full of food she could only nod. The Great Hall's hum faded to a whisper of sound and Kara looked up and across to the doorway. Her uncle strode into the room, flanked by several of his men and two of Hawkstead's men. Kara felt her stomach twist into a tight know but calmly took a bite of sausage and studied her trencher with apparent great interest though if questioned as to what the trencher contained she would not have been able to say. Lord Roffe strode up to the Lord's table and sat next to Kara. One of Hawkstead's men wedged his way between Kara and Lord Roffe and immediately lifted the lid off a pot, sniffing audibly at the porridge and seasoned apples it contained.

Lord Roffe was outraged, of course. "How dare you sit at the lord's table?"

Hawkstead's man looked up from the pot. He grinned. "Like I am a boil attached to your arse," he said.

Lord Roffe grunted and scowled at the man but did not say another word. Lord Roffe set about breaking his fast, picking up a sausage and eating half of it in one bite as he waited for a trencher. Kara had kept her gaze down when her uncle approached the table but now looked over at his hand as he reached for food. His knuckles had been cut but were already scabbed over and his thumb looked bruised and swollen. Kara glanced up at his face. His right eye had been black and blue but was already turning green and yellow.

Lord Roffe noticed her staring at his bruised face. "Admiring your handiwork?" he asked.

"What?" Kara asked in confusion. She was certain that she had not given her uncle a black eye. Kara was used to being blamed for what she had not actually done. Had Mrs. Smith done that to him with her broom handle? That day was blurred a bit but Kara only remembered Mrs. Smith hitting his back. It had to have been Hawkstead who gave her uncle the black eye. Why had he said he had not? Kara tried to remember just what Hawkstead had said.

"I am not to strike you ever again," Lord Roffe said. His scornful tone full of condescending rage was not the tone of a contrite man. "Did you fill your claimed husband's ear with *poor me* tales? When I have this marriage annulled you will come back to me. Remember that."

"Annulled?" Richard asked. He had settled onto the bench on the other side of Elyse. Lord Roffe had forgotten Richard was within hearing range but it did not change his attitude.

"This is not a sanctioned marriage," Lord Roffe said. "We did not have a contract. No notices were sent out." He smirked. "My lady niece did not say her vows."

Annulled? Kara had wanted the marriage annulled. Lord Roffe had thrown her at a stranger, the priest had pronounced them wed without her consent, and they had yet to consummate the marriage.

Now she no longer cared to have the marriage annulled. Could her uncle manage to do that? He sounded confident but he sounded confident about everything he talked about whether he was right or wrong. If her uncle managed to have the marriage annulled it would only be so that he could force her to marry someone he chose before she reached her majority.

"The contract is your permission in your letter," Richard said. "There will be no annulment."

Lord Roffe was as confident of obtaining an annulment as Richard was confident that there were no grounds for an annulment. Kara felt helpless, trapped. She no longer wanted an annulment. If her uncle managed to obtain one Kara would be at his mercy and she knew with certainty that she would not reach the age of majority without Lord Roffe trying to find a way of controlling her life even after she reached that age. Kara suddenly found it difficult to breath.

Chapter Eight

It took another two days before Kara was strong enough to venture as far as to the stable. Kara walked slowly, Elyse by her side again but not providing physical support. Elyse had not protested a visit to the stable. In fact, Elyse was eager to reach the building, often her eager steps taking her ahead of Kara before she remembered and slowed again to pace sedately next to her charge. Seeing the horses improved Kara's spirit and the pain of her ribs faded. Roger Murdock stepped out of the shadows. Instead of wearing his odd black clothes he was wearing a simple tunic and baggy linen trousers.

"Mr. Murdock," Elyse said in greeting. Kara glanced at her companion in surprise. Elyse's face lit up at the sight of the man and her voice had an excited tone to it when she said his name. No one else would probably notice but Kara knew Elyse so well that it was glaringly obvious that the woman was greatly excited to see Mr. Murdock and that she knew him well.

"Lady Ashton. Lady Hawkstead," Roger Murdock said, nodding his head in greeting. Though his tone was polite his eyes also revealed something more than polite greeting when they rested on Elyse for the briefest of moments.

"Mr. Murdock," Kara said. "I am surprised to see you. I thought you had gone with Hawkstead's men to Roffe Manor."

Murdock's eyes barely flickered to Elyse but Kara had been watching and caught it. "I wished to stay at the keep. I found mucking out stables a suitable pastime for earning my dinner."

Kara sighed. If this was the man who had Elyse's attention then she felt bad for her companion. A stable hand was not a suitable match for the cousin of the Duchess of Mael. Even if he was temporarily working in the stables to earn his dinner, he was not gentle born and therefore not someone who Elyse should be dallying with for she would only have her heart broken. Plus, the man gave Kara the creeps. Even in the security of the walls of the keep and not out in the countryside, he made her uncomfortable.

"I heard you had been injured," Murdock said. Though most of the visible bruising had faded the right side of her face was still yellow and brown. "It angers me greatly when a man feels he may abuse a woman. I would like to help."

"Help?" Kara asked, puzzled. Several thoughts rushed through her head, including an image of this man calmly slicing her uncle's throat. She shook her head to clear the unbidden images. "I do not know how you may help. My husband has already put in place measures to prevent it from happening again."

Murdock scowled. "A beating and an escort? Bah, what good is that? Memories fade with the bruises and escorts grow lax. What you need is to know how to protect yourself."

"Me?" Kara asked in surprise. Stand up to Lord Roffe? She had tried that when she was younger, resisting, fighting back. The beatings that resulted were worse. Weapons would do no good unless she was prepared to use them. Waving a sword around as a threat was a sure way of giving her uncle a weapon while he was in a rage.

"Your ribs are cracked or broken, yes? When you are able I will show you how to defend yourself. For now I can show you that it can be done," he said. "Men like your uncle, he is feeling lack of control. So he seeks to control you, something he can control."

"I cannot," Kara said. The pain of her ribs suddenly throbbed, reminding her how helpless she was against the strength and might of a man.

"You can," Murdock said. "What you lack in strength you must make up for in intelligence. I have been showing Elyse how to defend herself so that no man will harm her as you have been harmed."

Elyse shook her head slightly in warning when he used her given name but Murdock did not catch his mistake. Elyse turned to Kara. "Where he comes from they are more familiar and use given names. Once he found out my given name he has not used my proper name."

"This man has been showing you how to defend yourself?" Kara asked in surprise. The fact that he was teaching Elyse to fight outweighed the use of her given name.

Elyse smiled brightly. Once again Kara was struck by the transformation in her companion over the past few weeks. Her surrogate mother looked beautiful, not at all matronly as Kara was used to thinking of her. "It has been great fun, Kara. I wish I had been there when your uncle was hurting you." Elyse grew fierce. "I would have been able to stop him."

"Elyse, don't say that," Kara said in horror. "If you had stepped between us he would have hurt you. You know he would have hurt you even more for interfering." Just thinking about Elyse trying to stop Lord Roffe made Kara squeamish. Her uncle would have hurt Elyse severely. "We stand no chance against a man's strength."

"Let's show her," Elyse said, gripping Murdock's arm.

"What are you doing?" Hawkstead asked as he entered the stable. Elyse immediately dropped her hand, standing demurely with her hands held together in front of her waist.

"I am trying to convince your wife to allow me to show her how to defend herself if she is attacked by a man," Murdock said without hesitation.

Hawkstead frowned. Hawkstead opened his mouth to say something then snapped it shut and gave thought before he did speak. "She is not strong enough to wield a sword or any other weapon for that matter."

"Which is why I will not train her how to use a weapon. I will show her how to use physics," Murdock said.

"Physics?" Hawkstead asked, puzzled.

"A body in motion remains in motion. Opposing forces. Gravity is our friend," Murdock said. He stepped closer to Hawkstead and gestured with his hands, motioning for Hawkstead to approach. "Come, I will demonstrate."

Hawkstead hesitated. Hawkstead was a trained warrior with the advantage of height and bulk over the man facing him. Yet something about Murdock warned him that the man was also a warrior and a confident one. After considering, Hawkstead stepped forward and changed his stance so that he was relaxed at the hips, putting his weight on the balls of his feet. Murdock nodded and smiled. "Elyse," he said, gesturing for her to approach Hawkstead.

Hawkstead straightened. "What is the meaning of this? I thought you meant for *us* to wrestle."

"What will that show you? No, it is up to Elyse to show you and your wife what a woman is capable of with the right training," Murdock said.

"I'm not sure of this," Elyse said, looking up at Hawkstead in uncertainty. He looked very large next to her.

"Just remember what I taught you and don't let his size intimidate you," Murdock said. "Hawkstead, you try to grab Elyse from behind."

"It is Lord Hawkstead and Lady Ashton to you," Hawkstead said coldly. Murdock shrugged and gestured for Hawkstead to approach Elyse. Hawkstead looked up at a gathering of boys near the doorway. They scattered when they saw him looking then immediately first one face, then another and another again lined up along the doorframe and peeked back in. "This is a waste of time," Hawkstead muttered.

"Afraid to be shown up by a fragile woman?" Murdock asked.

Elyse turned her back to Hawkstead, glancing over her shoulder to invite him to come up from behind as Murdock instructed. Muttering under his breath, Hawkstead stepped up to Elyse as if to choke her. Elyse reached up and gripped each of his pinkie fingers and pulled. Stunned, Hawkstead felt her pull his hands away and was powerless to stop her. In addition to being unable to prevent her from pulling his hands away he felt his eyes begin to water. Elyse smiled and danced away, clapping her hands in delight.

"The smallest fingers have no strength," Murdock said in explanation to a shocked Hawkstead. Kara's attention was piqued and she watched with much more interest. "Now come up behind her and wrap your arms around her."

Hawkstead did not hesitate this time. Feeling confident that there would be no tricks she could pull to get out of his grip, he stepped up and grabbed Elyse from behind, closing his hands into fists so that she could not get to his little fingers. Instead of trying to get away, Elyse grabbed his forearms and stepped back, right up against Hawkstead then bent at the waist as she pushed her rear end against him. Caught off balance, Hawkstead toppled right over Elyse. Hawkstead lay on the stable floor staring up at the woman as she clapped and jumped up and down in delight over him. Kara actually laughed out loud then gripped her ribs in pain.

Hawkstead laced his fingers together behind his head to keep his head off the straw and stared off into the recesses of the stable in deep thought for several minutes. At first Hawkstead had thought it a bad idea for two reasons. First, he worried that Kara would be given a false sense of security if she thought that she could fight a man. Second, it was his job to protect her. Yet these tricks seemed to work and would at least buy her time to get away and find help if someone did attack her. Hawkstead had already learned that he could not always be there to protect her.

At last he stood, dusting dirt and straw off his clothes. "I see no harm in my wife learning such tricks from you," Hawkstead said to Murdock. He looked to Kara and added, "If that is what she wants."

Kara nodded once. Then she nodded again more firmly. "Yes. Yes, very much."

"You will never teach her without Lady Ashton or Mrs. Smith in attendance. There's an empty foaling stall at the rear of the stable that you will use. Hang blankets to cover for privacy."

When Elyse flipped Hawkstead over her head Kara had been shocked to her core. What Elyse did looked so easy. Hawkstead went right over the woman despite his greater size and strength. The thought of standing up to her uncle both terrified and thrilled Kara. Kara did not think she could really stand up to him but she was eager to learn these tricks and maybe, just maybe, be able to stand up to her uncle and know that she could at least make him hesitant about striking her again. Though Lord Roffe never came up behind her to attack her, Kara hoped Murdock also knew a few tricks for facing an enraged man with physical strength beyond her ability to stand up against.

***

Julia tugged on the collar of her wool dress as she walked through the keep. Wool might be the preferred fabric of the middle class in this dimension but it itched like crazy. Julia was alone, her escort of the first days relieved of duty. The day was dry but overcast and briskly cold. The wool might be itchy but it was quite warm and she was comfortable as she walked between the infirmary and the main building. A few days earlier Julia had also been moved from the infirmary to a room inside the keep which she shared with two other women. Julia hadn't asked either of them even their names, preferring to not get to know them. John Cho was well on his way to recovery and they hoped to leave that day yet.

When a man stepped directly in front of her from behind a low brick wall surrounding a garden Julia stopped in her tracks. Jensen smiled at her, nodding in greeting. "Julia. Roberts is it?"

"And you must be Roger Murdock," Julia said stiffly. Julia felt torn. It was so good to see him again yet she was angry with him as well. All the old feelings flooded through her as she looked into his eyes. Julia had loved him once. Until he had betrayed her.

"Anger? Ah, you think I was the one who shot your friend," Jensen said. He held his arms out to his side and swept his hands towards his body. "I am unarmed."

Julia raised her right eyebrow. "So you aren't currently carrying a weapon. That means nothing. They don't have guns in this dimension and we were attacked while passing through the zipper at your heels."

Jensen shook his head. "I am telling you that I did not shoot you. I did hear the shots and headed toward the sound to investigate," he said.

"You have every reason to attack us. I know that you know about the team and that we are here in England. What you are doing here is wrong," Julia said. She believed him when he said that he did not shoot her, since she had not been shot. The fact that he was careful to say the precise truth in an attempt to manipulate the truth made her distrust him completely. He never had been one to be reticent about throwing in some lies when it suited his needs.

"Wrong? What am I doing that is wrong?"

"Going through the zippers recruiting purple halos," Julia said.

"Purple halos? You mean people with the talent? That's what you think I'm doing?" Jensen asked. He leaned against the wall, crossing his ankles. "You Americans are so arrogant, thinking the world revolves around you. I can understand your keeping an eye on the zippers in the States but that does not give you the right to globally police all zippers."

"We're not," Julia said, frowning. Said out loud it did sound like it though.

"Where are you now, woman?" Murdock asked, uncrossing his ankles and straightening. "This does not appear to me to be the good ole' US of A."

Julia was quiet for a moment as she considered how to respond. He did not know that he was a wanted man and that that was why she had followed him. He thought that the team was here policing the zippers. Even if he was right about the team not having jurisdiction outside of the States, what he was doing was still wrong. Julia found it difficult to distinguish between him being a criminal and being an ex-boyfriend. For some reason the two became entangled in her thoughts. In this case he was not someone who had broken her heart he was someone who posed a threat to national security. Since she was standing in England it was a global threat.

"I'm telling you that I did not shoot at you," Jensen said. "Has it occurred to you what that means?"

"If that's true," Julia said. "Then someone else is here with weapons from our dimension."

"Or just outside this dimension," Jensen corrected. "It is possible someone tried to prevent you from entering the zipper."

Julia considered what he said. He was probably stretching the truth again as it was what he liked to do. The mere fact that Cho had been shot and not her made her believe it had been Jensen. Jensen had always had a soft spot for women. Jensen might lie to women but he could not bring himself to physically hurt one or to see one hurt. She would never get the truth from him. Something else was eating at her that she wanted answered and though she did not trust him to be honest with her, she could not resist asking. "Is it true? Can you detect someone with a purple halo?" Julia asked. She could not help but sound excited. It was an invaluable talent. "Is there someone here with a purple halo?"

"Tell me," Jensen said, stepping closer. "If there is someone here with a purple halo, what would you do?"

"Stop you from recruiting them, of course," Julia said without hesitation.

"Ah, that's why you followed me," Jensen said. He sounded disappointed. "And then what? Just let them be?"

"Of course not," she said too quickly. "Well, that is, we would want to at least talk to him or her, of course."

"Of course," Jensen said, shaking his head. "You followed me here, considering me a criminal because you think I travel between dimensions recruiting purple halos, when in fact, you would do just that if you had the ability." He turned to walk away then stopped and looked back at Julia. "Daniel Thomas found an already collected cache of keys. Did your team ever investigate where they came from to begin with?"

"That's classified," Julia said. Jensen grimaced and began walking away. Julia hurried after him. "Wait," she said. He kept walking. "Wait," she said again, coming up beside him. "How do you know about Thomas and the cache?"

Jensen smiled. "Maybe you should be nicer to me if you want answers."

"Why did you come to this dimension?" Julia asked.

Murdock shrugged. "The same reason I have visited other dimensions. Curiosity."

"I think the reason it's wrong is because you are pulling people from other dimensions. Why don't you stay within our dimension to recruit people? Are you not able to find them in our dimension?"

"You ask a lot of questions," Jensen said. "Why? When you don't believe what I am telling you anyway?"

"I am listening, Roger Murdock," Julia said, emphasizing the false name. "Why use an alias?"

"Calling the kettle black, pot?" Jensen asked.

"I married. I did not fully consider the result or I might have kept my maiden name," Julia said with an embarrassed smile.

"You married someone with the last name Roberts?" Jensen asked. He smiled but there was little humor in his face. "When did you get married?"

"It was long after your little episode with Bonnie Thieland," Julia said, eyes narrowing.

Jensen laughed and shook his head. "Bonnie. Yes, that was an adventure. Okay, I will tell you. I use an alias so that I don't leave an obvious trail yet someone from our dimension would be intrigued by the name. Sort of catching flies with honey theory."

Julia let him depart, watching him walk away. Julia knew that Jensen was heading to the stables. He even slept in the hay loft above the stalls. The conversation with the man irritated her. Jensen said he hadn't shot Cho but who else would have? Could have? Julia resumed her path to the infirmary. Every day Julia was in this dimension she regretted blindly following the man through the zipper. Even if Julia could get to the team and return to the zipper before he left, they had no legal right to detain him or anyone he brought through the zipper. Julia stopped in her tracks as an idea struck her like a lightning bolt. They had no right to detain him but there was no reason not to beat him to the punch.

John Cho was standing beside his bed when Julia walked around the wood screens in the rear of the infirmary. Cho nodded in greeting and stretched his legs, grimacing from the pain but slowly repeating the stretches. "Did you get a guide to the zipper?" he asked.

Julia shook her head. "I did not find Hawkstead. His steward said he was attending to some matter out on the estate and would return to the keep in a few hours." She watched Cho for a few minutes. "Jensen approached me. He said it was not him who shot you."

Cho was quiet for several minutes as he considered that. "Then does he know who?" Cho asked.

"He suggested someone with a key," Julia said.

"Do you believe him?" Cho asked, watching her carefully.

"I don't know. Let's say I am willing to consider other options, though they are far-fetched. If it was someone else, why would they shoot without asking questions first?"

"Someone saw the zipper open and panicked?" Cho suggested. He did not look convinced either. "The man is probably lying to you, Julia. There was no one else around."

"Cho, you were in the original group sent through the zipper in Minneapolis, right?" Julia asked, thinking out loud. Cho nodded. Julia knew the answer. "So why did no one investigate who had been living in the house Thomas house-jacked? I understand there were hundreds of keys. Where did they come from?"

Cho shrugged. "How do you know it was not investigated? There weren't hundreds of keys. There were a lot. Just not hundreds."

"But it's been years. I haven't heard anything about an investigation. Someone out there collected all those keys to open various zippers and then vanished."

"They were gone over twenty years before we found Daniel Thomas in possession of the house and the keys," Cho said. "Did Jensen bring this up?"

"But someone out there knew about the zippers and had keys. I heard one was a porcelain dog statue. How does a porcelain dog become a key to open a zipper? Does that mean someone out there is making keys?" Julia asked. "Do you think it could have been a group that Jensen belongs to? He hinted that we were amateurs overstepping our bounds. To me that suggests that he belongs to some team or group."

"I take orders," Cho said. "I follow orders. My orders are to keep you in one piece. You step through a zipper and I step with you. I don't worry about teams or groups or conspiracies."

"We know that he is here recruiting. I was thinking, maybe we should bring the purple halo back with us."

"What?" John Cho asked, straightening. "You know who it is?"

"Well, no," Julia said. "He's been spending all his time with only a few people though."

Cho grunted and switched from stretching his legs to stretching his arms. "That means nothing. Besides, we aren't here to kidnap possible purple halos."

"But if we can find the purple halo and bring that person back with us, that would be a great addition to the team," Julia said. "There are only a handful of us."

"No," Cho said. "We go back and make our report to Tabitha."

"But we might lose the purple halo to Jensen," Julia protested.

Sweat glistened on Cho's forehead but he continued pushing his muscles. "We are not going to recruit someone from another dimension in England," Cho said.

"I am not talking about recruiting someone," Julia said.

"Of course you are," Cho said. "Do we need this Hawkstead's permission to leave?

"What? No, I don't think so. I just thought it would be better manners if we waited until telling him. He did take a personal interest in us," Julia said. "I am not talking about recruiting someone. I am thinking we just bring those people with to the village, see if they react to the zipper. Then invite them with if they do."

"Huh," Cho said.

Julia wrinkled her nose. It *was* different than what Jensen did. They weren't traveling between dimensions looking for purple halos. Now that Julia suspected there was at least one purple halo here it was a shame to lose that talent. It had to be the explanation for Jensen to remain at the keep all this time. And it was not kidnapping. Julia would invite him or her or them to visit their dimension. How could they not want to leave this backwards dimension for a civilized dimension?

"You don't even know if he found purple halos," Cho said.

"Something has been keeping him at the keep," Julia said.

"Are you listening to what you are saying?" Cho asked. "We will not recruit potential purple halos from this or any other dimension."

"I thought your only job was to protect me," Julia snapped.

"Even from yourself," Cho said. He fell back in the bed and took several deep breaths. After a few minutes of rest he forced himself to stand again and start new exercises.

Julia frowned. Mentally she took a step back. It did sound like recruiting when said out loud. When Julia had gotten the idea it had seemed simple, keep Jensen from recruiting a purple halo by bringing that person back with them. Julia bent her head and covered her eyes with the palms of her hands. The goal of the team was to prevent people from entering the country from other dimensions, not exploit these other dimensions for resources, including people.

"The girl, the one that was beaten, I want to take her back with us," Julia said, standing up and walking to the stand next to Cho's bed to pour herself a glass of water.

"She is the purple halo?" Cho asked.

Julia frowned. "No, I don't think so. I just don't want to leave her here to get beaten again. She has scars, Cho. Bad scars."

"And if she carries a plague?" Cho asked.

"She isn't sick," Julia said adamantly. "She was not even born when the last plague went through."

"But she could be a carrier anyway," Cho said. "We agreed. When we go through the zipper we don't go more than a few yards from the entrance and call immediately for a quarantine tent until we can be tested."

"She can be tested at the same time," Julia insisted.

"You can't rescue every puppy, Julia," Cho said. "What makes you think she would even go willingly? This is where her life is."

"I heard her," Julia said. "She said that she had to get away from her uncle and there was nowhere here that she could go to escape him. If she agrees to go with us I am bringing her back with us. If I don't and the uncle hurts her even worse I would not be able to live with that."

"How would you even know?" Cho asked. He shook his head. "She has a husband. Are you going to bring him? Where does it stop, Julia? It isn't up to you to decide someone else's life."

Julia stared at Cho as his words sank in. "I just want to help," she said in a low voice. "It is painful to see what that girl suffered. It isn't right."

***

Kara watched Elyse and Murdock demonstrate how to block a blow to the head and then follow through with a punch to the opponent's stomach while they were occupied trying to hit the head. Kara had not healed enough to take part in physical exertion that extreme so she listened to Murdock lecture and lecture and then Elyse and Murdock would act it out. Then Murdock would have Kara go through the motions. Murdock called it training the muscles. He explained that her muscles would remember if Kara did the motions enough times.

"Keep your hand in a fist," Murdock said to Elyse, pausing to move her fingers into the right position.

"If I am not striking with a fist why does it matter if my hand is in a fist?" Elyse asked, not for the first time.

"It keeps your fingers safe," Murdock said. He glanced over at Kara, who was sitting in the thick straw piled on the stall floor, chin resting on her hand. She stared blankly at the floor, deep in thought. "Are you paying attention, Kara?"

"Fists," Kara said without even looking up. "How many times must you be told that it isn't appropriate to say my given name?"

"Fine." He pointed at Elyse. "You are Thing One." He pointed at Kara. "You are Thing Two."

"Thing Two," Kara said, nodding. "Got it."

"Why am I even teaching you?" Murdock muttered.

"I think the question is why are you repeating yourself so many times?" Kara said.

"Because that is how you learn," Murdock said. "That is what training is. Your body will remember the right movements without your having to think about it before acting. That difference can save your life."

"Where have you come from?" Kara asked. "That knowing this has saved your life? Where have you come from that you even know how to do this?"

"You ask a lot of questions for someone who probably hasn't gone more than twenty miles from where you were born," Murdock said. "Now pay attention. When someone grabs you like this, step into it like this." Murdock demonstrated with Elyse.

"I have traveled all over Europe," Kara said. "I have heard of a lot of things but I have never heard of anyone who fights like you or battles involving fighting like you do. Men like to talk about fighting. They talk about formations and head counts and cavalry and lay of the land. They don't talk about men tossing people around with their bare hands."

"Well, the world is bigger than Europe," Murdock said.

Kara stood and stretched slightly. She was only sore now if she moved too much. "I would like to try this physical training now," she said. "Teach my muscles what they must know."

Murdock considered. "Are you sure you're ready? It hasn't been that long since you were hurt."

"If I cannot learn by watching then it's time to learn by doing," Kara said.

Murdock nodded. He gestured for her to take Elyse's position and Elyse moved back to the wall and watched. Murdock moved his right hand to punch Kara in the face. She easily blocked his casual punch. Murdock nodded in satisfaction. Kara was holding her thumbs under her fingers correctly and staring him in the eye and stepped into the block with her right arm so as to not leave an opening when raising her left arm to block.

"You have been paying attention," he said. He threw several more practice punches at her and Kara effectively blocked each one exactly as he had demonstrated with Elyse, though Elyse had not been as quick to see beyond the first steps. Murdock picked up speed and Kara did not hesitate, matching each move. Murdock smiled and threw in something new, a roundhouse kick. Kara ducked under his leg and swung her leg out at the same time and made contact with the leg he was standing on. Murdock almost fell. It was because he was so surprised that he even wobbled a bit.

Kara grimaced and clutched her side. "Perhaps that is enough for today," she said.

"Have you seen this style of fighting before?" Murdock asked, surprised.

"No," Kara said, shaking her head. "If I had seen it before I would have used it."

"Then how did you know to drop and kick like that?"

"It seemed logical," Kara said. Her side and area just below her shoulder blade felt like someone had stuck her with a hot poker.

"Logical? You are a natural. Why did you never use this before?"

"I did not know about it before," Kara said, puzzled. Though she was a bit foggy from the pain she was sure she had already told him that.

"But…" Murdock started to say then stopped.

Elyse stepped away from the wall. "I think it's time to tell her our plans," Elyse said, slipping her arm around Murdock's elbow. "You can't tell anyone yet, Kara. Please promise that you will hold our secret."

"I promise," Kara said slowly.

"When Robert returns to his home I am going to go with him," Elyse said.

Kara stared at Elyse in disbelief. "But he's a stable hand. You are descended from kings."

"That does not matter," Elyse said. "He loves me and I love him. We'll be married and start a family. He says that it's common for women my age to have children where he's from."

"You're descended from kings?" Murdock asked in surprise.

"Oh, a long way back," Elyse said. "Second or third sons, several generations. And I know you're not a stable hand." Elyse turned back to Kara. "He is only mucking out stables so that he could stay here and be by me until he convinced me that he was the right man for me."

"So you're returning to your home?" Kara asked Murdock. "Where is that?" she asked Elyse. Elyse clearly did not know and looked startled at the question. Kara turned back to Murdock. "And why did you leave to begin with?"

"Yes, I am returning to my home today," Murdock said. "Elyse would like you to travel with us. At least until she's settled."

"Today?" Kara asked in surprise. "How can you just tell me now that you're leaving today? Today? Are you serious?"

"You are cousins, yes?" Murdock asked Elyse. "I see glimpses of kings in this one."

Elyse frowned. "Kara, dear, we just decided to go today. It will be an adventure. You wanted to put some distance between you and your uncle for a few months. This is perfect."

"Did you forget I am married?" Kara asked.

"Ah," Elyse said in surprise. "Now you remember that you're married. Can it be that you don't want to be away from your husband? In that case I understand if you won't want to go." Elyse smiled, happy at the idea of Kara finally accepting her marriage.

"I think it would be good for Elyse if you came with," Murdock said, not liking the turn of the conversation. "It will be a new land for her and it would be of great comfort for her to have you at her side. At least think about it. We can wait a few more days before we go."

"Yes, time to consider," Kara said, though she was thinking that it would give her time to convince Elyse not to make such a foolish action as to run off into the unknown with a man she barely knew just because he filled her head with flattery.

"Before I leave, I must collect some belongings I left outside the keep. Remember where we first met? Not so far from that village down the road? I would like it if you both came with me. We can pack a picnic lunch," Murdock said. Looking at Kara he said, "I would like you to get to know me better before condemning me as not suitable for your cousin."

Elyse's eyes lit up. "Oh, that sounds wonderful. Please say you'll come, Kara."

"No," Kara said, the idea of riding out made her uncomfortable. The man was just untrustworthy.

"Oh," Elyse said. The excitement faded but she was still hoping for a picnic with her beloved even if Kara did not join. "Maybe Mrs. Smith will join to provide company."

Elyse could not ride out alone with a man even with an escort, for propriety. Elyse did not look too hopeful that Mrs. Smith would agree to interrupt her duties with a picnic on a brisk, autumn afternoon. Guilt washed over Kara. Elyse looked so crestfallen.

Kara considered. "Very well," she said slowly. She was only agreeing to appease Elyse. What could it hurt to ride out to the village and eat lunch on a blanket?

A stable boy was sent running to the kitchen to request a basket for lunch. Murdock convinced Elyse to ride a horse instead of dragging out the wagon. Murdock watched the stable boy thoughtfully. "It will take at least half an hour for the kitchen to prepare a lunch. I have an errand to run in the meantime. Can you get the horses ready by the time I return?"

The stable boy returned in less than an hour, carrying a large basket. Murdock returned only a minute behind the stable boy. Murdock took the basket from the boy and lashed it to the horse designated for Elyse. He also slung saddle bags over the withers of the horse he was riding. The man was suddenly in a hurry and had no patience for Elyse's reluctance to mount her horse. Elyse quickly climbed onto the mare with the help of a stable boy.

The three rode out of the keep late morning with two of Hawkstead's men as escort. Kara had actually thought to inform Hawkstead that she was riding outside of the keep but he was out on an errand somewhere on the estate. It was a beautiful morning, crisp and brisk with the hint of winter but little wind and the sky was a robin's egg blue without a cloud in sight. Elyse was happier than Kara had ever seen her and though Kara wanted to be happy for her companion she could not bring herself to see anything positive about Elyse forming a relationship with this man.

They rode past the copse of trees where Kara had first encountered Murdock. When Murdock continued past the area Kara glanced around suspiciously and asked him why he was not collecting his belongings as he intended. "We will pick them up on the way back. There is no point in dragging them around with us. First we shall enjoy the delicious lunch prepared for us. I saw a doable spot perfect for a picnic just past the village," he said in explanation.

The horses walked slowly and Murdock and Elyse led the way, Elyse often giggling at whatever it was Murdock was saying. Kara's ribs hurt but it was bearable. Julia had said not to ride horse for several weeks yet so Kara kept Rhinney to a very slow walk and her even gait was workable. Hawkstead's men rode side by side behind Kara, occasionally talking and joking but mostly quiet, attention on the land around them. They passed the village and several villagers waved in greeting as they went about their work. Murdock led them off the road just past the village.

Kara looked around them then glanced to the other side of the road. Murdock was leading them into a grove of apple trees. A wind picked up and blew a blast of cold air against them. Kara shivered. The cold air funneled down the row of trees felt like a bad omen. Kara looked up at the sky. A few clouds had gathered in the distance but they were still white and fluffy. Murdock stopped and dismounted, immediately going to Elyse's side and helping her dismount, standing at her back with his hands around her waist. Murdock whispered something in her ear while she stood with her back to him and she blushed red to her neck but there was a smile on her face.

Kara glanced around them. She did not see anything special about this place but it was not horrible either. "This is your spot?"

"Just ahead," Murdock said. "This is the spot for the horses so we don't have to smell horse while we eat."

One of the escorting men frowned. "Not wise to leave the horses unattended."

"Then maybe you should stay with the horses," Murdock said. The two men frowned at him. "We won't be out of sight. I am completely capable of protecting these two lovely women."

"I'll stay with the horses and John will go with you," the man said.

"Very well," Murdock said. "We'll be sure to save some chicken for you."

Kara was still sitting on her horse, studying the area. There was not really much to see, just apple trees dropping dying leaves onto grass that the villagers kept trimmed by letting goats graze between the trees. A deep sense of melancholy struck her. She felt the strongest urge to return to the keep and find the security of Hawkstead's arms. Instead Kara swung her right leg over the horse's rump and kicked her left foot from the stirrup and slid down the horse's side, using the saddle for support to slow her descent. The dismount was relatively painless. She followed Murdock and Elyse as Murdock led them deeper into the trees. John followed, carrying the blanket and basket of food.

Murdock stopped under a tree that looked like any other tree growing in straight rows around them and gestured for John that this was the spot. Kara looked back the way they had come. As Murdock had said, the horses were still visible. At least their rumps were. Kara could even hear their loud crunching as the horses found fallen apples and ate them. There was no reason to feel so, so homesick. John spread out the blanket and Elyse opened the basket and pulled out bundles of food and set them on the blanket. Murdock invited John to sit with them.

"Winter will be here soon," Murdock said, shivering as another cold breeze gusted just enough to stir the dead leaves on the ground with a soft rustle. "This will be the last picnic of the year."

Elyse passed the paper wrapped roasted chicken and Kara selected a chicken breast before passing it on to Murdock. "How am I supposed to get to know you if you won't even tell me where you're from?" Kara asked.

"London," Murdock said. "I was born and raised in London. I do travel a lot, however."

"London?" Elyse asked, looking up in surprise. "Why that's not very far at all, less than a day's journey. I thought it would be a much longer journey." Murdock glanced at John meaningfully and Elyse ducked her head. "I thought you had traveled from a land far away," she said carefully.

"Funny how no matter how far you travel, chicken is the preferred picnic food," Murdock said, studying his chicken thigh before taking a large bite. He watched Kara as he chewed and swallowed. "Are you in pain, lovely girl?"

Kara shook her head. She ate her chicken breast without talking. Kara could not explain what she felt but she felt uncomfortable here and it was not pain from her ribs. Murdock continued to watch Kara as he ate. Elyse made small talk about the food and the weather.

"Are you sure you aren't in pain?" Murdock asked Kara again. "You are very quiet."

"I am fine," Kara said. "A little stiff but it is bearable."

Murdock nodded. "It takes a long while to heal from injured ribs. Where I come from men would go to jail for what that man did to you."

"He is her uncle and was her legal guardian before she married," Elyse said. She glanced at their escort, clearly uncomfortable discussing this in front of the man. "We have discussed this. Since it is his job to see to her upbringing and safety he has the right to discipline her. Well, had the right. He really should not have done it now that she is married."

"A real man does not strike a woman," Murdock said coldly. "Guardian or not. If I was your husband I would beat the bastard to an inch of his life."

Elyse sucked in her breath and Kara looked at Murdock in surprise. "My uncle is not a bastard. Do not say such things or it is you who could face discipline."

"It's a crazy world you live in where a man may beat women without reprisal but a man question's a man's parentage and is disciplined. At home a man who beats a woman is put in jail."

"Public whipping," Elyse said, shuddering. "Criminals are not left to sit in jail. There is too much need for bodies to work. If a public whipping does not successfully chastise a man's unruly behavior then he is put to death. Perhaps it is different in a city but here there are not men to spare to act as jailor. But Lord Roffe is a baron and only the king may order a public whipping of a baron."

"It is not the first time he has beat you, yes?" Murdock asked. "Then I would say he has not learned to curb his unruly behavior."

Something in his tone sent shivers down Kara's back. "I do not wish my uncle harmed, sir," she said, fearing that he was suggesting that Lord Roffe deserved to be put to death.

"Of course not," Murdock said. "You are not in pain. Is it something else distracting you? Perhaps you miss your keep already?"

Kara was startled to hear him ask so close to what she was feeling but she kept her face a mask. The man was paying far too much attention to her and her state when he should be focused on Elyse. Then Kara realized that he was probably trying to win her over so that she would grant approval of his relationship with Elyse and some of her tension with him eased.

Kara ate a boiled egg and a carrot, which was enough to make her feel full after the chicken breast and declined the little iced apple cakes Elyse found. The conversation had curbed her appetite. Murdock ate two of the little cakes. When they had eaten their fill Murdock requested John take the basket to their man guarding the horses. John did not even give it a second thought, quickly selecting an assortment of food to put back in the basket and carrying it to share. Murdock smiled as he watched John walk away.

"John forgot pickles. I think he would appreciate some pickles," Murdock said, standing. "Wait here."

"Please don't think ill of him," Elyse said as soon as Murdock walked away. "I am happy, Kara. Truly happy. I would like you to be there for my wedding. Please consider it."

"You know nothing of him," Kara said. "I want to be happy for you, Elyse. But it should not be a secret and it should not be so rushed."

"You were married the night you met Hawkstead," Elyse said sharply. She was immediately contrite. "I'm sorry. I know you had no choice. My head is in such a turmoil."

Murdock returned in a short time, carrying the saddle bags from his horse and suggested they stroll through the apple trees to settle all the food they ate. Elyse immediately agreed and Kara grudgingly got to her feet and trailed behind them. Murdock walked with Elyse nestled up to his right side, hand in hand. Murdock glanced back to make sure Kara was still with them. The man looked quite happy.

That was what Kara was thinking when a light flared in front of Murdock without warning, that the man looked happy and satisfied. Kara instinctively put her arm up to protect her face before realizing that there was no heat coming from the beam of light. Murdock had his arm around Elyse and reached back and grabbed Kara's arm and pulled them both right into the beam of light. Kara shrieked in alarm, still expecting to be burned though there was no heat. They passed through the light and several steps beyond without any ill effects.

On the other side of the light it was raining and it was dark. For a moment Kara worried that she had been blinded from stepping through the light. No, she could see Elyse's white face reflected from a light overhead. Kara glanced up, into the soft rain. A yellow light on a curved pole shone down on them. Kara turned her head. A row of curved poles with lights on the end went off into the distance on both sides.

"What has happened?" Elyse asked, clutching Murdock's elbow with all her might as she stared around them.

"Welcome to my land," Murdock said with a grin. "Let me introduce myself. I am not Roger Murdock. My name is Jensen Chaunders."

"I don't understand, Roger," Elyse said softly.

"I know, dear," Jensen said, patting Elyse's hand on his arm. "But it's Jensen, not Roger. Try to remember that." Jensen pulled a black rectangle out of his pocket and when he touched one flat side it became a light. He touched it with his thumb a few times than began to speak with it against his face. "It's Jensen. The zipper in Greeneway Park has yielded treasure. I'm heading there right now."

Kara turned, looking all around them. Soft lights glittered in the distance and there were noises coming from everywhere, even in the sky. There were no apple trees. The grass was manicured and they stood next to a road but it was a road like none she had ever seen, like the old road by the glass building but smooth and only a few feet wide. Behind them was a bench with its own yellow light on a straight, ornate pole. More benches, each with their own light pole were visible further along the narrow road.

Jensen put the black rectangle back in his pocket. The face had gone dark again. "Come, let's get out of the rain."

"I don't understand," Kara said, trying to take it all in but finding it overwhelming. "Where is the apple grove? Where are the horses? Where are the men? Why is it night?"

"Come," Jensen said, tugging on her arm. "We will get out of this rain and I will explain it to you."

"No," Kara said, turning. There was no longer a beam of light, just more of the same strange scenery. There should be an apple orchard at the foot of a small hill holding a walled village. Instead she was staring at buildings beyond another hundred yards of manicured lawn and more benches. "I don't understand. Where did it go?"

"It's gone. We are in another place now. Come. There is nothing else you can do right now," Jensen said.

Reluctantly Kara allowed Jensen to lead them out of the rain. Elyse was so in shock that she hadn't said a word, just stared around them with her mouth hanging open. Jensen put his arm around Elyse's shoulders as they walked. It took longer than Kara expected and eventually she trudged behind him with her head down as the rain increased in intensity. They walked for several minutes and Kara actually bumped into his back when Jensen suddenly stopped in front of her. He had stopped in front of a dark shape that came up to his chin. It had a door which Jensen opened, causing a light inside the structure to turn on. There was a fabric covered bench and two chairs. Jensen gestured to Kara to go inside the structure onto the bench. Kara was hesitant but the temptation to get out of the rain was strong and it was dry inside this thing.

Kara ducked her head and stepped head first into the contraption. Jensen muttered something under his breath and pulled Kara back out by her arm, gesturing and telling her feet first. With her skirts it was a struggle to fit her feet in the space between the bench and the chair but she did it. Kara wiped the rain from her face. Jensen pushed her skirt completely inside, pulled a strap down to hold her in place and shut the door and went to the other side of the contraption where he opened yet another door and helped Elyse as she struggled to sit on the bench next to Kara. Once Elyse was in and also strapped in place Jensen shut the door with a dull thud and opened yet another door and sat on the right sided chair in front of them. Jensen pulled a strap over himself and put a metal piece attached to the strap into the seat with a soft click. The light came on each time he opened a door as well as a bell making a ding ding ding sound.

"What is this contraption?" Elyse asked.

"It's a car. Much like your wagon but no horses needed to pull it."

"Why have you tied us in?" Elyse asked, pulling on the strap across her chest.

"It's a safety strap," Jensen said. "See, I am wearing one also."

"Perhaps I was wrong about you," Kara said, looking at all the glass surrounding them. "You must be very wealthy to afford so much glass just for a wagon."

Jensen chuckled as he started the car. Elyse shrieked in alarm when the metal wagon began to vibrate and loud sounds came from underneath. Kara would have shrieked as well but hearing Elyse's shriek froze her own shriek in her throat and instead clutched Elyse's hand as the metal wagon moved. Kara looked out the rain streaked window next to her. There were more cars all around them in neat rows. At least she thought they were cars as they were a variety of shapes and sizes. They both fell back against the back of the bench from the force as Jensen pulled out of the parking lot and drove onto a road.

Kara stared out the glass next to her. A green sign on the road said London 189 km. Several pairs of lights came straight at them then passed what felt like mere inches away from the side of the car where Jensen and Elyse sat. Kara closed her eyes as Jensen's car sped down the road, the speed the car traveled making her stomach roil while the continual sight of similar contraptions moving right at them was enough to give her heart palpitations.

The steady hum of the car and thud thud of the black sticks clearing the rain from the glass at the front of the car lulled Kara almost to sleep with her eyes closed so she opened them to keep from falling asleep. Lights and the noise of other cars around them as well as approaching them continued to make her feel terrified but gradually she realized that the approaching cars were now separated with a strip of darkness and sometimes with a lighter colored barrier between them. Green signs would occasionally show up above them on the road or to the side of the road. The distance to London was decreasing dramatically. Kara watched Jensen. There were lights on the wall in front of him as well as a wheel. He kept his hands on the wheel to guide the wagon he called a car and moved his feet to slow down or go faster.

"I am going to be sick," Elyse moaned.

"We will be there shortly," Murdock said.

"Where will we be?" Kara asked.

"London," Jensen said. "We are going to London."

"I wish to return to the apple orchard," Kara said. "There must be a way back. You went there once you must be able to return again."

"Oh, you will," Jensen said. "You most definitely will. If that is really what you want after you meet my, um, friends."

"I wish to return now," Kara said, sitting up straighter. "You control this wagon, right?"

"I have some friends who are looking forward to meeting you," he said. "But we have to go to London in order to meet them. It's late now so after a bite to eat and a good night's rest we will go visit with my friends. After you talk with them you may return to the apple orchard, if you still want to."

"I don't believe you," Kara said. She could see his face reflected from the lights in front of him. Jensen smiled. Kara's eyes narrowed. "What interest am I to your friends? Why would you have to drag us here without any warning if it was legitimate? What about Elyse? Did you even intend to marry her or were you just playing with her affections?"

"I have great affection for Elyse. Unfortunately I think marriage will have to wait," Jensen said.

"I really am going to be sick," Elyse said.

Jensen muttered something under his breath and slowed the car, turning the wheel to move the car to the side of the road. Kara watched him, paying careful attention to every move he made. Jensen pulled a small bar in the door and the door opened and the light came on above. Kara glanced at the door next to her and saw the same bar then looked at the door next to Elyse and saw the same bar. Jensen reached over Elyse and pushed a red button and the strap fell away from Elyse with a soft whirring sound.

Jensen had to help Elyse out of the car. After Elyse lost the contents of her stomach on the side of the road Jensen pushed her back in the car and pulled the strap over her chest and lap again. The end snapped into a small box on the bench.

Elyse was quite pale but trying to be brave. Kara felt the box her strap was attached to with her fingers as Jensen got back into the chair in front of Elyse and shut his door. Jensen was reaching for the strap above his shoulder when he glanced up at the mirror above his head and swore. Kara looked at the mirror. There were two lights on the side of the road behind them reflected in the mirror. A moment later red and blue lights began to flash above the two lights.

Jensen hit his palms on the wheel then put his left hand on the stick next to his chair and pushed his foot down and swung the wheel all at the same time. Jensen had not attached his safety strap across his chest and lap. The car shot out into the road right into the path of another pair of lights approaching behind them. There was the sound of a horn wailing and then a crack and crunch as the two cars collided. The car they were in spun and Kara was thrown hard against the strap across her chest.

Then they were rolling over and over and the strap Jensen had fastened across her chest and lap was the only thing keeping her from hitting the top of the car. Elyse screamed and Kara realized that she was screaming as well as the car they rode in dropped back onto its tires but did not move any longer. Elyse saw Jensen laying halfway out the broken window and screamed even harder. Blood covered the cracked glass and the door.

Time seemed to slow. Two men ran up to the car, one on either side. Kara saw the man talking to her. He had opened the car door and was talking to her but his voice sounded so far away and so slow. Blood dripped onto her face. Kara reached up and touched her head. Her forehead was wet. More blood dripped onto her hand. The man next to her kept yelling at her in slow motion and Elyse was screaming and crying. The man yelling at her shone a bright light in her face. That was the last Kara remembered.

Chapter Nine

Hawkstead returned to the keep to find chaos. He had gone out to collect the last of the rents from the tenants at the far edge of the estate and been wined and fed so it was dusk when he returned to the keep. The gates were wide open. Riders were out and milling about the road and gates. A huge bonfire burned in the fire pit near the gates, bathing the wall and riders in yellow light. When Hawkstead was spotted a small group separated and galloped to meet him, led by Richard.

"What is it?" Hawkstead asked.

"Your lady wife, my lord," Richard said. "John and Cory are dead. We sent runners looking for you. No one must have found you."

Hawkstead stared at Richard, a low buzzing filled his ears. John had pulled his rear end out of trouble more times than he could count. Cory, laughing Cory, silenced forever? Kara still alive meant possible torture at the hands of bandits. It might already be too late to save her. "Why did no one see bandits before they got so close to the keep?"

"Not bandits. There is no sign of anyone else having been in the apple orchard."

"Apple orchard? They were in the same place as the strangers appeared?" Hawkstead asked in surprise. "Lord Roffe? Is he responsible for this?"

"Accounted for. He never left the keep. In fact he is in no condition to do much of anything. The stranger, the one working in the stable, gave your wife's uncle a thrashing before he rode out with your wife and companion, Lady Ashton. John and Cory were the escort. When they were out longer than expected a boy was sent to check on them. It was a rather brisk day for a picnic, after all. He found John and Cory dead. The horses are still there but no sign of the other three. They have just vanished," Richard said

"They can't have gone far on foot," Hawkstead said. "The other strangers? Where are they?"

"Under guard in the infirmary. We questioned them, of course. The woman is quite upset. I don't believe they had any hand in it but I think she knows something."

"Of course she does," Hawkstead said. "The man, Murdock, he already attacked them. Who is the idiot who let him leave the keep with my wife?"

"You did not give orders that he was not allowed," one of the men spoke up.

"Can't you think for yourselves? Does it have to be spelled out for you?" Hawkstead yelled.

"You're just upset," Richard said. "How was anyone to know he would kidnap the women and kill two men in the process?"

"Damned right, I'm upset," Hawkstead said. "The man abducted my wife. We have to find her."

"We're ready to ride," someone shouted out and the cry was repeated by several.

"Not yet," Hawkstead said. The strangers might have information that would be helpful. "Julia Roberts could save us time from running in circles. First I talk to her."

Hawkstead found John Cho and Julia Roberts sitting in the infirmary with four armed men flanking them. Julia looked up when Hawkstead approached, the pain and worry in her eyes clear. She stood automatically and one of the armed men pushed her back down. Hawkstead waved him away and Julia again stood.

"I heard. Jensen killed two men and took the two women," Julia said.

"Jensen? It was Murdock. Do you know where he has taken them?" Hawkstead asked. He was trying to be polite but his voice was brusque and harsh causing Julia to wince slightly.

Julia and John exchanged glances. Julia shook her head. "I have no idea."

"London," John Cho said.

Both Hawkstead and Julia glanced at Cho in surprise. "He has a flat in London. He will go there first, then contact who he's working for."

"What if he goes directly to those people?" Julia asked. "We don't know where they are."

"If he's getting paid for them he will want the money before releasing them," Cho said.

"What if he's not getting paid?" Julia asked. "What if he's using them himself?"

"Then he would go to his flat in London," Cho said.

"Enough!" Hawkstead said. "I don't have time for this. If he's going to London he won't be going quickly. He left the horses." Hawkstead turned to leave and Julia stopped him.

"Wait," Julia said. "You can ride to London five times and back and not find him. He went, um, using, well, privacy please."

"Out with it," Hawkstead said.

"Have your men wait outside," Julia said. Hawkstead gestured without hesitation and the men walked out of the area immediately. Julia sighed. "This isn't going to be easy. There are many, many dimensions to our world." She paced as she talked. "Picture orange wedges. They taper and widen."

"What are orange wedges?" Hawkstead asked.

Julia stopped in her tracks. "You don't know what oranges are? Okay. Hmmm, well, where these dimensions get narrow and where they touch there are openings, sort of. They are called zippers because they can be opened. At least only a special few can open them."

"Zippers? I do not know what you are trying to tell me," Hawkstead said. He raked his fingers through his hair. "Dimensions? Measurements? Open but closed? This makes no sense."

"Imagine for a moment," John Cho said. "What if? What if the Golden Age still existed? What if disease hadn't gotten loose and killed off millions of people? We come from a land where that what if is what happened. There are places where doorways between those different lands can be bridged. First, you have to be able to find it. Second, you have to be able to open that doorway. The people I work with call them zippers. The man you know as Murdock is able to open that zipper and once through he closed the zipper. So to find your wife you require someone else who can open that zipper for you will never find your wife in this land."

Hawkstead considered Cho's words thoughtfully. He had heard childhood stories of fairy lands and that was what this sounded like. In the stories either people were pulled into the fairy land by fairies or had a talisman that opened an invisible door. Though it sounded preposterous, so did the arrival of these two and the disappearance of Murdock with Kara and her cousin.

"You can open this zip, zip, zip per?" Hawkstead asked John Cho.

Cho shook his head and looked at Julia. "I can," she said. "We just need an escort to the location you found us. I will do my best to find Kara and bring her back to you."

"Okay," Hawkstead said. "Let's go."

"Only you and one other man to escort us to where they disappeared," Julia said, caught off guard at how quickly he agreed.

"The less who know about the zippers the better. Someone who can keep his mouth shut."

"It will be only me," Hawkstead said.

Every delay shortened Hawkstead's temper. He ground his teeth in frustration when Julia struggled to mount and sit on the horse even with the assistance of two stable hands. She had never ridden a horse before that moment. Hawkstead was tempted to have her tied to the saddle so that she did not fall off at a gallop. Cho did not say anything when he put his foot in the stirrup and gracefully swung into the saddle but Hawkstead could tell that he did not have much experience on a horse either. What he lacked in experience Cho made up for in physical prowess.

Just as it appeared they were ready to ride out Mrs. Smith came rushing into the stable. She gripped Hawkstead's leg as she tried to catch her breath. Hawkstead frowned down at the housekeeper in alarm mixed with irritation. The woman gasped for breath for several agonizing minutes. Hawkstead waited patiently.

"I heard," Mrs. Smith said. She sucked in a deep breath and let it out slowly. "I heard. Here. Do not lose it." She held out a thick bronze ring with squared corners.

"I do not have time to waste, Mrs. Smith," Hawkstead said. He did take the ring and looked at it without interest. The ring would be uncomfortable to wear since it was so thick and roughly square shaped. Hawkstead tried to put it on his little finger and it went to his first knuckle but no further.

"It is a key," Mrs. Smith said in a low voice for his ears only. "Family relic. The leather cord was falling apart. Sent boy for new cord. Wear it around your neck. Keep it with you. Do not lose it. It is a key." Mrs. Smith squeezed Hawkstead's hand. He grimaced when the ring ground into his fingers. "I can't stress enough, keep it with you always. I did not have time to find a new cord."

A page came running up to Mrs. Smith and handed her a piece of leather cord. She patted the boy's hand in gratitude and held up the cord. Hawkstead took the cord and pulled the ring off his finger. He looped the cord through the ring and tied the ends in a knot. Mrs. Smith watched him anxiously.

"A key? A key to what?" Hawkstead asked.

"To return home," Mrs. Smith said in such a low voice that Hawkstead barely heard her. She looked up at John Cho and Julia, who were watching while they were waiting then hurried out of the stable without another word.

Hawkstead ran his thumb over the gnarly ring, feeling the smooth ridges and ribs. The ring felt like it had been molded. He stared thoughtfully out in the direction Mrs. Smith had gone. Hawkstead put the cord over his head and let the ring drop onto his chest under his shirt. He had no idea what the housekeeper was up to but it did not hurt to carry the ring with him. Though Hawkstead intended to escort the two strangers alone, once they were mounted and heading out of the keep at least thirty of his men rode up and joined them.

"Jax, take ten men north towards Mael. If you don't see any signs of them in an hour circle back. Ralph, take men north past Mael before circling back. Richard, head west with the rest of the men," Hawkstead said. Jax and Ralph called out the names of men and within minutes were riding north with most of the riders. Richard was not so easy to convince to blindly follow orders that made no sense.

"Where are you going?" Richard asked.

"To the village," Hawkstead said.

"Then you'll want us there," Richard said. "Though we searched immediately right after finding out that Lady Hawkstead had vanished."

"I want to see where she was abducted," Hawkstead said. "Then I would like to look within the village," Hawkstead said.

"There are only a handful of us left," Richard said.

"Very well," Hawkstead said. "Without horses they can't have gone far. You start the search within the village while I take a look at the apple orchard."

Julia wanted her horse to move over to Hawkstead. At least that is what it looked like she was doing to everyone but the horse she was on. She shook the reins and kicked her legs out to the side and did a scooting motion with her rear end on the saddle while the horse stood perfectly still and flicked its ears back and forth. Hawkstead guided his horse up next to her. "What?"

"This is too many people," Julia said, doing a head count with her pointer finger in the air. "That's eight more men."

"When we get to the village they will be busy searching buildings," Hawkstead said. "While the three of us can go out to the apple orchard."

They made it to the village without Julia falling off the horse she rode. Richard gestured for his men to go into the village while he stayed with Hawkstead's group riding the short distance to the apple orchard. The clouds covering the sky earlier in the day had cleared and the stars and nearly full moon provided enough light to allow them make their way to the right location between the trees. The clear sky also meant a quick drop in temperature and it was growing quite cold.

"Here," Julia said, dismounting by swinging her right leg over the horse's neck and jumping to the ground. She stumbled and held her arms out to catch her balance.

"How can anyone know so little of riding a horse?" Richard asked in surprise. He swung his right leg over his horse's rump and smoothly slid to the ground.

"I need you to keep an eye on things while I am gone," Hawkstead said to Richard. He handed the reins to his horse to Richard. "I don't know how long this will take. Don't let Roffe leave the keep while we're gone either."

"Gone?" Richard asked. "Where are you going?"

"I don't really know," Hawkstead said.

Julia walked with purpose several yards then stopped and turned around. "The zipper is here. I will do my best to find Kara and return her as soon as possible."

"I am going with you," Hawkstead said.

Julia frowned. She shook her head. "No. No. That's not a good idea at all."

"That may be true but I am still going with you," Hawkstead said. He gathered the reins to the horse Julia had ridden and handed them to Richard.

"What are you talking about?" Richard asked. "Who is going anywhere without horses?"

John Cho stood next to Julia. Though the moon made seeing shapes possible it was not enough to see facial expressions. Because Hawkstead knew Richard so well he could imagine that Richard's face would be showing confusion. By the tone of her voice, Julia's face would be showing that she was distraught. Cho's face would be expressionless but a hint of considering in his eyes.

"I will find her," Julia said. "You have to stay here."

"Let's see this zip per," Hawkstead said, growing impatient.

Julia stood where she was for several minutes, her shadowed face unreadable as she considered what she should do. Finally she turned and took another step away from the group. A beam of light flared from the ground up into the treetops. The light was about three feet wide. Richard cursed and stepped backwards, the horses milling about him. John Cho ducked into the light beam and vanished. Julia followed. Hawkstead took a deep breath and jumped into the light beam after them.

Hawkstead continued to run several steps beyond the light beam then froze in shock. Though it had easily been an hour after sunset when they stepped through the zipper it was now almost dawn. Seeing the lightening sky heralding the imminent arrival of the sun was his first shock. The second was that instead of an apple orchard they stood in a grassy area surrounded by buildings and structures. Metal wagons without horses or oxen moved along a road in the near distance. Tall metal poles curved overhead with lights that did not flicker but burned steadily. Hawkstead turned his head, trying to see everything but it was almost overwhelming. The beam of light was gone and the same foreign scenery stretched behind him.

"You should not have done that," Julia said.

"What is this place?" Hawkstead said, memorizing every detail he could see.

"Well, he's here now," Cho said. He pulled a black rectangle out of his pocket and used his thumb to rub the rectangle. "Damn, battery is dead. We need to get to an outlet."

Julia pulled out a similar rectangle and also swiped the top with her thumb after pushing the edge. Light emanated from the rectangle. "I turned mine off right away. It has just enough charge to send a text." Julia pushed the top of the rectangle and put the rectangle to her face. "At Greeneway Park in Greenestone. Phones need charge. Critical situation," Julia said into the black rectangle then pushed a button, studying the light in her hand. After a minute she visibly relaxed and pressed the edge of the rectangle again and the light went out. "They are nearby. She says ten minutes."

Cho nodded. "They must have been looking for us. How long were we missing?"

Hawkstead watched a woman running towards them. She wore her hair in a ponytail and had white strings coming from her ears. She also wore barely any clothing. He could see her bare legs below skin tight black under pants as well as her stomach below a thin bit of pink fabric covering her chest and upper arms. Patches of sweat darkened the pink fabric. At first he thought she was in distress and his hand went to the sword at his side but he did not see anyone chasing her and she was running at a steady pace. Julia put her hand on his sword arm and shook her head. Hawkstead looked at Julia and then at Cho. Neither of them was concerned with a half-naked woman running towards them. The woman glanced over at the three of them as she ran past on a narrow, smooth roadway, eyebrows rising at the sight of Hawkstead but she continued her steady pace right on by them.

"She was not in distress?" Hawkstead asked.

"She was jogging," Julia said. Hawkstead stared at her blankly. "Running for enjoyment," Julia said in further explanation. Hawkstead still stared at her blankly.

"That could be a problem," Cho said, shaking his head. He stepped up to Hawkstead. "You will see a lot of things here that might seem strange. Unless someone says the words help me, don't try to help them. Got it?"

"They're here," Julia said. The relief in her voice was apparent. She started walking along the same black strip of road that the woman had been using to run for enjoyment.

Two men had exited one of the metal wagons and were walking toward the small group. Hawkstead followed Julia, attention again on the surroundings. Without the buildings, poles with wires and lights, and roads the landscape was recognizable. It was the area outside the village. It was like the village had expanded beyond its current walls. Hawkstead glanced over his left shoulder. The keep should be only a few miles in that direction. Instead of open fields and trees more houses and buildings blocked the view.

One of the men greeting Julia was much like Cho, alert to his surroundings and in terrific physical shape. He was almost as tall as Hawkstead but without the large frame. He had blonde hair, blue eyes, and sun darkened skin. The other man was about the same height as Julia with a wild mop of curly black hair and a large hooked nose. He wore glass in frames on his face that rested on his striking nose. The second man was soft, his rounded stomach noticeable against his thin shirt. Both men had eyes on Hawkstead though they were talking with Julia.

"She's not happy," black haired man said. "Your traveling companion will make her even unhappier."

"First, Cho needs medical attention," Julia said. "I removed the bullets but he should be evaluated anyway."

"I'm fine," Cho said.

"No, you need to be checked," Julia insisted.

"Gunshot wounds at a hospital in England?" black haired man said, grimacing.

"Just need some antibiotics and I am good," Cho said.

"Is she here?" Julia asked.

"No," black haired man said, shaking his head. "She is in London, waiting for Jensen to show up."

"He hasn't arrived yet? If he was going to his apartment he should have arrived hours ago," Julia said. "He must have taken them somewhere else." She suddenly turned to Hawkstead. "Oh, sorry. Introductions are in order. Lord Hawkstead, Mike and Frank." Julia gestured to tall blonde man as she said Mike and swept her arm towards black haired man when she said Frank.

"Lord, huh?" Frank said.

"Lord Hawkstead, seventh Earl of Greenestone," Hawkstead said bowing his head slightly in greeting.

"Got a first name?" Frank asked.

"I do," Hawkstead said. "Come, we are losing time."

"Arrogant bastard, isn't he?" Frank said, taken aback.

Hawkstead stiffened. "You question my parentage?"

"It's an expression," Julia said quickly. "He isn't saying that your mother had you out of wedlock."

"Strange expression," Hawkstead said, fingers caressing his sword hilt. "To cast aspirations on my mother's character is no light matter."

"That's because it is common here for women to have children without being married, so it does not mean anything here," Julia said quickly to Hawkstead. She turned to Frank, missing the shocked expression on Hawkstead's face. "We should get out of the open before he actually decides to draw that sword and all sorts of attention."

"Yeah," Frank said, stepping back. "I take this zipper led to a dimension where they're a bit backwards?"

"From what I can tell, they were even more advanced until something happened to release massive global plagues that wiped out huge populations," Cho said. He held up his hand to quiet Mike and Frank when they both looked at him in alarm. "It's been at least two generations since the last plague struck. Julia and I discussed being quarantined but then decided it was safe. Neither of us noticed any symptoms in us or anyone around us."

"Sent back to the dark ages. A society can only handle so many redundancies in skills. Huge losses in a population would wipe out all sorts of skill sets," Mike said thoughtfully. He looked at Hawkstead. "What happened?"

"Roger Murdock abducted my wife and her companion and brought them here," Hawkstead said. He was growing impatient with their need to chatter incessantly while he felt the need for action.

"Roger Murdock?" Mike asked.

"He means Jensen," Julia said. "The priest said there was a failure in electricity holding diseases in storage. It must have been a long term failure."

"Scary," Frank muttered, shivering at the thought.

"The first plague wiped out most of the major cities. Or it could have been the nuclear fusion experiment that went awry and forced the complete ban of all electrishity. That was not substantiated, however. Other rumors were that the sun sent out a wave of energy, not a nuclear fusion experiment. I don't know," Hawkstead said, staring up and to the right, trying to remember the history. It was difficult to concentrate when his whole body screamed to get moving but he decided that if he satisfied their curiosity then perhaps they would start doing something. "With so many people dead, whole towns wiped out completely, by the time we recovered from the plagues we had lost all knowledge and ability to access information not written on physical items. I have heard many versions of what happened with electrishity but in the end it is all gone." Hawkstead had quoted almost word for word what Mrs. Smith had told him when showing him the relic room. The words did not really make much sense to him but his audience seemed to understand everything he said.

All four people around him stared at him in horror as he spoke. The idea that such a horrendous crisis had occurred clearly affected them. Hawkstead did not understand why they were so horrified over something that happened a century ago to people they did not even know. He did not realize that each person standing there was imagining their dimension experiencing the same horrific accident that could possibly unleash the many diseases kept in strict laboratory conditions for research, or even released on purpose by terrorists.

"How do you plan on following Murdock?" Hawkstead asked.

"Why did you bring him?" Frank asked Julia.

"I did not. He came through on his own," Julia said.

"Look, Lord Hawkstead, was it? I think you should go home and wait for us to find your wife," Frank said, speaking slowly and a little too loudly. "All right?"

"You do not wish for my company?" Hawkstead asked. He felt a growing dislike for the black haired man. Hawkstead looked around his surroundings, getting his bearings. Hawkstead did need their help but if they would not help he was not going to let that stop him from finding Kara. He could find his way to London on foot if necessary though it would take longer. Hawkstead would prefer to work with these strange people but if they would not cooperate he would do it on his own and he was not about to ask for help. The first step would be to locate a horse. Hawkstead took a deep breath. "I would appreciate working together but if you do not wish that I shall prevail on my own. Where can I find a horse?"

"A horse?" Frank asked. "Why would you need a horse?"

"It's faster than going on foot," Hawkstead said.

"We need to bring him with us," Julia said. "The last thing we need is him riding to London down the motorway on a horse."

"Just send him back through the zipper," Mike said.

"He's coming with us," Julia said. She turned and started walking in the direction the two men had come from when they arrived. "Let's go."

Hawkstead was surprised when the three men obeyed her without another word of argument. Cho gestured for Hawkstead to go ahead of him and they all walked quickly after Julia with Cho bringing up the rear. Mike caught up with Julia and then passed her by a few feet, leading the way to a parked metal wagon. He inserted a key in the door and unlocked it. Julia frowned when she saw the size of the vehicle.

"This is it," Mike said. "The giant outlander will have to sit in front with me and the three of you will have to squeeze into the back seat."

Hawkstead was very uncomfortable sitting in the metal wagon. He had to scrunch his shoulders in and hold his arms out in front of him and even then he was pressed against the door and brushing shoulders with Mike. Julia and Cho immediately stuck wires into round holes in the metal wagon and attached their black rectangles to the ends of the wire. It took all Hawkstead's strength of will to not shut his eyes when the metal wagon started to move on its own. After a few minutes he began to relax. By the time they were on the motorway Hawkstead was appreciating the speed with which they were able to travel. Green signs with white letters along the road periodically announced the distance to London as well as various towns between Greenestone and London. He had to find her. The thought of Kara in the hands of that man created a rage deep in his chest.

"Looks like there was an accident," Mike said, slowing the metal wagon. Several metal wagons in front of him moved slowly past a two metal wagons with flashing lights on the side of the road. A man stood at the side of the road, gesturing for the metal wagons to keep moving. A strange metal vehicle with a winch at its back was parked sideways, attached to a mangled metal wagon in the grass bordering the road by a taut cable. The mangled metal wagon in the grass crept slowly up towards the winch as the winch turned.

Hawkstead stared at the wreckage as they drove past at a crawl, shuddering to think of the same happening to the metal wagon he rode within. Mike rolled down his window, leaning out to ask the man directing traffic what had happened but the man would not talk to him, just gestured repeatedly to keep going. Mike glanced in the mirror above his head and kept going. There was a line of paired lights behind them.

"I did not see anyone," Julia said, sitting back on the seat. "It must have happened a while ago."

"That could explain why Jensen did not arrive in London," Cho said.

"Or he did not go directly to his flat," Julia said. "He knew we would follow him."

"I think we should check it out," Mike said, driving off the motorway onto a curving road and stopping at the intersection of another road. Cho swiped his black rectangle with his thumb and held it up to his face, black cord still attached and dangling. "Yes, it's Cho. We're near Mannington. Signs of an accident. Check nearest hospital."

"We're wasting time," Julia said.

"His flat is under surveillance," Mike said.

Hawkstead watched them with interest. He was confused but highly interested. Cho was listening to the black rectangle and occasionally nodding to himself. Mike and Julia continued to argue. The black rectangle appeared to be a source of information, which was confirmed when Cho lowered it slightly and spoke to the group. "A car hit a lorry. That's a truck here, right? Driver of car is at Norman Medical Center in critical condition. Driver of lorry was sent to hospital but already released. Two female passengers in car. No detailed info on them."

Chapter Ten

Kara woke in a bed in a quiet room. Her body felt stiff and sore and her ribs hurt as badly as they had the day after her uncle had beat her. Kara ran her tongue over her swollen lower lip. The smell was the first thing she noticed after the quiet. She wrinkled her nose. The smells tickled her nose. A second bed sat next to her bed. She hadn't noticed it at first because a curtain hung from the ceiling, blocking the view except for the foot of the bed. Kara struggled to sit up. Her clothes were gone and she wore only a paper thin cloth that tied at the back with two straps, leaving gaps in coverage. A black box hung from the wall that looked like a window with people doing things but it could not be a window because the scenery kept changing.

The door opened and a tall, dark skinned woman wearing white entered the room. Her short dark hair was frosted with gray and curled over her head like a cap. She smiled when she saw Kara. "I'll be with you in a moment, dear," she said. She went first to the other bed and only a moment later stepped around the curtain. "I am your day nurse, Claire. How are you feeling?" The woman placed a cuff around Kara's wrist and stepped up to a table on wheels, eyes on the lid of another black box even as she talked.

"I hurt," Kara mumbled. Talking felt strange because her lip was so swollen.

"I see you were in a car accident. I'll get the doctor. Looks like you were unconscious when they brought you in."

"Elyse? Where is Elyse? Where are my clothes?" Kara asked. Her words felt thick. She traced her lip with her tongue again, feeling the painful bump inside. "What's wrong with my mouth?" The bracelet the woman had put on her wrist was gaining pressure and squishing her wrist. "What are you doing?"

"Looks like you bit your lip. It'll hurt for a while but will heal. This is helping me take your blood pressure. It'll only be a minute or two more."

"My clothes," Kara said.

"I'm sure your clothes are in the closet," the woman said. She stepped away from the rolling table and took the cuff in her hand. The pressure immediately released. The nurse pulled a strap making a sound like cloth ripping, releasing the cuff and the cuff fell away. "Elyse? That would be the woman in the next bed." Kara immediately pushed the thin blanket aside and slid her legs off the bed. "Whoa," Nurse Claire said, pushing Kara's legs back up on the bed. "You need to stay put until the doctor arrives. Don't worry, your friend is fine, except for a broken leg. She's sleeping now but has been awake."

"A broken leg?" Kara asked in alarm. A broken leg was a serious injury. She did not understand why the woman was so casual about a broken leg. A broken leg meant months of being bedridden and most likely a painful limp for the rest of Elyse's life. If the leg was not set properly the consequences would be even worse than that.

"Do you remember what happened, dear?" Nurse Claire asked.

The woman fidgeted with the blanket, tightening and straightening, as she waited for Kara's response. Kara noticed that the blanket had writing along the edge. St. Agnes Hospital. Kara looked up at the nurse, noticing the gray hairs yet her face was smooth and she moved about like a young woman. Julia had been the same, a sense of maturity about her but little sign of the normal ravages of time. Did people not age here? Where were the sores, the wrinkles? Her teeth were as white as a child's and no missing teeth broke her smile.

"No?" the nurse asked gently, studying Kara's face. "The police also wish to talk to you." When Kara stared at her blankly the nurse frowned slightly. "It is clear you suffered injuries before the accident. Perhaps your boyfriend or father?"

"My uncle," Kara said. The words caught in her dry throat. She cleared her throat and said again, "It was my uncle."

"It will be better if you press charges," the nurse said. "They will arrest him anyway."

Two people entered the room, an elderly man and one was a short, serious faced woman both in identical blue uniforms. They both wore embroidered badges on their uniforms identifying them as members of the Mannington Police Department. Kara pulled the thin blanket up to her chin, feeling quite exposed. It was not at all proper for a strange man to enter her sickroom, especially when she was not properly clothed. They greeted the nurse then waited quietly and patiently for the woman to finish her tasks and leave the room. The nurse squeezed Kara's shoulder in an act of comfort then left the room. Kara stared at the two uniformed people. They looked so somber and serious.

"Your name?" the woman asked, gaze on a pad of paper in her hand, pen poised over the paper.

"Lady Kara Hawkstead nee Roffe, Countess of Greenestone, Duchess of Mael," Kara said.

The woman looked up sharply from paper to Kara lying on the bed. "Don't be fresh. Your name?"

"Lady Kara Hawkstead nee Roffe, Countess of Greenestone, Duchess of Mael," Kara repeated. She sat up straighter, holding the blanket under her chin when it started to slide down. "Who are you and what business have you to question me?"

"Police business," the woman said. "The hospital reported potential domestic abuse."

"Domestic abuse?" Kara repeated.

"Let's try this again," the woman said. "Your name?"

"Just note Kara Hawkstead," the man said to the woman. He smiled at Kara. "I am Officer Glenwyck and my partner is Officer Cook. We just want to chat with you a bit if we might."

"Odd place to receive visitors," Kara muttered.

"We understand that you were in the auto wreck on the motorway last night," Officer Glenwyck said, watching Kara with kind eyes. He took a deep breath. "But you have recent injuries from before the accident. Possibly stemming from a severe beating?" Officer Glenwyck said.

Kara nodded. "Yes," Kara said. "My uncle did deliver a beating." The beating was not a secret and for some reason Officer Glenwyck felt like an old friend. Though he was the oldest man Kara had ever seen he also had all his teeth and they were white.

"Would you like to press charges?" Officer Glenwyck asked.

"What does that mean?" Kara asked.

"If you give us a statement we will see that your uncle is prosecuted to the fullest extent of the law," Officer Cook said.

"A statement?" Kara asked.

"Tell us what happened. Identify your abuser for the record," Officer Cook said in her brisk voice. "We can arrest him but if you press charges there is a better chance that he will see jail time."

"The first step is to procure an injunction," Officer Glenwyck said. Kara stared blankly at him. "An injunction will provide relief for you because your uncle will not be allowed near you."

"I see," Kara said. "My husband has put a guard on my uncle to ensure that he does not attempt to harm me again. Since he is a lord it was not appropriate to have a public lashing. Well, not and risk the king's anger since a baron cannot have another baron publicly whipped. An injunction is a rule, yes? The guard is more secure than a rule."

The two uniformed police officers stared at Kara in silence. Officer Cook turned to her companion. "Was she hit in the head?" Officer Cook asked Officer Glenwyck.

Officer Glenwyck shrugged. "Perhaps we can try again tomorrow? Maybe they have her on medication?"

"Tell me, here, what do you do to the full extent of the law for a man who beats a woman?" Kara asked in interest.

"Here? Greenestone County has no tolerance for men beating up women," Officer Cook said. "He will be sent to jail, of course."

"The man driving the car you were in, is he your uncle?" Officer Glenwyck asked.

"Roger Murdock? No, he was my cousin's betrothed," Kara said. Greenestone County he had said.

"I have here his name was Jensen Chaunders," Officer Glenwyck said.

"Was? They told you then that he is deceased?" Officer Cook asked.

Kara looked at the woman in surprise. Though Kara hadn't known him well and he had used trickery to drag her to this bizarre world, a band of despair tightened across her chest at his loss. Elyse cared for the man no matter what Kara thought of him. The loss of life of anyone was sad. He was their only way to return home. "Deceased?"

"Sorry, thought you knew," Officer Cook muttered. "He was not the man who beat you?"

"No," Kara said. "My uncle, Lord Richard Roffe." Kara suddenly found it difficult to breath.

Nurse Claire stepped back into the room, gaze on the noisy machines next to Kara's bed. "Sorry, officers, I need to ask you to leave and come back another time."

"Certainly," Officer Glenwyck said, giving Kara one last compassionate look. "We will try again tomorrow, Kara."

"Lady Hawkstead," Kara said in a ragged voice.

The two uniformed officers stepped out of the room but encountered the doctor as he was on his way in to see Kara and their voices could be heard in a low unintelligible murmur. The nurse held a white tube with a needle attached to the end. The nurse stuck the needle in Kara's arm and before Kara could protest, a warm cozy feeling washed over her and the need for sleep pulled at her. Just before sleep claimed her Kara heard the nurse apologize in a low voice.

When Kara woke she was still in the hospital but in a different room. Kara had been moved to a private room, no second bed. This room was bigger and had a large window with a lovely view of a park. The black box with moving pictures was also larger and Kara stared blankly at it for a while before she realized that the sounds she heard matched the pictures on the black box. Words too fast to read scrolled across the bottom of the thing. Two people sat at a desk talking to her as much as to each other. At least they were looking right at her as they talked. The picture changed to a large ship for a few minutes then back to the two people at the desk.

Nurse Claire entered the room with a smile. "You are awake. How are you feeling?"

"Hungry," Kara said. "My companion. Where is she?"

"She is resting. Here's a menu. Pick out what you want and I'll order it for you," Nurse Claire said. "The tv remote is on the tray if you want to change the channel."

"What is a tv?" Kara asked.

Nurse Claire's eyes widened in surprise but gave no other sign that she found the question unusual. She pointed to the black rectangle on the wall. "That is a television, mostly called a tv. It has news, entertainment, and educational channels." Nurse Claire picked up a flat, black tube lined with buttons on every spare inch. "This is the remote control. This button turns the tv off or on. This button moves from channel to channel in order. The buttons with numbers up here will take you to specific channels. This button raises and lowers the volume. Play with it."

Kara took the remote control that Nurse Claire handed to her. She pushed a button. Nothing happened. "You have to point it at the tv," Nurse Claire said. Kara pushed a button and the noise from the tv became louder.

Nurse Claire left the room and Kara set the remote down on the bed and stared out the window. Her heart froze in her chest when a large object with rigid wings flew across the sky. She could hear its roar even at this distance. Though there was a park across the street there were roads below the window and at each side of the park. Those roads were filled with noisy cars like the one Jensen had used, some big enough for many people. Horns honked, engines revved, and tires squealed. In the room more noises bombarded her. Machines behind her beeped and in the hall heeled shoes passed her door several times. Though the door was closed Kara could hear people talking as well.

Kara looked up at the tv. She picked up the remote and pushed buttons. The images changed instantly when she pushed the button the nurse had said would change channels. A number appeared in the upper right hand corner then faded after a moment. A land of ice and ocean appeared in the tv window and a man's voice could be heard talking about global warming though he was nowhere to be seen. Kara pushed the button again. She instinctively covered her face with her arm when a building exploded as a car drove into it but there was no heat coming from the tv. Kara pushed the button again and again, sometimes lingering for several minutes on a channel.

When Nurse Claire returned she carried a covered tray and set the tray on a table that rolled over the bed. The nurse removed the lid and the smell of food wafted into the air with the steam that poured forth. Kara's stomach growled in response. A piece of chicken without its bones sat on a round, white piece of porcelain. Green beans and a roll sat next to the chicken. Kara picked up the chicken with her fingers and bit into the meat. She was so hungry.

"Nurse Claire, where is my companion? The other woman in the accident that put me here." Kara had swallowed her bite before asking but did not wait for an answer before taking another generous bite of the chicken.

"She is resting," Nurse Claire said. "You can visit her tomorrow."

That evening there was a knock on the door heralding the entrance of two clean shaven men. Kara looked up as they stepped into the room and shut the door behind them. They were not the police officers returning as promised. These men were dressed in pants and matching jackets. A business suit, Kara had learned from the tv that day. These business suits could be purchased at a local store at sale price through the weekend.

"Good evening, Lady Hawkstead," the taller man said. He had no hair. Kara looked more closely. No, his head had been shaved, for there was a faint outline of a hairline. "I am Sean Matthews. My colleague here is Amie Letvos."

Amie Letvos nodded his head in greeting when Sean Matthews said his name. Both men stared at Kara with interest. Kara pulled the blanket up to her chin. Sean Matthews was taller than his companion by a few inches but both were generally of average height. Amie Letvos had cropped brown hair. Both had blue eyes and non-distinct features. They were older men, at least in their forties if not older.

Kara was finding it difficult to judge ages in this land for they all aged more slowly.

"Right then," Sean Matthews said when Kara remained quiet. "We are colleagues of Jensen Chaunders, the man who brought you here. May we have a few minutes of your time?"

"If I say no you will leave?" Kara asked.

Amie Letvos frowned then smoothed his face to a pleasant, friendly demeanor. "Perhaps we should say we would like a few minutes of your time. Did Jensen speak with you of your, uh, talent?"

"Talent?" Kara asked. The only time she had spent with the man they called Jensen had been when he was attempting to teach her to defend herself and he had not mentioned that she had any talent at it. If anything, Kara felt that Jensen thought she had no talent at it. Jensen had been surprised that she had even been listening to him. "I believe he did not feel I had any talent."

Amie Letvos frowned again. He turned to his colleague. "Can it be true? Would he have brought her through otherwise?"

Sean Matthews shrugged. "He said he had someone." Sean Matthews spoke to Amie Letvos but his gaze was on Kara. "The other woman, perhaps?"

"But why bring them both?" Amie Letvos asked.

"Maybe he just did not say anything to her," Sean Matthews said.

"Or maybe he was just thinking with his little head again," Amie Letvos muttered.

The door opened and both men reacted strangely, sliding their hands under their jackets. When they saw Nurse Claire they relaxed and pulled their hands back out of their jackets. "Nurse," Sean Matthews said, nodding his head in greeting.

"Oh, it's you," Nurse Claire said. She looked uncomfortable. "I am not sure how much longer I can keep her out of sight. It should not have been a problem for a few days but there are people asking about her."

"The police?" Amie Letvos asked.

Nurse Claire shook her head. "Police were here already. It's others."

"I think we need to assume she's the one," Amie Letvos said. "Nurse, one more favor." He glanced at Kara, who was staring at them in confused silence. "One more move. Double the original price."

Nurse Claire nodded. She looked sad. "I will grab a syringe and be back in a few minutes."

"Have you talked to my companion, Lady Addington?" Kara asked. "She was in the accident also and I have not seen her yet."

"Yes," Sean Matthews said. "We are going to move you to a room with her now."

Kara felt relief. Kara had been so worried that something serious was wrong with Elyse, the way the nurse continued to be so evasive.

Nurse Claire returned, gaze locked on the floor as she entered the room. She could not look Kara in the eyes as she pulled a syringe out of her pocket and stuck the needle in Kara's arm. Kara jerked in surprise but Nurse Claire's grip on Kara's arm was strong. Within moments Kara felt the familiar warm and cozy need for sleep. Again Nurse Claire whispered an apology.

Kara woke in a darkened room. The noisy machines surrounding her in the hospital room were quiet. Kara turned her head. No, there were no longer machines to make any noise. A window right across the room let in meager light, enough to see the general outline of furniture in the room. She looked to the right where the window should have been but it was a wall now. It was quiet outside the room also.

Kara pushed the blanket aside then stopped and rubbed the fabric between her fingers. Instead of the paper thin piece of cloth covering the hospital beds this blanket was thick, soft, and luxurious. Kara grimaced as she swung her legs over the side of the bed. Every muscle in her body protested but Kara ignored the pain, certain that only sore muscles hurt, not anything more serious. Kara no longer wore the thin hospital garment either, instead she wore a thick flannel nightgown. This garment covered her backside.

Kara slowly walked to the door, hands out, feet testing the next step to avoid stepping on something or bumping into something. It took a few minutes to figure out how the door handle worked. Fortunately in her travels Kara had encountered similar round door knobs and after twisting the round knob back and forth she heard the click of the latch freeing. With the door open she could hear the soft murmur of voices beyond the hall. A dim light came from the same direction as the voices. Kara walked in the direction of the light.

The two men who had visited her when the nurse again stuck a needle in her arm to put her to sleep were sitting in a room at the end of the hall. On the sofa opposite of them were a man and a woman with their backs to the hall. Sean Matthews saw Kara slowly walking down the hall and jumped to his feet. The people with their backs to her turned and looked.

"Lady Hawkstead," Sean Matthews said. "You should not be out of bed."

"Where am I?" Kara asked. She leaned against the wall for support. "How did I get here?"

"You were released from the hospital into our care," the woman said. She stood and approached Kara. The woman was tall and thin, dressed in a tailored red dress that barely covered her knees. Her blonde hair was cut short and framed her face. "Sean, grab the girl a robe. Come, dear, sit here. You are trembling."

The woman took Kara's arm and guided her to the sofa and eased her down on it. Kara had barely been seated when Sean returned with a robe and draped it over Kara's shoulders. The man who had been sitting next to the woman stood to allow the woman to sit next to Kara. He was a middle aged man with a large build.

"You have met Sean and Amie. This man here is Stephen and I am Cassandra."

"Elyse. Lady Addington. Where is she?" Kara asked.

"She is still in the hospital," Cassandra said with a smile. "Her injuries were more complicated. Once she can be released she will be joining us though."

"I do not know you. Why would the hospital release me to you? Is it normal in this land to send people out of the infirmary to the care of strangers?" Kara asked.

Cassandra smiled. "But we aren't strangers, dear. We are friends of Jensen Chaunders. We feel responsible for you since Jensen was bringing you to meet us."

"I see," Kara said. She looked around the room at the faces staring at her so intently. Though it felt like a lie she decided that she was not going to pursue the topic.

"How are you feeling, dear?" Cassandra asked.

"Sore," Kara said.

"I am sure," Sean said. "That was quite the accident."

Kara looked around the room again at the smiling Cassandra, the cynical Amie, the friendly Sean, and the stone faced Stephen. They did not look like grieving friends of Jensen. No one wore black. No one looked effected by the news that their friend had died the day before. Kara's gaze wandered to the lights at each end of the sofa and up to the light on the ceiling. The same type of black rectangle as at the hospital hung on a wall but was black, the tv.

Music came from under the tv. The volume of the music was so low that she hadn't heard it while in the hall.

"When you are feeling better we can show you the sights," Cassandra said. "Jensen mentioned that where you come from was, well, not as technically advanced. We have so many wonderful things here."

"I see," Kara said.

"A dentist is the first step," Amie said, staring at Kara's mouth. "I'll bet they don't have dentists there."

Kara resisted the urge to cover her mouth with her hand. She did not need to visit a dentist. Dentists pulled rotten teeth. Kara did not have rotten teeth. Had the man looked inside her mouth while she slept? Regardless, it was the rudest thing anyone had ever said to her, suggesting she had rotting teeth. Kara knew that she had a good ten years before she would have to worry about getting teeth pulled. The man had a bad habit of talking about her like she was not even there.

"With Jensen gone it is even more critical to find a talent," Amie said. "We promised that delivery. We are going to run out of time."

"You want to test her now?" Sean asked in surprise. He glanced at Kara in concern. "Maybe in the morning? Give her a chance to rest and clean up."

Kara did not realize what she looked like. Besides her fat lower lip, which had turned black, she had a bruised eye, which was quite purple and stretched down her cheek. Kara's hair was a tousled mess. Tufts of hair had been loosened from her braid, creating a rippled ridge of hair that poked out in all directions down her back and she had a hair halo around half her head. Deep puffy bags under eyes made her look tired. Kara had been through the wringer and she looked like it.

"She's fine," Stephen said. He had been leaning against the wall and now stood up straight. "They were going to release her anyway. I agree, let's not waste any more time. Let's test her and find out if she will work. A little grooming won't make a difference."

Cassandra grimaced at the idea of doing what it was they wanted then nodded. She turned to Kara. "What the boys are talking about is seeing if you can help us with a little test, dear. It's nothing big. We have a room in this house that we will visit and just see if you notice anything special about it."

Cassandra stood without waiting for a response from Kara. Cassandra took Kara's arm and tugged her to her feet. Kara wavered a bit but steadied. She slipped her arms into the robe around her shoulders and tied the sash. A rug covered the floor from wall to wall so walking barefoot was not uncomfortable. The rug actually felt good under her feet, smooth and warm. Kara would prefer to put some clothes on and freshen up a bit but at that point did not really care anymore.

Cassandra led the way with Kara leaning against her and the three men trailed behind. Instead of going back up the hall where

Kara had been sleeping they went through the room with the sofas and to another hall with several doors. Cassandra led Kara into the first room off the hall, a sparsely furnished room compared to the room with sofas. As they entered the room Cassandra slid her hand on the wall just inside the door and light filled the room. Bookshelves lined the walls and a wood chair stood in the corner.

"Just explore the room, dear. Tell us what you think," Cassandra said, releasing Kara and giving her a little push further into the room.

Kara looked over her shoulder. All four of them stared at her with anticipation. Kara had no idea what they wanted her to do. She looked up at the light in the center of the ceiling then back at where Cassandra had touched the wall then back to the light on the ceiling. Since entering the hall leading to this room Kara felt the strongest need to go home. All Kara wanted was to leave this place and go home. Someone behind her cleared their throat, suggesting impatience. Kara glanced back. Amie actually leaned forward slightly, intently watching her. Cassandra flicked her first finger fingernail with her thumb pad repeatedly, a nervous habit that she was not even aware of doing, but gave Kara an encouraging smile.

Kara walked to one of the bookcases and tilted her head to read the titles on the spine. Perhaps they wanted her to see the wealth of books they owned? She walked to the chair, tempted to sit down. Kara glanced again back at her observers. The anticipation oozing from them was almost stronger than the feelings of homesickness bombarding her. Various objects decorated the top shelves of the bookcases.

Kara's gaze lingered on a clay horse statue. The piece of work was well done, very pleasing to the eye and her fingers itched to feel it, see if it was smooth or rough, warm or cool to the touch. Kara missed her horses. Kara hadn't ridden in days and felt a sense of emptiness settle over her. When she rode she felt whole.

"Feel free to move around, dear," Cassandra said.

This room was not covered with a rug from wall to wall like the halls and room with the sofas but instead had polished wood for a floor, yet the floor did not feel overly cold to her bare feet. Kara walked across the room to another bookcase and again tilted her head to read the titles on the spines of the books. Behind her someone sighed. Kara ignored the obvious signal of impatience. If they would not give her a hint of what they wanted then they could wait for how long it took her to solve their riddle without any rules.

"Try walking towards us again, dear," Cassandra said.

Kara looked back at them. Steven chided Cassandra for cheating. Amie's enthusiasm was fading and a scowl was settling over his face again. Between her and them Kara could see three faint vertical lines. The lines were the soft purple of spring lilacs, a glowing purple with black edges. If they hadn't been glowing Kara did not think she would have noticed them. The lines hadn't been visible a few minutes earlier, she was sure. Kara had many years of practice at keeping her face expressionless so showing no response to seeing the lines was second nature to her.

Kara nodded at Cassandra but walked back to the first bookcase she had investigated and pulled a book from the shelf. When she turned to face her observers the lines were not visible. Kara wondered if they were like the tv in the hospital, only visible when directly facing them. Kara walked toward the doorway careful to avoid the three lines. There were so many strange things in this land but she had the feeling that it was these three glowing lines that her captors wanted her to report to them. Kara decided that she was not going to assist them in that.

"Now go back to the bookcase with the horse," Sean Matthews said eagerly.

Kara turned. If she walked directly to the horse she would walk right through the glowing line to the right. Kara stepped back one step, moving slightly to the left, hesitating as she slowly scanned the bookshelf to find the horse. Kara walked back to the shelf with the horse, her shoulder only a foot from one of the lines, and turned. "Is it the horse or a book you wish me to see?" Kara asked.

"It must be the other one," Steven said. "Come, send the child to bed." Steven looked very disappointed. "The other one does us no good while she has her leg in traction. Jensen gone. We'll have to ask for help." He sighed. "It will cost us."

"Wait," Amie said. He glared at Kara. "Do you see the zipper?"

"Zipper?" Kara asked. She had no idea what a zipper was and did not bother to hide her confusion.

Amie swore and abruptly left the room. Cassandra clicked her nails more rapidly, staring at the floor in deep thought. Whatever she was thinking was not pleasant as she frowned, shook her head, and frowned some more. Kara walked along the bookcase, studying the various objects sharing the shelves with the books on her way to the door. Many of the objects glowed slightly. What a strange land this was. All Kara wanted at that point was to return home but she had to find Elyse first. And food. These people did not seem to realize that she needed to eat.

"Are you able to take me home?" Kara asked Cassandra.

Cassandra looked up, blinking as she cleared her thoughts. She sighed. "Not now, dear. It really isn't a priority."

"Priority? Perhaps not to you but it is to me," Kara said.

"I suppose it is at that," Cassandra said. She took Kara's arm and led the way back to the bedroom assigned to Kara. "But it will have to wait, dear."

"Am I to be fed while in your captivity?" Kara asked.

Cassandra grimaced. "Captivity sounds so, well, harsh, dear," she said. Cassandra stopped in her tracks. "Oh my, you must be hungry. Let's get you some food." Cassandra led Kara through the room with the sofas into an area with stools at a counter. "Sit. I will make you one of the things I do know how to cook. Grilled cheese sandwich."

Kara sat on the stool Cassandra led her to then watched
Cassandra prepare to make the sandwich. Cassandra repeatedly
opened a door of a white cabinet to pull out food. There was a light
in the cabinet. Cassandra's back was to Kara as she worked. Kara
watched everything but also gave thought to what had been
happening to her and around her. The room with the vertical lines
and glowing objects was a mystery Kara felt would be important to
learn more about but she felt it would be in her best interest to not
allow these people to know that she found these things interesting.

"Why did Jensen bring us here?" Kara asked.

"I think the less you know the better, dear," Cassandra said as
she spread butter on slices of bread.

"I already know that Jensen brought Elyse and me through a
bright light into this strange land."

"A zipper," Cassandra said without thinking. She paused and
looked over her shoulder at Kara. "The beam of light is a zipper."
Cassandra turned back to making the sandwiches. "Yes, I guess you
do know, since you came through a zipper. It's about money, of
course. It's always about money, dear."

Kara did not understand how Jensen hoped to gain money by
bringing them to this land. She looked around her. The place felt
very rich and luxurious. Kara was more interested in learning about
these doorways they called zippers. If she could see the glowing
lines in the room perhaps she could see the one in the park where

they had entered this land. Seeing it was one thing though, opening it was the critical information that she needed.

"A zipper is what Master Letvos wished me to see? There was no beam of light in that room," Kara said. "Did you see a beam of light?"

Cassandra shook her head. "The zipper does not glow until it's been opened."

"Is there a zipper in that room or were you hoping I would find one for you?" Kara asked.

"There is one in there and we were hoping you could find it, yes," Cassandra said.

"If there is one in there, then you can open it so I can go home?" Kara asked.

"I can't, dear," Cassandra said. "Only special people can open a zipper. Or a key. And it does not work that way. Different zippers lead to different dimensions. The zipper in that room won't take you home even if I could open it."

"And you thought I was one of those special people?" Kara asked, genuinely surprised. "Why?"

Cassandra opened the white cabinet door again. This time Kara saw the light turned on when she opened the door. "Because Jensen said he found someone with the talent. He came back, all excited because he had found someone with the talent, a woman, he said. Then he went back in to collect her. We thought it was you. He did not tell us he was bringing two and he never said a name. It must be your friend, dear. You still have to stay, of course."

"But I had never even heard of these zippers before he brought us through," Kara said. Something Cassandra had said tickled her ear. "You said people or a key. What is a key?"

"There are some objects which can open the zippers," Cassandra said. "The zipper in the room can be opened with a key, a carved piece of soapstone. But it leads to a dimension much like here. We need to go to the dimension where--"

"What are you doing?" Amie asked, coming up behind them, interrupting Cassandra.

"Making the girl something to eat," Cassandra said. "Do you want a grilled cheese sandwich, Amie?"

"What are you telling her? Are you out of your mind?" Amie asked, voice rising.

Cassandra dropped the sandwiches onto a griddle pan. The buttered bread sizzled on the hot pan. "Speak up or you go without."

"Forget the damned sandwich," Amie snapped. "Keep your mouth shut about the zippers."

"Yeah, it's like she did not know anything already after tonight," Cassandra said. "It does not hurt anything to talk about it."

"Are you out of your mind?" Amie yelled. "Telling her what we're doing?"

"I was not telling her what we were doing," Cassandra said but her cheeks flushed slightly as she realized she had gotten a little more detailed than she realized.

"The less she knows the better," Amie said. "We can't have her going around talking about zippers."

"Then Jensen should not have brought her through one," Cassandra said.

Amie glared at Cassandra then stalked away without further argument. Kara did not realize she had been holding her breath until she let it out in one big whoosh when the angry man retreated. "You are not afraid of him."

Cassandra turned in surprise. "Of course not. Why would I be afraid of him?"

"He seems very angry. It felt like he wanted to hit you," Kara said.

"Oh, he yells a lot but he's not a hitter. Besides, if he hit me I'd have his rear end in jail before you can say jacknapes," Cassandra said. She turned to look at Kara. "Oh, I'm sorry, dear. I forgot about your situation. With things that bad back home why do you even want to go back? I've heard it's quite primitive in that dimension. An abusive uncle, forced into marriage to breed in a land where women commonly die in childbirth, and treated like property. You would be much better off staying here."

"Staying here?" Kara asked in alarm. "No, I can't stay here." Kara was caught off guard that Cassandra knew so much about her and was wrong about half of it. "Murdock, uh, Jensen that is, said I could go home after I met his colleagues."

"Did he, dear? It must be the other one then. Or he lied. The man does tend to lie, dear. Maybe you'll change your mind after some time enjoying the modern conveniences, dear," Cassandra said. "Indoor plumbing, modern medicine, electric heat, public transportation, clean water. Um, I'm trying to remember my history. What else do you have to live with?"

Kara frowned. Stay here? Cassandra seemed to think that this place was so much better than her land but it was not. It was not at all. As Cassandra chatted merrily about the greatness of her land compared to the horrible, unhealthy, life could not be worth living land Kara came from, Kara drifted into thoughts about the room with the zipper. The three lines must be zippers, three zippers not one zipper.

Cassandra set a plate in front of Kara. Two pieces of burnt bread with cheese and ham between the bread sat on the plate, as well as three pieces of raw carrot. Kara picked up a carrot and bit into it, gaze on the black and brown grilled cheese sandwich, feeling a bit dubious about whether it was truly edible. Cassandra picked up the sandwich and scraped the bread with a knife, knocking off a small pile of burnt crumbs and leaving the bread more brown than black. Kara's stomach rumbled. Cassandra put another plate on the counter with another blackened grilled cheese sandwich, scraped that one to remove most of the burnt bread, and took a bite, eyes closing in enjoyment. Kara picked up the sandwich and took a bite. It was edible.

"What book did you take?" Cassandra asked.

Kara swallowed the food in her mouth. "It is called *The Black Stallion.*"

"I saw those movies when I was a kid," Cassandra said. Cassandra reached over the counter and slid the book across the table so that she could look at it as she ate.

"Movies?" Kara asked.

"Yes, it is popular to take a book and turn it into a movie," Cassandra said, gaze still on the book. "Movies are like plays but recorded so you can watch them over and over again if you want. Huh, I did not know it was a book first."

"Will it be a problem if I visit the book room for more books?" Kara asked.

Cassandra shrugged. "No problem. You'll need to do something while you're here." Cassandra pushed the book back towards Kara. "You like horses, eh?"

"Horses are my life," Kara said. She took another bite of the sandwich and another bite and it was quickly devoured, despite the bread being burnt.

"Not many horses here in London," Cassandra said. "The racing stables, of course. Some riding schools, I guess."

"London?" Kara asked in surprise. They had brought her all the way to London while she slept? Cassandra looked up in surprise at

Kara's startled exclamation. "My London is filled with horses," Kara said. "I can't imagine a London without horses."

Cassandra picked up the two plates and set them in the sink. "I'll take care of these later. Now let's get you cleaned up and in bed. Tomorrow is going to come early."

Cassandra showed Kara the bathroom across the hall from her bedroom and how to use everything, including an explanation of the multiple soaps and shampoos. Kara jumped in alarm when she saw herself in the huge mirror on the wall above the sink. Then Cassandra showed Kara the closet in the bedroom, complete with clothes and under garments. Kara's dress was not in the closet. Cassandra explained that the hospital had tossed it but she averted her gaze when she said that. Cassandra held up a pair of pants. They were blue and of a heavy fabric. Jeans, Cassandra called them.

"Women wear pants?"

"Sure," Cassandra said. "Everyone wears jeans, dear. Try them on."

"How do you get them on?" Kara asked, puzzled.

"The zipper," Cassandra said, pulling a metal tab down, opening the front of the pants.

"The same as the beams of lights," Kara muttered.

"Well I suppose the zipper works like the doorway so they called them that," Cassandra said. "I don't know what they called them originally, now that I think about it. Zippers haven't been around that long, you know? I am guessing the other zippers have been around much longer. But they work the same, dear."

Kara stared at Cassandra, totally confused by what she had just said. "What?"

"Closed. Open. Closed. Open," Cassandra said, pulling the tab up and down to show her how the zipper worked. "Well, you can play with your clothes. I have to get some sleep."

Kara used the bathroom first. It took a while to unbraid her hair and comb out the snarls. Water poured out of a spigot on the wall and she could adjust the heat just by twisting a knob. The liquid Cassandra called shampoo lathered into a foamy mass on her head. Kara took several deep breaths. The shampoo smelled so good. Kara used almost every cleansing product on the shelves. The product called conditioner did not make sense but when she finished with the shower and started the tedious task of combing out her hair she fell in love with conditioner. The comb moved smoothly through her long hair. If anything could tempt her to stay in this land it was hair conditioner.

Kara was not tired. She had been sleeping for days. Kara played with the light switch near the door to her assigned bedroom for several minutes. Up and down, up and down and the light went off and on, off and on. There was a tv on the wall across from the bed and Kara turned it on with the remote. This remote was different than the remote in the hospital and she pressed several buttons before getting the tv to change from a woman cooking to two people sitting at a desk talking. Kara dropped the remote on the bed and went into the closet. The closet had its own light switch and Kara played with that a few times. The tv was loud enough to clearly hear in the closet. Someone was talking about expanding public transportation use.

Kara picked up the blue pants Cassandra had called jeans and played with the zipper for several minutes, trying to see how it worked. Little pieces of metal were pressed around a strip of fabric and when she pulled the tab one way the metal pieces snapped together and when she pulled the tab another way the metal pieces were forced apart. Kara nodded thoughtfully. It was quite simple actually. There were several dresses and pants in the closet and all the pants and some of the dresses had zippers. Kara tried on each of the dresses. She quickly learned that closing the zipper while wearing the dress was not as easy as when holding the dress.

Kara chose a brown polka dotted dress made of a soft, flowing fabric and sleeves made of a transparent brown fabric. The nightgown she had been wearing had a lower hemline than all the dresses in the closet. Kara swished as she walked out of the closet. Walking around barefoot was a strange luxury. She dug her toes into the thick rug covering the floor from wall to wall. Kara picked up the book from the table next to the bed and left the bedroom.

The house was dark now but a fireplace burned in the room with sofas, giving her enough light to find her way. Kara paused and stared at the fireplace. There was no wood. Steady flames danced behind glass. There was a pattern to the flames' movement. After a few minutes the pattern repeated. Kara shivered. Fake flames? She continued on to the room with the bookcases, feeling along the wall for the light switch. Light flooded the room. Kara shut the door and stepped further into the room, studying the strange glowing lines. Now that she could look directly at them she could see that there was black edging framing the glowing lilac light at an angle, just like the zipper teeth.

Kara walked past the zipper to the objects on the bookcase that she had noticed were glowing. The glow was not coming from the shelf. This light was not from an artificial source, like the ceiling or cabinet with food. The light coming from the various objects was a soft lilac just like the zippers and was originating from the object. Kara did not touch anything that glowed. She walked along the bookcase to the horse statue again. The horse did not glow. Kara ran her fingers along the sculpted mane. Kara wanted so much to go home.

The door slammed open and Amie stormed into the room. Steven was at his heels. Kara looked up in surprise, wiping the tears from her cheeks. "What are you doing in here?" Amie demanded.

The man was not wearing a shirt. Amie wore loose trousers that tied around his waist but no shirt. Steven wore similar trousers but also wore a matching top. Kara quickly averted her eyes. Amie strode across the room at her. Kara glanced up in alarm just as he walked right through the vertical lilac line. Kara backed away into the corner, trying not to look at his bare chest. Amie picked up the horse statue, raising it up to look at it. Kara thought he was going to strike her with it and instinctively raised her arms to block the blow.

"What are doing?" Cassandra yelled, tying her bathrobe shut as she hurried into the room.

"She came back," Amie yelled, waving the horse around. "She's mighty fascinated with this statue." He strode into the middle of the room, waving the horse out in front of him.

"Come here, dear," Cassandra said, wrapping her arm around Kara's shoulders. "Amie, you're an idiot! Can't you see that you've scared the shit out of her?"

Amie was getting frustrated when waving the horse statue around did not open any zipper. "You think she's so naïve. I know better. She knows something!"

Sean Matthews joined the group. He was not wearing a shirt either. Sean was not even wearing trousers, just short pants. He yawned repeatedly and rubbed his head. "What are you doing, Amie? That horse isn't a key. The soapstone lion and jet penguin are keys." Sean Matthews yawned again. He noticed Kara, then looked at Kara with wide eyes. "Holy crap! She cleans up nice."

Everyone suddenly noticed that Kara was dressed and groomed. Amie stopped waving the statue around like a wild man and stared at Kara. He looked deflated as he studied her. "Maybe that's all it was. Maybe Jensen just brought her, because, well, look at her."

"Quit talking about her like she isn't here," Cassandra snapped. "I told her that she could use the books in here."

"Why are you dressed?" Amie asked. He still held the horse statue, hugging it against his chest. "It's the middle of the night."

Kara stared at him but did not speak. Kara could still feel her heart beating crazily in her chest. Kara had been convinced that the man was going to beat her, using the statue as a weapon. All of Jensen's training had fled her head when Amie had picked up that statue and she thought he was going to strike her with it. Cassandra pulled away from her, looking at her thoughtfully. Kara stared at the woman in shock. Her face was no longer youthful looking. She looked like she had aged ten years since saying good-night. Maybe this was all a bad dream.

"She's barefoot, Amie. Go back to bed. All of you," Cassandra told the men. She turned to Kara. "Why don't you stay in your room the rest of the night, dear? If you can't sleep then watch tv or read your book."

Kara fell asleep in her new dress while watching the tv. She woke to Cassandra knocking on the bedroom door once before opening the door and walking in without waiting for a response. The first thing Kara noticed was that Cassandra's face once again looked youthful. The second thing that Kara noticed was that Cassandra was wearing jeans and a pink sweater. Kara was so shocked to see the woman wearing men's pants that she could not speak. Cassandra looked worried, her face stern as she studied Kara.

"Steven is making breakfast. We have to leave you here for a while today, dear," Cassandra said. "Behave so Amie does not threaten to lock you in your room. I don't think it's necessary, dear. Where would you go, right?" Cassandra asked. Cassandra waited for some response from Kara. Kara nodded, unable to bring herself to speak. "Right then. If you're hungry then let's get out there before they eat it all."

Before joining the others for breakfast Cassandra led Kara into the bathroom, explaining that she would make her face. Kara allowed Cassandra to rub lotions and dust powders over her face without protest. Kara was learning that when Cassandra was distracted with something she would talk a lot. Kara avoided looking directly at the jeans. The woman could just as well be naked as wear the form contoured pants.

"Did you put the zipper in the room?" Kara asked, eyes closed as Cassandra rubbed peach powder over her eyelids.

Cassandra laughed in delight at such a far-fetched idea. "No. It was here so Steven bought the house."

"How did you know it was here?" Kara asked.

"You would have to ask Steven, dear," Cassandra said. "Okay, open your eyes and take a look."

Kara opened her eyes and looked in surprise at her reflection in the huge bathroom mirror. She almost did not recognize herself. The powders and lotions Cassandra had applied had almost completely concealed her bruises. They did not hide the swelling but the swelling was not as noticeable now. Kara glanced at the bottles and containers Cassandra had used to change her appearance and realized why Cassandra's face looked smooth and even again that morning.

While they ate breakfast at a table between the kitchen and the room with the sofas Kara was all too aware of the appreciative stares from Steven and Sean. Amie glared at her but stared at her just as much as the other two men. The stares made Kara uncomfortable and she kept her head down, gaze on her plate of scrambled eggs and toast. This toast was not burnt, fortunately. Next to her plate was a shallow bowl of fruits. Kara recognized the strawberries but did not recognize the green pieces or the yellow pieces.

"Rick is going to meet us at the wheel," Steven said to Cassandra. He glanced at Kara. "We have to decide what to do with her while we're gone."

"I told you, she'll be fine here alone," Cassandra said to Steven. She turned to Kara. "You will stay in the house and wait patiently, will you not, dear?"

Kara looked up from her plate. She nodded. As Cassandra had said, she had nowhere else to go. Not yet anyway. Amie snorted in disbelief. "Right. And as soon as we are out the door she is on the phone with the police."

"She does not even know what a phone is," Sean said. He smiled at Kara. "You know that we are your chance to get home, don't you?"

"You will take me home?" Kara asked eagerly.

"See," Sean said with a grin for Amie. "She would not even know who to call. She does not know anyone here. Call the police? And tell them what? That she wants to go back to her fifteenth century dimension through a beam of light in a park in Greenestone?" He looked back at Kara. "As soon as we can, we will send you home."

Cassandra looked uncomfortable. "Well, we need to keep her here for now. Don't tell her that we'll send her home."

"I said *when* we can," Sean said.

Kara nodded. They treated her like a five year old. An invisible five year old. Kara had spent a lot of time the night before thinking about her options before falling asleep. The first thing she had to do was get back to Mannington to the hospital to find Elyse. Kara did not know yet how she would get Elyse to Greenestone with a broken leg but she would cross that bridge when she got to it. As Kara figured it, she had two options. First, she could wait, learn some more about this land, and give Elyse more time to heal. Or she could rush out blindly and try to find her way south without money or transportation. These people were treating her fairly and she felt that biding her time would be beneficial.

The longer Elyse could remain immobile the better. Kara knew that. If Kara escaped these people and found her way to Mannington before Elyse was ready to be on her feet they would just find her. Kara did not know what they would do if they found her. Kara could not decide if they were holding onto her just because they were too busy to take her back or if they still felt they had a use for her. Now that they believed that Kara could not open zippers they would be turning their attention to Elyse, Kara realized.

So what if either of them could open these zippers, Kara wondered. Why would they go to such extremes to abduct them? Kara finished her food on her plate and put the bowl of fruit on the empty plate. Kara picked out the strawberries first and ate them, then tentatively tried the green piece of fruit. It was good. Some type of melon. The yellow piece made her mouth pucker and it took all her resolve not to immediately spit it out. Cassandra and Sean laughed out loud. Kara looked up to see them looking at her and laughing. Even Steven cracked a smile.

"Your face, dear," Cassandra said, laughing more. "It's pineapple. I guess you don't like it?"

Kara spit the pineapple out onto her plate. How could anyone eat that tart stuff? Sean speared a piece of pineapple from his own bowl with a fork and grinned as he pushed the entire piece into his mouth. Cassandra glanced at her wrist and jumped to her feet. She picked up her plate and empty fruit bowl and set them in the sink. "Help yourself to anything in the kitchen if you get hungry, dear. There are frozen dinners in the freezer. Oh, I suppose you don't know what a microwave is." Cassandra gave Kara a quick overview of the appliances in the kitchen, waving her arm at each item while

Kara still sat at the dining room table. "There's always bread and sandwich meat and you can make yourself a sandwich, dear."

A few minutes of flurry and they were gone, leaving Kara sitting alone at the table. Kara was still hungry. They had only given her a small portion of food. Kara was used to eating much more. Normally Kara was very active and burned through food quickly. The white cabinet with the light inside should have food. Kara got up and walked to the cabinet and pulled on the handle. It was difficult to open but a good tug did the trick. Glass bottles in shelves in the door rattled.

A bowl with more fruit sat on a shelf. A thin, transparent film covered the bowl. It did not take Kara long to figure out how to remove the film. Kara stood at the door of the white cabinet and picked out all the fruit but the pineapple and ate it with her fingers. Cold air came from the cabinet. The transparent film had crumpled into a ball when Kara pulled it off the bowl so she tossed it into the bowl when she finished and set the bowl back on the shelf. A package said ham and Kara tore that open and smelled the perfectly shaped, thinly sliced pieces of ham. It smelled like ham, so she ate that as well, putting the packaging back on the shelf.

Next Kara explored the rest of the house. The bedroom next to hers clearly belonged to Cassandra as it was littered with feminine clothes and the closet was filled with dresses and high heeled shoes designed for a woman's sized foot. There was a staircase at the end of the hall and Kara climbed the steps. Climbing the steps reminded her that her body had been through a lot recently and she clutched her side by the time she reached the top. Three bedrooms and an office were upstairs.

The bedrooms of the men were both neat, orderly, and sparse. The only reason she knew that the men were using them was because of the clothes in the closet. The third bedroom was not being used. The office had a desk with another black rectangle like the tv but smaller and with an attached remote. At least Kara thought it was a remote since it had numbers like the tv remotes but it also had all the letters of the alphabet but in a strange arrangement. Kara touched one of the letters on the remote and the tv screen went from dark to showing a white box with lots of words and pictures that moved and changed. Kara pushed another letter but nothing else happened. She pushed a few more and the same image remained unchanging.

At the end of the hall was a staircase with a foyer at the bottom. The front door was in the foyer. Kara looked out the window next to the door. It was raining. Kara could see townhouses across the street and cars parked and driving past in the street between the townhouses and this house. Kara walked through the foyer and was at the room with sofas. She walked down the hall with the room with the zippers. Kara walked past that room to the next door, which she opened. It was another bathroom. She went to the next door. It was just a small room with a sink and two square appliances. One had a door in the front side and one had a door on the top. Kara went to the last door. The doorknob was locked. There was a gap between the bottom of the door and the floor. Kara lay down on the floor on her stomach and looked through the gap. It was a large empty room with a car sitting in it.

Kara returned to her bedroom and turned on the tv. This one worked when she pushed buttons on the remote control. Kara stood in the middle of the room and changed channels with the button she had learned just moved the tv from channel to channel. She would stay on one channel for a few minutes and then switch to another channel. When she saw the same type of tv as in the office upstairs she watched with interest. It was called a laptop.

Kara did not hear him approach. When Sean stuck his head in the bedroom doorway she jumped in surprise. He smiled and stepped into the room. "It's good to see that you are indeed behaving yourself."

"You are checking on me?" Kara asked in surprise. She had not expected that.

"Yeah, Cassandra was convinced that you would be a good girl but Amie does not trust anyone," Sean said, coming right up to her. He touched her hair. "I'll bet that looks amazing out of that braid."

Kara stepped back away from him. "Now that you are satisfied that I am behaving myself you may go."

"In a minute," Sean said, stepping closer to her. He chuckled when she backed away again. He held his arms out. "All right. We'll have time later to get to know each other better."

"I am married, sir," Kara said. Her heart was racing. Kara had not expected this either.

Sean chuckled again. "It's not like you'll ever see him again. I can't get over how well you clean up. What a knockout."

"I have no desire for your attention," Kara said. Kara straightened and faced him defiantly. "Your attentions are unwanted. If you try to touch me again I shall be forced to harm you."

"Oh, I can be charming," Sean said. "Give it time." A noise of strange music suddenly came from his clothes. Sean pulled a black rectangle out of his pocket and swiped his thumb across the top as he held it up to his ear. The music stopped. "Yes, you were right. Our little girl is in her bedroom behaving herself. I'll be right out."

"Later," Sean said, blowing her a kiss and grinning when she pulled away from the imaginary kiss.

Kara stood frozen for several minutes, heart pounding. The man had seemed so pleasant to her until that morning. If he came back would the others prevent him from forcing himself on her? Kara had no desire for his attention and did not know why he suddenly thought that she would. Never see her husband again. They had no plans on returning her to her home land. Sean had been so casual about her not ever seeing Hawkstead again. When her heart finally calmed down Kara walked to the bed on trembling legs and sat down.

The idea of never seeing Hawkstead again made her feel like there was a heavy weight in the pit of her stomach. Breathing was an effort. Kara took a deep breath then another. She missed him. She missed his gentle teasing. She missed his annoying habits. Kara missed his ready smile. Kara missed his hard body snuggled against her in bed at night. It seemed impossible considering their unconventional meeting and sudden marriage that was not really a marriage but the thought of never seeing him again was worse than never going home.

Kara raised her head and looked around the room. This land was definitely different than her land but from the tv she had learned that people were still the same people, just with different types of problems. It would be a land her uncle would enjoy though she did not. Too bad Kara could not send Lord Roffe here to get him out of her way. Kara chewed on her lower lip. An idea was forming and the idea shocked her. The idea grew and expanded. Kara glanced at the tv screen. A family was bickering over a silly situation and an invisible audience laughed at several moments when the argument was funny.

Kara jumped to her feet and went to the closet. A large canvas bag with shoulder straps caught her eye and she picked it up. Kara took two dresses off their hangers. Kara needed shoes. Kara slipped her bare feet into a pair of brown mules and hurried to the room containing the zippers. She ignored the zippers and walked along the shelves, picking up any item that glowed. Kara wrapped the knickknacks in the dresses to keep them from knocking against each other and put them in the bag. The bag became heavy but everything fit inside. Kara also took a small globe made of various gemstones to represent each country and gilded in gold though it did not glow. Kara stopped in the bathroom and collected all the bottles of conditioner and stuffed those in the bag as well.

The front door was locked. Kara studied the doorknob, peering through the gap between the door and doorframe. She could see the bolts holding the door to the doorframe had corresponding knobs on the door. Kara reached for the first knob then hesitated. They might still be watching the house. Kara hurried back to the hall with the locked door leading to the room with the car. It only took a few minutes to figure out how to unlock the door and open it. The room with the car was cold and barren but it had a door at the back. Kara opened the back door and peered outside. The door opened to a walled garden, small to her eyes.

Kara stepped outside, shutting the door behind her. It did not take long to scale the stone wall even with her shoes in her hand. Kara was tempted to jump from the wall's top but her body still ached from all her recent injuries and she did not want to jar anything so she turned and slowly, slowly climbed down the other side. Kara walked away from the wall with a few minor scrapes but otherwise intact.

Chapter Eleven

Hawkstead felt frustrated as he walked into Elyse's hospital room. He had been in this land for days without being any closer to finding Kara and he was about ready to strike out on his own rather than listening to his companions. Hawkstead had promised Julia they could have two more days and if they came up with nothing new in that time he was going to tear every inch apart from here to London looking for his wife. Julia put a lot of faith in their technology, insisting that they were researching possibilities, yet Hawkstead had the feeling that they did not know any more now than they did when he first arrived in this land.

Elyse smiled when she saw him enter the room. Hawkstead looked quite striking in the clothes Julia had dressed him in to help him blend in this land. That morning they had put what they called a walking cast on Elyse's leg and had helped her walk up and down the hall to get used to it and get her muscles working after several days in bed. "They said I can be released tomorrow," she said in greeting. "They keep asking about insurance. What does that mean?"

"I don't know," Hawkstead said. "Tomorrow? That is good news."

"The doctor assured me that the leg will heal as good as new. I just need to leave the cast on for a few weeks," Elyse said. She studied Hawkstead's dour face as she talked, realizing that he was in a sour mood. "No word on Kara?"

Hawkstead shook his head. "London is much bigger here." He removed his jacket and draped it over the chair next to Elyse's bed before sitting. "Is there anything Murdock could have said that would give a clue?"

Elyse shook her head, wracking her brain for any clues. Elyse did not want to admit to Hawkstead that she had been so caught up in being romanced by the man that she had not paid attention to those details or dug any deeper into his life away from the keep. After being ignored as a woman for so many years it had gone to her head that this strong, attractive man seemed to desire her. Now Elyse could see that she had put up blinders but while going through it she had not cared who he was or what he did or where he came from. All that mattered was how good he made her feel about herself.

"She would not have left me," Elyse said. "I know that girl and she just would not have left without a word. Those friends the nurse talked about weren't friends. If she can, this is where she will come," Elyse said.

"I know," Hawkstead said.

They both settled into their own thoughts. Hawkstead looked over at the door when a tall, blonde woman knocked on the open door and stepped in at the same time. A man with a shaved head followed her into the room. The woman's attention was on Elyse. Hawkstead studied the man thoughtfully and decided that he matched the description the nurse had given as one of the men who had visited Kara. Hawkstead resisted the urge to jump out of his chair and shake the truth out of the man. Instead he pulled the cell phone Julia had given him a few days ago and pushed the buttons that dialed Julia.

"Hello there," the blonde woman said to Elyse, glancing at Hawkstead. She gave Hawkstead a second look. "And hello to you, too. Oh, sorry, did not see you were on the phone."

"Yes, it's good for a visit," Hawkstead said into the phone.

"They are there?" Julia asked.

"Possibly," Hawkstead said. The woman was talking to Elyse, introducing herself as Cassandra. Hawkstead listened with half an ear. "When the description fits then wear it."

"What? Oh, are they right there? Keep them there," Julia said. "It will be almost half an hour before someone can get there."

"You?" Hawkstead asked.

"I am so sorry to hear about your fiancé, Lady Addington," Cassandra said to Elyse.

"It was not an official betrothal," Elyse said, eyeing Cassandra dubiously.

"No. No I'm farther out," Julia said. "Um, are they there to see Elyse?"

"Oh, but he said you had agreed to marry him," Cassandra said.

"Yes," Hawkstead said.

"I agreed to consider it," Elyse said.

"Let's see what they will tell her," Julia said. "Leave the phone on and put it somewhere then leave the room."

"That's almost the same thing, isn't it?" Cassandra said with a smile. She glanced at Hawkstead again, gaze roaming from his head, down his broad shoulders, to his long legs.

"That sounds complicated," Hawkstead said. "I have a better idea. Bye."

Hawkstead slid the phone into his jacket hanging on the back of his chair. Seeing Hawkstead off the phone Cassandra immediately turned her attention to him. "And who might you be?"

"I am more curious who you are," Hawkstead said lightly.

Cassandra smiled, blatantly scanning him with her eyes and biting down on her lower lip suggestively. "I am Cassandra."

"Cassandra. I think you should call me Apollo," Hawkstead said.

Cassandra laughed in delight. "But Apollo was not at all kind to Cassandra."

"How can you say that?" Hawkstead asked. He tilted his head slightly and smiled. Elyse stared at him with wide eyes. "Because of Apollo Cassandra gained prophesy. Can you read the future now, Cassandra?"

"I saw a tall, dark, and handsome man in my future," Cassandra said. Behind them Sean coughed. Cassandra's smile twitched. "But first I must console my dear friend, Lady Ashton."

"I will give you privacy," Hawkstead said, standing.

"Wait," Elyse pleaded.

"I will be down the hall," Hawkstead said heading for the door.

"Wait," Cassandra said. "How do you know Lady Ashton?"

"Jensen worked for me," Hawkstead said over his shoulder.

"Indeed," Cassandra muttered, frowning. She looked up at Sean. Sean shrugged but looked puzzled. Cassandra turned back to Elyse. "It must be a great shock to arrive here and so quickly be involved in a car accident and lose your loved one."

"It has been a rough few days," Elyse said in agreement. "How do you know, um, Jensen?"

"We worked together. He helped us, well, with travel," Cassandra said.

Hawkstead lingered near the door, eavesdropping without any guilt. These people would know where Kara was. These people were responsible for her being smuggled out of the hospital. Hawkstead took a deep breath and stretched his fingers, resisting the urge to beat the information out of the man standing just inside Elyse's hospital room.

"Lady Ashton, may I call you Elyse?" Cassandra asked.

"You may call me Lady Ashton," Elyse said.

Cassandra chuckled. "Jensen did say that you were quite proper. He also said that he hoped you would be able to help us here. That is why he brought you to this land."

"Help you? How?" Elyse asked.

"Did he not talk about any special talent you might have?" Sean asked.

"No. He wished to bring me to his home so he could see that he was more than a stable hand," Elyse said. "I could not marry a stable hand, you see." Elyse looked uncomfortable that she had just confessed that marriage had been discussed. She wished to put the whole sordid business behind her.

"Why did he bring Kara?" Sean asked.

Hawkstead held his breath and counted to ten as he slowly let it out again. Whoever Julia was sending better arrive soon or he would not be able to hold back from getting the information from these people himself.

"Kara. You mean Lady Hawkstead, my cousin," Elyse said. Her voice could chill a room.

"Yes, Lady Hawkstead," Cassandra said. "I can understand Jensen wanting to show you his home but why did he bring your cousin?"

"It would not be proper for me to travel with Jensen alone. I may be long in the tooth but I am still a single woman and my reputation is intact," Elyse said. "How do you know about my cousin?"

"Why Jensen told us, of course."

Hawkstead looked up. Kara was walking down the hall toward him. At first he thought he was dreaming. When Kara saw him she stopped in her tracks in surprise, shaking her head. Kara closed her eyes then opened them again. When Kara realized that Hawkstead was really standing in the hall outside Elyse's hospital room in this dimension and not a dream she took a deep breath and ran the rest of the distance. Hawkstead moved at the same time. Hawkstead wrapped his arms around her and lifted her in a bear hug. Kara barely grimaced at the pain in her ribs but he noticed and promptly set her down. Hawkstead continued to hold her in his arms but not squeezing her ribs.

"You're here. You're really here," Kara said, feeling his face with the palm of her hand. "I thought I was dreaming."

Hawkstead smiled. "I have never been so happy in my life to see someone as the moment I saw you just now."

"Elyse?"

Hawkstead jerked his head towards the door to Elyse's hospital room. "She has company."

"Company?"

"Cassandra and Sean," Hawkstead said.

Kara's eyes widened and she glanced around Hawkstead at the door. Kara stiffened in his arms. Hawkstead looked over his shoulder. Sean was standing in the doorway staring at them. Hawkstead did not think the man could see Kara clearly enough to know who he was holding as his body completely blocked the view of her. Kara stepped back, pulling out of Hawkstead's arms and faced Sean. Sean stared at her in disbelief.

"How did you get here?" Sean asked.

"Public transportation," Kara said.

Cassandra stepped out of the room to see what was going on and forced a smile when she saw Kara. "Kara, dear, you were supposed to stay at home." Cassandra looked at Hawkstead standing protectively at Kara's side. "You know each other."

"My husband, Lord Hawkstead," Kara said.

Cassandra frowned. Sean turned a pale shade of gray, glancing between Kara and Hawkstead. Kara tilted her head thoughtfully, considering whether to remind Sean of his rude behavior earlier. Sean did not care to risk the chance of her calling him to count for his advances and took off down the hall without waiting, almost running. Cassandra watched Sean in surprise. Cassandra was left alone to face what was coming. She did not like not having Sean at her back but tried to make the best of the situation. Cassandra had been in worse situations and come out whole.

"We were just helping you, dear," Cassandra said.

"No you weren't," Kara said. "If you leave now I won't press charges for kidnapping me from the hospital."

"It was not kidnapping," Cassandra said. She tapped her fingernails together. "My how quickly you adapt. Jensen said that your land was a medieval timeframe. How in the world did you get from London to here without any help?"

"Why do you think I have no brain in my head? I have visited London many times. Horse or train or boat or bus, all that matters is money in the pocket."

"Where did you get money here?" Cassandra asked. Music came from Cassandra's bag on her shoulder.

"Pawn shop," Kara said.

Cassandra answered the phone, listening to someone yelling so loudly that she had to hold the phone a few inches from her ear. Cassandra stared at Kara as she listened. Though Kara could not hear the words clearly the voice belonged to Amie. Kara smiled. They had obviously discovered that she had taken items from the zipper room. Cassandra's face hardened and she glared at Kara as she listened. When Amie finished his tirade Cassandra simply said that Kara was there and hung up the phone.

"Give them back," Cassandra said in an icy voice.

"Find them," Kara said with a shrug.

"You little bitch," Cassandra said, stepping closer. Hawkstead immediately stepped between them. Cassandra looked up. "You don't scare me."

"You should be scared," Hawkstead said in a low voice.

Cassandra stepped back. "You don't know what you've done."

"I have an idea," Kara said. "Some of those trinkets opened those zippers in that room, right? Now you'll have to go on a scavenger hunt to find them."

"Tickets. They would have given you tickets, some type of receipt," Cassandra said. Rage was replaced by panic. "You can at least give me the tickets to redeem them." Kara just shrugged. Cassandra grew angry again. "I was kind to you. How can you do this to me?"

"Please hold the noise down," a white uniformed nurse said, coming down the hall.

Behind the nurse were Mike and Frank walking toward them. Cassandra literally growled when she saw the two men and walked down the hall in the other direction. Kara watched the two men approaching them with uncertainty but Hawkstead looked at them without concern so she relaxed. Hawkstead nodded at the two men in greeting. Having successfully resolved the noise issue the nurse went back to her station.

"That was her?" Frank asked.

Hawkstead nodded. Frank and Mike exchanged glances and continued walking in the direction Cassandra had taken, pace increasing to a trot. Hawkstead guided Kara into Elyse's room. The two women embraced. Hawkstead waited by the door while his wife and her cousin greeted each other. Now all he had to do was get them home. Hawkstead remembered the phone and walked to the chair. He pulled the phone out of his jacket pocket and put it up to his ear.

"Julia?"

"Hawkstead, what's going on?" Julia asked.

"My wife is here. We're ready to go home," Hawkstead said.

"Mike and Frank will take you to Greenestone," Julia said. "I won't get there until later tonight. Hawkstead?"

"Yes," Hawkstead said, staring at Kara.

"I'm glad you found her," Julia said.

"Me too," Hawkstead said. "Me too."

Hawkstead hung up the phone. Mike and Frank returned. Hawkstead introduced them to Kara as colleagues of Julia and Cho. Both men stared at Kara in appreciation. Hawkstead glared. Kara did not even notice. Kara went to the closet and found her own clothes but instead of changing into her own clothes she stuffed the dress into her shoulder bag. Kara picked up her boots and hugged them against her chest before she kicked off the shoes she was wearing and pulled on the boots. Kara stuffed the shoes in the bag. The bag bulged now and the zipper would no longer close.

"We'll take you to Greenestone in the morning," Frank said.

"No, it has to be now," Kara said.

"Lady Ashton won't be released from the hospital until tomorrow," Frank said. "We'll put you up in a hotel room and keep an eye on you until we get you home. You need Julia to open the zipper also."

"Okay," Hawkstead said. He had a strong desire to spend some time alone with Kara. "Let's do that now."

"But they're going to come after me," Kara whispered into Hawkstead's ear. "I sort of, uh, sabotaged their plans."

"Let's talk later," Hawkstead said.

Once they were alone in the hotel room Hawkstead pulled Kara to him and embraced her. Kara wrapped her arms around her neck and stood on her tiptoes to reach his face. They kissed hungrily, the stress and worry of the past few days transferred to animal passion that chased away all thoughts but the moment. The moment was about feeling alive in each other's arms. The moment was about becoming husband and wife in more than name. The moment was about committing to a life together as one.

It was almost dawn when Kara wrapped a sheet around her bare body, picked up her bag from the floor and set it on her lap. Hawkstead lay on his side next to her on the bed, head resting on his palm as he watched her. Hawkstead did not bother covering up his naked self. Kara held the sheet over her chest with her left arm and with her right hand upended the bag over the bed. A variety of objects fell out of the purse. Kara picked up a jet penguin and held it up for Hawkstead to see.

"It glows," Kara said. "I took everything they have that glowed."

Hawkstead took the piece of jet between his long fingers and studied it thoughtfully. "You lied to that woman then?"

"Well, I took something of value that did not glow and pawned it in a shop that gave me money for it. It was enough to get me here. I did not tell her that I pawned everything," Kara said.

Hawkstead grinned. "You made her think you did."

"I can't be blamed for her assumption," Kara said.

"I appreciate that you are sharing this with me but I don't know what it means," Hawkstead said.

"The beam of light that brought us here, the zipper. Remember last night when I told you that only special people can open them or they have to use keys to open them? I think they glow because they are keys."

"I was not really paying attention," Hawkstead said. "My mind was on other things."

Kara grinned. "Yes, you distracted me as well." Kara leaned over and kissed Hawkstead's cheek. "Thank you."

"For distracting you?" Hawkstead asked. "I am happy to distract you again now."

"For being here," Kara said. "I can't believe you came here for me."

"I did not manage to do anything but sit at that hospital waiting," Hawkstead grumbled. "And why would you think I wouldn't come after you?"

"Your being here is everything," Kara said.

"Did they tell you why they brought you here?" Hawkstead asked, shifting slightly, feeling uncomfortable with Kara's praise for something he saw as nothing.

"I think they thought that if I could open the zipper doorways that they would force me to do things for them. They did not even know that I could see glowing keys. I hope that they think I just grabbed whatever I could get my hands on." Kara stared off into the distance thoughtfully. "I don't think it occurred to them to test me on the keys, yet the one man tried to use the horse statue to open the zipper that he couldn't even see."

"You can see glowing keys to open zippers that you can see and no one but the two of us knows it?" Hawkstead asked.

Kara nodded her head. "They did not know about all of them. At least I don't think that they knew. Sean Matthews named two items as keys," Kara said. "And they only knew about one zipper in the room and I saw three zippers." Kara shrugged as she stared off into the distance again. "Unless they were just doing that to test me."

Hawkstead looked up at Kara over the piece of carved jet. "What are you saying?"

"Jensen brought me here because he thought I could open the doorways they call zippers. I can see them. I don't know if I can open them but I can see them. And I can see these things glowing and two of the things Sean Matthews said were keys to open the zipper glowed so I figure all the glowing ones are keys. So I took them all."

"I don't know what to think of that," Hawkstead said. He frowned. "What does that mean for us? Julia opens zippers for her government and look at the danger that put her in. I do not mind you managing a horse breeding program but I have no desire to have a wife who travels between dimensions willy nilly."

Kara stared at Hawkstead. For a moment Hawkstead thought that he had just said something wrong. Hawkstead did a quick mental review of his words to figure out what he had said that held her frozen in thought but instead of getting angry with him Kara bent over and kissed his cheek. "You are the best husband a girl could ever hope for," she said. "I prefer my horses. I have no desire to visit other dimensions."

Hawkstead let out his breath in long whoosh. "That's good."

"At least now. I don't even know if I can open them like Julia does or if these keys can ever be matched to their zippers. I like that I can see the zippers. At least we can find them and mark them so these people don't show up again." Kara took a deep breath. "But more than that, I want to bring people to our land."

"Who do you want to bring there?" Hawkstead asked, sitting up.

"Doctors and dentists," Kara said.

"You want to kidnap doctors and dentists?" Hawkstead asked in alarm.

"I never said kidnap," Kara said, taken aback. "Cassandra said something. She said people will do anything for money. I think that if we offer them enough money they will come."

"Doctors and dentists, eh?" Hawkstead said. He stared at Kara thoughtfully. "That is the most brilliant thing I have ever heard. But it might still amount to kidnapping people. Or you won't get people to leave their homes to get stranded in some strange land."

"I was thinking that my uncle could come here and stay here and recruit people," Kara said.

Hawkstead took a long time to respond to that statement. "Lord Roffe? You trust him to do that?"

"It would make him feel important. He needs to feel important," Kara said. She looked up at Hawkstead. "And he would be here."

"I am married to a very devious woman," Hawkstead said after letting the full impact of that statement sink in. He did not know whether to be impressed or nervous about that idea. "We don't know that he would come here."

"He will," Kara said. She started shoving all the trinkets back into the bag.

"What are you going to do with those?" Hawkstead asked, handing Kara the piece of jet that she had given him to look at.

Kara shrugged. "Maybe one will open the zipper in the apple orchard. Maybe they will open other zippers I might see. Mostly, I wanted to keep them away from those people."

Hawkstead nodded and laid back. He stared up at the ceiling. Those people would be very angry with her for taking those items. "Which two did they know about?"

Kara dug around in the bag until she found the two keys Sean had mentioned. Hawkstead took them and set them on the nightstand next to the bed. "What are you going to do with them?" Kara asked.

"I will hold them for now." Hawkstead looked at Kara thoughtfully. "I've had time to adjust to the idea of zippers leading to different dimensions but now I will need to adjust to the idea that you can use those zippers as well. How did Jensen know?"

"Maybe I glow, like these," Kara said, shaking the bag slightly. She leaned over Hawkstead. "Do I glow?"

"Let's see," Hawkstead said. He pulled away the sheet covering her, staring at her bare form with open admiration. "I can't believe you let me believe you had a previous lover."

"You came up with that all on your own," Kara said, reaching for the sheet to cover herself again, suddenly feeling uncomfortable. Hawkstead stopped her from covering herself, pulling the sheet out of her hands.

"I am sorry," he said. "I was an ass."

Kara smiled. "Yes, you were."

"Now that I know how devious you are I will be more careful to ask specific questions," Hawkstead said.

"Or maybe just don't assume the worse?" Kara said, pulling back.

"That too," Hawkstead agreed.

Both were showered and dressed when Mike and Frank knocked at the door of their hotel room. Hawkstead was eager to get home and he could tell that Kara was also. They went directly to the hospital to collect Elyse. Julia and Cho were already there. Elyse hadn't been released yet. Before the hospital would release Elyse they needed insurance information. When Julia explained that they did not have insurance there was some concern about the bill being paid. Kara assured them that they would pay the bill once they knew what it was but the hospital staff could not confirm the address.

Kara wrote an address on the form the administrator held. She pointed to Julia. "She will return later today with payment. Just tell us what the amount is."

The woman looked at the address and her eyebrows rose. "I will get the bill ready as soon as possible."

"What did you put there?" Julia asked in a low voice.

"The address where I was staying in London," Kara said. "I hope you don't mind returning but we don't have money with us."

"It's on the way back," Julia said.

"I have it," Elyse said. "I always carry a few hundred pounds in my skirt."

"Maybe they will be happier with a down payment," Julia said. "I am afraid the bill will be thousands of pounds, not hundreds."

Elyse gestured for the men to turn their backs and lifted her skirt to get to the money sewed into a hidden pocket. Elyse placed a handful of gold coins into Julia's outstretched palms. Julia stared at the pile of gold in shock.

Hawkstead suddenly remembered that he had been collecting rents when Kara was abducted. "I don't know if this is enough but I do have money also." He pulled his coin purse from inside his shirt and placed it in Julia's outstretched hand. To Elyse he said, "I will pay you back when we return."

Elyse looked surprised that he had to say it out loud. "Of course."

"Uh, this is gold," Julia said. "This is gold."

"Yes," Elyse said, puzzled by Julia's reaction. "Money is gold or silver."

"This is thousands of English pounds, not hundreds," Julia said.

"No, see the faces of the coins," Elyse said, pointing at the printed value.

"Gold is incredibly valuable right now," Julia said. "It is worth far more than the face value." She looked up at Hawkstead. "That is what they are doing. They are bringing gold back. Probably other precious metals." Julia pulled out her phone. "What was that address you gave?" Kara repeated the address and Julia typed it into her phone. "Yeah, that's one expensive area of town. They won't give it up easily. They'll go back for more."

"Jensen insisted he did not shoot you," Elyse said. Everyone looked at Elyse in surprise at the unexpected change in topic. "He was upset that you thought he would hurt you."

"He killed two of my men," Hawkstead said.

"But he does not hurt women," Julia said. She looked up from the phone and stared at Elyse. "That means someone on your side was working with them."

"You think they've been visiting our land?" Kara asked.

"He was confident when going to the zipper," Julia said, remembering. "He must have made the trip several times already." Julia handed the pile of coins to Frank. "Can you go pay the hospital bill?"

"With gold?" he asked in alarm.

"Figure it out. Find some broker and do the exchange first. Wait. Yes, just pay them in gold. Say your name is Sean Matthews and confirm the address Lady Hawkstead gave. That should get some attention from the English equivalent of the IRS," Julia said. She looked over at Cho. "Whoever it is might be waiting for them to return."

Cho nodded. He sighed. "I understand."

"I don't understand," Kara said.

"Cho will go through first to test the waters," Julia said. "Let's get going. Mike, you wait for Frank and follow us. We need two cars anyway."

Hawkstead held Kara's hand as they left the hospital. A nurse pushed Elyse in a wheeled chair. Elyse had dark bags under her eyes and a few times she could be seen drifting off into sad thoughts but overall was happy to be leaving the hospital and going home. Hawkstead stared at Elyse thoughtfully, seeing her differently now than he had before knowing that she had developed a relationship with Jensen. The woman was young enough to marry yet. Perhaps he should consider convincing Richard to take her for a wife. That way she could still be around Kara but have a life of her own. Elyse had remained unmarried too long.

Chapter Twelve

The drive to Greenestone Park did not take very long. It was a quiet ride as all of them had their private lines of thought to muse over from the past few days. Hawkstead touched the pouch hanging around his neck containing the odd ring that Mrs. Smith had given him. He had taken it just to appease the elderly woman when he was in a hurry. Now Hawkstead wondered how Mrs. Smith happened to have a key to a zipper and how she knew that it was a key. Hawkstead opened the pouch and pulled out the ring to look at it, watching Kara's reaction when she saw the ring. Kara's eyes widened and she looked from the ring to his eyes. Hawkstead nodded once ever so slightly and put the key away again. Kara clearly burned to ask him about the ring but she kept her tongue still. Julia watched them but showed no interest in what they were doing.

Hawkstead just remembered something Julia had said when he first met her. "Mrs. Roberts, you said that you came to south England to find relatives named Greene. Will you still look for them?"

"I don't think I'll have time now," Julia said.

"Our housekeeper is a Greene," Kara said. She frowned. "Does that mean you are related to Mrs. Smith?"

"Mrs. Smith is a Greene?" Julia asked in interest. She shook her head. "No, I don't think it works that way. There were so many drastic changes in your land that I don't think a genealogical line would remain intact."

"But there are the same people in lands that are in similar time lines?" Kara asked.

"No one has been able to answer that question yet," Julia said. "So far no one who is a purple halo has encountered their self in another dimension. Or anyone they know. That I know of anyway." Julia looked over at Kara and Hawkstead thoughtfully, as well as she could be scrunched in the back seat together. Elyse was in the front seat so that she had more room for her leg in its cast. "I think that it was a mistake for Jensen's people to underestimate you."

"Why do you say that?" Hawkstead asked.

"Well, we get a bit swollen headed about our knowledge and importance because of the technology that we use. It can be easy to think that people that don't have the world's knowledge at their fingertips are not so bright," Julia said.

"You have the world's knowledge at your fingertips?" Kara asked in interest.

"The internet," Julia said.

"What does it say about the zippers?" Kara asked in interest.

Julia wrinkled her nose. "The zippers won't be in there."

"So not everything is in there," Kara said.

Hawkstead looked out the window as the two women talked. Though he had thought to return to life as normal and forget all about the trip through the zipper he was realizing that Kara's plan was a good idea. Though his education on the Golden Age was minimal he knew that the reason they had slipped back into a simpler lifestyle was because of losing so many people. With the loss of all those people a lot of knowledge was lost as well. Though he had no desire to bring this land's way of living to their land, the thought of skilled doctors interested him greatly. Julia was not even a doctor and she had known more about medicine than their resident doctor, Father Tom.

So many women died in childbirth. So many children died before the age of two. Even if they were only able to acquire a doctor able to safely deliver babies they would already be gaining a major advantage. There were also workers who suffered a simple cut and infection took either their limb or too often their life. His squire could have been saved.

Hawkstead imagined going back through the zipper and trying to find a doctor willing to return. If the doctor was competent he or she would laugh at the idea of traveling through a beam of light to live in a land so different from this one. He remembered how he felt when Julia told him that she had arrived on his estate through a zipper from another dimension.

Hawkstead hoped that Kara was not serious about setting her uncle to the task of recruiting doctors. The more he considered the idea the more he felt Lord Roffe was the last man he would want in charge of such a task. Convincing Kara to let go of that idea might be the first obstacle they faced but it would not be the last. If they continuously made trips through the zipper someone was bound to notice and that would create more problems. Most of his enthusiasm for the idea of using the zipper as Kara suggested quickly faded into worry about using the zipper at all.

Hawkstead stared out the window as they drove along the busy highway with similar vehicles sharing the road at equally high speeds but he wasn't seeing the scenery, he was remembering a bright-eyed boy who died too young because of a simple scratch on his leg that went unnoticed. They would indeed make trips through the zipper to this land at least a few times. If Hawkstead could not buy a doctor he would find a way to get someone established at Greenestone who could treat the minor injuries that should not cost a life. A doctor would mean less risk of death at childbirth, less risk of infants dying before they saw their first or second year.

The car rolled to a stop in the parking lot at Greenestone Park. They all sat silently for a moment after Cho turned the key to turn off the engine and the car's soft hum faded into silence. Hawkstead opened the door and climbed out of the cramped back seat before turning and giving Kara a hand as she climbed out. Julia bounded out of the car and opened the door to help Elyse, starting with gently lifting the leg with the cast and setting it on the paved ground. Cho popped the trunk before exiting the car. Hawkstead quickly walked around the car to give aid. Elyse pulled herself out of the car using Hawkstead's arm for support.

While they were helping Elyse exit the car Cho had done a quick survey of the area and he returned to say that it looked clear. Kara looked around them. "You think they would still try to stop us at the zipper? But they are satisfied that I am of no use to them."

"They haven't ruled out Elyse yet," Julia said.

"What can they do?" Kara asked in disdain. "They are only a few against all of us."

"I like your optimism but there is plenty they can do," Cho said, gaze moving over the rooftops across the street. "Fortunately I am seeing no sign of anyone." He looked back at Kara. "Not in such a hurry anymore?"

"They are busy visiting every pawn shop near their house," Kara said. "That is more important to them."

"What?" Julia asked.

Kara looked a bit uncomfortable. "I took several items from the house. I needed money for public transportation. So I went to a pawn shop," Kara said. It was not a lie but it was definitely a misleading truth.

"And why are they satisfied that you are of no use to them?" Julia stared at Kara in horror. "They have zippers in that house. Were the items you took keys?" Julia asked. Kara nodded. Julia swore and pulled out her phone again. As she swiped and pressed the screen to make her call she was talking to Kara. "At the address?"

Kara nodded again. "Hopefully Tabitha can figure out where they lead. They could be waiting for us inside."

"Cassandra said the zipper led to somewhere more advanced than here," Kara said. "I thought she could open it to send me home and she laughed and said zippers lead to many dimensions."

"You took their keys? No wonder you were in such a hurry to get out of the hospital," Cho said. Cho became even more alert, if that was possible.

While the two women were talking Hawkstead was helping Elyse test her weight on the walking cast. Once Elyse was standing steadily Hawkstead reached into the car trunk for her crutches. Elyse and Hawkstead followed Cho deeper into the park. Elyse took a few awkward steps as she got the feel of how to use the crutches then settled into an almost steady pace. Hawkstead glanced back to make sure that Julia and Kara were following. The two women were still talking, Julia alternating between the phone and Kara. Hawkstead lingered, keeping an eye on Elyse as she followed Cho's path.

"Zippers or one zipper?" Julia asked Kara.

"Cassandra said there was one zipper in the room," Kara said.

"What did you pawn and where did you pawn them?" Julia asked. "Maybe we can beat them to the items."

"They won't find them," Kara said. "Let's get Elyse home."

"Why won't they find them?" Julia asked, not budging.

"Because they did not know what they had," Kara said.

Hawkstead stepped up and held out the two keys that Kara had given him. They lay in the palm of his hand. "Sean Matthews named these two items as keys." Julia reached for the two keys but Hawkstead closed his fingers over the pieces. "I'll hold onto them," he said.

"Be reasonable and give them to me," Julia said.

"Why?" Hawkstead asked.

"They have two keys," Julia said into the phone. "I don't know. I see. Okay. I'll call you after then." Julia slipped the phone into her pocket. "We'll see if they work on the zipper and if they don't then you may keep them there. Since our goal is to remove keys from action it will suffice."

Cho and Elyse were stopped and waiting for them in the general vicinity of the zipper. Hawkstead looked around for landmarks he had noted when arriving as they approached Cho and Elyse. Kara walked several steps beyond Cho before stopping and waiting. Julia walked up to Kara, staring at Kara closely. "How did you know it's here?"

Kara pointed at the bench nearby. "This is where we came out."

Julia nodded. "You have a good memory." Julia glanced around them. A young family walked along the bike path near them. "Once it's clear we'll test those two keys and then go through." Julia looked at Kara thoughtfully. "You don't have to go back, Kara."

"You will try to hold me as well?" Kara asked, letting the informality with her name pass.

"I am saying that if you want to stay here you can. Here you can be safe. No abusive uncle. No barbarian horde rushing to your door," Julia said.

"Probably Mongols," Cho said.

"What would I do here?" Kara asked.

Hawkstead shifted his weight from foot to foot, not liking the conversation. Kara held up her hand, palm facing Hawkstead before he could speak. Kara wanted to hear what Julia had to say.

"Do? Oh, I am sure we could find some job for you. After some training. You read and write? You like horses? Maybe you could work at the race track? Or something like that," Julia said.

"That is hardly motivation to stay here," Kara said. "At home I own four estates. I run a million dollar business breeding horses. I am married to a man who is friends with the king and has been assigned as marshal of the southern lands. Here I would be a landless serf. Why would I walk away from my life to come here and perform menial tasks to eke out a living? Away from all I love."

"But you would be safe," Julia said. "It is not safe in your land."

Kara smiled. "You may rest easy, Julia Roberts. I do not fear to live my life. It is my home."

"Since you found them you should test them," Hawkstead said, handing the two pieces to Kara. Hawkstead pulled the bag from her shoulder and held it, gesturing for her to step towards the zipper. Kara nodded, not happy about being given the key. Kara glared at Hawkstead. He tapped his chest once, right over the pouch under his shirt. Kara realized what that meant and made a face. Kara had forgotten about the ring hanging on his chest and that it was a key for this zipper.

"Wait," Julia said. They all looked at her. "Let these people go by first. And for God's sake, try to look casual."

Kara studied the two keys she held while they waited. She glanced up in the direction of the zipper, nodding thoughtfully. Kara turned to Julia. "Here, you try one and I'll try one."

Julia took the key Kara offered. It was a piece of jet carved into the semblance of a penguin. The young family came near them on the bike path. The woman was pushing a stroller with a toddler and the man was holding the hand of a girl just old enough to no longer fit in a stroller. They smiled and nodded as they passed by.

"You first," Kara said.

"It will have to be Cho since a key does me no good," Julia said, handing the key to Cho. Cho took the key and blindly waved it in front of him. "Here," Julia said, taking his arm and pulling him directly to the zipper. Nothing happened.

Hawkstead felt needles at the back of his neck. He raised his head and surveyed the area slowly, looking for the source of danger he felt. Someone was watching them. There. Two men were approaching at a run and behind them a third was pulling a weapon out of a car's trunk. Hawkstead estimated the time it would take to reach them at the pace they ran and grimaced. It would be close. He turned his back to the zipper and faced the approaching men.

Kara stepped up next to Cho and gestured with the key. The zipper opened and a beam of light burst forth. Kara took Elyse's arm and helped her through the zipper. Cho swore and jumped through after them. Hawkstead gestured to Julia to go next but she was already moving. Hawkstead glanced around them. The little girl had let go of her father's hand and was watching him. She waved. Hawkstead faced the men, his back to the zipper.

The men raised weapons as they neared Hawkstead. "Out of the way."

"You wish to go through?" Hawkstead asked. He recognized one of the men from the hospital, the one who had run in guilt when learning that he was Kara's husband. "You are a lot braver now," Hawkstead said to the man.

"Move out of the way," Sean repeated. "She stole something very, very valuable and she's not getting away with it."

"You stupid dolt," Amie said. "I'll shoot you dead if you don't move."

"You can try. If you go through you will find that being on the other side is my domain," Hawkstead said. "In my land I am the law."

"This is the law," Sean said, waving his weapon.

"You'll be dead," Amie said. "Doesn't that mean anything to you? You won't be on the other side to stop us because you will be dead."

Hawkstead noticed that though Amie was screaming threats the hand holding the weapon was shaking so he reached over and took the weapon out of Sean's hand. Sean was shocked but recovered quickly, lunging for the gun. The second man, Amie, was flustered and tried shooting Hawkstead but he had little control over the gun and it was moving from side to side when he pulled the trigger. Sean froze in shock then slowly looked down at his side. He turned on Amie, who was trying to fire a second shot but the gun jammed. "You shot me, fool!"

Hawkstead punched Amie in the jaw. The man crumpled like a rag doll. Hawkstead took Amie's gun as Sean sank to his knees. Hawkstead looked up at the third man approaching, at a walk, not at a run like the other two. "If I find you in my land…I will have no mercy," Hawkstead said to Sean. "Do you understand?"

Sean nodded. He clutched his side, blood seeping over his fingers. Hawkstead glanced back at the zipper. It was no longer visible. The third man had raised his weapon and kept it leveled at Hawkstead as he cautiously approached. Hawkstead looked for the family who had been out taking a morning stroll. They were running through the parking lot. Hawkstead backed toward the zipper and it flared to life again. Hawkstead ducked through the beam of light.

The other side of the zipper was quite chaotic. At least five of his men and Richard were waiting for them on the other side. No one seemed to have even noticed that he had been delayed in coming through the zipper. A cool breeze struck Hawkstead in the face and the setting sun had turned the sky a teal blue. Julia and Kara were already facing off over the key that Kara held. Julia was insisting that Kara give her the key. Kara was firm when she said, "I will keep it for now."

"But you need to give it to me," Julia said.

"Hawkstead!" Richard said, weaving his way through the crowd to reach Hawkstead. The two men shook hands and slapped each other on the back in greeting. Cho's eyebrows rose when he saw the two guns in Hawkstead's free hand but he said nothing.

"Have you been waiting here the entire time?" Hawkstead asked in surprise.

"I posted some men," Richard said. "This has actually been a busy place."

"What do you mean?" Hawkstead asked.

"Well, first someone arrived from the village less than an hour after you left and created the beam of light. I just happened to still be here, pondering life you might say."

"Pondering life?" Hawkstead asked. "Standing in an apple orchard freezing your arse while ponding life?"

"I was standing next to a tree, leaning against it as I considered how you could step through a beam of light and not come out the other side," Richard said.

Hawkstead grinned. "Forgot about that part."

"So I delayed him a bit. That set me to thinking that a watch should be posted," Richard said. Hawkstead nodded in appreciation.

"Only a day or two later the beam of light appeared again and a man stepped through. Jon and Kevin delayed him from whatever he was up to. A few hours later, yet another visitor."

"I had not realized how busy a place this apple orchard is," Hawkstead said, looking around their surroundings.

Hawkstead looked around. Richard had chosen well. The men gathered around them were all trustworthy and men who could keep their mouths from rambling. Hawkstead had no desire for others to learn about this zipper. Hearing that the zipper could be contained within a building had given him the idea that putting a structure around this one would be a good way of maintaining control, especially if Kara wanted to use it to bring skilled people back from the other land. Now he was convinced that building a structure around the zipper was necessary.

"Where are you holding them?" Hawkstead asked.

"Up at the keep," Richard said.

"Anyone I would know? The man from the village?" Hawkstead asked.

"You might," Richard said in agreement.

"So they were coming in, getting help from the village, all right under our noses," Hawkstead said, staring off in the direction of the village. "Not all of them though. Or they wouldn't have brought Julia and John Cho to us. They would have kept them hidden until we had gone on our way that day." He remembered Elyse with her broken leg. "Someone fetch a wagon for Lady Ashton."

"Kevin is already headed for the village," Richard said. He offered Elyse his arm. "Come, Lady Ashton, there is a bench here for you to rest on while we wait."

"A stool in an apple orchard," Elyse said, looking up at Richard in surprise. She stared at him openly for several heartbeats before taking his supporting arm.

"For the men. They have kept this area under constant guard," Richard said.

"Would they have been waiting for us when we returned?" Elyse asked in alarm. "It was your quick thinking that made our return safe."

Richard looked uncomfortable. "Well, it was my inability to deal with seeing Hawkstead step into thin air, so you could say my slow thinking."

Elyse giggled. Kara looked up in shock at hearing the woman giggle. A thoughtful gleam lit her eyes at the sight of Richard helping Elyse before she turned back to her discussion with Julia.

"What will you do with them?" Cho asked Hawkstead as they watched Richard carefully settle Elyse onto a bench. "The men you have in custody."

"I don't know yet," Hawkstead said. "I'm sure that you and Julia are anxious to get back to your lives now. I appreciate your assistance. I would like to reward you for all your assistance."

"We can't take gifts," Cho said.

"I'll take that key your wife won't let go of as a reward," Julia said.

"No," Hawkstead said at the same time Kara responded.

"You're in my territory now," Kara said. "I will hold onto it."

"There is a reason why we get rid of any keys we find," Julia said in a low voice. "If it's used repeatedly it will damage the zipper. It's *forcing* the zipper to open. People who have a purple halo can open the zippers without any consequence but using a key compromises the integrity of the zipper."

"It will not be used here," Kara said firmly, keeping her voice down also. "You have to trust me on that."

"The only way you can guarantee that is if it does not work on this zipper," Julia said. She sucked in her breath. "It does not work here does it? You opened it. You are actually a purple halo."

"I did not know I could open it until it opened," Kara said, looking in the direction of the zipper. "I could see the zippers in the house but they were just thin lights with black on the edges. Why are there three there but only one here?"

"I don't know. Tabitha understands those things. I don't," Julia said. "It's either three or one though. I have never seen two close together and never more than three."

"They are only aware of one in that room. What will you do with those people who abducted us?" Kara asked.

Julia shook her head. "There's nothing we can do. England is out of our jurisdiction."

"This is our jurisdiction so we will deal with them then," Kara said, meeting Hawkstead's gaze. He nodded.

Kara pulled Julia aside. Hawkstead gestured for his men to back away but remained where he could hear them. "England is in my jurisdiction," Kara said. "I think it's time to stop these people from robbing our dimension. It might be better if they came here though. Can you help them get here?"

Julia stared in Kara in surprise. "What would you do to them?"

"They kidnapped a duchess. Fortunately they did not mistreat me so I think hard labor would suffice," Kara said.

Julia shook her head. "I don't know. I don't feel right about that. Isn't it enough punishment that you stole their keys?" Julia asked, staring at Kara, now feeling a bit intimidated by the young woman. "I hope you aren't expecting us to bring them to you? How else would you be able to deal with them here? Wait. How do you actually know the key does not work?"

Kara held up the key. "See the pattern of the glowing light? There are patterns in the zipper also. I knew that it would not work because the patterns are different."

"I don't see any lights," Julia said.

Kara lowered the key. "Really? What do you see?"

"I feel the zipper," Julia said. "I get a feeling. First it's a feeling of homesickness. Then when I'm close enough I see a distortion, like a heat shimmer. I can't see or feel anything with a key. You are the first person I've known that can see keys glow."

"Oh," Kara said. She looked at the key in her hand thoughtfully. "Then how do you find keys?"

"Blind luck," Julia said. "Oh, Tabitha would love to meet you."

"And why do you think the keys weaken the zippers?" Kara asked, studying the key she held. "If it is a perfect match then it should not harm it. Perhaps they are using keys that are not exactly in tune. Do you know if that is the case? I wonder how it works if it is not a perfect match? How intriguing."

"What do you mean in tune? Do you hear music also?" Julia asked.

Kara shook her head. "No music. You didn't say, how do you know the keys harm the zippers?"

"Tabitha discovered that," Julia said.

Hawkstead decided that Kara was showing far too much interest in the zippers for someone who was going to leave them alone. "It's time to get Elyse to the keep. Julia and John Cho, you are welcome to refresh yourselves at the keep before you return to your land," Hawkstead said.

"We have to get back," Cho said.

"We do," Julia said sadly. She perked up as an idea struck her. "Maybe we can bring Tabitha to meet you?"

Kara looked up at Hawkstead. "I hadn't thought of that."

"I think that if you or John Cho want to visit that should be allowed. You went through a lot of trouble to help us. You will always be welcomed here," Hawkstead said.

"Yes," Kara said in agreement, looking over at Julia. She took Julia's hands between her hands. "If it had not been for you we might not have made it home."

"And Mike and Frank," Hawkstead said. "If any of the four of you want to come you may. Let's put a limit of four people at a time if you wish to bring others."

Hawkstead and Kara said farewell to Cho and Julia, watching as the two stepped back through the zipper. Someone had brought a horse for Elyse instead of a wagon and she was arguing that she wanted her wagon. Kara stepped up to convince Elyse to ride the horse back to the keep. Richard returned to Hawkstead's side.

"I have the feeling that this is going to be an interesting story," Richard said.

"Indeed," Hawkstead said. "You're going to have a few interesting stories of your own soon."

"What?" Richard asked, puzzled. The dull rattle of a wagon could be heard approaching even before it rolled into sight.

"I think it's time you get married," Hawkstead said. "Why don't you take the first step and help Lady Ashton onto that horse?"

"Married? Me? What?" Richard stammered, gaze automatically going to Elyse. "You know I have no property."

"What a silly reason to not marry. There is a big change coming, Richard. I married a woman who has done nothing but surprise me since the day I met her and I think it's just the start of what is to come," Hawkstead said. "Go on, get acquainted with your future wife. When we get back to the keep we will have Father Tom perform the ceremony."

Richard laughed. "Even if I am willing, which I am not saying I am, who is to say the lady is willing?"

"I think she will be willing," Kara said, coming up to stand beside Hawkstead. She looked up at Hawkstead. "I think it might not be this day yet. A woman likes to be wooed. Make her feel wanted."

"A man can't think too long or hard about it or he will put marriage off for years. It should be done before he has time to come up with reasons to not get married," Hawkstead said, gaze locked on Kara. "And when he realizes that marriage is the best state to be in he won't regret an impromptu marriage."

Richard laughed again, thinking the two were both joking. A wagon rolled into sight at last. Richard had a thoughtful expression on his face as he went to help Elyse into the wagon however. Hawkstead slipped his arm around Kara's shoulders and pulled her carefully up against him. After all, she was still recovering from multiple injuries. Kara put her hand over his hand on her shoulder and watched Elyse and Richard.

"How are you going to find the time to run Roffe Stables and make trips to that other dimension in search of skilled professionals to convince to come back with you?" Hawkstead asked Kara though he was also watching Elyse and Richard.

Kara looked up at Hawkstead. Her face lit up at hearing his question. "I was afraid you would try to stop me. I will hopefully have some help but I am sure it will be busy times ahead. You know, when I first met you I thought you were a bit of a jerk."

"That's only because I was," Hawkstead said, giving her shoulder a squeeze. "Does that mean your attitude has changed?"

"Maybe," Kara said, suddenly feeling awkward. Hawkstead turned so that they were facing each other. Kara stared at his chest. "We have a lot ahead of us. The barbarians are still headed this way. My uncle is never going to be cooperative. We probably have very angry people from another dimension out to get us now. But I am glad you are by my side to face all those things."

Hawkstead used his finger to raise Kara's chin so that their eyes met. "I am also glad you are by my side to face what is to come. Together we can face anything."

"So you don't want to get our marriage annulled?" Kara asked.

Hawkstead laughed. "Oh, it's too late for that. Besides, if you try to leave me I will follow you to the ends of the world."

"Are you saying that you love me?" Kara asked.

"Don't go expecting flowery phrases from me," Hawkstead said. He kissed her temple. "But I would like to hear it from you."

"You would, would you?" Kara said in a light, teasing voice. "A lady never says it first."

Hawkstead ran his hand down Kara's back. "If I say it now don't expect to hear it all the time."

"Oh, of course not," Kara said, kissing his neck. "A girl only needs to hear it once."

"What a relief," Hawkstead said. "I thought I would have to tell you all the time and that would just be redundant. You can, however, tell me all the time. Five times a day would even suffice. Yes, five times a day would be quite nice. A man needs to be reminded of these things."

"My Lord," Kevin said, coming up to them. "The wagon has started for the keep. Are you ready to ride?"

Hawkstead scowled at Kevin, who meekly stood waiting, oblivious to what he was interrupting. "Kevin, I am talking to my wife."

"Oh," Kevin said. He remained standing where he was, patiently waiting for Hawkstead to join the group.

Kara laughed and slipped out of Hawkstead's embrace. "I think it is time to go home, my Lord."

"Home," Hawkstead said. He pulled Kara's hand into the crook of his elbow and walked towards the waiting group with Kara beside him while Kevin trailed behind the pair. "Home," Hawkstead repeated. "Let's go home."

"I have so much to do," Kara said, almost bouncing as she walked. "We have to enlarge the stable. I have to make a list of who to, er, invite here. I think we should put some walls around this apple orchard. Oh, it's snowing!"

Hawkstead grimaced. "Don't I have any say in this?"

Kara smiled up at him, snowflakes drifting around her head and shoulders. "Of course you do. You get to decide if it will be stone or wood." She stopped in her tracks. "Oh, I should look at your ring and see if it matches the zipper."

"It matches," Hawkstead said, urging her to keep walking by not letting go of her arm. "Trust me, it works. I am curious to find out how Mrs. Smith knew about the key."

"How do you know it matches?" Kara asked, puzzled.

"I used it," Hawkstead said.

"Oh," Kara said, though she still sounded puzzled. "I think I missed something." Kara seized on Hawkstead's comment about Mrs. Smith. "If the Greenes had a key, maybe they have more."

Suddenly Kara was in a hurry to reach the keep and pulled on Hawkstead's arm as she hurried her step. Hawkstead released her arm and watched her race ahead. Kara smiled brightly at Jon who cupped his hands to provide her with a lift to the saddle. Kara put her foot in his hands and Jon swung her up into the saddle. Kara smiled at Hawkstead as he calmly walked the distance between them. Hawkstead felt the strongest sense of happiness that he could remember ever feeling and he grinned back at Kara. He was looking forward to going home with his wife at his side.

www.ingramcontent.com/pod-product-compliance
Lightning Source LLC
Chambersburg PA
CBHW071157250626
47159CB00001B/121